IG/TT

BURNED OUT

DEAN MAFAKO, M.D.

1

THE BEGINNING OF THE END

"What's the fucking ACT?" Dr. Porter yelled as he stormed into room 3 of the pediatric cardiac intensive care unit at Children's Hospital of Biloxi.

"The ACT is 140, sir!" replied the perfusionist managing the ECMO circuit.

"I told you I wanted the ACT to be 160–180. Why isn't it 160–180?"

"Well, sir, we are getting some conflicting orders regarding the ACT goal. Due to the massive amount of bleeding from the chest tubes, we had been told that we were not adjusting the heparin infusion based on ACT," explained the respiratory therapy supervisor.

"What is your name, son?" Dr. Porter asked rhetorically. As Gary opened his mouth to reply, he was rudely interrupted by the words, "Never mind your name. Who told you to think? I give the orders and you follow them, that's how this works," screamed Dr. Porter.

I had just walked through the entryway doors leading to the pediatric cardiac intensive care unit to meet Dr. Slovak, one of my cardiac intensive care colleagues, so that she could provide patient hand off, as I was taking over service responsibilities for the week. We looked at one another as we heard the commotion that appeared to be coming from room 3 of the CICU, so we both rushed down the hall to see what was going on. Astrid and I arrived at the doorway of room 3 to discover a scene best described as a hybrid between a low-budget horror film due to the massive amount of blood hemorrhaging from the patient, and a 1980s human resource video showing an extreme example of workplace violence. Astrid and I looked at one another with shock and disdain as we witnessed Dr. Porter's tyrannical behavior, his face cherry red, radiating unfathomable rage, in such an uncontrollable manner it screamed pathologic, suggesting a source housed deep within. His surgical mask rested misplaced, exposing his somewhat long, pointed nose with beads of sweat tumbling down until finally reaching the tip and falling to the floor, as if drops of water dripping one at a time from an aged, leaky farmhouse faucet.

"Phil!" I said, attempting to get his attention, but there was no response. "Phil!" I repeated in a much louder voice, again vying to capture his attention and break him from this trance of rage.

The room was comprised of Dr. Porter and his five victims, who believe it or not, also happened to be employees and human beings as verified by human resources, and by anyone with a damn conscience for that matter. Each of these poor souls stared nervously at the floor. Following my second attempt to capture Dr. Porter's attention, their eyes cautiously shifted upward, just enough to discretely search the room for the source of the voice. However, their heads refused to relinquish their downward gaze, remaining unaltered and motionless as if cemented like a statue. Their eyes resembled those of beaten dogs, once caring, loyal and innocent, but now looked upon me with uncertainty and ambivalence, questioning without saying a word, whether I still maintained a sliver of authority that would allow me to rescue them from the bullying toxicity, which had now become customary and mundane.

The seed of mistrust had been planted during Dr. Porter's previous behavioral outburst as the staff watched the hospital administration ignore their complaint, blatantly refusing to hold him accountable for his despicable and infantile behavior.

"Phil let's go outside the room and discuss this," I said a third time, more loudly. Dr. Porter momentarily ceased yelling as he turned toward the sound of my voice, eventually making eye contact with me as he stomped angrily toward the door. As he reached the doorway, we exited the room in unison as he continuously shook his head side to side, muttering to himself like a spoiled toddler who had just been told they cannot have ice cream before finishing their dinner.

Phil Porter was a somewhat legendary physician in the field of pediatric cardiac surgery. He was world-renowned for two major skills, the first of which was his elite technical surgical skill and in particular his ability to operate with great precision on even the tiniest of babies with complex congenital heart defects. Prior to joining the team as the chief of congenital heart surgery at the Children's Hospital of Biloxi, he held the prestigious position of chief of pediatric cardiac surgery at the Children's Hospital of Pennsylvania for nearly a decade. Children's Hospital of Pennsylvania was long recognized as one of the preeminent congenital heart programs in the world. Since his departure, Phil had held two other chief positions, both of which were short-lived. His most recent position lasted two years, while his leadership position prior to that lasted an astonishing two months before he was asked to leave. Which leads us to the second skill that Phil Porter was nationally renowned for, BEING A WORLD-CLASS ASSHOLE! Previous staff and colleagues were quick to share that after a decade of his shenanigans in Pennsylvania, he was asked to leave, and speak to this day of the glorious celebration that occurred upon his departure. While Dr. Porter claimed his voluntary departure, it was said that if he stayed much longer, the choice would no longer have been his to make.

Dr. Porter had left Pennsylvania to assume the role as the chief of pediatric cardiac surgery at the University of Idaho, which was respected as a small-to-medium-sized congenital heart program with a solid reputation for good clinical outcomes. Dr. Porter lasted a whopping two months before he was asked to leave. Perhaps asked is the wrong word, more accurately, he was told to leave. As in, immediately! Beyond his notorious reputation as a bully and a toxic leader, he was specifically known to despise and torture pediatric cardiac intensive care unit staff and most infamously, the cardiac intensive care physicians (aka cardiac intensivists). When he arrived in Idaho, the culture deteriorated so quickly and the cardiac intensivists were treated so poorly, that they took a stand and said either Phil Porter goes or all six of us go. So, the hospital played the smart odds and asked him to leave. Dr. Porter was clearly an intelligent physician, but he was also an exceptionally skilled sociopath, who knew he was on the cusp of being terminated in Pennsylvania; however, the University of Idaho, who was to become his new employer, did not. Dr. Porter had little faith in his ability to control his behavior issues, or at least he had no interest in doing so, and being the master manipulator he was, he negotiated his contract with the University of Idaho to state that in the event that his employment was terminated, he would be compensated for the entirety of the multi-year contract he had negotiated. In his mind, this allowed him free rein to act as he pleased, unopposed. Such opportunism would become an important factor leading up to his next employment opportunity and more importantly it would have implications pertaining to his negotiated employment agreement at Children's Hospital of Biloxi.

Following his brief, two-month stint in Idaho, he found employment at North Dakota Health, a large hospital system that consisted of a pediatric wing, housed within the adult hospital. They had a thriving adult cardiac program with a successful cardiac transplant program and had shown significant interest in developing a pediatric congenital heart program for some time. They saw the hiring of Dr. Porter as a no-lose situation. They had struggled mightily for years to find a congenital heart surgeon to begin building their program. The state already had another congenital heart program that was successful, which only added to their difficulty in recruiting. In this scenario North Dakota Health was aware of his behavior issues in Idaho and was cognizant of the payout he received for his multi-year contract after only two months of employment. Therefore, they used the money Phil was paid from his short stint in Idaho to subsidize a much lower salary offer. So, for them, it truly appeared to be a no-lose situation as they not only scored the pediatric cardiac surgeon they had so desperately sought, but one with a nationally recognized name, and for dirt cheap! Win-win, right? Well, Phil lasted two years in North Dakota before leaving on his own terms, or as was suggested by colleagues and staff once again, if he didn't leave it would no longer have been on his own terms. During his two years in North Dakota, he accumulated several staff complaints related to his bullying and abusive behavior, one of which involved shoving a nurse.

Dr. Porter was also known as a risk taker when it came to congenital heart surgery, which means that he was willing to operate on babies who have such severe heart disease that they are deemed inoperable by most institutions because their disease is so severe that they are unlikely to survive surgery and instead will endure substantial suffering. Taking such risk, which leads to an almost certain mortality at a program such as Children Hospital of Pennsylvania, which performs approximately one thousand cardiac operations annually, will have minimal impact on the overall mortality rate of the program, due to the large number of overall cases they perform. However, taking such risk in North Dakota, with an annual cardiac surgical volume of perhaps two hundred cases, where the program is new and working to build its prominence in the community, two to three mortalities involving complex cases can have irreversible repercussions on the program's reputation. Well, the CEO in North Dakota began to sour on Dr. Porter when his mortality rate began to surpass the number of complaints received by human resources regarding his behavior. While the M:C ratio (mortality to complaint ratio) is not a current metric understood by anyone on this earth, except me, because I quite literally just made it up, right now, in Dr. Porter's case, I am here to suggest perhaps anyone entertaining the idea of employing him, should consider it. By history, Dr. Porter appears to start with an M:C ratio far less than one because he is almost certain to have several complaints from the start, but few or no mortalities. However, over time, the mortalities begin to increase at a rate similar to the human resource (HR) complaint rate, resulting in an M:C ratio approximating one. Now, here are the features that delineate Dr. Porter from most pediatric cardiac surgeons. For most pediatric cardiac surgeons, an M:C ratio greater than one at baseline may be the norm, due to the fact that some mortalities are sadly unavoidable, and due to the fact that most pediatric cardiac surgeons can behave as adults, which implies that they can function reasonably in society among other humans, therefore complaints to HR should be few or nonexistent. However, when Dr. Porter's M:C ratio exceeds the number one, it suggests the time to terminate his employment is imminent, because we already know his HR complaints are off the charts, so when a rising mortality rate exceeds an exorbitant number of complaints, then it signifies that your risk far exceeds your benefit as an institution. All right, enough of my foolishness. Ultimately, North Dakota health had tired of Dr. Porter as a leader and a surgeon, and by now he had sharpened his awareness, enabling him to sense his impending termination, arriving at the conclusion that it was time to develop an exit strategy. So how did Phil Porter end up at Children's Hospital of Biloxi? That part of this story is yet to come.

I led Dr. Porter out of room 3 and around the corner of the cardiac intensive care unit (CICU), attempting to distance ourselves from the patient rooms and the high-foot-traffic zone near the front desk. At this point I knew Dr. Porter well enough to predict with relative certainty which direction our "discussion" was headed.

"Eric, I told them I want the ACT 160–180; nobody is following my order!" Dr. Porter screamed in my face as he obsessively fidgeted with the surgical mask that remained misplaced with his beak-like nose protruding over the top.

I calmly replied in my monotone voice, "Phil, the patient is hemor-rhaging his entire blood volume every hour and has been doing so for the last five days."

"I want the fucking ACT 160–180, no questions asked," he demanded. ACT, or activated clotting time, is a measure of how quickly a patient's blood forms clot and is reported in terms of how many seconds it takes for clot to develop. To explain, a result of 160 means it takes approximately 160 seconds for the blood to form clot. ECMO, which is an abbreviation for extracorpo-real membrane oxygenation, is a machine that uses a pump to remove deox-ygenated blood from the patient's body, subsequently circulating it through a device called an oxygenator, which as the name implies, oxygenates the red blood cells, essentially doing the work for the lungs. Lastly, the oxygen-ated blood is pumped back into the body where it is utilized by the cells and organs. The ECMO circuit can essentially perform the work of the entire body for a finite period of time before the organs inevitably succumb to the complications of the ECMO circuit, which can include the breakdown of red blood cells and multi-organ failure, among others. When patients require ECMO, they also require blood thinners such as heparin that help keep the blood from clotting while flowing through the circuit. There are a few differ-ent ways physicians can monitor the adequacy of the blood thinner, one of which is by measuring the ACT. Now back to Dr. Porter and my "discussion."

"Eric, when I say I want something done, I want it done, no questions asked. I said I want an ACT of 160–180 so God dammit, I want it 160–180," said Dr. Porter with progressively increasing levels of agitation, as he resumed the behavior of compulsively pulling his surgical mask up and down as it slowly became saturated with the sweat abundantly prevalent on his nose.

Suddenly, I felt my steroid rage surging. I had just returned from Mayo Clinic the night before and as directed, I had doubled my prednisone dose due to worsening of my autoimmune condition. I knew this familiar feeling all too well, and it usually wasn't good. After three-plus years of high-dose steroids, I had failed to learn to control this feeling when it reared its ugly face, and for someone who prided himself on his ability to handle difficult and stressful situations by managing his emotions and maintaining a calm demeanor, it was helplessly frustrating to say the least.

"Phil, please! Enough with the fucking ACT, the patient is actively hemorrhaging. We should be stopping the heparin infusion or at least be adjusting our anticoagulation goals to a much lower level and quite frankly, you should be surgically exploring the patient to search for the source of bleeding. This patient is losing 500 milliliters of blood from the chest tubes every hour! That translates into half a liter per hour, which equals his entire blood volume that is being lost and replaced every hour. To allow this child to bleed so profusely, without aggressively pursuing the source of bleeding, and to be so irresponsible with blood utilization, particularly in the middle of the COVID-19 pandemic where the entire nation is suffering from a shortage of blood, is wrong and bordering on unethical! The other laboratory markers of anticoagulation suggest that our heparin use is excessive. We developed an anticoagulation protocol two years before you arrived, due to the fact that we had longstanding issues with bleeding because changes in anticoagulation were being dictated by ACT alone, and without physician oversight. After extensively reviewing the literature, we found no clear, universally adopted marker of anticoagulation while on ECMO, so we chose to use anti-Xa as our marker of choice. While our review revealed no clearly superior value, it did suggest that ACT alone was an inadequate marker of anticoagulation, and such a practice is outdated. Since implementing our protocol, bleeding complications have been relatively infrequent. Our staff have been trained to follow the pathway tightly, which has led to our ability to standardize this approach of anticoagulation among all of the intensive care units through-out the hospital. The sole use of ACT to guide anticoagulation is prehistoric, so please, for the love of God, stop obsessing about it and to state it bluntly, in this particular scenario, forget about the anticoagulation markers alto-gether, BECAUSE THE PATIENT IS EXSANGUINATING RIGHT BEFORE OUR EYES!"

I suddenly snapped out of my "roid rage," as though I had transiently blacked out and suddenly regained consciousness, and my heart rate began slowing, as if exercised from a demonic possession. I attempted to regain my composure, as I sensed approaching footsteps behind me. I turned to catch a glimpse of Tim Kowatch, the chief of pediatric cardiology, as his head peeked sneakily around the corner, resembling that of a child failing miserably at a game of hide-and-seek. As he caught my gaze, he quickly receded behind the wall. I stood in awe. "Where the hell am I right now?" I thought to myself as I prayed for someone to wake me from this awful and bizarre nightmare. Suddenly, I saw Dr. Kowatch's entire body emerge slowly from behind the wall. His movement appeared odd as his feet were still, yet inch by inch his body revealed itself from behind the wall. "Was he levitating? Was this some type of reverse moonwalk he had been mastering in his free time?" I thought to myself with a baffled look on my face. As his entire body finally emerged from behind the wall, I could now visualize two black arms that appeared to be pushing Dr. Kowatch against his will from behind the wall. Seconds later, the body that was attached to those arms revealed itself. It was Ms. Lewis, the unit clerk. Ms. Lewis was an older woman in her sixties whom I labeled the sweetest woman in the universe, yet you didn't want to cross her, because she could become feisty in an instant. Here she was pushing Dr. Kowatch, against his will, reminiscent of a temperamental child throwing a tantrum, toward Dr. Porter and me, attempting to force him to intervene in our heated "discussion." I later came to understand that Ms. Lewis had literally chased Dr. Kowatch down the hall as he attempted to flee the confrontation, as she sought to force him to intervene, in hopes of defusing the situation that was rapidly deteriorating between Phil and me. You can't make this stuff up and it is impossible for me to refrain from shaking my head in disbelief as I type these words. This was the behavior of our two, and I hesitate to say fearless, leaders who have roamed this earth for more than sixty years. The two co-directors, leading the entire Heart Center!

"Uh, guys, what's the um, problem?" Dr. Kowatch said timidly, in a voice riddled with crackling anxiety, wearing a pink button-down shirt covered with sweaty armpit stains the size of Manchuria.

"Tim, I want the ACT 160–180 and they aren't listening," Phil obsessively repeated.

"Tim, this is absurd and bordering on unethical. The patient is bleeding to death, yet he continues to obsess about the ACT and insist that we increase the anticoagulation, while he verbally and emotionally abuses my staff," I explained after reestablishing some semblance of emotional stability.

"Um, guys, can we just take a couple deep breaths? You both have valid points. Let's go to surgical rounds and discuss this later," Tim suggested while his voice continued to crack with extreme anxiety.

As we walked toward the conference room, Phil looked back at me with pure rage in his eyes in what I can only describe as an acute psychotic state, and said, "I want the ACT 160–180, I mean it, 160–180!"

That was it. That was the moment I realized it was over. In retrospect, I had been in denial and unable to completely process the futility of the situation, that is up until now. His compulsive use of the same words combined with that sociopathic, dissociated look he had in his eyes as he stared at me, couldn't have made it clearer, his actions were those of a man incapable of modifying such disturbing behavior, and I felt like a fool for failing to recognize it sooner. I had seen that look before, three years earlier on the face of the previous cardiac surgeon, Dr. Rostri. Once you have seen the look of a sociopath, it is impossible to forget it. Perhaps the use of the term "sociopath" is a bit harsh; however, in this scenario, it appeared accurate. For some, like Dr. Porter, I came to believe that there must be some deep, underlying pathology to explain such behavior, which rendered him refractory to repeated attempts at intervention. Others I had encountered during my career, such as Dr. Rostri, shared subtle hints, suggesting that hidden somewhere, deep inside, existed a genuine individual with a kind heart, who began the practice of medicine with relatively normal behavior. However, somewhere during the course of their career, something occurred, causing them to lose their way. The etiology of this remained elusive to my discovery; however, eventually, I concluded that events accumulating over the entirety of their career reached a critical point, causing them to stray from their original purpose, one guided by doing the right thing for the patient, to one dominated by the need for being "right" and for maintaining control. It was no longer about collaboration and intelligent discussion to determine the best possible avenue leading to a good outcome for the patient; instead, it was 100 percent motivated by the need to retain control at all costs. The experience I had just witnessed was disturbing but admittedly, as a scientist, I found the pathology equally fascinating. In hindsight, as I reflect on this event, it was there in that moment, as I witnessed the possession of Dr. Porter's body by an acute psychotic state, that I concluded after a mere four months of working together, that this marked the beginning of the end for me and for the cardiac program at Children's Hospital of Biloxi.

2

THE LIFE-CHANGING PHONE CALL

It was spring 2016. I had been working as a pediatric cardiac intensivist for nearly ten years at a small-to-medium-sized congenital heart program at a children's hospital in Fort Myers, Florida. I had joined the program straight out of my pediatric critical care training and had come to love and admire the group of physicians I worked with. It was a small group, but it was filled with high-quality physicians who were national experts in their respective subspecialties, and together we formed a strong, cohesive team, delivering excellent outcomes to the patients. While the cardiac surgical volume was small-to-medium-sized, the complexity of the surgical patients we cared for was high, due to the fact that the children's hospital was directly connected to the Women's Hospital where the majority of the city's high-risk deliveries occurred. I was one of five cardiac intensivists who worked exceedingly well together, and I was thriving both personally and professionally in Fort

Myers. I was blessed with two beautiful daughters and a kind and beautiful wife. Life was good, we had recently purchased the house of our dreams and just one year earlier I had been promoted to associate director of the pediatric cardiac intensive care unit. Everything in my life appeared perfect from afar; however, recently, I began to notice thoughts enter my mind that suggested maybe I was too comfortable and perhaps a bit unchallenged professionally. Though I was now associate director, I began to contemplate what the future held for me professionally at Fort Myers Children's. As I further dissected these incessant thoughts, I was bothered by the fact that my current medical director, and close friend, was not much older than I was. He had formed solid roots in the Fort Myers area and appeared content in his current position, with no intention of trying to further his career by going elsewhere. As a result, I entertained thoughts that I felt were normal for anyone in my position, at this stage of their career. However, as I would soon realize, feeling unchallenged and uncertain about my future in Fort Myers, would leave me vulnerable to making drastic decisions that would forever change my life.

May 15, 2016, I received the phone call that would change my life forever. I was sitting at home on a wicker chair on our rear patio, adjacent to our pool, relaxing. I had just completed a long week of clinical service and was looking forward to some much-needed rest when my cell phone rang. It was a number I didn't recognize so as most people do in such a scenario, I debated whether or not to answer it. "It's almost certainly a spam call, so I will just let it go to voicemail," I said to myself, but for some reason, at the last minute, I decided to answer the phone. "Hello, yes, this is Eric Philson. Who is calling please?" I asked.

"Hi, this is Todd Burnely, I am the owner of a physician leadership search firm called Burnely and Associates. I have been hired by the Children's Hospital of Biloxi to lead a national search for the next medical director of their pediatric cardiac intensive care unit. Thank you for taking my call, I was given your name as a potential candidate by a colleague of yours," Mr. Burnely explained.

"Oh, thanks for considering me as a candidate, but I am happy at my current job, and I am not really interested in leaving," I said.

"Would you at least consider listening to me explain the specific details about the position?" Todd asked.

I paused and contemplated for a moment. To this day, I still reflect on that moment with regularity and consider how different my life could be if I had reiterated my original answer of no. Should I blame my parents for raising me to be polite and respectful to others? Perhaps I should direct the blame toward the restless uncertainty that consumed my mind at the time, or maybe the feeling of being unchallenged at work? Irrespective of cause, after a brief pause, the word "Sure" left my mouth.

"Wonderful," Mr. Burnley said as he explained the details. "It is a well-established congenital heart program that has been around for more than twenty years. It is a medium-to-large-volume surgical program that performs approximately 350 cardiac surgeries per year. It has a dedicated cardiac intensive care unit; however, it is currently run exclusively by the cardiac surgeons, and—"

"Wait, could you repeat that?" I interrupted.

"Yes, I realize it's unusual and an outdated model of postoperative care, but the program has been set back as a result of two major hurricanes and by a lack of resources, but this position is now fully supported and financially backed by the University of Southeastern Mississippi. The new medical director would be provided the financial support needed to hire all necessary staff and to purchase all necessary equipment he or she considers vital to building the cardiac intensive care unit from scratch. It is truly a rare opportunity these days," Todd continued.

I thought to myself, wow, a cardiac ICU run exclusively by surgeons with no resources and medium-high volume, sounds like a nightmare, but morbidly, I couldn't help but feel intrigued. I had to admit, the opportunity to build a cardiac intensive care unit from scratch would definitely be challenging and quite possibly a once-in-a-career opportunity, and to do so in an established medium-high-volume cardiac program guarantees that I will be busy with plenty of surgical volume.

The truth was the combination of these two factors was exceedingly rare. Normally, you are either hired to build a CICU for a start-up congenital heart program and left with the uncertainty of the surgical volume or in another scenario, you are hired as the medical director and plugged into a well-established CICU and congenital heart program, which typically makes it more difficult to implement substantial change, meaningful enough to create a brand of your own. The part that left me skeptical was the fact that the CICU had been managed by cardiac surgeons for many years, which could prove difficult to implement change. As I pondered these factors in my mind, I was transported back to reality as I heard the words, "What do you think, would you like me to set up a phone interview with the chief of pediatrics and the chief medical officer (CMO)?" Todd asked.

Without fully contemplating the situation, I hastily answered, "Yes."

I spoke to Ana, my wife, about the call and she understandably shared my skepticism. We had built a pretty incredible life in Fort Myers and for the first time in our lives, we were established and were beginning to put down roots. During our first several years together, we moved two separate times to different cities for my medical training. In Fort Myers we owned a wonderful house, and we were fortunate to have made some great friends. We enjoyed watching our kids grow and thrive at their school. "Why would you want to move?" she asked.

"I feel bored professionally here in Fort Myers and I feel like I need to be challenged at this stage in my career. Can we at least see how the phone interview goes without any commitment and then we can take it from there, once we have more information? Does that sound reasonable?" I asked.

"OK, I guess," she said, reluctantly agreeing.

Two months later, following a one-hour phone interview, I felt more reassured and optimistic about the program in terms of the support that would be provided by the hospital and the university. Both the CMO and the chief of pediatrics assured me that they would provide what was needed to build the cardiac intensive care unit. Dr. James Deeton, CMO of Children's Hospital of Biloxi, explained to me in great detail that the cardiac program had recently undergone an external review performed by experts in the field who had overwhelmingly stated in their report that a CICU developed and staffed by cardiac intensivists was essential in order to progress the program in a direction that would allow it to achieve its goal of establishing a care model that mirrored that of top programs around the country, both functionally and from a quality standpoint. "Were there any other deficiencies identified during the review?" I asked Dr. Deeton.

"That was really all they identified. What do you think? Would you like to come for an in-person visit?" Dr. Deeton asked.

Satisfied with their answers, I replied, "Sure."

3

FIRST VISIT TO CHILDREN'S HOSPITAL OF BILOXI

I had never visited Biloxi before, or anywhere in Mississippi for that matter. As I sat on the flight from Fort Myers to Biloxi, I began to imagine what the city looked like. I tried to erase any preconceived notions my mind had constructed based on stereotypes of the Deep South, including toothless residents baring shotguns in the rear window of their rusted out trucks with Dixie flag stickers plastered on the bumper. When my plane finally landed, it appeared as though my imagination may not be that far from the truth. While I walked through the airport I received a text message reading, "Hi Eric, this is Luke Leblanc, chief quality officer at Children's Hospital of Biloxi (CHOB), I am currently en route to pick you up at the airport and transport you to your hotel. Be on the lookout for a grey Honda Civic."

"Thank you, Luke. That is very kind of you. I will meet you curbside shortly," I replied as I proceeded to make my way toward the airport exit. As I walked, I thought to myself, "You really shouldn't be so judgmental and jump to the conclusion that all people from Mississippi are rednecks." I walked out the automatic doors exiting the airport and immediately spotted Luke's Honda Civic, which appeared just as he had described. I opened the passenger door and was subsequently greeted by three empty Coca-Cola cans that fell to the street making a loud clanging noise. "Well, perhaps I prematurely dismissed my stereotypical thoughts regarding rednecks, although there doesn't appear to be any shotguns or Dixie flags upon first inspection," I said to myself, fighting back the urge to laugh aloud. I sat in the passenger seat, managing to push the dozen or so empty soda cans to the side with my feet, just enough to reassure myself that indeed there was a floorboard to rest my feet, and not a hole with a direct connection to the pavement. I closed the door and proceeded to inhale a scent that I can only describe as a mixture of cow manure and three-day-old urine-drenched diapers, leading me to regurgitate the snacks I had eaten on the airplane into the back of my mouth. I was struggling to clear the image of cow shit and old dirty diapers, which complicated my ability to swallow, returning the contents in the back of my mouth to their place or origin. After fighting with my mind and my epiglottis for what felt like an eternity, I successfully returned the half-digested vomit to my stomach. I thanked Luke again for picking me up at the airport. The ride to the hotel was very informative as Luke gave me a brief tour of some very beautiful areas of Biloxi while giving me the historical background of the city.

At the conclusion of Luke's tour, I checked into the hotel and rested a bit before my scheduled dinner with Dr. James Deeton, chief medical officer of Children's Hospital of Biloxi, Dr. Richard Potts, the chief of pediatrics for the University of Southeastern Mississippi, and Dr. Gerald Rostri, chief of pediatric cardiac surgery. Before I knew it, Dr. Potts was texting me, informing me that he was outside the hotel to pick me up for dinner. I hurried to put on my suit coat and hopped into Dr. Potts's Toyota Camry, which was void of guns or Dixie flags as well, and thankfully smelled normal. We drove down the pothole-filled streets of Biloxi passing beautiful plantation homes intermixed with dilapidated and abandoned homes. We pulled up to the restaurant called Rick's on the Park, a beautiful, and as I would learn, historic restaurant that had been a favorite in Biloxi for decades and had survived several major hurricanes, most notably Hurricane Kelly, which had wreaked havoc, flooding and destroying much of the city nearly twelve years ago. The restaurant specialized in Southern cuisine and per the recommendation of Dr. Rostri, I ordered the turtle soup.

"Well, tomorrow you will meet several of the team and hopefully you will get a feel for what we are about," said Dr. Deeton.

"Dr. Rostri, what are your thoughts about the results of the external review?" I asked.

"Uh, I think there are always areas that all programs can improve. Which part are you referring to?" he asked.

With what I can imagine must have been a look of sheer confusion, I directed my gaze toward Dr. Deeton. Dr. Deeton quickly responded with a stern voice, "Uh … as I … told you before … the cardiac ICU is what … uh … we were told needs … uh … attention, which is why you are here today."

In hindsight this was the first sign of the deception I would come to experience, which would haunt me for years to come, but at the time I was too naive to understand the importance of persisting with my questioning, plus I wanted to mind my manners and be respectful while we were enjoying dinner. Dinner finished and we said our goodnights as Dr. Potts drove me back to the hotel. "Rest well," he said. "Tomorrow you will get to see the hospital and meet the team."

Morning came quick and before I knew it Dr. Potts was in the lobby of the hotel waiting for me and we were soon off cruising once again down the pothole-filled streets of Biloxi. "There is the children's hospital," said Dr. Potts as he pointed out the front window of his Toyota Camry. As I looked with great interest, I could begin to make out the front of the hospital with a sign that read Children's Hospital of Biloxi. As we approached the hospital, it was clear we were in a suburban area of Biloxi, surrounded on both sides of the street by beautiful, historic Southern homes, most in pristine condition. As we drove in front of the hospital, I saw what I would describe as a historic building constructed with white, somewhat weathered bricks, old yet well-kept. The grounds across the street though were straight out of a horror movie and consisted of two abandoned plantation-style homes that were falling into ruins; however, they paled in comparison to the massive four-story psychiatric hospital, towering behind them, which had been closed for many years, with several of its windows covered by plywood. I wondered if Freddy Kruger, Michael Myers, or perhaps both were squatting in the building. "Keep in mind that we are six months away from starting a $300-million campus transformation that will renovate these dilapidated properties and essentially leave us with a brand-new children's hospital, including a brand-new, state-of-the-art CICU, two new cardiac operating rooms, and two new hybrid cardiac catheterization labs," Dr. Potts hurriedly explained as he tried to counteract the shock and disbelief I must have displayed on my face.

The interview day was informative and started by meeting Doris Geisinger, a junior cardiac surgeon who had trained at Boston Children's. Doris was extremely intelligent and well-spoken. She appeared to have profound insight related to the institution and its goals for the future. During our brief time conversing, she managed to convince me of the limitless potential present at Children's Hospital of Biloxi. She spoke of a few talented physicians who shared her same vision regarding the potential that existed, painting an elaborate picture in my mind as to what the future could look like at CHOB. They were simply awaiting the final piece of the puzzle, which consisted of a fully staffed and well-developed cardiac intensive care unit. She also managed to sell me on the wonderful people who lived in the city of Biloxi. She spoke of salt-of-earth people who were grateful for the care that they received, despite the fact that it was not yet to a quality that matched the standard of care around the country.

I asked her specifically, "What are your thoughts about the care being provided in the CICU?"

She replied, "Honestly, it is below the standard of care, but most of the problems are fixable, and low-lying fruit for the right person with the right vision. We recently began participating in the pediatric cardiac intensive care national database and we have collected one full quarter of data."

"Great. How does it look?" I asked.

"It's pretty bad; we are among the worst in many of the metrics measured, particularly in hospital length of stay and duration of mechanical ventilation. Many of our patients, even those undergoing the simplest of surgeries, arrive to the CICU from the operating room intubated, and remain mechanically ventilated and medically paralyzed for at least a few days," Doris responded.

"Excuse me?" I replied trying to hide my shock.

"Look it's bad, but it's fixable, and you can make it your own," she said.

"Wow, thanks for the information. It was truly a pleasure meeting you," I said as I shook her hand. It was overwhelming, but I appreciated her candor. I sat and allowed myself a brief moment to recover from the shock of what I had heard and the images of the dilapidated buildings I had just witnessed, while allowing my mind some time to mentally digest the information I had been provided, as I waited for my next interview. "Wow, that is crazy, but I have to admit, so far it all appears easily fixable," I thought to myself.

The next two interviews that day would also prove to be memorable, involving both of the interventional cardiologists. The first was with Dr. Kajay Swami, a young, soft-spoken interventional cardiologist with five years of experience, who echoed a sentiment similar to that described by Doris regarding the good people of Mississippi. "They are so thankful, yet they deserve better cardiac care than what is currently being delivered. The foundation for success is here at Children's of Biloxi; we now need someone such as yourself to help deliver a fully functional and staffed CICU capable of delivering high-level clinical care," Kajay explained passionately. Next up was Eric Saltiel, an experienced interventional cardiologist who originally hailed from the Midwest. He found his way to Biloxi as a contract physician when the hospital desperately needed interventional cardiology help. However, following his arrival, he fell in love with the city, the people, and the culture, so he accepted a full-time position but flew back and forth to see his family regularly. Eric was extremely intelligent, and as a person he appeared to be as genuine and real as they come. He had a plethora of clinical experience and even more life experience that would prove to be invaluable for me in the future. Eric validated Kajay and Doris's claims regarding the potential that existed for the program and volunteered his love for the wonderful people of Mississippi. I left their interview feeling positive about the potential that existed. I felt like I was developing a strong understanding of the place as I headed into the final interview, which was scheduled with Dr. Gerald Rostri, chief of pediatric cardiac surgery and his partner, Dr. Terry Penton, another pediatric cardiac surgeon with twenty years of experience, only a few years less than that of Dr. Rostri.

I sat alone in the room for ten minutes, waiting for the cardiac surgeons to arrive. I felt anxious but confident and hoped that I would feel the same vibe from the two of them that I felt from the others I had met, which I summarize as optimistic and hopeful for the future. I sat pondering the possibility of taking the job, when suddenly, in strolled Dr. Rostri and Dr. Penton, both wearing the look of stone-cold killers on their faces. I stood and shook both of their hands, still no smile. As we sat down, Dr. Penton said, "Thanks for coming."

I replied, "Thanks for having me."

Dr. Rostri followed with, "What questions can we answer for you?"

"What would you like to see happen with the CICU?" I asked.

"Well, we understand that practices you may see in the unit may not be what you are used to, but we have done our best without being provided much in the way of resources. We would like to see someone work with us as a team while continuing to keep an open mind regarding the way we practice intensive care medicine," said Dr. Rostri.

"Sounds reasonable," I replied.

Dr. Rostri was in his early sixties and had a full head of grey hair. He was approximately five foot nine and Russian with an obvious accent but who spoke clearly and intelligently. He always wore a serious look on his face that gave you the feeling you were being analyzed and interrogated by the KGB even when he was silent. It was quite intimidating, especially at first. Dr. Penton was a balding man in his mid-fifties, approximately five foot ten. He too regularly carried a serious look on his face but would offer the occasional smile. He seemed unimpressed by our conversation, and I got the overall feeling that neither surgeon really wanted me, or anyone for that matter, to be the leader of the CICU if that meant relinquishing any sort of decision-making control over the care in the CICU. Despite this gut feeling, they remained cordial during the interview and as it ended, they thanked me for visiting. On the way out Dr. Rostri said, "We would show you the CICU but we have to run to another meeting."

"No problem," I replied. In retrospect, this was another warning that I simply overlooked, which would come back to haunt me in the not-so-distant future.

4

THE SECOND VISIT

After returning home to Fort Myers, I shared the details of my visit with Ana. I was excited about the challenge and the potential that existed. I told her about my visits with Doris the cardiac surgeon from Boston as well as Kajay and Eric the interventional cardiologists. But most of all I shared my experience meeting with Dr. Rostri and Dr. Penton, the cardiac surgeons. It was that meeting that tempered my excitement and made me hesitate to commit to anything. "Well, if you like it, let's go take a look as a family," said Ana, in her typical supportive manner.

The following day I received text messages from several of the staff at Children's Hospital of Biloxi I had met with, thanking me for visiting and stating how much they enjoyed meeting me as well. Two days later Dr. Potts the chief of pediatrics called to hear my thoughts regarding my initial visit and to see if I had any interest in bringing my family along for a second visit. "Yes, Richard, I enjoyed my first visit very much. It helped me get a feel for the potential that exists at Children's Hospital of Biloxi. I spoke with my wife,

Ana, and my two daughters and we are definitely interested in coming for a visit as a family," I explained.

"Great, I will have my assistant contact you with potential dates, and we will get it set up. Talk to you soon," Dr. Potts said with excitement.

July 2016 arrived, and we were on our way to Biloxi, Mississippi. As the plane touched down on the runway of Biloxi International Airport, we were immediately overwhelmed by the humidity. Even as we sat inside the airplane, the windows began to fog, and as we exited the plane and entered the ramp to the airport, we were immediately saturated with sweat due to the extreme humidity. Fort Myers was hot, actually on average, the daily temperature was hotter than that in Biloxi; however, the humidity was unlike anything I had encountered, even in Florida. We grabbed our luggage and exited the airport in search of a minivan taxi capable of handling the four of us with all of our luggage. "Would you mind taking us through the historic district of Biloxi, so that I can show my family some of the beautiful, historic plantation homes?" I asked the driver.

"Of course, sir. Is this your first time in Biloxi?" he asked politely, with a strong Southern accent.

"Yes, sir, and only my second," I replied.

"Wonderful. What brings y'all here?" he asked.

"I am interviewing for a job at Children's Hospital of Biloxi," I explained.

"Wow, that is wonderful. Children's is the best around. Yes, sir!" he replied proudly.

Ana looked at me with confusion, as she gathered from my description of the hospital following my visit that while I enjoyed the team and felt that there was massive potential, the children's hospital that I described was far from a national leader. I nodded my head and gave her the "I will explain to you later" look. While clearly Children's Hospital of Biloxi was not currently a national leader in health care, the driver's statement spoke volumes to me about how proud the people of Biloxi were of their city and their children's hospital, but even more so, it was the first time I was able to experience the "salt of the earth," always grateful type of attitude displayed by the people of Biloxi that so many others spoke so fondly of during my first visit. It made me feel warm and happy to be around someone so grateful and proud of their home. It was not something I had experienced. Gratefulness, yes, but not gratefulness for what appeared to be medical care that was substandard in comparison to the care that was being delivered by most children's hospitals around the country. It was humbling, yet it left me feeling sad and inspired, an odd combination of feelings to experience simultaneously, but it made sense oddly enough, because I realized that the opportunity before me provided a chance to contribute to something meaningful, which could help balance an unfair and inhumane deficit in health care that the people of Biloxi didn't even realize existed. The feeling I felt was indescribable and profound. It added an element of humility to the prospect of the job and made the challenge that lay ahead appear even more appealing and provided a motivation that superseded anything I could possibly experience with any other medical director position that would become vacant in my lifetime.

As we drove down St. James Avenue through the historic district of Biloxi, it was nothing short of awe-inspiring. We passed homes that must have been multimillion-dollar plantation-style homes, in pristine condition, some dating back to the early 1800s. I couldn't help but feel as though I was transported back to a time of Southern elegance and class as we drove down this historic street, which was lined with massive old oak trees, covered in Spanish moss, that could tell stories of slavery, civil war, as well as hurricanes, flooding and death. The trees were beautiful and magnificent, appearing weathered but durable, as if symbolic of the people of Biloxi who could accurately be depicted the same. Both had endured catastrophes and suffering dating back to the 1800s, but remained resilient and proud, living on to tell future generations of their suffering, adventures, and resiliency. We arrived at our hotel on St. James Avenue as I returned to reality following my brief trip back in time. I reached for my credit card to pay the fare as the driver pointed toward the center of the street and said, "Look, here comes a streetcar." We looked up to find an old, shiny and refurbished green streetcar passing on railroad tracks, completely full of passengers. "It comes by here about every ten to fifteen minutes. It is only a couple dollars to ride. There is a schedule there on the sign, just across the street. Right there. Y'all see it? Or you can look it up on your phone," the driver said with great pride.

"Yes, sir. Thank you so much," I said as I handed him my credit card. "Thanks again for the ride, the tour, and the hospitality!" I said.

"My pleasure. Y'all enjoy your visit and good luck on the job, Doc," he replied.

"Thank you, sir, have a great day!" we said waving goodbye as he drove away. We checked into the hotel, while my amazement at the sincere kindness of the driver continued on in my mind. But as I would come to see over time, this was simply a way of life in the South and in particular the city of Biloxi.

Dinner that night was planned at the home of Luke Leblanc, chief quality officer. Despite my first impression of Luke, which started with olfactory-induced memories of cow manure and stale diapers followed by soda cans littering the streets as I entered his Honda Civic, I found Luke to be a great guy. He was extremely intelligent, honest and straight to the point, which I appreciated as that is how I prided myself on being as well. Luke and I hit it off from the very start. Well, after I got over the whole car odor trauma. He was a pediatric critical care physician who had practiced for many years. Luke was a couple of years senior to me in terms of clinical experience, but of my "same vintage," as I would learn was a favorite saying of his. The fact that he understood the profession and that he understood the challenge that lay ahead gave me solace knowing I had a sounding board to share my thoughts and concerns with. No other, outside of him, could have a true understanding of the challenges as they pertained to the job as well as those challenges and deficits related to the university system that I was considering joining. But most importantly, I needed someone who could summate all of these factors and validate that the potential I perceived to exist before me was indeed real. I also needed to rely on his knowledge of the field and of the Biloxi health-care system, to help me ascertain if this mountainous challenge was actually surmountable.

Dr. Potts, always punctual, sent me a text message notifying me of his arrival at the hotel at 5:45 p.m. sharp, to pick us up for dinner at Luke's house, which was scheduled for 6 p.m. in the historic district. Dr. Richard Potts was a tall man, at least six feet in height, intelligent and kind with razor-sharp instincts allowing him to read situations and people better than anyone I had encountered in my life. He was born and raised in Northern Louisiana. He had joined the University of Southeastern Mississippi as clinical professor and the chief of pediatrics a mere six months prior to my first visit to Biloxi. He and James Denton, CMO of Children's Hospital of Biloxi, were the two primarily tasked with my recruitment for the position of medical director of the pediatric cardiac intensive care unit. As Ana, the kids and I walked to the front of the hotel, Dr. Potts exited a burgundy sport utility vehicle and simultaneously the passenger door opened as a beautiful English woman in her early sixties exited the vehicle with a friendly smile, extending her arms to greet us all with a hug. Dr. Potts shook my hand as he introduced his wife. "This is my wife, Naomi," he said.

"Pleased to meet you, dear," she said.

"Likewise," I replied.

She moved on to Ana and introduced herself while offering her a warming hug, which Ana graciously accepted. "Who are these adorable little ones?" Naomi inquired.

"This is Heather, our seven-year-old daughter, and this is Erica, our five-year-old daughter, and you have already met my wife, Ana," I said. We finished our greetings and introductions and proceeded to pile into Naomi's burgundy Toyota 4 Runner. As we drove toward Luke's house, Dr. Potts did his best to avoid the numerous potholes, although I now understood such a goal in Biloxi was virtually unobtainable. As he drove, Dr. Potts explained about the unfathomable damage the city suffered at the hands of Hurricane Kelly back in 2005. The roads of Biloxi were nearly in ruins and while the biannual placement of layer upon layer of pavement were valiant attempts at repairing each pothole, the harsh reality was that these measures merely temporized the problem as if placing a Mickey Mouse Band-Aid to treat a cut measuring twelve inches long and two inches deep, until once again the potholes were reborn a few months later in the same location, often worse than before, while birthing multiple newly formed potholes. I asked Dr. Potts, "Why is there so much digging ongoing and why does it appear that there are so many drainage pipes being placed beneath the streets."

"Believe it or not, this is still replacement of the city drainage system that began following Hurricane Kelly nearly twelve years ago," he replied. "The physical damages sustained by the city of Biloxi were astronomical and those you see are some of the measurable damages. The repercussions felt by the health system as it pertains to multiple staff and in particular physicians who left the city is immeasurable and we are still recruiting to replace the loss of over half our staff nearly twelve years later," said Dr. Potts.

"Wow, so sad, but strangely fascinating. I would have never guessed the long-term, lingering consequences of such a storm and how long the recovery process can last," I replied. I was shaken by this realization, but I was also humbled by the resiliency of the people of Biloxi and by the dedication of people such as Dr. Potts who understood the challenges, yet they saw beyond the destruction and envisioned the future and how he himself could contribute and be part of the slow, painful recovery process. It was inspirational.

"Here we are," said Dr. Potts as the car pulled in front of Luke Leblanc's home. Luke's home was beautiful, modestly sized but well-kept. It was a classic Southern-style home known as a "shotgun" house, which in actuality, described the design of the home, long and thin and divided down the middle into two separate living residences, like a double-barrel shotgun—a logical explanation for the name, though locals would say that the name "shotgun home" arose from the concept that if you were standing at the front door, you could shoot someone trying to leave the backdoor after robbing your house with a clear line of sight. Both were fascinating explanations, purely descriptive of the rich Southern history I would come to admire about Biloxi. As we exited the vehicle, Luke stood on the porch with his beautiful family who affably greeted us with open arms. "Welcome, everyone!" Luke said as he waved to us with sincerity. "This is my wife, Emily, and my three daughters, Cindy, Alexis, and Josephine," said Luke.

"Nice to meet y'all," Emily said with a smile.

"Nice to meet you too. This is my wife, Ana, and my daughters, Heather and Erica," I replied.

"Hi," Erica and Heather replied nervously.

"Girls, why don't you go show Erica and Heather your room," said Luke.

"I hope you don't mind but we prepared some traditional Southern food, red beans and rice," said Emily.

"That sounds wonderful," I replied.

Dinner was lovely and even the kids loved the red beans and rice, which was a testament to how delicious the food was. I felt a real sense of connection with Luke and Dr. Potts and their respective family. Nothing was forced; instead, everything and everyone radiated a sense of sincerity and genuine kindness. The ambiance matched that of a close family gathering where there had been an extended absence, yet the reconnection was as if nothing had changed, and the conversation flowed naturally and uninterrupted by any feelings of anxiety or reservation. Dinner was complemented by bread pudding for dessert, another classic Southern favorite, which was mouthwatering and delicious.

"What do you say we have a drink and take a stroll down the street to Bayou St. James?" suggested Dr. Potts, as he glared at my reaction, interpreting my expression in real time and with great ease. "Don't worry, it is legal in Biloxi to walk down the street with alcohol," he said.

I chuckled and said, "Sounds good. It is incredible how well you can read people," I replied. He responded with a wise grin that said everything without speaking a word. The wives and children stayed at the house as we took the short stroll down to the bayou. When we arrived at what appeared to be a tiny lake, we stopped near the water's edge. I looked at Dr. Potts with what I can only imagine to be complete confusion and asked, "Is this the bayou?" Being a forty-two-year-old man who grew up in the Midwest, I was admittedly naive to many customs of the South. I expected the word bayou to describe something more reminiscent of a swamp, while this appeared to resemble nothing more than a retention pond, which were small, numerous, man-made bodies of water known to riddle the suburban communities of Florida.

Dr. Potts again in his wise professorial voice said, "Bayou simply describes a slow-moving body of water. So the South is littered with bodies of water that are termed bayous."

"Ahh, I understand. It really is quiet and peaceful," I said. I stood and reflected on the concept of a bayou, a word that appeared to be the perfect metaphoric representation of the pace at which things moved in the South, and at the time provided me the foresight that I hoped could curb my lofty goals were I to accept the medical director position at CHOB. A slow-moving "bayou of progress." I hoped to store this lesson in my mind and call upon the analogy should I decide to accept the job, as a way of remembering that things move slowly in the South, like the drainage pipes I witnessed being laid today, twelve years after Hurricane Kelly. Slow moving, bayou progress, but progress nonetheless.

The magical evening came to an end, and we thanked Luke and his family for the marvelous food, drink, and company. "See you tomorrow at the hospital, Luke," I said as I closed the door to Naomi's vehicle.

"Hope you enjoyed the evening," Dr. Potts stated.

"We did!" we all replied in unison. The ride back to the hotel was quiet. Food coma and the drinks had settled in nicely. Very few words were spoken, and the only audible sound consisted of the obnoxious resonation of the vehicle tires as they took turns plunging into each pothole as if being temporarily swallowed then subsequently regurgitated back onto the street, rendering the tires once again viable prey, vulnerable to an all but certain attack by the endless packs of potholes lurking in the dark. As I stared out the window at the large oak trees and old historic Southern homes I felt overcome again by this sense of warmth and home. It simply felt right or perhaps the two glasses of bourbon I consumed had me feeling a bit tipsy. It was impossible to know, but I was content. As I looked over at Ana and smiled, she returned a cautious smile that said to me that she wasn't sold on the prospect of moving to Biloxi, not yet.

My alarm sounded promptly at 6 a.m. and I awoke stealthily, attempting not to awaken Ana and the kids. I showered and put on my suit and as I finished tying my yellow-striped tie and putting on my navy-blue suit coat, I felt my cell phone vibrate. It was Dr. Potts, punctual as ever, sending a text. "Morning Eric, I'm down in the lobby. Take your time." I dashed down the hall to the elevator and hit the button labeled G for ground floor. As the elevator door opened there stood Dr. Potts looking dapper in his brown sport jacket and tie. "Are you ready, or do you want to eat some breakfast before we head to the hospital?" he said.

"I am good; let me grab a quick cup of coffee on the way out the door and I am ready to go," I said. I filled the disposable cup full of black coffee and off we drove down the pothole-ridden streets of Biloxi.

The second interview agenda consisted of a more diverse group of interviewers than my prior visit. This time I would be meeting with a few members of the congenital heart team that I was unable to meet during my first visit. Otherwise, the majority of my scheduled interviews were to involve the C-suite administrators, including Nancy Ogylview, the chief executive officer, Justin Telen, the chief operating officer, John Wozniak, the new chief nursing officer, and once again I would be meeting with the James Deeton, the chief medical officer. The final meeting of the day would again be with Dr. Rostri and Dr. Penton.

The first meeting of the day was with Nancy Ogylview, chief executive officer of Children's Hospital of Biloxi. Nancy had been in her current role as

CEO for a little over a year. Nancy's story was fascinating as she had worked her way up through the children's hospital system, which as I would come to understand, is the path most administrators would follow as they eventually assumed leadership positions at Children's Hospital of Biloxi. She began her career as an outpatient clinic nurse, followed by a five-year stint as manager of a few different outpatient clinics before she obtained her Master of Business Administration. Her husband was a well-respected and well-connected clinical professor of adult neurology, employed by the University of Southeastern Mississippi. As I would also come to understand, in the Deep South, and in particular Biloxi, connections mattered far more than your education or anything else for that matter. The feeling among those I met was that Nancy was egregiously unqualified to be a CEO. However, in Biloxi she had the one attribute that trumped all others, the gold standard of all qualifications in the Deep South, and that was quite simply her connections, and it ultimately thrust her into the role of hospital CEO. Dr. Potts had given me an extensive yet politically correct review of Nancy's meteoric rise to the position of CEO. Her hiring predated Dr. Potts's arrival at CHOB and it became quickly apparent that he harnessed significant reservations related to her ability to move Children's Hospital beyond the recovery efforts of Hurricane Kelly and into a new phase of medicine reminiscent of the top children's hospitals around the country. During my first visit I had heard rumblings from some of the CICU nurses that Nancy had recently announced controversial changes, which she decided necessitated her implementation. Let's just say labeling them as "unpopular" by the staff was a gross misrepresentation of the resultant after-effects of her decision. These changes included a substantial downgrade in health benefits for nonphysician employees and negation of all accumulated sick leave exceeding one hundred hours, which many long-term employees had accumulated for years. So, as I prepared for my interview with Nancy, I felt it was important to discuss these changes in order to understand her perspective and reasoning for such a decision because after hearing the concerns of the CICU nurses, it became crystal clear that this had led to unhappiness and mistrust of the administration, which for me translated into to substantial risk of nursing turnover. Such a downwind effect could sabotage any hopes of building and evolving the CICU, should I decide to accept the position. Dr. Deeton's secretary led me from the waiting room into Nancy's office and told me she would return for me in thirty minutes to escort me to my next interview.

"Welcome," said Nancy. "Please have a seat."

"Thank you," I replied.

Nancy proceeded to give me a detailed summary of herself, explaining how Children's Hospital had a long-standing history of service to the Biloxi community. "We have managed to break even or operate in the black for the last several years from a profitability standpoint. 'We run thin,' but we do the best we can with what we have," she said.

As I came to understand, the Biloxian saying "we run thin" when translated into English, in fact means "we cut staff, salary, and resources or any cost in general, in any manner necessary, in order to ensure an annual profit, even at the expense of staff and patient care." I hope you're picking up my sarcasm because I am laying it on pretty thick. I couldn't believe what I was hearing, but "we run thin" would become a theme repeated by countless staff members as if it was a slogan representing a way of life. I thought to myself, perhaps they should make T-shirts and instead of Nike's "Just do it" or "Run Hard" they could say, Biloxi "Run Thin"! The sad part of this slogan was that everyone had simply adopted it, but to me it meant that they had found a way to convince the staff that running a hospital, which they actively starved of resources, likely resulting in suboptimal patient care, so that the hospital finished the year financially in the black, was acceptable. She said these words in such a way as if she was proud of it. I saw no way to interject my opinion without being offensive, so I let her continue to talk, which consumed twenty-five of the thirty minutes scheduled for our interview.

When she was finished and glanced at her watch, she asked, "Well, do you have any questions?"

I replied, "Yes, I have a couple. I know you said you 'run thin' but are there any subspecialties that have consistently been profitable here, which may represent an opportunity to invest and grow that specialty in order to improve your revenue stream, so you don't have to 'run so thin'?"

"Well, right now we don't have a lot of money to invest because of the upcoming hospital renovations, so outside of our commitment to invest in the staffing and development of the CICU, we don't have any immediate plans for expansion in any specialty," Nancy replied.

"I am happy to hear you say that you are investing in the CICU, but unfortunately that is not a revenue-generating specialty. Hopefully we can promote and grow the cardiac surgical program, which will ensure filling the CICU and generate revenue," I said as gently as I could, trying hard not to upset her while still attempting to get my point across.

"Maybe we can reconsider investing in the future. Well, time is almost up," she said as she rustled papers on her desk in a random and aimless manner, I can only assume with the intent of convincing me that she was extremely busy, so I would leave her office as soon as possible. "Any other questions?" she asked insincerely, hoping that the answer was no.

"Just one last question. Do you think there will be any major repercussions relating to nursing turnover following your very difficult decision to change health-care benefit structure and alter sick day limits?" I asked as I desperately attempted to appear impartial, but I am certain I unintentionally came off as a smug prick. How could I ask that question in any way that wouldn't fan the flame of her insecurity after making such an appalling decision with the goal of making money for the hospital while showing a complete lack of remorse for the effects on the staff, who were now busy "running extra thin" as a result of her actions.

"Uh, where did you hear that?" she asked angrily.

"I met with some CICU nurses during my last visit here and they seemed quite upset about the change and were considering other options for employment. It does concern me a bit to hear of their displeasure when I am considering taking over leadership of the unit. Nursing turnover in such a specialized unit can be crippling to a CICU," I said, hoping I appeared sincere and non-aggressive.

"Yes, we may lose nurses, but we will hire new ones. Actually, it may be more cost-effective to hire younger nurses who are less expensive," she responded snidely as suddenly her face turned to one of relief as there was a knock on the door signaling that my time was up. "Oh, looks like our time is up. Enjoy the rest of your visit!" Nancy said. I was deeply disturbed by her answers, her thought process, and even more so by her lack of empathy for her employees.

"Thank you for your time," I said as I shook her hand. Although I desperately fought the urge to say, "Nancy, I know you're busy with your whole aimless paper rustling thing, so I won't consume any more of your precious time, but I wanted to tell you that 'I believe your business strategy will soon have you running thin for your career.' Anyway, back to reality. Red flags two, three, four, shit I lost count at this point. Let's just agree that a significant number of red flags had just flown right over my head and while I understood her logic was flawed, I was again far too naive at that point to understand the tragic consequences that can result from poor leadership, when administrators fail to have the best interests of their employees and patients in mind. I would soon learn that poor leadership inevitably trickles down the hierarchical ladder, negatively impacting everyone.

Angie, Dr. Deeton's administrative assistant, led me to my next interview, which was with Justin Telen, chief operating officer. Justin was a younger guy in his late forties, clean-shaven, with a short military-style haircut. He had been in his current role for just under two years. He had a business background and held an MBA. He had joined Children's Hospital of Biloxi following a two-year stint as COO of Oklahoma Children's Hospital in Oklahoma City. "Please have a seat, Eric. How are you, sir?" asked Justin.

"I am doing well, thanks," I replied.

"How has your day been so far?" asked Justin.

"Informative," I replied. Following introductions and small talk, Justin and I spoke in great detail pertaining to his opinion about the state of Children's Hospital of Biloxi and what he felt a glimpse into the future would look like. It was clear to me by the time our visit concluded that Justin was a very sharp guy, leading me to believe there were two possible avenues as they related to his future. One possibility included him as the future CEO of Children's Hospital of Biloxi, but several other changes would need to line up for that to occur. More likely, I felt his future was likely to lead him to another institution where he would certainly do great things. Why did I think that he would end up elsewhere and not as the future CEO of CHOB? He lacked one major characteristic. Can you guess what that was? You nailed it! He lacked "good ol' boy" connections! Regardless of where his path led, I felt reassured to have him as a leader at Children's Hospital of Biloxi, even if for a brief period of time. It helped reassure me that his intelligence and vision may help balance or stabilize the clear intellectual deficit resulting from the CEO, particularly after experiencing what I could only describe as a very concerning interview with her.

"Follow me, Dr. Philson, we are headed to John Wozniak's office, the new chief nursing officer, which is just down the hall," said Angie.

John Wozniak was in his early fifties. He had joined Children's Hospital of Biloxi just three months prior to my visit. While he was still adapting to his new role, he was making impressive changes, including emphasizing the importance of supporting and developing the nursing staff, a philosophy which had been nonexistent for decades. John came from an impressive pedigree. He was educated at the University of California, San Francisco, and had previously held the CNO position at Stanford University and at Columbia University. "How is your day going, Eric?" John asked.

"It is going well so far," I replied.

"Since I am new here, I figured this would be a good time for you to ask about all the dirty secrets I have uncovered and the challenges I have had to deal with since I arrived, so ask away. Go!" said John.

I was shocked but grateful for the honesty and transparency. I started with what I considered the most important question. "Are you happy with your decision to come here?" I asked.

"Great question!" he replied. "The answer is yes. I will tell you that this has so far turned out to be the most challenging position of my career. I have been in much more prestigious places but never in a place that was so in need of change and outside influence. I know that may sound arrogant, but I can promise you it isn't. It's the truth. When the same people stay and are promoted within the same system, things become stagnant and too comfortable. Add a catastrophic event like Hurricane Kelly to the mix and suddenly you have an institution that has been set back ten to twenty years as staff leave the city and state at record rates, resulting in a hospital that essentially functions inside of a bubble—totally disconnected from the evolutionary changes in medicine that are occurring all around them. I couldn't believe the staffing ratios when I arrived here, and everyone just accepted it as if it was the norm. If I have to hear the saying, 'We run thin' one more damn time, I am going to vomit!" said John with great passion.

I smiled and laughed aloud as I said, "You have no idea how happy I am to hear you say that. Hearing others passionate about changing things for the better, helping the community, and improving the care for the children of the State of Mississippi is what is truly drawing me to this place," I replied.

"Look, if you decide to come, there is so much work to be done, but it is an opportunity to bring change and you will have the opportunity to make the cardiac ICU your own and that is a rare thing these days!" John said.

"That is so true," I replied. Our thirty-minute interview seemed like seconds, and it left me wishing we had more time to talk about his plans and goals for the future but alas, Angie was in the doorway, waiting to whisk me away to my next interview, which was with the CMO, Dr. Deeton.

"Two more interviews to go, Dr. Philson. I am sure you are ready to finish and get back to your family," said Angie.

"Yes, I am, but I have enjoyed the day and it has been very informative," I replied.

Angie knocked on Dr. Deeton's door. "Come in," Dr. Deeton said loudly.

"Dr. Deeton, here is Dr. Philson," Angie said as she anxiously turned and exited the room.

Dr. Deeton stood and offered his hand in greeting. "Great to see you, Eric. Have a seat," he said. James Deeton had golden blonde hair, which must have been dyed. He was a short man at five foot five although as a result of a progressive kyphotic posture he suffered from over the years, his actual measured height while standing was probably closer to five foot. He was a Mississippi native, born and raised in Biloxi. He projected a serious demeanor at all times and was well-known for his extremely short fuse, with a propensity for using the word "fuck," often multiple times in the same sentence. When angry, which was frequent, his face would turn beet red, resulting in a rather frightening appearance, which suggested to bystanders that at any moment he could rupture a cerebral aneurysm. He was responsible for many changes over the years that had positively influenced CHOB and the city of Biloxi. He constructed the entire anesthesia department at CHOB and was also responsible for building and maintaining the ECMO program at Children's Hospital of Biloxi. He was a man blessed with many talents and gifts; unfortunately for everyone else, the gift of speech was not one of them. Conversations with him were exceedingly awkward and painful. They were often filled with long, random pauses of uncertain origin, which left you scrambling for reasons to explain what the hell was happening? You were often left wondering, was he thinking about what he should say next? Was he intentionally pausing to build suspense, adding dramatization to the moment, allowing him to really drive home his point? Was he waiting for me to speak? Or was he waiting for me to reply to his last comment, which could be problematic because between the monotone voice and snail-like pace of his speech, by the time the pause had occurred, I had either stopped paying attention LONG ago or I may have actually dozed off for a brief moment. Either way, I often had no idea what he had said, which made it nearly impossible to respond without appearing foolish. As a result, you were left confused, and for this reason, I never looked forward to one-on-one conversations with him.

Dr. Deeton spent his career as an anesthesiologist, practicing mostly cardiac anesthesia, which meant he worked closely with Dr. Rostri and Dr. Penton before obtaining his MBA and being hired as the chief medical officer of Children's Hospital of Biloxi. During his time practicing pediatric cardiac anesthesia, he observed areas he felt could be improved upon, which were primarily deficiencies involving the postoperative care in the CICU. He felt anecdotally that the mechanical ventilation times appeared long, as did the hospital length of stay, particularly for those patients undergoing simpler cardiac surgeries. His assumptions were later confirmed when CHOB began contributing data to the national CICU database, which tracks CICU outcomes and allows you to compare yourself to other institutions across the country. Beyond the ventilation times and length of stay concerns, there were frequent complications occurring in the middle of the night with no in-house physician present to respond immediately to emergencies. While the cardiac surgeons lived close to the hospital, even a five-minute delay can be fatal when dealing with these fragile patients. This left the CICU nurses alone to recognize and address problems without proper oversight and guidance. As a result, cardiac arrests were not an infrequent occurrence in the CICU, occurring at a rate that subjectively appeared higher than one would expect, an observation that was also validated once CHOB began participating in the national CICU database. In addition to lacking 24-7 in-house physician coverage, there was little to no input from the pediatric cardiology team and there were no critical care physicians involved in the care of cardiac patients. Dr. Deeton recognized these deficiencies and proposed the hiring of cardiac critical care physicians to direct the postoperative care in the CICU and to implement 24-7 coverage. This was viewed as unnecessary by the cardiac surgeons who felt the care that they provided in the CICU was adequate, leading Dr. Deeton to hire unbiased experts in the field to do an external review of the program, ultimately resulting in a report that led to the creation of the position I was currently interviewing for.

"Eric, how have you enjoyed … uh … your …"

"Oh shit! Here we go!" I thought to myself. The pause seemed like an eternity. It felt as though it must have been at least an hour. What was happening? The first time I witnessed this uncomfortable pause, I was certain he was having an absence seizure. Or perhaps a stroke? At one point I considered activating a rapid response announcement overhead? I even contemplated initiating CPR. The silence was so uncomfortable. However, I now considered myself a veteran, approaching expert-level experience when it came to dealing with JDPs (aka James Deeton pauses). "Remember your training," I said to myself, as if I was Luke Skywalker in the movie *Star Wars*.

I took a deep breath and waited, as he finally blurted out the words, "Visit so far?"

"It's been going quite well, thanks," I said uncomfortably.

"Well, uh … so far … uh … the feedback has been uh … exceptional, Eric!" he finally finished.

"Thank you, sir. I have equally enjoyed meeting everyone," I replied.

"We uh, …" Each pause became progressively more difficult to tolerate. "We uh … would uh … really like you to … uh think …"

"Jesus, please help him finish so I can get the hell out of this room," I said to myself as I squirmed in my seat, repeatedly checking the time on my watch.

"About the possibility of joining us. Why don't you … uh …"

Suddenly there was a knock at the door. "Yes! Thank you, Lord, for answering me. My time must be up, and Angie is here to save the day," I celebrated to myself.

"Dr. Deeton, you have a phone call on line one," said Angela.

"Noooooo … For the love of God, please let him finish!" I screamed in my mind.

"Tell them I … uh … I will call them … uh … back," he said.

"It is Dr. Rostri," she replied.

Dr. Deeton picked up the phone. "Uh-huh, uh-huh. OK. I will let him … uh … know. Eric, … Uh … Dr. Rostri and … uh … Dr. Penton are still in the … uh … operating room and won't be able to make their meeting with you, but … uh … they want you to know that … uh … they will … uh … call you … uh … tonight. Now, …uh … where was … uh … I?" he said as he smiled awkwardly at me.

"I have no frickin' clue," I said to myself.

"Eric, we would like you to consider joining us, so why don't you go home, talk with your wife and kids and let us know what it would take for you to join us," Dr. Deeton said with surprising speed and clarity.

I turned my head to look behind me and around the room to see if there was anyone else who could verify the miracle I had just witnessed! "What the hell just happened? He said a complete sentence with absolute clarity and void of a single pause in ten seconds flat, while he struggled to finish a five-word sentence over the last twenty minutes," I said to myself, utterly confused. Regardless of the cause, I would take it. I wasn't sure if I was happier to hear him offer me the job or to know that I could finally get the hell out of that room as quickly as possible. "That sounds wonderful, Dr. Deeton," I replied as I stood up from my chair to shake his hand.

"Angela!" he yelled at the top of his voice.

"Yes, Dr. Deeton?" she inquired as she nervously rushed into the room.

"Please … uh …" (long pause)

"For the love of God! Please let him finish!" I prayed silently to myself. Just then, my prayers were answered, as he completed his thought.

"Uh show ... Dr. Philson out and ... uh call him a cab. Safe travels, Eric."

"Thank you, Dr. Deeton, I appreciate everything, and I will be in touch with you next week after discussing everything with my family," I replied.

I felt a sense of relief as I departed Children's Hospital of Biloxi on the way back to my hotel. Yes, it's true, I felt as if I may have actually lost about twenty IQ points after being stuck in Dr. Deeton's office for the last thirty minutes, but overall, the visit was positive, and I was able to get a good feel for the potential that existed. I arrived at the conclusion that there was a strong foundation of physicians residing at CHOB who shared a vision and a passion for evolving the program into one that rivaled top cardiac programs around the country. I acknowledged that accepting the job also meant accepting some risk, as there were clearly some concerning aspects that revealed themselves during both of my visits to Biloxi; however, I believed that the potential to make a difference and the likelihood of eventual success far outweighed these risks. In hindsight, I admit that I was oblivious to the many shortcomings, which may have altered my optimism were I capable of recognizing them at the time. I was disappointed that I didn't get a chance to tour the inside of the CICU or meet with the cardiac surgeons again; however, I understood that they were busy operating. Besides, what could be that different about this CICU when compared to every other ICU I had seen? The answer awaiting me was, A WHOLE LOT!

I arrived at the hotel and excitedly discussed my day with Ana. She had spent the day with Naomi, Dr. Potts's wife, who was kind enough to take her and the girls to the park for a picnic. Ana was happy to see the joy on my face, but I could see the hidden displeasure in her eyes. I finished telling her about the day as we packed our things and called a cab to take us to the airport. As we rode to the airport, I could sense a mixture of emotions and energies that were passing throughout the cab. My excitement was intermixed with what I perceived as uncertainty on the part of Ana. However, I would later come to realize that it was not uncertainty but instead a sprouting resentment that would ultimately grow, spread and fester to a point where it would overtake and consume her thoughts and emotions, like an invasive species in a foreign land. As we approached the airport, Dr. Rostri called and apologized for his inability to meet and offered his support for my hiring and passed on the same sentiment on the part of Dr. Penton. We arrived home to Fort Myers safe, with a lot to discuss and think about.

5

THE LIFE-CHANGING DECISION

For the next week discussions between Ana and I intensified. "You know I support you and if you want to go then we can go. I understand now that this seed has been planted in your mind and even if it is not Biloxi, it will be somewhere else. I just feel sad because we have finally established roots here in Fort Myers, we have wonderful friends, the kids have a great school, and we live in our dream house. Now all of that will change and we will need to start over, once again," Ana said.

"You are right. I don't feel challenged here and I feel like this is the right move for me. I know it is hard to start over, but we can do it. We have done it before. I will not only be challenged but we will financially be far better off," I replied.

"I don't care about the money. You will be home much less," Ana said.

"Yes, you are probably right," I replied.

I had already made the decision in my mind; now I needed to do some research regarding the financial commitment that would be required from the hospital and university in order to successfully build the CICU from scratch. I spent days researching the structure of some of the most successful cardiac intensive care units in the country. This included calling and emailing colleagues around the country to get their input regarding staffing, salary ranges, necessary equipment, as well as the cost of such equipment. After a week, I had compiled a list of requests, which consisted primarily of staff and equipment needs that I felt were essential for building the cardiac intensive care unit from scratch. I once again sat down with Ana to share with her the list I had complied, which I subsequently intended on sending to Dr. Deeton and Dr. Potts. I spent time discussing with her the increased salary that I was to request, hoping it would help convince her that the move would be worth it. She couldn't have cared less about the money, and once again she repeated her support for me; however, I could see her disguised disdain for the move. She attempted to hide it by offering a fabricated smile as she hugged me and said, "I am happy for you."

"Don't you mean happy for us?" I replied.

"Yes, happy for us," she said, again with her best attempt at covering her sadness. She walked out of the room, hiding her tears but I sensed their presence.

I sent a text to Dr. Potts and Dr. Deeton, notifying them that I had finshied compiling a list of requests that I felt were necessary to build the cardiac intensive care unit and that I would like to review it with them. They replied with excitement at the fact that I had been able to generate such a list so quickly. Dr. Potts called me and suggested that I email Dr. Deeton and him a copy of the list so that they may review it and investigate the feasibility of my asks in advance. He suggested we set up a phone call the following day to discuss their thoughts regarding my requests. I agreed and sent the list to the two of them via email with the plan to call Dr. Potts the next day at 1 p.m.

Time seemed to fly and before I knew it, 1 p.m. the following day had arrived. Dr. Potts being his punctual self, called me at 12:58 p.m., just as I was picking up my phone to dial his number. "Eric, Dr. Deeton and I have reviewed your requests and we have discussed their feasibility with Children's Hospital leadership as well as leadership from the University of Southeastern Mississippi and we believe we can meet all of your demands. So, I guess that means welcome aboard," exclaimed Dr. Potts excitedly.

"That is great news, Dr. Potts. I am very grateful and couldn't be more excited to start this next chapter of my life," I said.

"I was thinking March 1, 2017, would be a reasonable start date for you, which should provide ample time to obtain your Mississippi medical license and to get you credentialed at Children's Hospital of Biloxi. What do you think?" asked Dr. Potts.

"I think that sounds great. I will get started on the application for my Mississippi medical license tomorrow. Thank you so much for everything and please pass on my thanks as well as my excitement to the rest of the team," I replied.

"I most certainly will," he said. As I hung up the phone, I was overcome with relief and excitement. Ana engulfed me with a massive hug and kiss, expressing her congratulations as tears trickled down her face. She made valiant attempts to pass them off as tears of happiness and joy, but I wasn't fooled, and I couldn't help but sense the resentment that continued to build inside of her.

6

WELCOME TO BILOXI

As part of the employment agreement, The University of Southeastern Mississippi paid our moving expenses, so in the weeks leading up to the move, our Fort Myers home was placed on the market, and we had a plethora of movers in the house packing our dishes and belongings as they whisked them off and loaded them onto the moving trucks to commence the three-day journey to Biloxi. Ana and I each drove one of our two vehicles, the girls, and our two dogs to Biloxi over a two-day period, planning to arrive at our new home before the moving trucks. We decided to break up the trip by spending one night in Tallahassee, Florida.

When we arrived in Biloxi, it was the first time Ana and at the kids had seen our new home in person. The original house we had placed an offer on was found to have significant termite damage, so we backed out of the contract. At the last minute I flew down to view a beautiful three-acre estate property that needed some interior work but was in an excellent school district and the property itself was breathtaking. We placed an offer without Ana actually seeing the home in person because we didn't want to place any additional burden on the kids after already moving against their will from Florida by requiring them to move into a rental property and then subsequently move again, into our permanent home, which could require changing schools twice. Surprisingly, when we arrived, Ana and the kids immediately fell in love with property. It was a private gated property with two ponds that were stocked with fish, a pool, and a massive yard, which the girls had never had in Florida.

Much to our surprise, our belongings actually arrived on schedule and without major damage. However, there was one problem, which was the fact that the long, winding driveway leading to the house was lined with beautiful apple blossom trees that contained large overhanging branches, making it impossible for the moving trucks to enter the driveway and park near the house. So the movers had no choice but to transport our belongings down the driveway using dollies. Needless to say, there were some very unhappy movers that day. Spring was near and the weather was gorgeous. There was a cool southern breeze with clear sunny skies, and the grass was beginning to morph from the dying brown color synonymous with the winter to the vibrant, rejuvenated green that announced the arrival of spring! The apple blossoms were blooming, and there were swarms of white petals wafting through the air with each gust of wind, which pissed off the movers even more. When the wind ceased, the white petals of the apple blossom trees gracefully receded to the ground, covering the entire driveway, resembling a remote country road freshly blanketed by a winter snowstorm. It was magnificent and peaceful.

I had two weeks off before my official start date at Children's Hospital of Biloxi. It gave me an opportunity to help Ana unpack and also gave me some time to spend fishing with the girls in the pond present in our new front yard. Our new neighbors were friendly, each taking time out of their day to stop by our house and welcome us to Biloxi with gifts such as a king cake, cookies, wine, and homemade shrimp gumbo. I looked at Ana and said, "In all the places we have lived, not once have we known our neighbors by their first names, nor have they stopped over to bring us gifts."

Ana replied, "I will agree with you about that, it is nice to have friendly neighbors."

One week after our arrival to Biloxi, I received a text from Dr. Rostri, which read, "Hi Eric, hope you are settling in well. I would like to meet for coffee this week prior to your start date if that is OK with you?"

"Absolutely! Tell me when and where," I replied.

"How about tomorrow, 11 a.m. at Starbucks on Mainstreet, in Old Town Biloxi," Dr. Rostri responded.

"Perfect, see you then," I replied. My curiosity began to eat at me, as I wondered why he wanted to meet with me in advance. Perhaps due to the fact that we never had the opportunity to meet during my second visit to the hospital? The numerous potential explanations ran uncontrollably through my mind, which kept me awake tossing and turning that night. I awoke at 5 a.m., finally giving up after multiple failed attempts at falling back asleep. I tried not to wake Ana as I quietly crept to the bathroom and showered. After dressing and making a cup of coffee I walked outside and sat on the front porch. It was strangely quiet, a silence reminiscent of my childhood days, growing up on a farm in the heart of Michigan. I missed the quiet; however, my body had become unaccustomed to it after years of living in and around the noise inherent to large cities and after years of being immersed in the noise and commotion of the cardiac intensive care unit and its incessant warning alarms. Our new home was peaceful, and it gifted me a moment that was precious and memorable, allowing me to experience peace and tranquility in the simplicity of silence, surrounded by nature. I could never have imagined this meaningful moment would represent one of only a handful of times over the next several years where I would actually have the time or the right presence of mind to truly be alive and in the moment, enough to enjoy this gorgeous estate in the manner it deserved.

As Ana and the kids woke, we sat down and ate breakfast together. The girls were anxious about their new school, and I did my best to calm their nerves by reassuring them that, "We all get nervous" and empathized by sharing that I too was anxious about my new job. After years of proving myself and establishing myself as a strong clinician, I would have to start all over and prove myself once again to a new group of colleagues and staff. I said, "Whether it's a new job as the medical director or as a new student at a new school, new experiences force us out of our comfort zone and that makes us anxious, but it also provides opportunity for personal growth and the experience eventually makes us stronger. But if you just carry on being yourself, everything else will sort itself out because when you are yourself, you are sharing who you are and you are showing others what you are all about, whether it be at school or at the hospital." As we finished eating and talking, it was time for me to leave for my meeting with Dr. Rostri. I changed my clothes, got in my car and headed down the pothole-filled streets of Biloxi on my way to Starbucks.

I arrived at Starbucks five minutes early to find Dr. Rostri already seated at a table. "Eric, let me buy your coffee," he said.

"Oh. Thank you, but that's not necessary," I replied.

"I insist," he said. I reluctantly submitted to his offer, and after grabbing my double espresso, we sat down at the table. "Eric, I am glad you are here, but I want you to understand some things before you start. Biloxi is a complicated place to understand, and Children's Hospital of Biloxi is even more complicated to understand. This institution has a long-standing history of financial success. Yet, it also has a long-standing history of refusing to invest in the hospital staff and services, which has led to the substantial understaffing of physicians, nurses, and other ancillary services, which has continued to worsen over time. Are you seeing the connection I am implying, Eric? And in terms of support within the congenital heart program, let me tell you, we haven't been given much. The recruitment for your position is the first time in twenty years that the administration has committed substantial amounts of money toward investing in the growth of any specialty within the congenital heart program. They continue to cut funding and the number of ancillary staff continues to decline each year. Yet, the hospital boasts a profit year after year. Do you understand what I am getting at?" Dr. Rostri asked again.

I nodded my head in agreement; however, I began to notice a stirring anxiety build inside me, birthing a large glob of saliva that had accumulated in the back of my throat, inducing the involuntary and uncontrollable urge to swallow, certain to produce the audible "gulping" sound universally synonymous with "Oh shit!" I didn't want Dr. Rostri to sense my concern, and as such, I struggled desperately to manage the growing pool of saliva. Yet with each word he spoke, my anxiety and the quantity of saliva increased exponentially and linearly, until I was left with no choice but to sip my espresso, allowing me to clear the saliva in a premeditated and controlled manner, thereby concealing the escalating concern building inside me that I may have made a big mistake accepting this job.

"You are going to encounter some intensive care unit practices when you start that may seem odd or outdated to you. I ask you to keep an open mind and try to understand that we have done the best we can with what we have been provided," said Dr. Rostri.

"I understand, Dr. Rostri. I am a team player, and I will do my best to remain impartial and open-minded. We both share the same goal, which is taking excellent care of the patients. In this same regard, Dr. Rostri, I ask that you keep an equally open mind toward new suggestions that I may make, even if they are outside of your usual pattern of clinical practice," I replied.

"Of course," he responded. "There is one more thing I would like to bring to your attention. It is in regard to Dr. Geisinger, our junior surgeon," said Dr. Rostri.

"Of course," I replied with what I can only imagine must have been a puzzled look on my face.

"As you know, the practice of congenital heart surgery is extraordinarily competitive, and programs are constantly being evaluated under a microscope when it comes to patient survival and postoperative outcomes. As a consequence, it is far too risky for me to allow her to perform complex surgeries and she is not ready anyway. Yes, she is from Boston, but the congenital cardiac surgery fellowship program is merely one year of training, which is simply an insufficient amount of time and exposure, and I cannot put my program at risk by allowing her to operate, when it could result in a bad outcome. As a result, Dr. Geisinger is upset that she is not being permitted to perform complex cardiac surgeries and instead is only being allowed to do some simpler cases," exclaimed Dr. Rostri as he waved his arms in the air with great passion.

I was extremely confused. Doris had told me nothing of this. "Dear, Lord, please don't let her leave after I have just arrived here. She is one of the major reasons I decided to join this program!" I thought to myself, doing my best not to panic. As I tried to compose myself, I replied with sincerity, "I understand what you're saying. Obviously, I am not a cardiac surgeon so I have to defer to you; however, isn't there a way you can coach her through a complex case after having her watch you perform several?"

"No, too risky!" he snapped back.

"Well, what is the long-term plan for her necessary professional development as a congenital heart surgeon? At some point she needs to perform complex cases, correct?" I asked, now somewhat annoyed.

"I was pushed to hire her by Dr. Deeton. I didn't want to hire a junior surgeon, too much risk! She will have to decide if this program is right for her," he said with a scowl on his face.

I took a couple of deep breaths to calm myself and stood up to offer Dr. Rostri my hand, which was now ice cold, as a consequence of the profound "fight-or-flight" response and resultant adrenaline surge my body had just experienced, due to this concerning discussion. I imagined my face must be pale, as if I had just witnessed a ghost. I thanked him for the conversation as

I explained that I needed to get home and help my wife unpack our belonging from the move. This was the first time I fully acknowledged the obvious display of controlling behavior exhibited by Dr. Rostri. Feeling uneasy following our conversation, I knew my next course of action must involve a one-on-one conversation with Doris Geisinger, the junior cardiac surgeon. I needed to gain some clarity on this situation by hearing her point of view, which would hopefully provide me clarity as to her long-term plans for future, in particular, to confirm whether or not CHOB was to be part of those plans. As I walked to my car, I worked to shake off the shock I had experienced while I composed a text message to Doris. "Hi Doris, it's Eric. My start date at the hospital is March 1. I am looking forward to working together. Can you and I sit down and talk that morning? How about 8 a.m.? I can meet you in your office if that works for you?" I wrote.

"Hi Eric, glad to hear from you. Glad you are here, and I am excited for you to start working. That sounds perfect. I will meet you in the lobby of the hospital a little before 8 a.m. and we can walk up to my office together. How does that sound?" she replied.

"Perfect, see you then," I answered.

7

FIRST DAY AT CHILDREN'S HOSPITAL OF BILOXI

March 1 arrived without warning. I felt a mixture of emotions ranging from excitement to anxiety. I was excited about the possibilities and challenges that lie ahead as they related to the construction of the pediatric cardiac intensive care unit; however, admittedly, my excitement was curtailed by a moderate amount of anxiety regarding the massive amount of work ahead, but even more so, uncertainty pertaining to the possibility that I could be walking into a nightmare that may not be fixable. Had I been so focused on finding a new challenge that I overlooked major deficiencies within the hospital and in the congenital heart program that were beyond my control? Was I even qualified to do this job? As I parked my car and walked toward the main entrance of the hospital, I attempted to reassure myself that these were normal feelings and reservations for anyone assuming this type of role, just as I had tried to reassure my daughters about the anxiety they felt related to their new school, but sadly my attempts at self-reassurance weren't working.

As the automatic doors to the hospital slid open, I stepped into the lobby, where I was overcome by the sound of a metal ball clanking as it slid down a massive, beautiful handmade roller coaster maze. At least a dozen children occupied every inch of the viewing space surrounding this man-made marvel, as the metal ball continued down the maze, in a course predetermined by gravity and its creator—each child with their hands and face plastered to the glass barrier protecting this masterpiece. I became increasingly mesmerized by this maze, when I was abruptly awakened from my trance by the words, "Eric!" I looked to the right and saw Dr. Doris Geisinger, cardiac surgeon, standing near the center of the hospital lobby.

Doris was a young, attractive female in her early forties. She was quite short, measuring five foot two, while wearing hospital clogs, which appeared to add an additional two inches to her actual height. She had brownish-blond hair and brown eyes. She carried a serious look on her face at baseline, but when in the company of those she trusted, this defensive fortress she had masterfully constructed over the years, necessary to survive male-dominated, malignant thoracic and congenital cardiac surgical fellowships, could disintegrate, producing a smile that was genuine and kind, and far more representative of the person she was inside, once you got to know her. When she did, she blessed the world by sharing the kind and compassionate person she was at her very core. Doris was extremely intelligent and had trained at some of the top programs in the United States. She held a Master of Public Health and was the only member of the congenital heart program employed by the University of Southeastern Mississippi who boasted her own research lab, including funding for several ongoing projects and for a research assistant.

As I walked toward her, we naturally bypassed the professional handshake and instead embraced in a quick hug. The first time we met, I could tell that we shared a mutual connection as it pertained to our outlooks on life and in particular the practice of medicine. As we released one another from the hug, we shared mutual smiles of admiration as she said, "I am so glad you are here."

"I am too, Doris," I replied.

"Let's grab a coffee and head up to my office," she said. As we walked through the lobby toward the cafeteria, I paid careful attention to areas of the children's hospital that I had not toured during my previous visits. The hospital interior was old, just as the exterior; however, well-kept nonetheless. It was obvious that the interior had required several face-lifts over the years; however, it appeared clean and the unique and historic nature of the toys in the lobby offered an individualistic touch unparalleled by other children's hospitals I had seen. As we grabbed our coffees and walked toward the elevator leading to Doris's office, it became very apparent that there was a paucity of windows throughout the hospital. As a result, the long hallways we traversed relied on fluorescent lighting, which gave an eerie, almost claustrophobic feeling as if walking through tunnels in a coal mine.

We entered the elevator as the doors closed, subsequently followed by a *ding*, announcing the arrival at our destination, as the automatic doors opened, spitting us out onto the third floor of the hospital. "This way," Doris said, pointing. "This hallway leads to all of the cardiology offices and the cardiology clinic, while this door leads to the cardiac surgery offices. Dr. Rostri, Dr. Penton, and I all have offices in this area," Doris explained.

As we walked through the main door to the three offices, we were greeted by a blond woman who must have been in her early sixties, attractive and well-dressed, who greeted us with a big smile as she said, "Good morning!"

"Good morning," I replied.

"Lisa, this is Eric, he is the new medical director of the pediatric cardiac intensive care unit. Eric, this is Lisa, she is the administrative assistant for our cardiac surgery group," Doris explained.

"Pleasure to meet you, Lisa," I said.

"Same here," Lisa replied.

After exchanging pleasantries, Doris and I stepped into her office and I shut the door behind me as we both sat on opposite sides of her desk. "You have a very serious look on your face, Eric, what's up?" Doris asked.

"Wow, you can read me well. Yes, I am a bit worried after the conversation I recently had with Dr. Rostri," I replied.

"Oh boy, I can only imagine," she said rolling her eyes.

"What is going on between you and Dr. Rostri? He made it sound as though you weren't being allowed to perform complex surgical cases. Is that true?" I asked. I could see the distress in her face as she fought back tears.

"Eric, it is awful. I have been asking to do more cases and in particular more complex cases, but he is refusing to allow me to do them. I have gone to Dr. Deeton but he has been no help whatsoever. He keeps telling me to be patient, but I am required to perform a certain number of surgical cases per year in order to maintain my board certification. Also, in this field you have a finite number of years to develop before you become marginalized, making it virtually impossible to advance your career as a congenital heart surgeon and ultimately find a senior cardiac surgery position, particularly when you are a woman in this field," Doris explained. "Dr. Rostri has told me that I won't be performing complex cases anytime soon and perhaps I should find another job," she said, now fighting back tears with every ounce of her will. "I have spoken to one of my mentors from my fellowship who has reached out to a couple of senior pediatric cardiac surgeons around the country, on my behalf, to see if someone might consider mentoring me while I am still working here. There is a cardiac surgeon in Alabama who is willing to do it," she explained.

"How exactly would that work?" I asked.

"I spoke with Dr. Deeton and he has agreed to allow me to go every other week to Alabama. Dr. Vazquez, the chief of congenital cardiac surgery, at the University of Alabama has agreed to arrange several cases during the weeks I am there, and mentor me in performing complex cardiac surgeries. Then, I will return to Biloxi and continue to work here in hopes that Dr. Rostri will gain confidence in my ability to perform complex surgical cases. My only other option is to leave Biloxi and I really don't want to give up after only two years and put my family through the stress of another move," Doris explained.

"No, please, don't do that. While this is a very unusual arrangement, I don't know what I would do if you left immediately after moving my family here," I replied. I left Doris's office feeling somewhat relieved that she was not leaving, at least in the short term, that is. However, the controlling and manipulative behavior exhibited by Dr. Rostri left a foul taste in my mouth and left me wondering just how far his controlling hands reached throughout the Heart Center and Children's Hospital of Biloxi. As I walked by Lisa's desk toward the exit of the cardiac surgical offices, I was perplexed. Suddenly, I remembered, "Shit, I still haven't physically seen the cardiac intensive care unit that I am supposed to staff and build." I turned around and knocked on Doris's office door and opened it a crack, just enough to peek my head in and ask, "Any chance I could get you to walk me through the CICU."

"Sure," she said as she stood up from her chair and led me out of the cardiac surgery offices, waving goodbye to Lisa as we walked toward the elevator.

The elevator descended and the doors opened, presenting us the first-floor hallway that would lead us toward the cardiac intensive care unit. After a brief walk, we turned left, following the sign hanging from the ceiling above, which contained an arrow pointing toward both the CICU and the morgue. "This must be a joke," I said as I looked in disbelief at Doris.

"Oh, I assure you, this is no joke. The morgue is directly across from the rear doors of the CICU, aside the doors leading to the trash dumpsters for the entire hospital," Doris said with a sarcastic smile.

"Where the hell am I?" I said to myself as I prayed this wasn't some type of hellish omen as to what the future would hold for me.

As we stood at the double doors outside the front entrance to the CICU, Doris fingered the entry code on the touchpad attached to the wall. Suddenly, the double doors automatically opened outward, allowing us access to the CICU. As we stepped through the doorway into the CICU, I was overwhelmed by a strange yet somewhat familiar feeling. I couldn't immediately identify the feeling, but it resonated with an uncanny familiarity to me, as if I had experienced it at another point in my life. As I looked around the unit, it appeared dark and congested, as I observed about ten staff members distributed throughout the CICU. Oddly, I failed to notice a single smile on the face of the staff members present in the unit. As we advanced toward the front desk, we were suddenly sideswiped by a nurse dashing past us on her way toward the exit, rolling her eyes while sighing aloud as she waved her hands in a manner suggesting her displeasure with something that had occurred. Then it dawned on me, I suddenly recalled that familiar feeling I experienced as we had entered the CICU as traumatic memories attached to that awful feeling came rushing back from my subconscious like a freight train. Toxicity! That's it! I had previously endured a three-year, one-sided, emotionally abusive relationship with toxicity during my pediatric critical care fellowship. On a daily basis we were relentlessly criticized, scrutinized, ridiculed, verbally and emotionally abused, all while being enslaved in a sleep-deprived state, with the morbid belief that in some manner this inhumane behavior would make us more successful and compassionate doctors.

As these emotions came flooding back, they were entangled with complex memories of the past, and I couldn't help but feel nauseous. As I looked at Doris, she looked at me and shook her head and said, "Yeah, it's a pretty miserable place right now. Changing that dynamic may be your biggest challenge." I shook my head in disbelief and proceeded to verbally abuse myself for accepting such a job without first experiencing the CICU in person for myself.

We walked around the unit past each patient's bedside, with some of the nursing staff taking the initiative to introduce themselves to me. Doris went through each patient's history briefly. Some were long-term residents of the CICU; however, she glanced over specific details such as the duration of their stay. I guess she was trying not to overwhelm me on my first day. As we walked by the last patient's room, Doris said, "I gotta run. I have a research meeting in fifteen minutes."

"No problem. Thanks for the quick tour and for the talk this morning," I said.

"Of course. See you later," she said as she rushed out the CICU doors leading back to the hallway. Just as she reached the door, she turned back and said, "Hey, you need to talk to Justin. I will tell him to stop by the unit tomorrow."

"Sounds good," I replied. Justin Thorn was a cardiac intensivist who had recently completed his cardiac ICU training just three months prior to my arrival. Justin was born and raised in Biloxi. He was the very first pediatric cardiology fellow trained at Children's Hospital of Biloxi through a newly developed fellowship created by the University of Southeastern Mississippi. He had been hired by Dr. Deeton in advance of me accepting the position of medical director. He had been covering several nights in the CICU over the last three months preceding my arrival. I had heard good things about Justin; however, after my recent meeting with Dr. Rostri and after witnessing the toxicity in the CICU, I immediately became concerned about his longevity and ability to survive without my support. I urgently yelled, "Please send me his contact info," to Doris as she disappeared down the hall.

Seconds later my phone vibrated, revealing his contact information, acknowledging that Doris had in fact heard my request. I immediately sent a text to Justin, asking if he was able to meet with me tomorrow morning in the CICU for rounds with Dr. Rostri. He quickly replied, "Sure, see you then."

"Boy, I hope he is alright," I said to myself.

With Doris gone, I figured now would be a great time to introduce myself to more of the staff while also taking advantage of the opportunity to become more familiar with each patient's medical history. I slowly walked to each bedside, introducing myself to the nurse caring for each patient. I spent time asking each one their name, how long they had worked at Children's of Biloxi, while also attempting to gauge their satisfaction with the care currently being provided to the patients and their overall job satisfaction as a nurse in the CICU, and as an employee of Children's Hospital of Biloxi. I found most of the nurses enjoyed caring for the congenital heart patients; however, there was a blatant and unfathomable disdain directed toward the hospital administration due to the perceived lack of support, which was obviously exacerbated by the recent downgrade in health insurance coverage and cap placed on the number sick days allowed, recently implemented by the CEO, Nancy Ogylview. As I met some of the more experienced nurses, there was an obvious mistrust of an outsider such as myself, particularly one who stood to disrupt and oppose the current decision-making hierarchy in CICU, which had remained unchallenged for decades. The senior nurses were far more reserved, displaying hesitancy to share any meaningful information, including whether they were happy or displeased with the current environment in the CICU. They responded to most of my questions with vague, impartial answers as they pertained to the CICU; however, they were quick to share their hatred and mistrust for hospital administration. I met two experienced nurses willing to share their concerns regarding toxic cliques that had formed and thrived within the CICU, who exhibited bullying behavior toward several younger nurses, resulting in their resignation. This was my first revelation as to the etiology of the rampant nursing turnover that was prevalent in the CICU upon my arrival to CHOB. This meant that young nurses rarely remained on the job long enough to even complete their new hire training, which typically lasted six months, before resigning due to the toxic environment. High nursing turnover can be especially problematic when it occurs in a specialized unit such as that of the CICU, where new hires require months of education and precepting by experienced nurses before they are allowed to care for patients independently. However, realistically, such a job requires several years of exposure before a CICU nurse can truly be considered "experienced." If a unit is unable to retain new grads, how can it ever become fully staffed with experienced nurses?

While the workings and consequences of such a cycle may be obvious to some, it remains worthy of explanation because if the cycle is not successfully broken, the consequences can be crippling to a unit such as the CICU. So, an understaffed unit often has no choice but to hire inexperienced nurses to fill vacant positions, so that they have the staffing required to safely care for critical patients. Experienced nurses are necessary in order to provide mentorship and education to these new nurses. So, if there is repeated turnover of new nursing staff, this places additional burden on an already insufficient number of experienced nurses who must now continuously provide mentoring and education for a large number of new nurses. After a period of time this endless burden placed on the few experienced nurses who remain, ultimately becomes intolerable, placing them at risk of burnout and subsequent resignation, thereby perpetuating the repetitive nature of this "revolving-door phenomenon," defined by the constant resigning and rehiring of nursing staff. This crippling phenomenon can ultimately result in an entire nursing staff void of meaningful cardiac critical care experience who are overcome with the feeling that they are unsupported, thereby contributing to or exacerbating their unhappiness.

I was deeply concerned, so I decided to ask some of the more vocal, experienced nurses for their suggestions as to how they recommended remedying such a situation. Some were kind enough to recommend that I set up one-on-one meetings, in private, with some of the several nurses who had recently given their notice. I asked, "Did you say several nurses?"

Laura, one of the more vocal and experienced nurses, replied, "Yes, I believe there is a total of eight nurses who have resigned."

I shook my head in disbelief and said, "Would you mind sharing their names with me?"

"Sure, let me get the list for you," she said.

"Thank you so much," I replied. I was appreciative of Laura's candor; however, admittedly, I was feeling quite down, as I grasped the gravity of the nursing situation. I was beginning to question my decision to take this job. Despite my concerns, I was here, and couldn't possibly go home to Ana and the kids and say, "Oops, I made a mistake. Let's go attempt to buy back our dream house and move back to Fort Myers." That was not even a possibility. I tried to reassure myself that this was simply the first day. "It couldn't possibly get any worse, right?" Oh, how I wish that were true. In hindsight, I learned an important lesson that day; things can always get worse!

I read through the paper chart of each patient—nope, that is not a typo—it was the year 2017, and Children's Hospital of Biloxi was still using paper charts. The same paper charts that were essentially eradicated in the United States several years ago when a national law was implemented, mandating the use of electronic medical records by health-care institutions. As I opened the physical chart with my actual hands, instead of the click of a mouse, I felt as though I was instantly teleported back to my days as a pediatric resident, nearly twenty years ago. This trip down memory lane required me to confront post-traumatic flashbacks of struggling to decipher the handwriting of fifty different clinicians in a single chart, as if trying to crack the damn DaVinci Code. Suddenly, I unintentionally heard two of the staff members recalling their own personal experiences during Hurricane Kelly, each speaking of the homes they had lost, one of whom witnessed water levels surpassing the roof of their house. As I heard of their awful experience, I came to a humbling realization, far more important than the simple annoyance and inconvenience I was experiencing as a result of paper charting. The archaic concept of paper charting, which spurred such irritation and a reflexive sarcasm that had regretfully led to my silent ridicule that such a practice still existed in the modern world, upon deeper reflection, now provided me with my first true understanding of the devastating effects unleashed by Hurricane Kelly on the city of Biloxi, and how such effect still existed to this very day. I felt shameful for my arrogance and silent ridicule of the hospital for something so silly, and quite frankly, out of its control.

Yes, paper chartering was obnoxious and inconvenient, but upon further self-reflection, I realized that my inexcusable judgment had actually blessed me with a lesson that would help me better understand the residual effects of such a catastrophic event, and even more so, further down the road, it would help me empathize and relate with the staff and people of Biloxi on an entirely different level. The paper charts now suddenly appeared to me as if they were a time capsule buried in the mud, once the water had receded twelve years ago, and my incidental discovery unearthed a treasure of knowledge, including a legend, which allowed me to slowly grasp the gravity of this traumatic natural disaster and how it had in essence, halted medical progress. The community and hospital enacted the most primitive reflex inherent to all living things, the instinct to survive, and as a result they created a metaphoric cocoon, which provided safety; however, it did so at the expense of disconnecting and losing contact with the rest of the outside medical "world." As a result, the staff had been involuntarily forced to "run thin" and "make do" with the resources they had at the time, and when you combine this with a hospital leadership who enabled the false narrative that it was acceptable for the hospital to function in this manner, without any substantial investment over the years, the result is an entire staff who had no choice but to adopt this philosophy as a way of life. I had no idea such a profound message could be housed within something as simple as "paper charts." However, as time went on, I began to realize that very few things in Biloxi were as they seemed, and rarely were such discoveries easy to understand without maintaining an open mind and a desire for further inspection. While it was a nightmare to deal with from a documentation standpoint, the paper records were indicative of the fact that Children's Hospital of Biloxi had been left in the rearview mirror of medical progress, forgotten, abandoned, and left to fend for itself, exactly as the people of the city had been following Hurricane Kelly. But as I learned over time, the resiliency of the people allowed Children's Hospital of Biloxi to persevere by utilizing the strategy of survive now and live to fight another day. I also realized that luxuries are in fact, just that, they are luxuries, which by definition implies that they are unnecessary. From that day forward, I made a conscious effort to remember that. Throughout the world and in particular in third world countries, luxuries are not afforded, yet they continue to provide excellent and passionate care to their patients in their absence. As I mentally digested this complex lesson, I couldn't help but feel that this lesson was a crucial step, signifying that construction of the road map to success over the coming years, had commenced.

As I returned to reality from my contemplative state, I continued reading through the medical chart, which for this particular patient, appeared to be missing some information. "Excuse me, Laura, I think part of this chart is missing," I said.

Laura chuckled sarcastically, as she opened the bottom drawer of the medical cart sitting outside of the patient's room. My philosophical reawakening had been short-lived as I was painfully returned to reality by a metaphorical kick in the nuts as Laura revealed three more completely full paper charts, which must have weighed twenty-five pounds each, while smiling, as if presenting me with the entire Encyclopedia Britannica series for my review. "She has been here in the CICU for nearly two years," Laura said with a fabricated smile.

"Wow, it is going to take me a while to get to know this little one. I will have to come back to her after I have reviewed the thinner charts first," I replied.

Laura again chuckled and said, "You're not going to find many thin charts in this unit." As I moved on to the other rooms and began reading through the charts and orders, I realized she was right. At least half of the cardiac ICU patients had been in the hospital for at least six months. I would indeed need to spend some time over the next couple of weeks getting to know these long-term residents of the CICU; however, I didn't have the time today.

As I read through some of the smaller charts, I asked the nurses about some consistent patterns of practice, which were unfamiliar to me over my previous ten years of practice. When I inquired about the reasoning behind such practices, the response I received every time was, "That's the way we have always done it." As I completed a full loop through the cardiac intensive care unit, I realized that I had successfully introduced myself to each of the staff members working that day and had completed reviewing each of the patient's charts who were not considered long-term residents of the unit, and I had formulated a plan to review the charts of the more chronic patients over the next week or so. As I left the hospital that day, I was mentally exhausted; however, I could conclusively say one thing, the only words I heard with greater frequency at Children's Hospital of Biloxi than "we run thin" were "that's the way we have always done it"—a statement which I had learned over the years was frequently representative of an underlying resistance to change, and typically consisted of learned behavior that had been passed down from leaders atop the institution. I knew among many other things, that indeed my work was cut out for me.

8

CICU ROUNDS WITH DR. ROSTRI AND THE FLOCK OF GEESE

I woke the next morning with a newfound sense of excitement, ready to start my actual first day of clinical work. Dr. Rostri had informed me that rounds started at 7 a.m. He explained that we would meet sharply at that time in the CICU and would subsequently walk as a group to each patient's bedside. I arrived at 6:50 a.m. to find that Dr. Rostri, Justin Thorn, the young cardiac intensivist who had just finished his fellowship that I was scheduled to meet with that morning, and the charge nurse, Erin, had already begun rounding without me and two of the cardiologists, who had just entered the CICU with aspirations of joining rounds. As the three of them walked hastily toward the bedside of the next patient, Dr. Rostri saw me standing at the front of the CICU, offering a weak, ingenuine wave of his hand, as he stopped at the patient's bedside and immediately redirected his gaze toward the paper chart, showing a complete absence of remorse for starting rounds without me. As I walked toward the three of them, Dr. Rostri barked instructions at Justin as he aggressively pointed to the yellow order form inside the paper chart, tapping his right index finger repeatedly until Justin started writing. "0.5 mg of Lasix intravenous, every 12 hours. Write it!" he demanded. I looked at Justin with confusion as this was a very small, homeopathic dose of Lasix, particularly for a child weighing ten kilograms. As I looked closer at Justin, he resembled death. He was struggling to keep his eyes open, and the whites of his eyes were faintly visible through the two-to-three-millimeter slit-like opening between his eyelids. His lower eyelids appeared anchored by the dark bags of edematous skin below his eyes that spoke of pure sleep deprivation. His appearance was disheveled, and his beard appeared unkempt; however, most concerning of all was the complete absence of emotion displayed on his face. This was my first-time seeing Justin in person. He couldn't have been more than five feet two in stature. He had short blond hair that looked as though he just rolled out of bed and a full-grown blondish-brown beard. He was dressed neat although appearing as if he was headed for a nature hike down in the bayou, minus the camouflage. He walked with short, quick steps but with a somewhat downward gaze, adding to my concern for his physical and mental well-being. His appearance resembled a man who had been verbally and emotionally abused like a dog over the last few months in my absence, but I needed to speak with him alone to be certain. His appearance was not consistent with how I envisioned the energetic and optimistic man I had spoken with on the phone prior to my arrival. I was sincerely concerned for his well-being.

I had heard about Justin several times from others during my two interviews. Just prior to finalizing and signing my contract, I had set up a meeting for the two of us to talk by phone. During the conversation, I was impressed. He appeared passionate and caring, well-spoken, and clearly the staff who were involved in his training spoke highly of his decision-making ability and collegiality. Following our conversation, I had concluded that he was an honest and sincere guy with a lot of heart and who shared similar interests with me, including a love of the outdoors and traveling. Given that Justin was a Biloxi native, I felt for the first time, his presence provided me at least some semblance of stability, as he shared with me his desire to improve the postoperative care being provided to the congenital heart patients in Biloxi, due to the major deficiencies he had observed during his years as a pediatric resident and pediatric cardiology fellow at Children's Hospital of Biloxi. He exclaimed, "I am here for the long haul." Though at the time I hadn't met him in person, I immediately liked him, and I knew we would work well together.

I looked at Justin with great concern, as Dr. Rostri closed the paper chart and without hesitation, proceeded to the next patient's bedside, while the others followed closely behind. Erin, the charge nurse, looked toward the three of us who had been left behind, waving her hand, as if saying, "Come on, join us." Before we reached the bedside, *slam* sounded the paper chart as it was aggressively closed by Dr. Rostri, signifying that they were off to the next patient on the other side of the CICU. As I tried to catch up, Dr. Rostri appeared to intentionally speed up his pace, making it virtually impossible for me to walk side by side with him.

Justin looked at me and whispered, "Trust me, don't waste your time attempting to walk next to him, he will only walk faster to ensure he is first and to mess with your mind. It's a power thing." I rolled my eyes, as the three of us were finally able to catch up to the group as we appeared to naturally fall into two single-file lines that could only be described as upside-down V shape resembling a flock of geese migrating south for the winter, with Dr. Rostri at the point, leading the flock. As the flock came in for a landing at bed number 20, their final landing spot for the day, I pushed my way to the front, now standing beside Dr. Rostri as I looked over his shoulder, attempting to read and analyze the flowsheet containing all the labs, vital signs, clinical data and fluid balance for the previous twenty-four hours. As Dr. Rostri finished scanning the document, he handed it to me as he walked toward the front doors of the CICU, exiting without saying a word, presumably on his way to the operating room to begin the surgical case for the day.

I looked back at the remaining team members who appeared confused and said, "I guess that means no changes for the day?" They chuckled and shrugged their shoulders as the group disintegrated and exited the unit.

Justin walked over to me and said, "The coffee truck is here today, should we go grab a coffee?"

"Coffee truck? That sounds wonderful. Let's go!" I replied.

I followed Justin toward the back doors of the cardiac intensive care unit. As the automatic doors opened, I was overcome with the repugnant odor of trash. I quickly remembered where I was as I saw a sign reading "Morgue" directly across the hall as well as the open doors to my right, revealing several trash dumpsters, which were the obvious source of this horrific smell. Just as we were about to exit, Justin stopped before the double doors exiting the CICU and pointed to a door on the left, at the very edge of the unit with a sign reading "Physician Call Room." "That's the call room we use when we take in-house call at night," Justin explained. He pulled out a key from his pocket and opened the door revealing a small room, no more than ten feet by ten feet in size, with a twin bed, a bathroom, a shower, as well as a desk and dresser that were in shambles. The room was filthy and there must have been an inch of dust layered on the desk and dresser and maybe two inches of dust layered on the carpet beneath the tiny bed, which surely must have accumulated over a year or more. The room felt humid and musty as if some vagrant had been squatting there for years.

I turned to Justin and said, "We need to get this deep cleaned immediately." Justin chuckled and nodded in agreement. "You have only been taking night call here for a few months, how have you accumulated so much stuff?" I asked.

"No, these things aren't mine. They belong to Jose," Justin said.

"Who is Jose? Oh wait, never mind, now I remember," I said. Jose Colmenares was a fellowship-trained pediatric congenital heart surgeon in his early sixties, who was born and raised in Bolivia, South America. He joined Children's Hospital of Biloxi after his previous program in Pensacola, Florida, was destroyed by Hurricane Henry and never reopened. He had joined CHOB just before Hurricane Kelly unleashed her wrath on Biloxi. He needed a job, so Dr. Rostri hired him; however, he had been marginalized and functioned more in the role of an advanced practice provider, assisting at times in the operating room (OR), but mostly assigned to the CICU. He spent many nights at the request of Dr. Rostri, sleeping in the hospital and had accumulated a lot of junk in the call room as a result. I recalled meeting Jose briefly during my second visit to CHOB. I remembered him as a short man with long black hair, appearing weathered and frail when I first met him, which I assumed were a consequence of the years of sleepless nights he endured in the CICU, which had clearly taken a toll. I recall how he willingly appeared to display the irreversible damage inflicted on his body, representative of a CICU soldier who had survived several tours of duty, as if heeding a warning to those considering such a career. I also remember being overcome with a sense of peace while speaking with him. He emanated a feeling of zen, as if he had discovered a way to tune out the toxicity, disrespect and physical exhaustion omnipresent in the world where his body suffered, while his soul functioned unaffected, in some parallel dimension, allowing him to remain optimistic and focused on helping the patients. As I thought respectfully on our prior meeting, I said to Justin. "I really enjoyed meeting Jose during my last visit, where is he?"

Justin looked at me with shock and said, "You didn't hear?"

"No, what?" I asked with great curiosity.

"He is in the hospital; he had a heart attack last week and has a near complete occlusion of his left main coronary artery. His left ventricular function is severely depressed and due to the extent of the occlusion, the adult cardiac surgeons at Biloxi General don't think he is an operative candidate," Justin sadly explained.

"Wow, that is awful," I replied. Justin went on to explain that Jose had apparently worked several night shifts over the last couple of weeks, which was his typical schedule; however, early last week he began to feel short of breath and physically exhausted, which was later followed by what he described as mild chest tightness. He tried to fight through it and continued to do in-house night call. By Wednesday of last week, he was walking around the CICU wearing a nasal cannula while pulling a portable oxygen tank on wheels behind him. The staff urged him to go to the emergency room to be evaluated; however, he refused. His symptoms worsened to the point where he asked one of the echocardiography technicians to perform an unofficial echocardiogram so he could take a look at his cardiac function. The echocardiogram revealed that his function was severely depressed, and the staff immediately sent him to the emergency room at Biloxi General where they confirmed the diagnosis of a myocardial infarction. "That is absolutely awful. I hope he can get through this," I said sincerely.

As we finally walked through the back doors of the CICU, past the morgue, through the gauntlet of trash dumpsters and out to the street, I heard the sputtering of what sounded like a generator. My eyes explored the surrounding area for the source of the sound, until they came upon a tiny green truck parked on the street, near the curb. The truck looked as though it was from a film shot in the early 1900s, but while old in appearance, the exterior shone without a hint of rust, as Justin proceeded to explain that it had been renovated to perfection a few years back. There was a large window on the side of the truck, facing the hospital, which was wide open, sharing the stunning smell of fresh coffee with all those fortunate enough to be walking by. A sun visor hung above the open window, trying its best to shield the Biloxi heat, while a stainless-steel shelf was mounted below the window, which admirably functioned as a viable countertop.

"Hey, Dr. Thorn. You want the usual?" asked a thin, frail woman in her early forties, standing inside the green coffee truck, wearing a tank top that revealed a sleeve of tattoos covering both arms.

"Sure," Justin said.

"Great, double espresso coming right up. What about your friend here?" she asked.

"This is Dr. Philson, the new medical director of the cardiac intensive care unit," Justin explained.

"You can call me Eric. I will also take a double espresso," I said.

"Coming right up, Big Pappi!" she replied, labeling me with a nickname that would be repeated by her at every subsequent visit to the little green truck over the next few years. We thanked her and grabbed our freshly brewed drinks.

As we left the coffee truck and headed back to the CICU, I continued to be bothered by Jose's situation. I admired his dedication, but I was deeply concerned for him and thought to myself, "I wonder why he continued to work despite the development of symptoms and especially after his symptoms worsened to the point of requiring oxygen?" Regardless of his reasons, I wished him the best. I contemplated the fragility of life and how in an instant, your entire life can change. I also thought about how personal health is a gift, one that we are fortunate to have and that all the riches in the world cannot buy. I failed to realize in the moment that Jose's tragic situation was nothing short of a premonition, offering me a glimpse of what my future may entail if I ceased to learn from his unfortunate circumstances. Unfortunately, I overlooked this warning and remained clueless to the fact that his situation would ultimately hit very close to home for me.

9

STRATEGY FOR CHANGE

After arriving to Dr. Rostri's morning rounds ten minutes early, the day prior, only to be left playing catch up with the rest of the flock, I decided to arrive at the hospital even earlier to avoid being left behind. I walked toward the CICU as I looked at my watch and celebrated silently to myself, saying, "Yes, 6:35 a.m.! Ha, there is no way he will beat me to the unit and start without me today!" I punched in the door code to the CICU and walked through the automatic doors as they opened. I immediately looked to my left, toward the computer behind the desk where we were to meet to review morning X-rays before we proceeded with bedside rounds. "Yes!" I said triumphantly to myself as I saw that I was the first to arrive. As I waited for the others, I walked by each room, greeting the bedside nurses and asking if any major events had occurred overnight. Over the next twenty-five minutes, Justin and a few of the pediatric cardiologists began to arrive and gather near the computer where we normally assembled to review X-rays. I walked over to join them as we exchanged pleasantries and small talk. I checked my watch and saw that it was now 7:15 a.m., with no sign of Dr. Rostri. I checked my phone to be sure he hadn't sent a text message explaining his tardiness, but there was nothing.

The four of us who had congregated began to ask where Dr. Rostri was. "Why don't you text him, Eric," they suggested, appearing to be somewhat fearful of doing so themselves.

"Sure," I replied.

Just as I removed my phone from the pocket of my white button-down shirt, the doors of the CICU main entryway opened and in strolled Dr. Rostri without the slightest sense of urgency. He walked behind the desk and pushed his way through the four of us while grumbling a barely audible "Good morning." He proceeded to double-click on the X-rays of each patient without an apology or explanation for his tardiness. The four of us looked at one another in disbelief and shrugged it off as we became engaged in the review of each X-ray. Five minutes later he stood up from his chair as we instinctively and unknowingly fell into formation, revealing a perfectly shaped upside-down V, signaling to Dr. Rostri that the flock was ready for migration to commence. I was annoyed by the lack of respect for others' time displayed by Dr. Rostri, so I attempted to break the flock rules and assume the lead position next to Dr. Rostri, head goose. However, he picked up his speed such that it would have required an all-out sprint for me to keep pace with him. Feeling defeated and even more annoyed, I reluctantly receded and assumed my position in the migration line as we went from one bedside to the next while he proceeded to shoot down input suggested by each of us, making entirely unilateral decisions for each patient. The average time spent on rounds each morning, including reviewing X-rays and passing by each bedside at warp speed, averaged between twenty and thirty-five minutes, even when the unit was filled to capacity with critical patients.

I reflected on Dr. Rostri and my prior conversation over coffee, now nearly a month ago. At the time he had asked that I observe for two weeks, so that I could learn the Children's Hospital of Biloxi system and take the opportunity to try to understand his approach to managing these complex patients in the CICU. After enduring two weeks of repeated rejections when it came to my patient management suggestions, as well as those suggested by my colleagues present on rounds, I decided it was time for a new plan. Following morning rounds that day, I asked Dr. Rostri if he, Dr. Penton, and I could sit down weekly, to discuss changes I was interested in implementing in advance, so he would have an understanding of both what I was planning to do, as well as what to expect as a result of the change I was suggesting. I thought this might help avoid confusion while also keeping communication lines open and helping to prevent the temptation of reverting back to "the way we have always done it" each time I left the hospital to go home. Additionally, I felt as though regular meetings could allow each of us an opportunity to reflect on our perception of how we felt things were progressing, while also permitting time for us to discuss any concerns that may arise. He agreed and said, "Sure. Let's start now. We can meet in the conference room across the hall."

"Sure. Sounds good," I said. I followed Dr. Rostri out the doors of the CICU and across the hall, where he unlocked the door to the conference room, a room I had no idea even existed, nor did I understand that I would come to despise this same room due to the numerous, traumatic meetings I would endure over the next year at the hands of Dr. Rostri. The room was dimly lit and frigid. The wall separating the room from the hallway was made of glass windows that were frosted, making it impossible to peer inside or outside the room. A rectangular table sat in the middle and consumed most of the room. There was just enough space to slide any one of the eight chairs on each side of the table out, thereby allowing you to sit. If you were more than a bit overweight, you would have to sit in one of the two chairs on each end of the table, as they afforded more space. The lighting in the room appeared yellow and dim. As I sat in one of the chairs across from the window, suddenly Dr. Rostri shut the door. He assumed the chair immediately adjacent to Dr. Penton, both directly across the table from me. They both shared the same stone-cold, emotionless look on their face, which I could only assume developed from decades of working closely with one another.

I looked at Dr. Rostri as he gave an uncomfortable attempt at a smile and said, "So, Eric. How do you think things are going?"

"Uh, I would say I am adjusting to a new system. I am taking the time you suggested to absorb and understand your current practices while also thinking creatively of ways that I can implement some new practices to help progress patient care, perhaps a bit faster, while maintaining the same quality and safety that are important to us all," I replied cautiously, trying to get my point across without appearing offensive in any way.

"You're not ready," he said. "You have only been here two weeks; you need to observe for a longer period of time in order to understand how we practice."

"Wait, I thought our agreement was a two-week observation period?" I responded.

"Eric, I will tell you when you're ready. What I need you to do is to start covering some of the night shifts," Dr. Rostri said with a scowl.

"Of course, I am happy to help share the night coverage. Justin and I will each begin taking five night calls per month," I said.

"That is not enough. Jose was taking much more than that and now he is unable to work," he replied, irritated.

"I understand, Dr. Rostri, but we need to play the long game here. My job is to build the CICU, which includes recruiting more staff with the goal of eventually providing twenty-four-hour-a-day, seven-days-a-week, day-and-night coverage. However, in the meantime, I don't want to burn myself or Justin out. I have posted job openings and have been reaching out to colleagues, gauging their interest while generating referrals for other potential candidates who may be interested. In the meantime, I would like to start implementing formalized medical rounds starting daily at 9 a.m., which are to be directed by the cardiac intensivist on service. I would also like to start inviting a dietician and a social worker to round with us at that time. Additionally, I have received approval from Dr. Deeton to hire a dedicated CICU pharmacist and I am in the process of posting this position," I explained.

"Why would you need to round again? I already carry out the rounding each morning and why would you need all those people? I am capable of determining the nutritional needs of our patients and I am extremely well versed in pharmacology. We don't need to waste money on a pharmacist," Dr. Rostri responded as if insulted by my plan.

"Listen, I am amazed at everything you two have done with virtually no support from administration. When I took this job, I saw it not only as an opportunity to build the unit, but also as an opportunity to build a team, and not just a CICU team, but an entire congenital heart team. I also saw it as a way to obtain essential resources for the entire Heart Center, which had been unavailable in the past. I am sorry but this is my plan, and I am telling you in advance so you understand it, and it would really mean a lot to me if you would simply support it. You don't have to agree with my idea, but I am asking you to at least keep an open mind. To start with, the medical rounds I am proposing will not be contradictory to your rounds. I will use them as a way to build rapport and collaboration with the staff, while also providing an opportunity for the nurses to report their concerns during rounds, so they can feel as though they are being heard. I also want to incorporate social work, nutrition, and eventually pharmacy into medical rounds, asking their input daily as it pertains to their individual field, thereby building a team where each person can share their expertise, which only improves the care we can provide for the patients; however, it still leaves you at the very top of the decision-making hierarchy. In the early weeks of starting these medical rounds it will be mostly symbolic. Any major decisions will be run by the two of you. But in time, I hope to relieve some of your responsibilities. The fact that the two of you have been performing all of the surgeries, while also managing the patients postoperatively 24-7, is impressive. That is dedication, but it is nearly impossible to stay on top of the clinical minutia that constantly evolve and unfold throughout the day and night, while you are in the operating room or when you are at home getting the rest that you need to operate the following day. We can relieve some of that burden while still keeping you informed on pertinent changes. And once we have a full complement of CICU staff, we can monitor and progress the patients twenty-four hours a day," I explained passionately, again attempting to avoid coming off as offensive.

"Let's give it a shot, Gerald," said Dr. Penton with a shrug of his shoulders. As if to say, why not.

"OK, but no major decisions without speaking to me first," Dr. Rostri responded authoritatively.

"OK, no problem. One last proposal. I realize that the approach here has been to keep patients intubated for at least a couple of days following cardiac surgery, but I would like to suggest that for nights when I am taking in-house call, I would like to extubate some of the simpler surgical cases in the CICU, on the same day as surgery. I would do it while I am here in the hospital, so I can be sure that the patient is safe and watched closely, since this would be a new process for the CICU," I explained.

"I don't think that's a good idea. The patients need time to heal," said Dr. Rostri, waving his hands in disbelief at the mere suggestion of early extubation.

"I realize that this is different than your typical approach, Dr. Rostri, but the majority of the simpler cases are extubated in the operating room at most institutions around the country," I explained.

"I don't care what other institutions are doing. What makes them better than our program?" he screamed.

"Calm down, Gerald. Let's give it a chance," said Dr. Penton as Dr. Rostri stormed out of the room. "Don't worry. He will be fine. In fact, he will be back in this room in less than two minutes, guaranteed! Eric, I respect the fact that you are trying to evolve things here, but you have to understand that change is not easy here and it takes time," Dr. Penton explained with great wisdom.

"I do understand and thank you for the support. I definitely need it," I said.

Just as I finished my sentence, the conference room door flew open and Dr. Rostri reentered the room just as Dr. Penton suggested he would. As he did, Dr. Penton pointed at him as if announcing his arrival while simultaneously shooting a gloating grin across the table in my direction, as if saying, "I told you so!"

"OK, Eric. I will agree with your request, but you need to promise that you will monitor the patients very closely with regular follow-up," Dr. Rostri exclaimed.

"Yes, Dr. Rostri. I certainly will, in fact, I don't know how to do this job any other way.

10

MEDICAL ROUNDS AND MY FIRST NIGHT SHIFT

I scheduled my first night call two days after my meeting with the cardiac surgeons, on a night when they were closing an atrial septal defect on a five-year-old boy who was otherwise healthy. He appeared to be the perfect candidate to become the first patient in the history of the Children's Hospital of Biloxi to be extubated the same day as their cardiac surgery. That same day marked the beginning of the first medical CICU rounds, which started at 9 a.m., where we were joined by a dietician and a social worker, both of whom were extremely helpful and shared with me that following my request, Dr. Deeton was working diligently on dedicating a dietician and social worker specifically for the CICU. Admittedly, medical rounds were met with a lukewarm response from the nursing staff. "Why are we rounding again?" many of the nurses asked. As frustrating as it was to hear those words, I understood that changing from the lightning rounds in the morning, which left me wondering what the actual plan was for the day, to a detail-oriented, time-consuming dissection of the minutia, was not going to be a simple transition that would happen overnight, but I was confident over time they would come to understand and eventually appreciate that I was actually seeking their expertise and input since they were the only ones at the bedside for twelve hours a day and who were able to see minute-to-minute changes that occur throughout the day.

Time passed quickly that day and the patient arrived to the CICU following cardiac surgery around 3 p.m., in stable condition. I had reviewed the extubation plan with the nursing staff and the respiratory therapist. The process was a bit more complicated than simply removing the breathing tube when the patient started to wake. Step one was reassuring the staff that extubating the patient on the same day as surgery was safe and was in fact routinely performed at most institutions around the country and around the world for that matter. I also explained some of the benefits of early extubation including reducing the risk of ventilator-associated pneumonia, reducing narcotic and sedative use, allowing for earlier institution of enteral feeding, decreasing patient agitation, and permitting patients to awaken, which provided the ability to monitor mental status more accurately after major surgery, among others. This led me to the next challenge, which was convincing the staff that all postoperative patients didn't need to be medically paralyzed and instead could be safely cared for on the ventilator with sedation or even reassurance alone. For twenty years, every single patient who returned to the CICU following cardiac surgery was medically paralyzed for a minimum of twenty-four to forty-eight hours to keep them from "harming themselves" while on the mechanical ventilator. As a result of such a practice, the nurses had learned that it was unsafe for a postoperative patient not to be paralyzed. After reassurance, the nurse caring for the patient who was to be extubated, reluctantly agreed with the plan. The third challenge in preparing to extubate a postoperative cardiac patient on postoperative day zero for the first time in the history of the hospital, was to develop a sedative plan in the CICU designed to adapt to the anesthetic algorithm used by the cardiac anesthesiologists at Children's Hospital of Biloxi. During my training and for the last ten years in Florida, I became accustomed to the anesthesiologist either extubating the majority of the patients in the operating room or to the practice of reversing paralytics and minimizing narcotic use toward the end of the case in order to keep from suppressing the patient's respiratory drive, thereby preparing for extubation when the cardiac intensivists saw fit. The anesthesiologists at CHOB were a great group who were also skilled clinicians; however, over the years, the group had practiced what I would describe as a fentanyl-heavy anesthetic regimen at the direction of Dr. Rostri. As a result, patients returned to the CICU heavily sedated, often ceasing to move for several hours. It is important to understand the somewhat unpredictable nature of fentanyl due to its variable metabolism among different patient populations. Newborns, those with large amounts of subcutaneous fat, and those with liver or kidney dysfunction are often vulnerable to slower metabolism leading to longer awakening times post-anesthesia. One challenge is when the patient suddenly awakens and either attempts to sit up or alligator roll in the bed while the breathing tube is still in place. The inexperienced clinician may inappropriately assume patient readiness and therefore proceed with extubation. However, premature removal of the endotracheal tube typically results in a patient who is no longer agitated; meanwhile, fentanyl that had accumulated in the subcutaneous tissue during surgery continues to spill into the bloodstream, leading to an overly comfortable and sedated patient who may now be vulnerable to the respiratory effects of fentanyl, including a loss in their ability to protect their airway, slowing of their breathing, or periods of no respiratory effort at all, which can lead to lung collapse and decreased oxygen saturations. Now, you can always administer Narcan to reverse the effects of fentanyl; however, that's just cruel to acutely reverse the analgesic effect in someone who has just had their sternum cut open. In the past, I would simply hold all sedatives until the patient awoke; however, as I stated earlier, patients may suddenly sit up in bed, without warning, and attempt to or succeed at, pulling their own endotracheal tube out in an uncontrolled manner, which may lead to the complications I previously outlined as well as others, such as trauma to their airway. So, in an attempt to adapt to the heavy use of fentanyl by anesthesia, while also retaining tight control of patient wakefulness, allowing me to progress the patient toward extubation in a much more controlled manner, I began to utilize infusions of shorter-acting sedatives such as dexmedetomidine and propofol for a period of two to six hours, allowing the body ample time to eliminate the majority of fentanyl from their system. I would choose the sedative based on each patient's medical history, including the type of cardiac surgery they had undergone. During this two-to-six-hour infusion period, I would repeatedly evaluate vitals, patient movement, and respiratory effort, which would guide the timing and rate of my sedative wean and ultimate extubation.

Honestly, none of what I am describing is rocket science by any means. The point I am probably belaboring here is that a very important lesson I learned is that in a system that has been forced to operate in the same unopposed manner for many years, void of critical thought and in the absence of essential resources, things we clinicians may consider simple or routine, such as "early extubation," cannot be implemented by simply removing the endotracheal tube when the patient wakes up. There are systemic deficiencies that are hidden EVERYWHERE and if they are unrecognized and if you are ill-prepared to react to them, they will inevitably lead to your failure. I learned this the hard way, not today, but further down the road. I found that if you wish to succeed and make progress in such an institution, you must understand that resilient people will find ways to adapt and "make do" with the resources they do have. As a result, it is vital to investigate and understand the institutions current practices and procedures, the equipment used by the staff, what resources are available to you, what has worked or failed in the past, what are the current limitations (perceived or real) that could obstruct your path to success, and what is the staff training and comfort level for carrying out your proposed change. If it seems like overkill for completing the simple task of extubating a patient who underwent a straightforward atrial septal defect repair, right, I can promise you, in this environment, nothing is straightforward or simple and if you believe it is, you will fail! I learned quickly that enumerable deficiencies and risk factors for failure reveal themselves at an alarming rate the minute you decide to go searching among the minutiae. Additionally, the interconnectedness of these deficiencies that unfold is quite astonishing. What I mean by such a statement is this: If there were no exhaustive preparations or troubleshooting algorithms prepared in advance and your plan consisted simply of pulling the endotracheal tube when the patient awakens and sits up in bed, at a high-functioning institution, there would likely be no adverse consequences. Hell, the patient could probably sit up in bed and pull their own endotracheal tube in a very uncontrolled manner and when this occurs in the setting of seasoned nurses and staff, armed with extensive resources and well-established algorithms for such unplanned events, the patient would likely suffer no adverse outcome. However, in a system starved of resources, suffering from massive nursing turnover for more than a decade, simply pulling the endotracheal tube without preparation or having troubleshooting algorithms in place may seem logical; however, this approach fails to adjust for systemic deficiencies such as the heavy use of fentanyl and the practice of not reversing medical paralysis by cardiac anesthesia, outdated noninvasive respiratory support to assist a struggling patient following endotracheal tube removal, an entire nursing staff with zero early extubation experience or comfort with the procedure, an inadequate number of cardiac intensivists to provide 24-7 care, the added pressure of cardiac surgeons who are uncertain about the safety of your intervention and a nursing staff that is still attempting to grasp the new hierarchy of decision-making in the CICU, among others factors. I found that talking through the process of early extubation, the result expected, as well as proposed algorithms for addressing any complications that may arise, with the staff caring for the patient, in advance, helped familiarize them with the process while offering reassurance that we had exhaustively considered and prepared for all possible outcomes that may arise. I also realized the importance of building on each success in the CICU, regardless of how minuscule it may seem, because each success strengthens trust among your teammates, permitting forward momentum to continue, which eventually presents the opportunity to implement more complex changes in the future. Failures, on the other hand can be catastrophic, even small ones. In an institution resistant to change, failures can destroy trust, and in a toxic culture, these failures quickly sprout and fertilize uncertainty regarding your capacity to do the job, which can infuriatingly reintroduce deeply engrained beliefs such as "we should have done it the way we have always done it," which can instantly erase every inch of progress you have achieved. While today's early extubation was successful and would help establish a small bit of trust among the staff, I recall other failures that resulted in detrimental setbacks or slowing of progress. Those failures, however, became lessons learned that eventually helped me develop a more complete understanding of the critical importance of preparing for all deficiencies that could impact your likelihood of success—a valuable lesson that would nonetheless prove exhausting over time.

After the first successful early extubation on postoperative day zero at Children's Hospital of Biloxi, I felt pleased. I thought to myself, wow, it feels odd to feel such gratification over something that has literally been performed by most institutions in the United States for more than ten years. But, as I looked at the bedside nurse's radiant smile as she shared her personal experience with the other nurses who had gathered at her bedside and detailed the preparation that took place in advance and outlined the actual steps we had followed during the process of early extubation, I was quickly reminded as to the importance of enjoying every success, as they were each individually vital. However, more importantly, their effect was in fact additive and functioned to increase trust among the team, ultimately increasing the likelihood of future success. I was obviously happy that the patient did well, but the real victory was apparent in the smile and happiness of the bedside nurse that day, which cultivated curiosity that was sprouting among the other nurses who were hungry to learn about the process.

As I wallowed in the success of the first early extubation performed in the history of the Children's Hospital of Biloxi, I carried out my usual night-call routine, which involved going bedside to bedside, checking data trends, analyzing the flowsheet, and asking the nurse if she had any concerns.

Suddenly, as I looked up at the clock on the wall, I quickly validated the time with that on my watch, realizing that it was indeed 8 p.m., signifying that it was time to perform my other night-call ritual, which was to FaceTime with my daughters before their bedtime. So off to the call room I went for a few minutes of privacy.

My FaceTime call couldn't have lasted more than twenty minutes. When I exited the call room, one of the night nurses said, "Dr. Philson, Dr. Rostri was just here."

"OK, thank you. Do you know where he went?" I asked.

"I saw him go that way," she said, pointing toward the front of the CICU. As I strolled slowly by each bedside in the direction of Dr. Rostri's last reported sighting, I noticed that each paper chart was opened to the yellow order page and that each patient had new orders written. Knowing that I hadn't written orders in the last twenty minutes, I moved closer to further examine the orders and to determine who was responsible for writing them. As I looked at each chart, I confirmed that they had all been written by Dr. Rostri, who had arrived at the unit, walked to each bedside without speaking to me or asking if any relevant changes had occurred with the patients that could ultimately influence the orders he had just written without my consultation. I became immediately infuriated. From a physician standpoint, this is considered poor etiquette and more importantly, it is considered a patient safety issue. The safety issue arises when a provider involved in the care of a patient, who is not the managing physician, actively caring for the patient, writes an order for a medication without obtaining an updated clinical course from the managing physician, which leads to an adverse event negatively impacting the patient. Suddenly the managing physician is called to the bedside of a decompensating patient but has no idea that the patient has received a different medication, because there has been no communication, thereby leading to a delay in recognition of the problem, which could have a serious or even fatal consequence. For safety and to a lesser degree professionalism and common courtesy, it is understood that if the ordering physician is different from the managing physician, there should be direct communication between the two regarding the new order. As a result, I was upset and rightfully so. Not only was I the managing physician who was in the hospital, on-call, at the bedside following Dr. Rostri's incessant demanding that I do more night calls, but now he felt it was acceptable to come in from home, presuming he understood what had happened throughout the afternoon/evening in his absence, and proceed to write orders on the patients without communicating this with me. This was unprofessional and unsafe on so many levels.

As I stormed toward the front of the CICU in search of Dr. Rostri, I could hear him speaking in the corner room closest to the front entrance. "You need to call the mom and get her on the phone immediately, so I can tell her we are going to place a peritoneal dialysis catheter in place and start dialyzing as soon as possible," Dr. Rostri explained to the bedside nurse. As I entered the room, Dr. Rostri ignored my presence. I could see the look of horror on the nurse's face as she picked up the phone to call the mother and explain that Dr. Rostri was demanding that a peritoneal dialysis catheter be placed.

I walked directly over to Dr. Rostri, stopping within a foot of him. I harnessed my anger to the best of my ability, attempting to maintain professionalism, as I looked into his eyes and said, "Can I speak with you outside the room, please?"

When he finally acknowledged my presence, he responded by saying, "No, you can speak to me here," dismissing my suggestion.

"No!" I said as I raised my voice. "We need to speak outside." I walked out the door of the room and stood in the main walkway of the CICU. By now, I could see that the attention of several of the nursing staff had shifted in our general direction. Dr. Rostri grudgingly exited the room and met me where I was standing in the general CICU area, away from as many of the staff as possible. "Dr. Rostri, I am extremely upset at the fact that you came into the hospital while I am here all night, clearly showing mistrust, while proceeding to write orders on all of the patients without at least notifying me of the changes you made," I explained.

"First of all, you are overreacting. It's not a big deal. Second of all, these are MY PATIENTS! I don't need your permission to do anything," he shouted, now attracting more staff attention.

"Wrong, I said, they are OUR patients as I pointed around the room. You, me, the nurses, cardiology, everyone! You may operate on them, but it is an entire team that cares for them and an entire team that is needed to get them home with their family. Additionally, it is unsafe for anyone to write orders without communicating those changes with the managing physician," I reminded him.

"You weren't here. Where were you?" he asked.

"Dr. Rostri, I speak with my children every night at 8 p.m. when I am on-call. I was in the call room speaking with them," I said.

"Well, for all I know you were sleeping," he said in a passive-aggressive tone.

"Dr. Rostri, it's 8:30 p.m., I was most certainly not sleeping. My eighty-year-old grandpa doesn't even go to sleep at 8:30 p.m.," I replied.

"OK, fine. Next time I will call you. Now let's focus on something more important," he said. "This patient needs a dialysis catheter, she is not making enough urine and she is fluid overloaded," snapped Dr. Rostri. The patient he was referring to happened to be one of several long-term residents present in the CICU upon my arrival to Children's Hospital of Biloxi. This particular patient was not the most senior of the long-term residents, she was somewhere in the mid-range, which at the time meant she had been in the CICU and in critical condition for nearly nine months. Fortunately, earlier that same day I had been able to find the time to get through volumes one to three of her medical record. This patient had extremely complex congenital heart disease. She had undergone two surgeries, one of which was the reversal of her original surgery because it was felt that her heart was not tolerating the new circulation. She was briefly on ECMO to support her heart following the second surgery. After being removed from ECMO she had remained critical, and her long-term ventilator dependence led to the placement of a tracheostomy. She had chronic feeding intolerance, requiring long-term total parenteral nutrition (nutrition delivered intravenously). Feeding intolerance combined with poor heart function had led to the development of liver failure as well as two pathologic bone fractures from severe malnutrition. She had been medically paralyzed for more than a few weeks because she experienced hemodynamic instability when she would awaken. Her poor heart function had also led to chronic kidney failure, which was now progressing to anuria (no urine being produced). She showed clinical signs suggestive of severe neurologic injury; however, she had not been given a more precise diagnosis and prognosis due to the fact that she was too unstable to be transported downstairs to undergo computed tomography (CT scan) of the brain at the time. Her course had also been complicated by several infections. As I recalled each of these details, which I had read just three hours earlier, in the three-volume series making up her medical record, I also remembered that I had intended to discuss this patient with Dr. Rostri in the morning; however, the conversation I was intending to have was instead occurring right now and was headed in a much different direction than I had intended. Unfortunately, in this career, there are patients who are born with cardiac disease so severe that they will simply never survive regardless of our attempts at making them better. The challenge in caring for these patients is having a team approach and having each branch of a congenital heart program, that is, cardiac surgery, cardiology, cardiac intensive care, anesthesia, the nursing staffs, and most importantly, the family, all on the same page when it comes to formulating a plan. Attaining unanimity is not essential when developing a plan; however, establishing a clear majority is, in my opinion. For some patients, surgical intervention, interventional catheterization, and medical management may all fail, and in such an instance it is important for the entire team to be on the same page regarding the long-term plan, when the patient's suffering begins to outweigh any real possibility for survival. Some patients may become heart transplant candidates, but as in this scenario, a patient who is too unstable to tolerate cessation of medical paralysis, and who is also suffering from progressive multi-organ failure, is unlikely to be accepted for consideration for a new heart nor are they likely to survive the waiting period required to find an appropriate donor. Therefore, having a consistent team approach for discussing futile situations where the patient is suffering remains a real challenge for many congenital heart programs. First and foremost, we all come to care deeply for our patients and often as physicians, our emotions can cloud our ability to make difficult decisions such as the decision to provide comfort care in futile situations. But instead, because there are procedures or medications we can always try, we feel the obligation to exhaust all options, even when they are futile, rather than allowing the suffering to end and the patient to pass comfortably, free of pain, in a more controlled and humane manner, while providing the family time to hold their child and appropriately grieve their loss. Too often, there is no advanced directive, and we are left performing chest compressions on a patient who has no hope for survival, and doing so is not only traumatic to the family but also to the staff performing the futile CPR, and it results in the unnecessary prolongation of suffering for the patient.

Earlier that same day, I had read through the chart of this patient, and clearly, she was one such patient who had fought hard but her disease was too severe, there was no hope for survival, and she was not deemed a viable heart transplant candidate. She was truly suffering, and the parents were in this limbo period of not knowing what the future held because with each deterioration she experienced, its significance had been minimized by Dr. Rostri as a minor setback, and that there remained hope for her survival. It was clear to me; this was not the case. In fact, this was one of the worst patients I had encountered in my career as it pertained to the degree of suffering that she endured and continued to endure on a daily basis. My plan had been to speak with Dr. Rostri tomorrow morning, so that I could suggest a palliative approach to her care, which meant discussing her futile state with the family, while suggesting that we should focus on ensuring she was comfortable from a pain and sedation standpoint followed by the discontinuation of all life-sustaining medications, thereby allowing her to pass naturally, ending her suffering. However, instead, I was being told that we needed to place a peritoneal dialysis catheter in this patient. Just as I had finally calmed myself from the whole Dr. Rostri orders debacle, I began to become agitated once again as he directed me to call the family. "You need to tell them, not ask them, that we are placing a peritoneal dialysis catheter in their child," he said with the authority of a five-star general.

I was appalled by this plan because I knew it would only add to her ongoing suffering without increasing her chances of survival. "No! I will not! First of all, I will never call a family and demand anything, this is their child and they have a say in her care. Second of all this patient is suffering immensely and any further escalation of care is futile, in fact, it is bordering on unethical for us to place a dialysis catheter in this child. What is the long-term plan? Her heart is the primary problem, which is causing renal failure; a PD catheter will not help that. We need to consider switching to comfort care and discussing withdrawal of support with the parents. This patient has had enough," I said to Dr. Rostri. I had become very emotional, and I noticed that I was speaking quite loudly, calmly, but loudly; however, nearly the entire nursing staff had turned their attention toward the two of us in the middle of the ICU.

"I will never quit!" he yelled in defiance. "Give me the phone," he yelled to the nurse. "And get me the consent for PD placement and dialysis," he replied, annoyed.

"OK, since I am new and you have cared for this patient for the last nine months, I will give you the benefit of the doubt and let you proceed but I don't agree with this. We haven't even consulted nephrology for their input or to prepare for dialysis," I said.

"Ha, I don't need nephrology to determine if I need dialysis and I certainly don't need them to perform dialysis, I have my own orders I use. I never involve them, they are worthless," he said. Placing a PD catheter without the blessing of nephrology is poor etiquette but refusing to consult nephrology at all and performing dialysis without their guidance as to dextrose content, fill volume of the dialysis fluid, fill time, dwell time, and drain time was definitely not the standard of practice.

As I stood there shocked and overwhelmed by all that was occurring, Dr. Rostri walked to the phone as the nurse said, "I have Mom on the phone, sir." I shook off my disbelief and walked toward the phone because I wanted to hear how he obtained consent from the family, and I also wished to hear how he summarized the patient's condition to the family. Sadly, it was just as I thought. The mother was told that we were placing the dialysis catheter, rather than asking if we had her permission to do so. It was explained that this was merely a minor setback, and that her kidneys merely required our help for a couple of days, after which she would be fine, which was clearly not the case. I was disgusted.

The general surgeons agreed to place the catheter at the bedside, and she tolerated the procedure surprisingly well. Dr. Rostri wrote his own dialysis orders and dialysis was commenced that evening. As he left the hospital I sat down in the break room, feeling down. Suddenly the charge nurse, the bedside nurse, and one other senior nighttime nurse entered the break room and said, "Thank you for that, Dr. Philson."

"For what? She now has a dialysis catheter, and her suffering continues," I said.

"Yes, we know, but you stood up to him. We have watched this same approach with other futile patients over the years and no one has ever stood up to Dr. Rostri. It gives us hope that things might change if we have someone who is an advocate for the patients and the nurses," they said sincerely.

"Thank you so much. You have no idea how much I needed to hear that," I said. The evening quieted around 3:30 a.m., so I walked to the call room and proceeded to lay on the bed, resting my head on the pillow as I reflected on a very bizarre yet slightly successful day. My resistance to Dr. Rostri's demands for placement of a PD catheter had failed; however, it gained me some unexpected support and trust from the nursing staff, as did the successful early extubation that occurred that day. As I closed my eyes, I smiled because I was beginning to see what I perceived as a shift in the support being displayed toward me by the nursing staff, which would be essential for me to have any hopes of long-term success. Just as I dozed off, I heard a loud sound. I wondered what it could be as it continued to happen again and again. I could hear men talking clearly as though they were right outside the call room door. I got up to investigate and when I opened the door and looked to the left, I realized it sounded as if it was right outside the door because it was actually right outside my door! The sound that I heard was the back doors of the CICU opening and slamming closed via a sensor that was activated each time the environmental staff walked by to take the trash out to the dumpsters, which appeared to be about every ten minutes at 4 a.m. As the doors slammed it was as if they fanned a fresh whiff of rotten food and trash right under the opening beneath the call room door. Clearly this call room was not meant for sleep, but I was so tired at that moment that I would take what I could get and proceeded to rest my eyes for at least a few moments.

11

CHALLENGES IN HIRING AND IMPLEMENTING CHANGE

As weeks went by, change was slow, painfully slow! Dr. Rostri remained in agreement with extubating less complex cases; however, he was still only permitting me, not Justin, to do so, unless it occurred during the daytime while I was there to "supervise," which was ridiculous. I had already worked with Justin long enough to understand that he was a solid clinician who would continue to develop with time and mentoring. Justin was inexperienced but had uncanny clinical instincts, a skill that simply cannot be taught. Dr. Rostri, however, did not see Justin in my same regard. He treated him as if he was a medical student, at best. Several staff members shared stories of Justin's all too frequent berating at the hands of Dr. Rostri. Now, thinking back to Justin's personal condition, and in particular his mental well-being, upon my arrival to Biloxi, I realized that had it been much longer before I arrived to offer him support, he would most certainly have left. Admittedly, I continued to feel as though the odds of him becoming fed up and ultimately resigning were 50:50, at best. Seeing him treated like this was agonizing and it left me feeling inadequate as his leader, but I knew that I needed to tread lightly and continue to practice patience as I gained Dr. Rostri's trust, all the while communicating my plan transparently with Justin, which would eventually result in his ability to practice and be treated as he deserved. I did my best to reassure him that this was part of the game we were going to have to play. I told him, "Look, Justin, he treats me like a first-year ICU fellow at best. This job has required that I swallow my pride and look at the bigger picture and toward the long-term goals I have for the unit. It has been extremely difficult for me as well, but I am trying my best to drop my ego and direct my focus toward succeeding in any manner possible, regardless of how small these successes may be. If I need to 'supervise you,' or if I need be near you while you extubate a patient, to at least give the appearance of such, in order to put Dr. Rostri's mind at ease, so that we may continue to advance the complexity of the patients we can extubate next, then I will swallow my pride and do it. You and I both understand that quite literally, I will not be doing anything other than providing the perception, that I am 'supervising you.' You do as you see fit and call me if you need help. I am standing nearby to appease Dr. Rostri while helping to put his mind at ease, that's all! I trust you. Believe me, I do," I said.

"I know you do; I can see that. It's just difficult being treated like this," Justin replied.

"I know, try not to think about it as how you and I are being treated; try to think of it as obstacles we must overcome in order to build a unit that we can call our own, which can function at a high level, ultimately leading to something that we can be proud of and run in the way we see fit. Thus far, swallowing my pride and tolerating being treated as if I am a fellow once again has been my greatest challenge. However, in this particular scenario if we are going to have any chance of making this work, I feel it is necessary to take this long approach. Thinking of our success down the road is what keeps me going! That and a whole lot of alcohol when I get home," I said with a burst of laughter.

Justin laughed and said, "For sure."

Sadly, I wasn't joking. The more time I spent at the hospital, the more we continued to make small improvements, and as we did so, additional gaps and deficits within the CICU as well as those affecting the entire institution continued to reveal themselves at an alarming rate and prevalence, adding to my burden. I quickly realized, "When you put your finger in the dyke it only reveals more leaks"! The amount of work required to build and develop the CICU appeared endless and overwhelming, as new tasks and obstacles accumulated by the day. Please allow me to elucidate further that this staggering workload was 100 percent clinical in nature, and neglected to account for the substantial burden incumbent upon me as medical director, which was veritably the primary intent of my hiring, and ultimately comprised the recruitment of a vast number of additional staff, providing education and training for these staff members, evaluating our institutional data to identify areas of weakness, which would then require additional intervention, and implementing clinical pathways and protocols with the goal of standardizing patient care, to name a few. As my workload increased, hours spent at the hospital increased exponentially, as did my stress level, which would become problematic to a level of detriment I couldn't possibly predict or understand.

Most people who know me, understand that I am a very reserved and introverted individual when it comes to sharing my feelings or emotions. People frequently say, "Eric is so relaxed all the time. He is never stressed." Well, let me respond to this inaccurate perception by saying I have an exceptional poker face, which allows me to conceal even the most intense internal anxiety, sadness, or anger and dissimulate it with an expression of calm tranquility. Admittedly, I instinctively submit to the tendency toward "bottling everything up" and pushing it down deep. And I am talking down to the deep abyss, like gasping for air, where plant and aquatic life ceases to exist and the Loch Ness Monster may indeed rest, type of deep! This description details my behaviors and inclinations at baseline, pre-Biloxi. Consider summation of such a tendency, now confounded with a disproportionate degree of newfound stress, which I was enduring on a daily basis, and you can begin to conceptualize that my omnipresent sleep disturbance evolved into a full-blown sleep disorder. And where do introverts tend to turn for help when the deep abyss of the subconscious mind becomes saturated with unprocessed and unacknowledged feelings and emotions? Some seek guidance from Uncle Jim, Cousin Jack, twelve-ounce Tammy, Napa Valley Nancy, or in my case I reunited with my long-lost Great Uncle Scotty who resided in the Highlands of Scotland. I began by consuming a four-fingered Scotch on the rocks each evening, questing for a mere hour or two void of this gnawing anxiety that resonated and metastasized within me. It provided momentary relief, granting me a few dismal hours of sleep, but it came at great expense because as you can envisage, neglecting the mind and body's incessant demands for reprieve while soliciting Great Old Uncle Scotty to function as your psychotherapist is a recipe for disaster. As I assume is the case with most, I unquestioningly acknowledged this was a poor decision, barren of even the slightest indelible long-term disposition, but I was desperate and craved expulsion of this demonic anxiety that had infested my body and mind and I was willing to sell my soul to attain such a state, even if only for an hour or two upon arrival to my home each evening. Hours, days, and weeks flew by as if a high-speed train passing in the night, though appearing as if one boundless day, deepening my angst and my thirst for companionship with Great Uncle Scotty.

One major hurdle that I encountered quickly was the fact that Biloxi is an extremely arduous city to recruit to, which I would come to learn over time, stemmed from multiple etiologies, the first and most prominent of which is the fact that the city of Biloxi resides in the state of Mississippi. I know, I know, I am an elitist Midwesterner stereotyping all Mississippians as rednecks with no teeth, Dixie flag tattoos on their neck, with no education who drive dilapidated pickup trucks with shotguns in the rear window, right? Not true! OK, so there is a minuscule amount of truth to that statement, but the reality is, Mississippi is the poorest or at minimum, it is among the top three poorest states in the United States, depending on the year. There is a considerable amount of poverty, a paucity of high-paying jobs, the school system is spotty at best, violent crime is rampant, and Southern Mississippi, in particular Biloxi, is vulnerable to flooding and hurricanes. There are other factors rendering Biloxi formidable to recruiting health-care professionals, but these were the crippling ones I had learned since my arrival. Convincing physicians and other health-care professionals to listen to my sales pitch long enough to explain the details of the job opportunity in Biloxi appeared an insurmountable task. It would take a real idiot, I mean a complete numbskull, to take on the responsibility of recruiting highly desired professionals to a city like Biloxi. I mean, honestly, who would assume such an obligation? Wait, I did! OK, so let me retract the idiot numbskull adjectives and replace them with the word naive. So, let's say hypothetically, by some miracle, you are fortunate enough to find someone foolish enough to listen to you describe the job opportunity, upon completion, or perhaps midway through characterizing that the pediatric cardiac intensive care unit has been run exclusively by cardiac surgeons for the last twenty years, the usual response consisted of an abrupt *click* … "Hello? Hello? Are you still there?" I am joking but not joking. The truth is, most were polite enough to resist the urge to hang up on me; however, there was nearly always a prolonged period of silence following my explanation of that final, critical detail to potential candidates. "I need to think about it. Or I need to speak with my family about the opportunity," were the overwhelming majority of responses I received, which were inevitably followed by relentless avoidance or flat-out ignoring of all correspondence attempts on my behalf. I wish I was joking. I spent the first couple of months uncompromisingly pestering friends and colleagues, cold-calling institutions with fellowship training programs and asking to speak with their upcoming graduates, posting job opportunities online both via the University of Southeastern Mississippi and via online sites where jobs in the field of pediatric cardiac intensive care were typically posted. Despite these exhausting, time-consuming, and sometimes demoralizing ventures, there was a paucity of applicants outside of a few foreign graduates with visa requirements, which was not a deal-breaker; however, these applicants were either untrained in pediatric cardiac intensive care or had not worked in the field for several years.

The other roadblock that Justin and I were experiencing was the fact that beyond the five night shifts we were each working per month, we struggled to contrive additional, meaningful change in the CICU due to the vacancies monopolizing the remaining twenty to twenty-one nights of the calendar month. Consequently, as soon as we left the hospital and departed for home, the plan would eminently revert back to "the way we have always done it," as demanded by Dr. Rostri. It was becoming increasingly frustrating because we were attempting to instrument the use of evidence-based protocols or pathways hoping to standardize certain clinical practices, thereby removing the temptation or inclination for individual physicians to haphazardly practice "as they pleased" or in this circumstance revert to practicing "as they had always been done." The idea, which had already been adopted by many CICUs throughout the United States, was to help assure, as much as possible, that each patient receives the same standardized, evidenced-based care regardless of the physician who happened to be working that evening, day or week for that matter. Justin and I had spent hours of our precious time at home, because we had no set-aside or free time for that matter at work, researching and constructing our first attempt at a formidable standardized neonatal feeding pathway. We were both in agreement to focus our efforts on developing a feeding protocol due to extreme variation in feeding practices we observed among the physicians in the CICU, in particular, Dr. Rostri, who often required a century or perhaps longer, to advance the feeds of newborns, both in terms of achieving their goal volume and caloric density. For example, oftentimes he would inaugurate feeds at one-quarter strength, which essentially means watering the formula down to 25 percent of the strength of normal formula, which in turn means the babies are getting 25 percent of the calories they would get from full-strength formula. Then he would advance as slow as one milliliter every twelve hours. So, on average it would take approximately five to ten days to reach the goal volume and another three to five days to advance to the caloric density required to gain weight. So, on average, it required a minimum of ten to fourteen days for a baby to receive approximately 80 percent of their calorie demands, all with an underlying assumption that the feeds are not stopped at any point along the way. The nurses had been taught if there was a "problem," which I came to understand was an extremely subjective and broadly ambiguous definition that was only found in the Rostri-Webster Dictionary and only understood by Dr. Rostri himself, to stop the feeds. Consequently, the feeds were stopped frequently and resultantly, the previously predicted ten to fourteen days required to attain 80 percent of feeding goal, now in reality translated into a period of weeks before achieving such a goal. Irrespective of my sarcasm, I am not trying to be critical of conservative management when it comes to these fragile neonates with complex congenital heart disease, but this was nonsensical. If you provided me with a choice to work with a colleague who practices pediatric cardiac intensive care medicine conservatively versus one who practices as a "cowboy" and manages all patients aggressively, I will choose conservatism every time. It's much safer. However, practicing overly conservative brings a whole new set of complications with it, because it causes patients to linger in the hospital for prolonged periods of time and as a result, they experience significant morbidity. And with increasing morbidity, the risk of mortality increases. So as a result, practicing too conservatively can be just as bad as practicing too aggressively. Recall the suffering baby I described previously with pathologic fractures as a result of severe, long-standing malnutrition? Cases such as this, fortunately, are a rarity in the United States. It is uncommon even in the most critical of patients and in my previous thirteen years of experience, I had encountered pathologic fractures from malnutrition only once, and it left me scarred. As it turned out, upon my arrival at Children's Hospital of Biloxi, the CICU housed three patients, simultaneously, who suffered from multiple bone fractures as a consequence of severe malnutrition. Yes, I acquiesce that severe critical illness often plays a substantial role in such pathology. However, for a program of this size to harbor three patients, simultaneously weathering such tormenting morbidity, spoke to a glaring abnormality in patient care, which fell several standard deviations outside the norm, and therefore required immediate investigation and intervention. Upon completion, I met with Dr. Rostri and Dr. Penton and explained in great detail the feeding pathway we had developed and provided references for our evidence-based approach. Dr. Penton appeared onboard with the change, although he was clearly skeptical, while Dr. Rostri grudgingly agreed while rolling his eyes as he read the protocol and said, "This increase in feeds is too fast. The babies will get necrotizing enterocolitis." Necrotizing enterocolitis (NEC) was among the most feared complications when it came to enterally feeding fragile newborns with complex heart disease, particularly those with single ventricle heart disease and unbalanced circulation. I acknowledged Dr. Rostri's concern and agreed that indeed, an expedited timeline for achieving feeding goal could theoretically increase the risk of NEC; however, with close observation and education of the nursing staff, the benefits of attaining feeding goals much sooner, far outweighed any perceived risk. I also highlighted that a pathway was merely a road map that could be deviated from if patients were deemed at higher risk. "This approach is utilized throughout the country and will help prevent malnutrition and fractures while promoting strength and wound healing among other benefits," I said, which was quickly followed by muttering the word, "Shit!" to myself, as I acknowledged that I had made a grave error by carelessly implying that his feeding practices were responsible for the baby's fractures.

"Fractures? You think the way I feed these babies is responsible for these fractures?" he said angrily. "Who do you think you are? I have been practicing twice as long as you have. These babies are abnormal, that's why they have fractures," he yelled as a large vein in his forehead, which I had ceased to recognize before, pulsated with each word he screamed, threatening to burst at any moment.

"I apologize, Dr. Rostri, I meant no disrespect, and it was certainly not my intention to imply that you were responsible for these fractures," I said as I tried to remove my foot from my mouth. Although these babies were in extremely critical condition with complex cardiac disease, likely unamenable to correction or survivable palliation, there was clearly an issue with the current nutrition practices in the CICU, as the likelihood of having three patients concurrently with fractures in the same unit, at the same time, was far too implausible to chalk up to mere coincidence. I saw this anomaly as an opportunity, or more accurately as an obligatory need to improve patient care, and the reality was that if the problem couldn't be independently explained by defective nutritional practices, then it likely reflected an urgent need to refine palliative care practices as well, which was a shortcoming that would reveal itself to me soon enough.

"Fine, you can start your protocol, but I reserve the right to change the timeline for increasing the feeds at any point and as I see fit," Dr. Rostri exclaimed.

"Of course, anyone who observes something that concerns them, should feel empowered to modify the schedule or stop the feeds accordingly," I replied calmly. As he stated his final disclaimer at the end of the conversation, I translated his words from the language of Rostri to English, and summated them to mean at the first opportunity, "he would change things back to the way they had always done it." Sure enough, three days following its implementation, the feeding protocol was abandoned by Justin and I due to the fact that each day we returned to the hospital, the protocol had been aborted and the feeding schedule reverted back to "the way we always do it"!

My frustration and fatigue continued to escalate. I was unable to sleep at home both as a result of the stress and my inability to stop thinking about the monumental work that was ahead of me. I began to feel increasingly troubled as I familiarized myself with the extensive clinical histories of the five chronic patients who resided in the CICU, which certainly weighed on my mind as well, exacerbating the ever-present and evolving sleep disturbance I was suffering from. The histories of these five patients were uniformly tragic. Three suffered from the pathologic fractures I outlined earlier, among other issues, while the two other babies were equally, if not more disconcerting. All five were born with complex congenital heart disease, which was sadly unamenable to surgical repair or palliation, stripping them of even the briefest reprieve from critical illness, neglecting them of essential bonding time with their parents, who themselves lingered in the purgatory of uncertainty as it pertained to any viable hope for their baby's survival. They remained imprisoned in the CICU, kept alive in physicality by mechanical devices and medicinal support, inexorably suffering. I revered their resiliency, though I struggled to understand whether they were truly resilient or if this was a descriptive term I used to assure myself that what we were doing was just. Could they merely represent physical beings at this point, molecular derivatives of carbon and water, void of souls that had moved on months prior once the universe had delivered their inevitable fate, simply kept alive by us physicians, who ourselves clutched desperately to the most favored of our prehistoric binary measures of success: life? The battle between survival and death in the physical sense is a daily occurrence in the world of CICU medicine, but when the war is complicated by concerns of futility or survival at the expense of extreme suffering and morbidity, which carry the potential of conveying life without quality or meaning, decisions can no longer be based solely on survival alone. Neglecting acknowledgment of this evolutionary shift in medicine can lead to convoluted decision-making by physicians, bordering on unethical at times. Yet how can we criticize physicians who care deeply for the patients but have themselves failed to upgrade outdated psychological and intellectual software to the latest version, which now no longer exclusively use survival at any cost as the sole measure for our individual and patient successes.

There are many scenarios where the window of opportunity for meaningful survival may have closed, yet we persist. Some reasons include the medical team's insistence on persevering, the families' wishes to continue care at all costs, and religious beliefs, among many others. If you have never been involved with caring for a patient whose care is clearly futile, yet we as health-care providers refuse to give up, escalating medical support, though it is blatantly obvious to most that the patient, staff and family are all suffering immensely, I promise you, as a parent, there are few things in this world that are worse. These experiences are traumatic to all involved, and sadly, in medicine we battle to recall the names of the numerous patients graced with a magnificent outcome; however, most can recall with ease the poor little ones burdened by unnecessary suffering and morbidity, as they await their incumbent mortality. So, to care for five unfortunate yet beautiful babies in the same unit simultaneously, four of whom I would classify as the worst cases of patient suffering I had witnessed in my career, was awful, to say the least. The responsibilities and obstacles to achieving my goals continued to accumulate in my mind but being exposed on a daily basis to this degree of patient suffering was a burden I was unprepared for mentally. Unfortunately, as I would learn over the next several months, the worst portion of this dilemma was the fact that at the time, I was virtually powerless to change the situation. The question before me was, could I change this situation over time, to prevent such suffering for babies under our care in the future?

My frustrations continued to mount due to what I perceived as my lack of success at implementing change at CHOB and the lack of support displayed by Dr. Rostri when it came to helping me carry out such changes in the CICU. I was beginning to have the realization that my only path toward success relied heavily on having a team of cardiac intensivists that could help me provide twenty-four-hour-a-day, seven-days-a-week coverage in the CICU; otherwise, practices would simply continue to revert back to "the way we have always done it." I decided I needed to meet with Dr. Potts and Dr. Deeton to voice my frustrations regarding my inability to recruit cardiac intensivists and to implement change as a consequence of Dr. Rostri's insistence on resisting change in the CICU. I called Dr. Potts and he promptly set up a meeting with the three of us for 11 a.m. the following morning.

The next morning the three of us met in the administrative conference room, which was larger than the conference room across from the CICU and far brighter and warmer. With the three of us seated at the table, Dr. Potts started the meeting by saying, "Dr. Philson asked to hold this meeting today to discuss staffing challenges and obstacles he continues to encounter as he attempts to implement process improvement initiatives in the CICU. Dr. Philson, would you mind elaborating on these concerns?"

"Sure," I said. "For starters, I have exhausted every method I can think of as I attempt to recruit additional cardiac intensivists, including calling all of my colleagues and contacts across the country, posting job positions online, calling graduating CICU fellows whose names I have obtained after reaching out to fellowship program directors, I have practically begged the pediatric intensive care unit physicians here at CHOB to help me cover the night calls, and I have even asked some of our pediatric cardiologists here within our program to assist me with night coverage, all without a single promising lead. So far, I have spoken to a few graduating fellows on the phone; however, as soon as I begin to characterize that the cardiac ICU has been run by cardiac surgeons for twenty years and I illustrate the current rounding model, I subsequently lose the candidates' interest. I always cautiously describe the proposed plan to evolve the current model into one that assimilates a model they are familiar with; however, by this time I have lost them," I explained with frustration.

"Well … uh … don't fucking tell them that part … Eric," said Dr. Deeton, authoritatively as his face became flushed and bright red.

"I refuse to do that, Dr. Deeton! I need to be honest, because if I am not, they will almost certainly resign shortly after they arrive, and the congenital heart community is very small, and word of mouth travels fast, which I believe is a large portion of the reason I continue to struggle to find others willing to entertain this opportunity. People simply don't know anything about this program, and what they do know is based on a negative narrative, which has been spread by the few disgruntled employees who have left following a brief stint here at CHOB. I spent an excessive amount of time investigating this program before I accepted this position and almost no one I asked knew anything substantial regarding the intricate details of this program, and the few details I did learn were far from complimentary.

Honestly, if I knew what I knew now, I would not have accepted this job!" I said somewhat passive-aggressively to Dr. Deeton.

"Uh … are you … uh saying … I uh … lied to you … uh, Eric?" Dr. Deeton asked angrily.

"Lying is a strong word, Dr. Deeton, but I would most certainly say that I was told the incomplete truth, in particular the fact that the cardiac surgeons don't appear to want to change, nor does Dr. Rostri even appear to want me here in this role whatsoever! The current model of care and rounding is so outdated that trainees view this as a major red flag and quite frankly, I agree with them. The current environment is toxic, and this is not a system set up for mentoring or developing junior faculty because it is so outdated. It will be impossible for me to tell an inexperienced cardiac intensivist, directly out of training, 'Don't do what you are seeing take place at this moment; instead, just remember that you should do it the correct way in the future.' That will simply not work," I said. "I am stuck in a repeating loop that goes like this: The system is outdated, and I don't have adequate staff to successfully carry out change because Justin and I are covering ten nights total per month, so as soon as we leave the hospital to go home, Dr. Rostri reverts the management back to his way, therefore attempts at change fail. Because we are unable to implement change, the system remains outdated, and we are unable to recruit additional staff to cover all of the nights that would otherwise allow us to implement more change. Do you see what I am getting at?" I asked.

"Uh … tell … uh … Dr. Rostri … that I said … to … stop … reverting … it … uh back," Dr. Deeton screamed.

"I think that needs to come from you, sir," I said.

Dr. Potts said, "Yes, Dr. Deeton, that would be best if it came from you. In the meantime, let's brainstorm regarding some ideas for getting you some help. What about a headhunter? What about asking Dr. Borland, who has recently joined us as a pediatric cardiologist? He had covered some nights in the CICU, the month before you arrived, and he enjoys inpatient medicine. He is quite busy developing the cardiology clinic, but he may be willing to help."

"Those are both great ideas. What about offering some money for people to pick up night shifts? That may increase the likelihood that they may do so," I asked.

"Why don't … uh … Justin … and … uh … you both … pick up … uh … more … night shifts? We will compensate … uh $150 an hour … for uh … each … extra … uh … shift," said Dr. Deeton, speaking at a pace that appeared to slow by the minute.

"I will talk to Justin. We might both be able to pick up one or two more night shifts, but I have concerns about longevity and sustainability. This is already a mountainous amount of work, and I am worried about the possibility of physician burnout," I replied.

"Yes, I agree we don't want to burn out our current staff, that would be short-sighted," agreed Dr. Potts. "So, Dr. Deeton, you will work on hiring the recruiting firm we used to find Dr. Philson as well as speak to Dr. Rostri about not interfering with changes?" asked Dr. Potts.

"Uh … yes … Dr. Philson … will tell … uh him … that I said … to stop interfering, and yes … I will … talk with … the … uh recruiting … firm," said Dr. Deeton, as he attempted to weasel his way out of talking with Dr. Rostri.

"I still believe that should come from you, Dr. Deeton. In the meantime, I guess I will take a couple extra night calls each month, and I will ask if Justin is willing to do the same. Also, I will inquire to see if Dr. Borland would be willing to help cover some nights. Can we follow up in a couple weeks to discuss progress?" I asked. The three of us agreed. "One last thing," I said as Dr. Potts and Dr. Deeton arose from their seats, preparing to leave. "A week ago, I placed job descriptions online for our pediatric cardiac pharmacy opening and for several of our nurse practitioner or physician assistant openings. The postings were approved and were placed online by human resources. So far, we have had no applicants for these positions. I am a bit surprised we haven't had at least one applicant."

"I would suggest reaching out to HR to verify that there have been no applicants and that the openings were indeed posted. Let's just say that HR has been a work in progress. I would suggest reaching out to Mark Rhiner. He is currently the head of human resources," said Dr. Potts.

"OK will do," I said as the three of us rose from our chairs and exited the room. Little did I know that I was about to unleash a massive hole in the dyke, which hid an entire lake of inadequacies at CHOB.

Over the next several days I was able to make some progress on my checklist of tasks. Justin and I both agreed to increase our night call number to seven per month each, which in the field of pediatric cardiac intensive care is about twice the number considered standard of practice, particularly for a medical director, who often work fewer nights, so that they have sufficient time to perform administrative duties, something that was simply not possible at the time. After speaking with Dr. Borland, he agreed to help cover four night calls per month to start with. He explained that he was busy covering and opening different clinics around the state, which meant that a substantial amount of his time was spent driving between clinics. As a consequence, some evenings he may not be able to arrive to the CICU to take hand off of the patients until 6 or 7 p.m. I explained that I was appreciative of his help and that I would take what I could get, so a late arrival on his part would be fine.

Lastly, I called human resources (HR) and asked to speak with Mark Rhiner. I was told that he was not in his office right now but when he returned that they would have him call me back. I waited all morning for a callback but nothing. I recalled meeting Mark briefly, a couple of days after I started the job. Mark was a friendly guy in his early fifties with brown hair. He had joined CHOB about six months before I arrived. He was a pleasant man who had worked as the head of human resources at a hospital in Nebraska prior to taking over as the head of HR at CHOB. I decided to walk to the physician's lounge to get a coffee, and as I passed by the cafeteria, something caught my eye, causing me to do a double take. As I looked back, I saw Mark sitting at the table talking with another HR employee drinking coffee. I thought to myself, "Oh, he must be taking a break or having a work-related meeting over coffee." I grabbed my black coffee and headed back to the CICU to perform medical rounds with the team. Two hours later, I finally finished medical rounds in the CICU and was yet to receive a return call from HR, so I decided to head to the cafeteria to get a bite to eat. As I paid for my food and walked toward the exit, much to my surprise, there sat Mark Rhiner, still at the same table, now by himself eating lunch. I thought to myself, "Perhaps he just finished his meeting and now he was having lunch."

I didn't want to bother him as he ate, but at the same time, I needed an update to determine where we stood with recruitment for our cardiac ICU pharmacist and advanced practice providers for the CICU, as I had still received no applications for these openings, which seemed odd. I decided to turn around and go talk to him. As I arrived at the table, I said, "Hey, Mark, I apologize for interrupting your lunch, I am not sure if you remember me or not, but my name is Eric Philson. I am the new medical director of the cardiac intensive care unit; we met briefly a couple months back."

"Of course, Dr. Philson, I remember. Nice to see you again," he said.

"Likewise. Hey, I wanted to ask you if we have received any applicants for the cardiac ICU pharmacist opening, as well as for the CICU nurse practitioner / physician assistant positions that we recently posted?" I inquired.

Mark looked at me with great confusion. "I am not aware that we have approval for these positions, nor am I am aware of any such postings," Mark said.

"Please tell me you are joking. I received approval for the openings from Dr. Deeton more than a month ago and your assistant had confirmed with me via email that indeed the openings had been posted online more than two weeks ago," I replied somewhat agitated.

He paused then said, "Oh yes, now I recall. Yes, yes, those positions have definitely been posted but unfortunately, we haven't received any applicants yet."

"OK. Well, please keep me updated and let me know if that changes. Have a good day," I said disappointedly as I walked back to the CICU.

12

ONGOING STRUGGLES

Two more months passed, as we continued to slowly advance our early extubation practices, which was clearly beginning to result in an expedited recovery time and shorter hospital length of stay for our simpler surgical patients; however, other changes continued to fail due to the fact that they continued to be reverted back to "the way we have always done it" by Dr. Rostri as soon as I left the hospital to go home. It was taking a toll on me, both physically and mentally. I felt stressed about the lack of progress and even worse, I was unable to make any progress convincing Dr. Rostri to consider comfort care for any of the five patients we continued to flog in the CICU as they continued to suffer helplessly. Unfortunately, this translated into an escalating dose of alcohol each evening when I returned home, as my inability to relax intensified, now mandating this ritual in order for me to get a mere two hours of uninterrupted sleep. Ana began to notice a difference in my personality and a flattening of my affect as I became more emotionally distanced, although at times, involuntarily, I found myself spontaneously crying after sharing an abbreviated version of the ongoings at CHOB with her in the evening upon my return to the house. I tried to hide my anxiety and sadness from her and the kids, but it was overwhelming, and I felt as though I was going to explode as my subconscious now appeared to resist and actually reject any further deposits of unprocessed emotion into the abyss. I vaguely explained to Ana that it was an overwhelming amount of work and that there were several patients not doing well at the same time and that I didn't want to talk about the details, so she left me alone.

At work, I was yet to hear anything from Mark Rhiner or anyone in HR regarding the pharmacy or nurse practitioner / physician assistant openings. "Time for a follow-up phone call," I said to myself. I called HR and was able to speak with Mark Rhiner. "Hey, Mark, it's Eric Philson in the CICU. How are you? I am just following up to see if by any chance we had any applicants for our openings?" I asked.

"Hi, Eric, which openings are you referring to?" he asked in a confused voice.

"Are you frickin' kidding me," I said to myself, after which I said aloud, "Um, recall the cardiac ICU pharmacy opening and the nurse practitioner / physician assistant openings we posted?"

After a brief period of silence, which was anything but reassuring, Mark said, "Oh yeah, right, right. Um … nope, nothing yet, Eric. But I promise as soon as we get some applicants, I will let you know."

I sighed and said, "Wow, none huh? That's odd. OK. Well, please call me if anything changes."

"Sure, will do, Dr. Philson. Take care," Mark said as he hung up the phone. Frustrated, I hung up the phone and walked back to the CICU to start medical rounds.

Outside of some early extubations, the only other change that I could say Justin and I had managed to sustain over the preceding month was consistently performing daily medical rounds with the team in the CICU. Though again, mostly symbolic in nature, Justin and I had pushed to continue medical rounds daily, even on days where we had been on call the night before, which meant that we would continue clinical care for thirty-six hours straight before handing off to the other person. Each day, we painstakingly sifted through each patient's data to be sure nothing was missed and used much of the time to engage the nurses, nutrition, and social work to be sure they understood that we valued their input. It was also time that we used as an opportunity to educate the staff about the different heart lesions and cardiac physiology while explaining potential complications that we may expect postoperatively and how we would manage them, should they occur. I could begin to tell that the nurses were starting to buy into medical rounds as they had never received dedicated teaching in the entirety of the program, and it was obvious that they appreciated the opportunity to have their voice and concerns heard and to be treated as a teammate whose opinion was valued. I felt the nursing staff harnessed so much untapped potential and they were slowly becoming more supportive of change; however, they were still clearly missing a leader and they were in desperate need of a structured education program, which had never been provided to them, nor had they ever been provided a dedicated nurse educator to help deliver such a program. During my contract negotiations, I had asked for and been granted the authority to have a significant say in the hiring of the nurse manager for the CICU and I also received approval to hire a dedicated cardiac educator for our unit. Once I had the approvals in place, and I had accepted the job, and after a LOT of convincing, I was able to recruit two exceptional candidates whom I had worked with previously in Florida—one agreed to accept the nurse manager position and the other, the CICU nurse educator position. Following a substantial amount of pressure on behalf of the CNO and myself, we were able to push HR to offer the salary necessary to convince them both to join us.

Ruth Hofstra was the colleague I had convinced to accept the nurse manager position. Ruth was a pediatric cardiac ICU nurse in her early forties, with more than fifteen years of CICU experience. She was the best cardiac nurse I had ever worked with, and she had significant leadership experience as a charge nurse. She had left Fort Myers Children's about a year before I had accepted this position due to the fact that she had applied for the nurse manager role in Fort Myers but was not chosen. When the new nurse manager, who had been hired instead of her, started, they failed to see eye to eye so she moved on and accepted a leadership role in the CICU at a nearby hospital that was considered a competitor. Ruth was extremely intelligent, with incredible instincts as a bedside nurse; she was also blessed with emotional maturity and intelligence and was a natural-born leader. She was very motivated and dedicated to making sure patients received the best care possible and I trusted her to get the job done, regardless of what that job was. We had always worked exceptionally well together, and I knew she was the perfect fit for the position. Maddie Morgan was also an excellent cardiac ICU nurse with more than a decade of experience. She had recently accepted the cardiac educator position at the same hospital Ruth had joined. She was a very kind, intelligent, and dedicated nurse. She had one of the most positive attitudes of anyone I had ever known, and she was a survivor of ovarian cancer. She was truly an amazing woman, both professionally and as an individual. It definitely helped that the two of them were inseparable and were the best of friends and always carried a positive attitude. I was excited for their arrival; however, that was still three months away, which felt like an eternity. I could hardly wait, knowing that they were joining me gave me some hope and something positive to look forward to, and I desperately needed that, as I continued to struggle physically and emotionally, and I hoped that I could last until they arrived.

One day after I had spoken the Mark Rhiner in HR, I received a call from him. "Hi, Dr. Philson. It's Mark in HR. Good news, we have received three applications for the pharmacy opening but still no applicants for the nurse practitioner / physician assistant openings."

"That is great news, Mark, could you please forward me their information so I can review them and give them a call to set up interviews?" I said excitedly.

"Sure, Dr. Philson, I will email the applications right now," Mark said. I was beyond ecstatic.

"Finally, a break," I thought to myself. I obsessively hit the refresh button on my email inbox until the message from Mark finally arrived. I opened the email and began reviewing the candidates' applications, in an instant, my excitement was replaced with horror. "These applications were submitted more than a month ago!" I read in disbelief. "Why did Mark not know about this and why was I not notified about their application?" I became very upset, as this was simply unacceptable. Cardiac-trained pharmacists are in extremely high demand, so failing to respond for more than a month almost certainly meant they had either found another position or at minimum it meant that they may begin to have reservations about an institution that ghosted them following submission of their application. However, I thought to myself, before I call Mark and question what happened and get upset, I had better call and see if any of these applicants were still available or remained interested in setting up an interview. Unfortunately, my instincts were correct; two of the three applicants had already committed to other institutions while the third was no longer interested and while they would not share their reasoning, I suspected that they questioned the lack of response for more than a month. Meanwhile, the following week I received an email from the University of Southeastern Mississippi containing an application submitted by a cardiac intensivist who was completing his training. Would you believe that the application date was also from nearly two months earlier? I again made the effort to reach out to the applicant who was irritated by the fact that he had not heard a response since his application. Despite my persistent attempts at apologizing, he was no longer interested. I was irate and entertained the idea of throwing my computer against the wall. The obstacles to success here at Children's Hospital of Biloxi continued to mount and these were merely the ones I had uncovered thus far. Such a lack of concern displayed at so many levels was deeply concerning. I wasn't sure how much longer I could take this. I felt defeated and broke down into tears, alone in my office. I wanted to quit, and it had only been a few months since

I began. I also felt trapped, I had moved my family here against their will, I had convinced Ruth and Maddie to move their families to Mississippi and I couldn't possibly leave Justin here to rot alone in this godforsaken place. I had no choice but to persevere. But how, I wondered?

That evening, I returned home and proceeded directly to set up a meeting with my Great Uncle Scotty, which ultimately led to two stiff drinks that night, to escape my misery and I proceeded to fall asleep for a couple of hours on the couch. I awoke and went into our bedroom where Ana was sound asleep. I spent the night tossing and turning, which became my habitual routine. My mind raced, struggling to identify a resolution or at least a temporary solution to make this situation tolerable and allow a chance for success. I finally gave up trying to fall asleep around 4 a.m. and got up to shower and prepare for another day of failure.

On my drive to work, my phone rang. I wondered who was calling me this early? It was Dr. Mitch Borland. "Good morning, Mitch," I said as I answered the phone.

"Good morning, Eric, how are things?" he asked.

"Well, Mitch, it's been rough. Please don't tell me you are calling to inform me that you can no longer assist me with night call," I pleaded.

"Oh no, I am planning on it and happy to help as needed. I wanted to tell you that I have been working with a physician assistant student in one of my cardiology clinics. She is wonderful. She is so enthusiastic, intelligent and she wants to work in pediatric cardiology. She has a couple clinical rotations remaining before she graduates and I suggested she rotate through the CICU and if she likes it, you may be able to recruit her as a staff physician assistant (PA)," Mitch said.

"That sounds wonderful, Mitch. Thank you so much. Why don't you tell her to give me a call?" I said.

"Will do. See you tonight when I arrive after clinic to take night call," he said.

"Sounds good. See you tonight. Thanks again," I said as I hung up the phone. "Finally, a glimmer of hope. I will take it," I said to myself.

That night when he arrived to take night call, Mitch shared the PA student's cell phone number with me and informed me that she was expecting my call. He repeated, "She is very friendly, a hard worker and is eager to learn pediatric cardiology." I thanked him again and said I would reach out to her tomorrow.

That evening as I arrived home, I was admittedly still excited at the potential lead from Dr. Borland, and randomly thought to myself, "I wonder what my friend and colleague Tim Short is up to?" Tim Short was a physician assistant and a good friend of mine who worked with me in the cardiac intensive care unit in Fort Myers for several years. He had resigned a couple of years before I decided to accept this position, to take a job in the adult emergency room because the job paid more money and had better hours, allowing him more time with his family, which was definitely hard to argue with. Tim was a great guy, loved by the staff, easy to get along with, funny, smart and had great clinical instincts. He was my same age and was originally from New York with a patented Long Island accent. He was beloved by the staff in Fort Myers due to his friendly, joking, sometimes inappropriate personality, and for his clinical competence.

I decided to send him a text message and see how he and his family were doing and see what he was up to. Tim quickly responded, explaining that things were going well and that he was still working in the ER and that he and his wife were enjoying life with their three kids. As I congratulated him, I explained what I was up to and confided in him the extreme challenges and duress I was under. I thought about it for a moment and thought hell, why not, so I proceeded to ask if he would be interested in joining me as a CICU PA. He chuckled and said, "I think I might have a tough time convincing the wife to move to Biloxi!"

"Yeah, I hear you my friend, sounds very familiar, yet here I am in Biloxi!" I messaged as I laughed out loud to myself. "Well, I understand but if you change your mind, or want to come take a look at the place and program, let me know. Hell, even if it's just as some part-time shift work, that would be a huge help for me. I would take any help I can get at this point my friend," I replied.

"Let me run it by my wife. I don't think the move idea will go over well but let me ask about the shift work. Out of curiosity, how much would the shift work pay?" he inquired.

"Not sure Tim, I hadn't even considered the idea until this very moment, but I can promise it would be worth your while and we would pay for travel and accommodation as well. How about this, you ask your wife, and in the meantime, I will investigate the compensation and get back with you. How does that sound?" I asked.

"Sounds like a plan my friend. Talk to you soon," Tim replied. That night, I slept better. Only requiring one four-fingered Scotch on the rocks, I slept four straight hours, which was the most I had enjoyed in quite some time. Maybe it was pure exhaustion or perhaps it was due to a microscopic amount of optimism building as I pondered the possibilities of what could be, if we were able to hire a couple of staff members, in addition to the impending arrival of Ruth and Maddie. Either way, I would take the much-needed rest.

Morning came and I almost felt a bit refreshed, which was now an unfamiliar feeling. I showered, made my double espresso and I was back on the pothole-filled streets of Biloxi, headed to work. When I arrived to CHOB I reviewed my plans for the day in my mind. First on the agenda was to reach out to the PA student Dr. Borland had connected me with, whose name was Martha Sandister. I arrived at my office, resting my bag on the chair aside my desk as I proceeded to dial her phone number. Martha and I spoke for approximately thirty minutes. Mitch was right, she seemed very sweet, energetic and enthusiastic. Martha was a Mississippi native and was certain she wanted to work in pediatric cardiology but felt like she wanted to focus on inpatient cardiology, rather than outpatient medicine, which limited her options to the CICU since the inpatient cardiology service was not well established at this point, which is the reason that Mitch referred her to me. She seemed very excited for her upcoming CICU rotation. I explained to her that all she would need to do is forward me the necessary documents from the University of Southeastern Mississippi and I would make sure it was forwarded to the appropriate hospital personnel. The plan we discussed was for the rotation to begin in two weeks and it was to last for one month with the possibility of doing an additional one-month elective rotation should she enjoy her time in the CICU. Her elective rotation would be her final student rotation prior to graduation. I was excited. Yes, she had no experience and I likely appeared desperate on the phone, but I didn't care. Someone fresh out of training can sometimes be a good thing if the person is motivated enough because they can be trained without the need to overcome preconceived notions learned from another system or institution that may be different and counterintuitive to the style you are trying to establish. Now if I could convince Tim to help out, that would be incredible not just because of the obvious need for help, but the bonus would be that since he was so experienced, he would be the perfect mentor for Martha's development as an advanced practice provider in the CICU.

Next on my agenda was to talk to the CNO, John Wozniak, who fortunately had assumed the responsibility of overseeing all advanced practice providers, which had become the politically correct terminology for describing a nurse practitioner or a physician assistant since they both can perform the same job. Rather than specifying whether they were a nurse practitioner, also known as an NP or a physician assistant, also known as a PA, they were now referred to collectively as advanced practice providers, also known as the abbreviation APP. John Wozniak had given me his cell phone number after our first meeting, so rather than going through his assistant, I sent him a text message asking if we could meet at his convenience. He responded with a text saying, "Sure, how about today at 11 a.m.?"

I responded, "Perfect, see you in your office at 11 a.m.," to which he quickly replied with a "thumbs up" emoji.

I passed through the CICU to find Justin carrying out medical rounds, spending time educating the staff, and engaging the dietician and social worker as he asked for their input: admittedly it felt good to see the budding signs of teamwork beginning to show. As I passed by each patient room, the patients were doing relatively well, except for the five "warriors." Justin and I had used the name to describe these patients, because despite our inability to end their suffering, they continued to fight, or at least that's what we told ourselves to get through each day. Sadly, it had come to the point where Justin and I would discretely increase the dose of their sedatives and narcotics without Dr. Rostri noticing, making any attempt we could to ensure that they were as comfortable as possible; however, oftentimes they were so unstable that they simply couldn't tolerate even the smallest increase in sedation, without experiencing a drop in blood pressure, which only highlighted the fragility and futility of their clinical state. It was awful and there are no words I can find to accurately depict the nature of their suffering, which appeared endless. I continue to have nightmares about their suffering to this day. Four of the five warriors appeared clinically unchanged but one of them, the patient who had undergone recent placement of a peritoneal dialysis catheter, had worsened, which I didn't realize was possible while still maintaining a palpable pulse. She had progressed to multi-organ failure, she remained anuric and we had been unable to remove fluid using her PD catheter for dialysis anymore. Such a scenario can occur when the peritoneum becomes scarred or "burned," from long-term dialysis or more commonly as a result of prolonged exposure to high concentrations of dextrose, which was likely the etiology in her case, because Dr. Rostri had been ordering the PD fluid without nephrology input and had been rapidly escalating the dextrose content in an attempt to remove more fluid. I had never seen such a high dextrose concentration used in my entire career. As a result of her renal failure and PD dialysis failure, her entire body had become swollen like a water balloon, as a consequence of being massively fluid overloaded. To make the situation even more horrific, and again, I honestly didn't know that was possible in her current state, but I would come to find out, indeed it was, she had developed a very unusual and psychologically traumatic infection. Now, please allow me to apologize and provide advance warning regarding the description of her infection, but unfortunately, I feel it is necessary to describe it in order to accurately elucidate to you the horrendous condition this poor, beautiful baby was in. So, if you are squeamish, please skip to the next paragraph. The infection that she developed involved the globe or in layman's terms, the eyeball. Due to her clinical instability, she had been medically paralyzed to keep her from moving and to allow the mechanical ventilator to perform its job, and to prevent her body from consuming too much oxygen, which occurs during everyday activities such as normal body movement and during involuntary activities like breathing. Short-term medical paralysis can be lifesaving as it conserves oxygen and energy that is normally replenished by blood, which is circulated by the heart. With each beat of the heart, red blood cells deliver oxygen to the organs, muscles, and cells, which is necessary for survival. When the heart is not functioning well, medical paralysis conserves oxygen, ensuring that the vital organs, like the heart, brain, and so on, get first dibs. After a period of time, if your heart cannot function well enough to deliver the necessary oxygen needed for cells and organs to function, then life cannot be sustained. So this poor, beautiful little baby's heart was the primary problem and unfortunately, nothing in the world, or universe for that matter, could help her heart. Medically paralyzing her was simply a Band-Aid that had become old, dirty, and was falling off and underneath remained the same poorly functioning heart. So as a result, she had begun to experience the effects of prolonged paralysis, one of which can be extremely dry eyes due to the inability to blink, which can lead to corneal dryness, damage and infection. While this side effect is managed with the regular application of lubricant and artificial tears, long-term paralytic use, prolonged critical illness, and severe malnutrition left her immunocompromised and as a result she developed a severe bacterial infection of her right globe (eyeball). I had never observed an orbital infection such as this in my career. The iris, which is the colored portion of the eye, located centrally in the eyeball, became darkened and essentially disappeared due to an overlying film that developed as a result of the infection, eventually leading to the rupture of the orbit and resultant drainage of pus that flowed like a polluted river, down her face, leaving the eyeball decompressed, with an almost fattened and foggy appearance. She had been receiving intravenous antibiotics for some time; however, her immune system was far too compromised and unable to prevent this overwhelming infection. It was the worst thing or at least in the top two most hideous things I have ever witnessed in medicine. Ophthalmology repeatedly insisted she emergently proceed to the operating room so that they may surgically remove the eye; however, she was far too unstable to move anywhere. I begged Dr. Rostri to let us talk to the family about comfort care and withdrawing support so that we may finally end her suffering.

"I will never quit!" he exclaimed defiantly.

"Dr. Rostri, you're not quitting, her body gave up long ago. Please, spare her more suffering. Please!" I begged on the verge of tears.

"She has fought too hard, and I have spent too much effort keeping her alive, I cannot quit on her now. There is always hope," he repeated.

I shook my head, overcome with a plethora of emotions, including disappointment, sadness, and guilt. "I am sorry, Dr. Rostri, but false hope is not hope! We are not helping her, and we have failed to do so for some time now, we are merely contributing to and prolonging her suffering, including the suffering of her family, and that of our staff," I said, fighting back tears.

Dr. Rostri proceeded to place his hands on her feet and said, "Feel these pulses? These are excellent pulses and not the pulses of a dying child. She is not done fighting," he exclaimed with great passion. I shook my head in contention to his comments and walked out of the room furious.

I briskly walked to my office to gather myself by taking a few deep breaths as I was suddenly overcome with the flooding of tears, which I had been fighting to hold back in the CICU. I glanced down at my watch and realized that it was nearly 11 a.m., and the time was rapidly approaching for my meeting with John Wozniak. Dealing with loss and suffering while practicing pediatric cardiac intensive care was by far the most difficult part of the job and somehow it managed to worsen over the years, particularly following the birth of my own children. After my daughters were born, I found it increasingly difficult to deal with death and the process of dying, I found it particularly agonizing witnessing families wail in tears following the loss of their beloved child. I imagined losing one of my daughters and it seemed as though it would be an unsurvivable pain that would cripple you and instantly crush your desire to continue on with your own life. I couldn't imagine the pain they must experience and relive each morning that they woke up after almost certainly crying themselves to sleep the night before, only to recall and relive the nightmare reality that their beautiful child was gone and was never coming back. When my children were born, I finally understood the reason I was alive. The love you feel is indescribable, it consumes you and it becomes the purpose of carrying on and the reason we continue to fight through adversity each day. Without that, I imagined it felt as though you were living a life void of purpose, constantly searching for a way to fill the emptiness in your soul, which once felt fruitful. The disturbing part is that no one teaches us how to deal with death at any point during our medical training, or even during our lifetime for that matter, particularly in a field such as mine where death was an inevitable certainty for some patients. While it is true that most children survive, in fact, it is incredible to see the resiliency of children, especially when compared to adults, nonetheless, death is an inevitability for some patients, and when it does occur, it can eat away at your soul. Yet we are left in isolation, to desperately search for ways to deal with loss and the emotions which are attached to death, and as quickly as possible, because there are other patients who are critical and in need of your assistance to help fend off the grim reaper. As a result, there is no uniform way of dealing with death; some excel at processing and dealing with these horrendous feelings, while some turn to drugs or alcohol. Regardless of the method you choose to adopt, these feelings associated with death are so vile that you will do nearly anything to prevent them from returning, and as a result you find yourself working harder to prevent death. For this reason, I understood why Dr. Rostri and so many others, including me, fight so hard to prevent death, and as a result, we may get lost and stray from the path, allowing us to forget that our options are not exclusively binary, and that we must edit the equation to adjust for confounding variables such as quality of life, suffering, and futility. This part of the job was dreadful, and it takes a toll on professionals in this field over time and is a major contributing factor when it comes to physician burnout. Especially for people, such as me, who tend to be less adept at processing complex emotions. The stress of this job, the recruitment challenges and all of the obstacles I was encountering, were a lot for one person, and in particular one who happened to be feeling a lot of emotion, but who was relatively incapable of processing or sharing these feelings with others who may be able to help process them. The emotional burden of watching these five warriors concurrently suffer in the CICU, albeit at different stages of their inevitable death, while being helpless to do anything meaningful that could put an end to their misery, would prove to be my greatest personal challenge, one that I had failed to consider or prepare for mentally. I was clueless to the fact that these five special little babies would live on in my mind, in the form of traumatic memories that appeared as flash-backs in the middle of the night, occurring with regular frequency, leaving me soaked with sweat and a profound sense of guilt and shame due to my involvement, for many years to come.

After contemplating the deep realities of death and dying for what appeared to be an eternity, but in reality, was a mere ten minutes, I rushed off to John Wozniak's office for our scheduled meeting. I knocked on his office door, as my watch hit 11 a.m. exactly, just as the calendar alert on my phone reminded me of the scheduled meeting. I opened the door after hearing John say, "Come in." I entered the room as he was hanging up the phone. He looked exhausted. "How are you, Eric? You look tired," he said.

"I am," I said. "No offense, but so do you," I responded with a smile.

"That's because I am tired too. There is a lot of work to be done here," he said as he shook his hide side to side and laughed.

"Isn't that the truth!" I replied.

"How can I help you, Eric?" John asked sincerely.

"I wanted to speak with you regarding the challenges I continue to encounter as I tirelessly work to recruit advanced practice providers for the CICU. For starters, I now understand that a major hurdle impairing my ability to hire APPs is that the state of Mississippi does not have a university that offers an acute care nurse practitioner training program and as a result, we have not received a single NP applicant since posting our open positions. The University of Southeastern Mississippi does have a physician assistant training program; however, in the twenty-year history of the CICU at CHOB, PAs have never been hired or incorporated into the workflow, so therefore the reality that has now unfolded before my eyes, is that we are unlikely to receive applications from any APPs with CICU experience, unless we convince individuals we know with such experience to move to Biloxi and join us here, or if there happens to be a scenario where someone with experience or training from another state moves to Biloxi due to family reasons, or a spouse. I currently have a PA student who has agreed to perform one of her clinical rotations with me in the CICU in the coming weeks, and if she enjoys the rotation, I would like to be prepared to make her an offer at the conclusion of the rotation, so I would like to discuss these details with you in advance to be certain we are making a competitive offer. I would prefer to have an understanding of the salary that HR will offer in advance, because I am worried if they lowball her, we could lose her to another specialty. I say this because let's just say my initial experience with HR thus far has been concerning to say the least," I explained.

"Yes, Eric, I like the forethought. I have similar concerns and in fact that is why in addition to my responsibility of overseeing the APPs at CHOB, I have additionally been tasked with reviewing the current state of the human resources department, which involves reviewing salary data to be sure it is up to date and in line with what is being offered both locally and nationally. My preliminary review of the salary data suggests the salary ranges being utilized by CHOB HR department are quite outdated. I can promise you that I will be certain we make your candidate a strong offer if she entertains joining your team," John explained, helping to put my mind somewhat at ease.

"Thank you so much, John. The other topic I wanted to discuss with you is that, given the unlikely scenario that experienced cardiac ICU APPs will be moving to Biloxi in hordes, anytime soon, I have reached out to an experienced APP colleague of mine and asked if he would be willing to help. He is a close friend and colleague who is a PA and happens to have about eight to ten years of pediatric cardiac ICU experience. We worked together in Fort Myers. He currently works in an adult ER in Fort Myers because the salary is generous, and the schedule is more amenable to spending greater amounts of time with his family. I asked if he thought he and his family would ever consider moving here to join me and he said his wife was unlikely to agree to that; however, he did mention his willingness to consider working some per diem shifts to help me out. I figured if we can get him here, even to help cover a few shifts each month, it will not only help me cover the CICU, but if the PA student, Martha, decides to join us, he could serve as a mentor and help train her as well," I said.

"That is a great idea. What will it take to get him here?" John asked.

"Quite honestly, I don't know what the current rate for locum APP shift work is, but I believe if we offer him a competitive hourly wage, cover his airfare, rental car, and accommodation, that he will strongly consider it, plus you never know, he may like it and could potentially convince his family to move here," I replied.

"Why don't you give me his contact information and notify him that I will be contacting him in the next day or two to negotiate a rate to get him here," John replied. I was ecstatic.

"Thank you so much, John. You have no idea how hard these first few months have been. It is so comforting to have someone understand the challenges here, and for me to see even a glimmer of hope means so much," I said while my voice cracked as I fought back tears.

"Trust me. I know how hard it is. Remember I haven't been here much longer than you and I am realizing as you are that the more you learn about the system, the more holes you uncover," he said shaking his head in disbelief. "But, I believe that this job, if we manage to get through all of this, will be the most rewarding of my career, not because it will advance my career professionally, but because we are essentially performing mission work in the United States, which is truly unheard of, and quite frankly, the people of Biloxi and the people who work at this hospital deserve so much more after all they have been through," he said.

"I couldn't agree more, John," I replied. There, in that moment, as I continued to fight back tears, I realized for the first time since arriving in Biloxi, I didn't feel alone in John's presence. We were both outsiders, new to the system, who shared the same vision and we both saw the opportunity as so much more than a steppingstone for professional advancement. Instead, we saw the once-in-a-lifetime opportunity to truly make a difference, and the only way to do so in such a complex environment was to open your mind and take the time to get to know the amazing people who made up CHOB and the city of Biloxi and all they had been through, because failing to do so made it impossible to comprehend that not only was changing the system to provide better care possible, it was essential.

As I thanked him, he said, "You and I need to think about a long-term solution for the lack of acute care nurse practitioners available in the state. Otherwise, this will be an ongoing problem for the CICU and for all of the units within the Children's Hospital of Biloxi."

"Yes, I couldn't agree more. The University of Southeastern Mississippi has a physician assistant program, it would be great if they would develop an acute care nurse practitioner program as well," I said.

"I was thinking the exact same thing. Let me look into that. I could help develop that," John said confidently.

"If you could do that, we could use the CICU as a designated clinical rotation site for training prospective students, while also utilizing the opportunity to find students interested in joining the team upon completion of their education," I said excitedly.

"I think this is a great idea with a lot of potential, which could provide acute care NPs to CHOB for years to come. I need to speak with Dr. Deeton about this idea, but perhaps we could offer two or three of your current CICU nurses the opportunity to study tuition-free as part of the inaugural class, in exchange for a three-year post-graduation commitment to work in the CICU. What do you think?" John asked.

"I think you're a genius," I said with a huge smile on my face.

A week later I received confirmation from both John Wozniak and Tim my physician assistant friend that they had been able to work out an agreement. Tim would start working four to six shifts per month, starting after his state licensing and hospital credentialing was complete, which was likely to take approximately one month. It was still at least a month away, but it was a welcomed start, and I was happy to have Tim on board to help me out. It was a huge bonus that along with Tim's clinical experience, he was simply an all-around great guy with a team approach to patient care. The current environment at CHOB was toxic and the more positivity around, the better the influence on the staff.

A few days following John's news regarding Tim, I received a text message from John asking if we could meet at 2 p.m. in his office. I replied, "See you then!"

When I arrived at his office, he had a huge grin on his face as he said, "Have a seat, Eric." As I sat in the chair across from him at his desk, he said, "Eric, I have some good news."

I replied, "I love when a conversation starts with those words." John went on to explain that he had several in-depth conversations with the dean and other staff from the University of Southeastern Mississippi regarding the possibility of developing a pediatric acute care nurse practitioner doctorate program. Not only were they overwhelmingly supportive of the idea, but they wished to expedite it and have the inaugural class commence this spring, which was a mere eight months away. I was overwhelmed with excitement and quite frankly I was even more in awe of John's efficiency. Yes, I understood that while this likely meant that it would be approximately four years before the first class would graduate, it had much greater implications for the state of Mississippi, as this program would become a means of producing pediatric acute care nurse practitioners that could staff every intensive care in the entire state. It truly was big news.

"John, you are incredible," I said.

"We did this together, Eric. You and I brainstormed the idea, and you are providing clinical training for our students." I was thankful for his thoughtful inclusion, but I truly felt this incredible accomplishment was primarily his, and I was amazed at his efficiency for moving it forward so quickly. Honestly, I believed after our last conversation that if he were to be successful, that it would be a minimum of one to two years before such a program would be developed. Especially seeing the speed at which progress appeared to occur in Biloxi.

"I can't thank you enough, John," I said as I stood from my chair, shaking his hand while preparing to leave and share the good news.

"Hold on. We aren't done yet. I have a project for you," he said with a smile.

"OK, whatever you need," I responded.

"Well, do you recall our idea of gifting tuition to two to three of your CICU nurses who are interested in studying to become an acute care nurse practitioner in exchange for a three-year commitment to work in the CICU following graduation?" John asked.

"Yes, of course," I replied with great anticipation.

"Well, I spoke with Dr. Deeton, who has agreed to pay for three of your CICU nurses to study in the inaugural class in exchange for a three-year employment commitment following completion," John said with a big smile.

"You are amazing!" I said, bypassing a handshake and going straight for a hug as I thanked him.

"It is up to you who you choose; however, I need their names within the next four weeks so we can get their applications processed," he explained.

"No problem. I will speak with Ruth, the incoming nurse manager, and we will come up with a fair way to decide. John, again, thank you a million times over. This last week, you have given me hope that this CICU build I have taken on just might be possible," I said, fighting back tears once again.

"You are most welcome," he replied with a satisfied smile on his face.

13

ARRIVAL OF LONG-AWAITED HELP AND DR. ROSTRI'S POWER

Three weeks had passed since John and I met and the time had arrived to provide him with the names of the three nurses who would be granted free tuition as the inaugural class of the newly formed pediatric acute care nurse practitioner program at the University of Southeastern Mississippi. Ruth and Maddie were literally in the process of moving to Biloxi so I engaged their input by telephone and the three of us brainstormed and eventually contrived the idea that interested nurses would submit an essay, no more than two pages in length, explaining their reason for becoming a bedside nurse and why they deserved to be chosen to receive free tuition to study in the brand-new program. The deadline for submission was today and a total of six applicants had submitted their essay for consideration.

Ruth, Maddie and their respective families had just arrived in Biloxi over the weekend and today was their first day at Children's Hospital of Biloxi. The three of us read through the essays with great interest. The decision was extremely difficult, so to help minimize bias, I concluded it was best if the two of them chose their top three applicants since they could not associate the name with the essay yet, with the understanding that I would function as the tiebreaker if needed. All six applicants did a phenomenal job and I wished we could provide the opportunity to all of them, but that was not possible, so ultimately, we chose the top three essays.

I was elated to finally have Ruth and Maddie physically in Biloxi and to learn that morning that Tim had received his PA license and was nearly credentialed, with plans to begin working in the CICU the following week. I attempted to restrain my excitement but couldn't help but feel a glimmer of optimism as I saw budding signs of progress, at least in terms of staffing the CICU. Martha, the PA student, was enjoying her rotation and had decided to complete her final elective in the CICU with me, which meant another two weeks of clinical exposure and I hoped we could convince her to join us following graduation. I had even received an application from a cardiac intensivist who was an MD, PhD from Yale whom I had arranged a phone interview with later that day.

While staffing momentum was on the rise, clinical change in the CICU remained painfully slow! We had lost a total of eight nurses since I arrived. While most were young and inexperienced, it was a dismal sign nonetheless, representative of the degree of toxicity that ultimately affected patient care. We desperately needed to break that cycle and usher in a new era, consisting of a positive and nurturing environment, which focused on nursing reten-tion. Beyond the detrimental effects the environment had on nursing, it was simply miserable for everyone to function at a job that was already stressful at baseline, when you were constantly surrounded by toxicity. Though Ruth had just arrived, I immediately burdened her with the task of addressing staff turnover as her top priority. I had inferred that a portion of the issue stemmed from Dr. Rostri and his posse, who appeared to have unfettered power and autonomy, to say and behave as they pleased, without fear of repercussions due to his protection, which often meant ridiculing and criticizing inexperienced nurses for making mistakes that were inherent with inexperience. This coupled with public criticism from Dr. Rostri during "migration rounds," were the primary reasons, I had concluded, responsible for so much nursing turnover.

One observation that had puzzled me since my arrival was the lack of visibility in terms of oversight, displayed on behalf of hospital administration. I had yet to see any administrator enter the pediatric cardiac intensive care unit in my brief four months at CHOB, including James Deeton, CMO, the person primarily responsible for recruiting me, and Nancy Ogylview, the CEO. I sensed the etiology of this absence was an underlying fear of Dr. Rostri. Dr. Deeton, despite working directly with Dr. Rostri as a cardiac anesthesiologist for nearly twenty years, appeared terrified to confront him with anything that could be viewed as confrontational, as witnessed by my last meeting with him where I spoke of his unwillingness to allow change in the CICU, to which Dr. Deeton repeatedly replied, "Tell him that I said to stop interfering with change." Despite Dr. Potts and me repeatedly saying that it would be best if those words came directly from him, he deferred it to me and was yet to speak to Dr. Rostri.

I wondered how deep Dr. Rostri's power and influence reached at Children's Hospital of Biloxi and within the preeminent hierarchy of the university? It was evident that there was a deep "good ol' boy" network within CHOB as well as within the University of Southeastern Mississippi. I had learned that the hospital once had an entire floor dedicated to research; however, with leadership goals focused on continued profitability and no apparent business plan to develop money-making specialties to improve revenue streams, their goals were achieved by cutting costs and "running thin," which translated into the entirety of the research floor, minus one minuscule research lab, being converted into office space, due to a lack of funding. Rumors throughout the hospital circulated that research funding from the university was virtually nonexistent now because the money was being distributed among the "good ol' boys," higher up in the medical school. News stories of whistleblowers would subsequently break years later, validating these rumors.

During my first few months at CHOB, at the peak of my desperate search for physicians willing to help staff the night shifts in the CICU, I had asked some of the pediatric intensive care unit staff if they might consider working some nights to help fill coverage gaps with the promise of additional compensation. In speaking with them, they provided an unprovoked, somewhat historical perspective on their relationship with Dr. Rostri. They stated that there was a brief period where they had offered coverage of his patients; however, due to incessant toxicity and his unabated insistence on micromanaging the patients, particularly in scenarios where they felt the patients were being mismanaged, the group arrived at the unanimous conclusion that they would no longer offer their assistance. They also shared that over the years, when patients of his were admitted to their unit, he continued his controlling behavior, leading to their team's eventual submission and deferral to his management, as the fight became futile and perceived as unworthy of the time and headache associated with such a battle, particularly when the administration appeared unwilling to intervene. I heard a similar story in the neonatal intensive care unit, where babies with congenital heart disease, including those yet to undergo cardiac surgery, were managed exclusively by him and even the pediatric cardiologists submitted to his plan, despite the frequent disagreement in management style. I heard a similar story when I had asked the dietician to join us daily on medical rounds in the CICU, sharing my desire for their opinion regarding such things as formula type and recommended daily calorie goals for each baby. Interestingly, the first week or so when I actively sought their valuable input, she commented how different it felt to be asked for her advice because Dr. Rostri had previously ignored their input and in fact told them to cease writing their recommendations in the chart, though they were required to do so for each inpatient in each of the intensive care units in the hospital. I was astonished by her words. I inquired further about her recommendations related to total parenteral nutrition, also known as TPN, which consists of intravenous nutrition given to sick patients unable to tolerate enteral nutrition. I had noted some very unusual consistencies when I observed the TPN being administered to many of the cardiac ICU patients. To understand what I am about to say, it is important to understand that TPN, like a regular diet, requires a combination of carbohydrates, protein, and fat. First, I noted that the dextrose content, which makes up the carbohydrate component of TPN, was rarely advanced beyond 10–12 percent, resulting in an inadequate delivery of calories for a newborn baby, which makes up the majority of patients requiring TPN in the CICU. Typically, a baby requiring TPN for a week or more may be advanced to 20 percent or even 25 percent dextrose at times. Secondly, I noticed that the protein content was rarely advanced beyond two grams per kilogram a day, well below the goal of three grams per kilogram a day required for babies to build or at least maintain muscle mass. If there is inadequate protein delivered to the body, it will result in a catabolic state, meaning that the body will actually break down its own muscle and utilize it for calories. Finally, lipids were not used at all in the cardiac ICU when I arrived. Lipids are the fat component that is calorie rich and provide essential fatty acids necessary for the body to heal and resist infection. As I mentally digested these atypical practices, I finally began to comprehend how such a degree of malnutrition could be achieved, severe enough to result in pathologic fractures in three patients concurrently. The slow advancement of enteral feeds or in the instance where enteral feeding was not tolerated, the continued delivery of inadequate nutrition via TPN, could definitely explain the concurrent pathologic fractures suffered by three of the warriors housed in the CICU, particularly over such a prolonged period of time. When I queried nutrition as to the reason, they had not been documenting TPN recommendations in the patient's chart over the years, she replied that she was told by Dr. Rostri that they lacked the knowledge and understanding of the nutritional needs of cardiac babies and therefore he didn't need their recommendations. I was appalled! I thought, wow, all of these behaviors exhibited by Dr. Rostri, including performing dialysis without nephrology input, were all about control and these were merely the ones I had discovered in my brief tenure at CHOB, and worst of all, these actions were negatively impacting patient care. From what I had observed, Dr. Rostri had also displayed control over the pharmacy department, or at least an extreme disregard for responsible antibiotic use. I agreed that our patients in the CICU represented an extremely vulnerable population, most of whom have undergone complex surgery, have many invasive devices in place, and have some degree of acquired immunodeficiency due to many reasons including periods of malnutrition. As a result, the empiric use of antibiotics was frequent and necessary, because overlooked infections can silently fester and turn fatal. Antibiotic prophylaxis, on the other hand had become somewhat controversial. Antibiotic prophylaxis consists of administering antibiotics in an attempt to prevent infection rather than to treat it. These practices have changed over the years and while antibiotics such as cefazolin continue to be used for surgical site or chest tube prophylaxis, it is typically for brief, defined periods of time, such as twenty-four to forty-eight hours, which can vary among institutions. When I arrived at CHOB, the practice was to continue prophylactic antibiotics for an indefinite period of time while any indwelling device, such as chest tubes or central venous lines, remained in place. The most extreme example of such a scenario included a baby who remained inpatient in the CICU for nearly two years, during which time the baby continued to receive antibiotics for the entirety of her stay. The concerns regarding prolonged antibiotic use are that the body is full of bacteria and certain organ systems are dependent on bacteria to function normally, such as the gastrointestinal tract. Therefore, long-term use can decrease the normal bacterial flora in the intestine, which are essential for digestion, leading to bloating, gas, diarrhea, malabsorption, and in severe cases it may allow bacteria such as Clostridium difficile to flourish due to unopposed reproduction, leading to bloody stools, which may cause children or adults to become extremely ill. Additionally, following prolonged exposure to antibiotics, commensal bacteria may become resistant to the antibiotics and if these bacteria are passed on within the hospital or in the community and result in infection, they can become extremely difficult to treat.

Pharmacy and the infectious disease physicians at CHOB had failed on several occasions to modify Dr. Rostri's antibiotic practices. When I arrived, the infectious disease doctors urgently requested my help in addressing this concern. They set up a meeting with me to share data they had accumulated over the preceding years, regarding antibiotic use around the country in comparison to that at CHOB and found that we had the highest use of antibiotics in the country and the majority of that was utilized in the cardiac ICU. Astonishingly, our use was at least twice that of children's hospitals housing double the number patient beds and annual patient volume—certainly a "top" statistic no institution should be proud of, by any means. Again, evidence continued to accumulate, suggesting that the source of this and other issues I previously outlined stemmed from an underlying control issue, or more accurately an "out of control" issue, in my opinion. Dr. Rostri had become too powerful and felt the only rules he was required to follow were his own, which he constructed anecdotally at will! But, as I would later learn, the origin of such behavior resulted from a long-standing lack of support, incubated and fertilized by absent, cowardly, and incompetent administrators who failed to hold him accountable for such actions. I remained in awe as to the degree of control and power Dr. Rostri displayed, which had been constructed in isolation over decades, eventually leading to his incorporation and eventual self-promotion to supreme leader of Children's Hospital of Biloxi, subservient to no one, including the hospital CEO or dean of the medical school. But as I learned from other CHOB staff members, his rise to power was also silently fueled by his connections within the board of directors of Children's Hospital of Biloxi and his connections within the "good ol' boy" leadership network of the University of Southeastern Mississippi School of Medicine. Rumors ran rampant among the medical staff detailing previous unsuccessful attempts at a coup to dethrone him, which were inevitably defended and blocked by hospital board members and university leaders. After my extensive review of Dr. Rostri's connections and power, it sadly led to a clearer understanding of the unorthodox practices occurring in the CICU and how he continued to successfully resist change and managed to practice in isolation for so long, because there was no one willing or capable of holding him accountable. I also became enlightened as to another chilling realization, my hiring was indeed partly to build the CICU; however, I now believed the fine print of my employment contract, which was surely inscribed with invisible ink, secretly detailed that 50 percent of the job duty consisted of the impossible tasks of challenging and holding Dr. Rostri accountable for these practices, due to the fact that hospital and university leaders were incapable, and terrified to do so themselves.

As I attempted to process this complex network of cause-and-effect relationships, which had resulted from years of ineffective leadership, the time for me to call the candidate from Yale was rapidly approaching. In the days leading up to this call, I had arrived at the conclusion that despite my previous failures, I refused to compromise my ethics or deviate from my approach of honesty and transparency when it came to summarizing the state of the hospital and the congenital heart program to the candidate. However, I felt differently this time, as if we had a fighting chance at recruiting him, because this time I was entering the interview armed with a new set of successes, consisting of the new hires we had been able to recruit. We now had Ruth, Maddie, Tim, potentially Martha, and with John Wozniak's help, we had been able to gift three of our nurses a free education in the newly constructed acute care nurse practitioner program who would subsequently become APPs in the CICU for a minimum of three years. The one new piece of information I had surprisingly discovered that morning, while reviewing our CICU data, was that despite the snail-like pace of progress in the CICU, our data revealed a substantial reduction in our mechanical ventilation time and a dramatic reduction in our hospital length of stay. While I fully understood that when you are among the worst performing programs in the country when it comes to hospital length of stay, implementation of an early extubation program, involving even the simplest of cases, will help narrow the data gap between you and every other program, simply because your patients had been staying far longer than the typical three-day average observed at other programs. It was substantial progress for us, and I was happy to see that we were now performing similarly with our colleagues for such cases. I felt that the right candidate would see through the fog of our dysfunction to visualize with clarity the potential that lie in the distance, much like I did. It not only gave me optimism about our chances with the candidate, but also provided me some much need self-confidence that what we were doing was indeed making a difference in the care we provided to our patients, which was the ultimate goal.

Leading up to this interview, I had done some digging into the candidate's background, including his research interests. I had a friend who had trained at Yale who asked some of his old colleagues about him. The candidate's name was Adam Bhuttoni. He was obviously very intelligent but had struggled a little clinically and had been away from bedside management for a year doing mostly basic science, laboratory-based research. He had studied and trained at some of the top programs in the country. So appropriately, as I dialed his number, I asked myself the obvious question, why the hell would he be interested in coming to Children's Hospital of Biloxi? As the phone rang twice, I heard a voice say, "Hello."

"Hi, is this Adam?" I asked.

"Yes it is," he responded in a friendly voice.

"Hi, Adam, this is Eric Philson from Children's Hospital of Biloxi. Thanks for taking the time to talk with me today. How are you doing?" I asked.

"I am doing well, Eric. Thanks for calling me," he replied.

"Adam, I thought I would start by providing you a little background information about the program here at Children's Hospital of Biloxi, including changes we have made over a short period of time, as well as changes we are planning in the near future. Then after that you can feel free to ask any questions that you may have. How does that sound?" I asked.

"Sounds perfect," he replied.

"Great. So, the program has been around for more than twenty years, and it varies between medium and large volume, with two senior cardiac surgeons who perform an average of 250–350 cases annually. I joined the program as the medical director approximately four months ago with the goal of building the CICU from scratch. Believe it or not, there was already a separate CICU in place when I arrived; however, the patients were exclusively managed by the cardiac surgeons, which as we both know is an outdated model, but I now understand this model continued due to the severe repercussions of Hurricane Kelly back in 2005, which set the city and the program back at least a decade. So, while there are quite a few outdated practices here, they are things that I view as completely fixable with a full complement of team members. It has definitely been challenging to implement change with surgeons who have practiced a certain way for twenty years, but it is a unique opportunity to help evolve the medical care for the kids in the state, which simply is not where it needs to be. So far it is me and one other cardiac intensivist who recently completed his training. We have a new nurse manager and unit educator who came with me from Florida. I also have a senior APP who worked with me in Florida who has agreed to help by doing some locum shifts and hopefully I can convince him to join us full-time. I also have a PA student who is weeks away from graduation who I am hoping will join us as well. In the meantime, we continue to recruit for more physicians, APPs, and a cardiac-trained clinical pharmacist. We have approval right now for four additional cardiac intensivists and four to five additional APPs. There is a lot of work to be done. Things you and I take for granted have not been practiced here, such as early extubation. We have had to convince the surgeons that these changes are safe for the patients, so that has been the biggest challenge so far. Shortly after I arrived here, we began extubating the simpler cases in the CICU on the same day as surgery, which has gone well and has already resulted in a significant reduction in our hospital length of stay based on our CICU data. Right now, the surgeons have only agreed that we can do it on days when someone stays in-house at the hospital at night. So, with Justin and myself each working seven nights per month and Mark Borland, a pediatric cardiologist with some ICU experience helping us out, we have a little over half of the nights covered each month. That's why we need more people like you to join us so we can cover more nights and increase the complexity of the changes we are trying to make. So, tell me, Adam, why are you interested in Children's Hospital of Biloxi?" I asked, taking a deep breath after completing my sales pitch.

Adam responded by saying, "Wow, sounds really interesting what you guys are trying to do. Well, I have actually been to Biloxi several times with family and friends. I love the rich history of the city as well as the architecture and it is one of my favorite places to visit," he replied.

"Hmm. Interesting. You have to be the only person I have met, who is not from here, that loves the city of Biloxi, which is wonderful! Do you have any questions regarding the program?" I asked. Adam proceeded to ask some general questions related to the subspecialty support at CHOB as well as the expected number of calls and service weeks per month he would be required to work. As we concluded the phone call, I finished by asking, "Adam, I very much enjoyed speaking with you, would you be interested in coming for an in-person visit to meet the rest of the team?"

"That sounds great," he said.

"Wonderful, I will have the administrative assistant for the university reach out to you and arrange a time to visit that works best for you. Please feel free to call me with any questions. Take care," I said as I concluded the call and hung up the phone. I turned in my desk chair and said, "Yes!" as I celebrated for a brief moment in solitary. While I understood that Adam's visit was merely an interview without any guarantee of joining us, I viewed it as a small victory, because just three months ago, I failed to get most candidates to even return my phone call or email. So, for the time being I would take the small victory as progress.

14

CONTINUED CICU OBSTACLES

In the CICU, one of our little warriors passed and as sad as it was to witness her family in tears, I felt an overwhelming sense of relief as did most of the staff that her suffering had finally come to an end. Her body couldn't take it anymore and finally she was at peace. We exchanged hugs with the parents and among ourselves and I told the nurses how much I admired them. They remained dedicated to these patients, even in the worst of scenarios and they came to work every single day to care for patients even when they could do nothing to end the suffering, yet they persevered just as the warriors did. I was so proud of them. I could slowly feel a trusting connection building with many of them.

Ruth and Maddie spent the next couple of weeks introducing themselves to the staff, as they each branched off and started individually asking the nurses about their perception of the current state of the environment in the CICU. They inquired about the perceived deficits, suggestions for improvements, and the difficult question of whether they felt there had been any positive change that had occurred since I had arrived. The last question I only learned of much later and had nothing to do with, but I appreciated it, nonetheless. I was not surprised to find that most were still resistant to change and preferred the "way they had always done it" and were hesitant to trust the two of them, mostly when it came to sharing honest thoughts regarding the toxicity in the unit as well as the perceived source of it. Dr. Rostri continued to lead the flock of geese each morning on "migration rounds" and continued to play mind games with me regarding the start time of said rounds. When I arrived early, he arrived late, making us all wait. When I arrived five to ten minutes early, he was already rounding with whoever the first person to arrive was that morning. Frustratingly, this would go on for months! In my mind, it was almost certainly intentional on his part, which I began to term "KGB psychological warfare tactics," and I had to admit, he was masterful! Justin and I continued CICU medical rounds with consistent attendance from nutrition and social work and with increasing input from each of these specialties. The decisions we made during medical rounds remained relatively limited, but we continued to use much of the time reviewing all clinical data to be sure the team wasn't missing any relevant details vital to the care of these complex patients. The one opportunity I saw during these rounds was to focus on discovered deficiencies in patient care, which appeared to have an adverse effect, things that Dr. Rostri didn't tend to focus much of his attention toward. So, Justin and I focused on TPN for which we engaged the dietician for her input. We advanced the calories daily as tolerated, including advancement of the protein content and for the first time in what must have been decades, or perhaps ever, we started intralipids on all patients requiring TPN. Again, a small victory for us individually but a huge victory for the patients collectively!

Each morning on "migration rounds" with Dr. Rostri, I relentlessly continued to offer suggestions, though the best response I could get from him was "Let me think about it," which I came to learn was another high-level KGB psychological warfare tactic that made you think he was considering your suggestion, when in actuality he was only delaying the inevitable "no."

I continued to identify new variations in practice that deviated far from the standard of care as it pertained to the practice of pediatric cardiac intensive care, discovering new deficiencies each day. One such practice was the frequent transfusion of small volumes of blood. In our complex babies with heart problems, blood carries essential oxygen to the body and organs, so having a normal hemoglobin, particularly in the most critical patients, was vital and therefore, the transfusion of blood was commonplace and often necessary. However, for many of our most complex patients with what we term single-ventricle heart disease, who were committed to undergo a series of three separate palliative surgeries over the first three to five years of their life, as their heart can never truly be "fixed," and ultimately at some point during their lifetime, were they to survive the palliative surgeries, they would eventually require heart transplantation. Each time a patient is exposed to a blood transfusion from a different donor, they develop antibodies to that donor, so the more blood transfusions, the more exposure to different donors, the more antibodies the patient develops. When the time comes for transplantation, the more antibodies a patient has developed due to exposure to multiple blood donors, the more difficult it may become to find an appropriate match, due to the increased risk of rejection, which may lead to longer waiting times for finding an appropriate donor heart. Therefore, one thing most institutions attempted to adopt was responsible blood transfusion practices. Babies with complex heart problems don't always tolerate a lot of fluid so we often give fluid boluses in aliquots of 5 milliliters per kilogram at a time. However, to limit antibody exposure, the typical practice is to give 10–15 milliliters per kilogram of packed red blood cells; however, due to the increased volume of this fluid, it is often administered over a longer period of time, perhaps three hours, for example, instead of one hour for a 5 milliliters per kilogram fluid bolus.

Dr. Rostri had practiced the concept of ordering 5 milliliters per kilogram of packed red blood cells (blood) when a patient's hemoglobin was low. Our complex patients frequently developed low hemoglobin due to daily lab testing, blood gases, and the natural process of red blood cell breakdown that occurs in the body on a daily basis, and as a result the change in the hemoglobin concentration that occurred following a 5 milliliters per kilogram blood transfusion was minimal. So, the following day or perhaps two days later another 5 milliliters per kilogram of blood would be given. These small transfusions may be repeated several times per week for certain babies, thereby exposing them to multiple donors, which could result in massive antibody production. This practice was by no means unethical and commonly occurred in medicine years ago; however, it was outdated, due to the continued advancement in our understanding of antibody production and its ultimate effect on transplant candidacy. Additionally, more and more literature continued to be published suggesting the potential adverse effects of repeated blood transfusions beyond donor exposure.

When I asked Dr. Rostri during "migration rounds" if he would consider changing this practice, he responded with a hard "no." I attempted to explain by foolishly saying, "Based on recent publications …," to which he responded quickly by stating, "These publications don't take into account how complex our patients are here in Biloxi, so I don't want to hear it!" I would learn over time, he truly believed the patients we cared for in Biloxi were different and more complex than those cared for in other CICUs across the country, which was obviously not the case. I came to understand that in his mind this belief somehow justified his practice of outdated medicine, void of the faintest resemblance to evidence-based medicine. However, much like the TPN deficiencies we had identified, I saw a window of opportunity to change this easily fixable practice due to the fact that during "migration rounds," he simply voiced aloud what he wanted, and expected the rest of the team to fill out the blood transfusion documentation, which was also still on paper at the time. "Ding, ding, ding. Opportunity!" I said to myself as I looked at Justin and smiled. So, Justin and I began filling the transfusion documentation out, ordering 10 milliliters per kilogram blood transfusions. No, I didn't feel great about the deceptive nature of what I was doing; however, it really wasn't about me, or even Dr. Rostri for that matter, it was about the patients, and following the repeated rejection of my suggestions that I experienced on a daily basis, well, desperate times lead to desperate measures, or so they say. These rejections were becoming increasingly frustrating, and I needed to capitalize on any opportunity that presented itself. So I did. This was not going to produce a measurable outcome, but it was the right thing for the patients, so again, I took the small victory; however, this one was in discretion!

That day the scheduled cardiac surgery was slightly more complex, and I was on call that evening, so I asked Dr. Rostri if I could extubate the patient that evening if everything went well with the case. He said, "Let's see how the case goes and we can speak afterward."

"Sure," I replied, as I thought to myself, "Another KGB mind trick that will lead to another 'no' I am sure," but I decided to wait and see.

Later that afternoon, the patient arrived to the CICU in stable condition as Dr. Rostri explained the details of the surgery, reporting that the only issue during the case was that the patient experienced brief periods of intermittent complete heart block for which he was being paced via temporary external pacing wires, which most patients have placed in the OR in case they are needed during the first few days postoperatively. Heart block is a type of irregular heartbeat where the electrical system of the heart is not conducting normally. Most commonly this heart rhythm resolves, and a normal rhythm returns spontaneously, but it is not unusual for patients to require temporary pacing, for a brief period of time.

After Dr. Rostri finished reporting the details of the surgery to me, he said, "If you want to extubate the patient tonight, that is fine."

"Wonderful, I will plan on it, unless I see something that concerns me later this evening," I said.

The patient did exceptionally well that evening, although he continued to require pacing for heart block but remained stable hemodynamically. I followed my usual algorithm to prepare the patient for extubation, which included starting Precedex and versed infusions at low doses in order to allow time for the high doses of fentanyl used during the operation to be metabolized and excreted from his body. Again, this approach was designed to prevent the patient from abruptly awakening until I had an opportunity to wean the ventilator and until I felt comfortable that the fentanyl load in the body was appropriate for extubation and would not suppress his respiratory drive. Four hours later, the patient was breathing and showed some purposeful movement, so I weaned the sedatives and placed the ventilator mode to continuous positive airway pressure, a mode that allows the patient to do the majority of the work of breathing, while providing a minimal amount of support. This helps test the patient's strength, ability to spontaneously breath, and helped me to test if he appeared ready to remove the breathing tube. The patient did well, so I stopped the versed infusion and continued a very low dose of Precedex to help keep the patient comfortable while also providing some analgesia to help ensure he would take deep breaths. The extubation went smoothly, and the evening continued uneventfully.

The following morning Dr. Rostri arrived on time for "migration rounds." Of course, I had been at the hospital all night so there was no need to alter his arrival time in order to continue his ongoing mind games with me. The flock migrated in their typical pattern from one patient room to the next, as I laughed to myself and said, "Indeed, our flock formation that morning appeared impeccable," which I am certain was humorous only to me in my delusional, sleep-deprived state.

We arrived at the bedside of yesterday's surgical case as the flock landed masterfully. I stood next to Dr. Rostri, offering a brief summary of the patient's clinical course overnight. Dr. Rostri gave a half-hearted effort, pretending to listen or even care in the slightest about the words that came from my mouth for a maximum of approximately ten seconds before walking directly to the temporary pacing box that was hung next to the patient on an empty IV pole, as he proceeded to unplug the cables to evaluate the patient's underlying heart rhythm. He nervously and rapidly plugged the cables back into the pacer box, for the underlying rhythm consisted of a flat line, confirming dense heart block without an escape rhythm, which meant that the patient was completely dependent on the pacer as his own electrical activity was one that would not sustain life without the assistance of the pacer. As he looked over at the patient's medication infusions, he said aloud angrily, "Precedex? No wonder he has heart block. Why is he on Precedex?"

I proceeded to explain that I had used it to prepare him for extubation and left the smallest dose possible on for pain control. "Nonsense, that is why he still has heart block. Don't you know that Precedex causes arrhythmias?" he screamed.

"Actually, you are referring to bradycardia, which is the most common side effect in terms of abnormal heart rhythms, that may be seen with Precedex use. In fact, for that reason, it is often used to prevent or treat tachyarrhythmias (fast heart rates) such as supraventricular or junctional tachycardia, but your point is well-taken, Dr. Rostri. He has an irregular heart rhythm so we can at least take that out of the equation as a reason the rhythm persists and we can easily stop it now, no problem. However, it is unlikely to be the cause of his heart block since he arrived from the operating room yesterday on no Precedex and was being paced at that time due to heart block that he acquired during surgery," I replied calmly.

"That is dangerous. That's why I don't ever use Precedex," he yelled.

"I disagree. Everything we do in medicine has risk and we must always weigh the risk to benefit of every intervention. I have used Precedex more than any other sedative in my career and yes, there are side effects like all medications. I have seen bradycardia but never have I seen it 'cause heart block.' As I said, I agree that it is reasonable to stop it at this point, but it didn't cause his heart block, surgery did, and it will most likely recover. I would appreciate if you would avoid making accusations that are untrue, they break trust among the team. Also, I don't deal in absolutes by saying things like 'that's why I never' or 'that's why we only do it this way.' Those are dangerous statements that ultimately discourage critical thinking and prevent progress," I replied calmly but with a firm voice. Dr. Rostri stormed out of the unit. I looked at everyone and calmly said with a smile, "Well, I guess that's the end of rounds for today." The group disassembled as I slowly walked to my office for some deep breathing exercises.

I sat down in my office and tried to relax. This was getting old. I missed the days of collaboration and evidence-based discussion with the unified goal of providing great care to the patients, which was how the team practiced in Fort Myers. The current environment at CHOB thrived on control and ridicule, which appeared to be mechanisms adopted to assist in resisting change at all costs. I didn't know how long I was going to be able to tolerate this behavior or environment, it had only been a little over four months and I was at my wit's end, but how could I possibly leave when Ruth and Maddie had just arrived, I just moved my family, my kids just started a new school, and I had just convinced Tim to come help. More than anything I was bothered by the idea that if I left without completing the job, who would possibly be foolish enough to replace me, which meant the patient care would remain below the standard of care and the children of Mississippi deserved better. I was beginning to realize that I made a huge mistake when I took this job but for the reasons I just mentioned, I felt trapped. But more importantly, for some reason, I felt an enormous amount of responsibility for these patients, not just the warriors and the current patients recovering in the CICU, but the children of the state who would have surgery and receive CICU care at CHOB in the future, they deserved high-quality CICU care that other children around the country were already receiving. I was naive and overlooked so many red flags prior to accepting this job; however, prior to my decision, the institution had been searching for years to find someone to fill this role, unsuccessfully, and as a result, I truly felt that there was no one foolish enough to take on the impossible role that I did.

As I contemplated these thoughts and emotions, there was a knock at my office door. The door opened and in walked Justin. "Hey, Eric, how are you doing? I heard about rounds," he said.

"I am fine. What exactly did you hear about rounds?" I asked.

"I walked through the CICU for rounds and the nurses told me that you and Rostri got into it about Precedex or something?" he replied, shrugging his shoulders with a confused look on his face.

I shook my head back and forth as I said, "Yeah, it's absurd. He was trying to blame me for heart block that he caused in the OR because the patient was on low-dose Precedex."

Justin laughed as he said, "Don't worry about it. Hey, did you see Jose Colmenares in the CICU talking to Dr. Rostri? Apparently, he is doing well after coronary artery bypass surgery and wants to come back to work."

"No, I didn't. Glad he is doing better but does he really want to come back? I am not sure that is good for his physical or mental health, or mine for that matter. Nor do I think adding Rostri's loyal sidekick, who has been trained like a beat dog to facilitate his outdated plans, is going to be constructive for the unit and is likely to disrupt what little progress we have made," I replied.

"Yeah, me neither," he said.

Justin and I walked back into the CICU so I could prepare for medical rounds, which were scheduled to begin in thirty minutes. As we walked through the double doors, there was Jose speaking with Dr. Rostri. Both were seated on the blue sofa underneath the large, colorful paintings directly across from the entrance to the CICU. They both glanced at us as Jose gave a friendly wave and Dr. Rostri appeared to intentionally turn away, projecting that feeling, with near certainty, that they were talking about us, or at least about me. As Justin and I walked around, I updated him on the patients, when suddenly behind us appeared Jose. I turned and shook his hand. "Good to see you, Jose. How are you feeling?" I asked.

"I am doing good. My function is better, still moderately to severely depressed but better and I am ready to come back to work. The doctors have cleared me to come back part-time," he said with a smile. "Eric do you and

Justin have a couple minutes to meet with me in the conference room?" he asked.

I looked at Justin as he nodded yes. "Sure," I said in agreement. The three of us walked together across the hall into the dark, cold conference room. We each found the nearest chair and proceeded to sit.

Jose said, "Eric, how do you think things are going so far since you started?"

"I would say they are going OK. It's been a bit of a challenge to say the least. I had hoped to be able to institute change a bit faster than I have and I was hopeful it wasn't going to be quite so difficult to recruit people here, but since I have readjusted my expectations somewhat, I can see that progress has occurred although quite slowly," I responded.

"You know, Eric, things here are different, our patients are more complex, and you need to realize that we have a certain way of doing things, which has worked for years and therefore, doesn't necessarily need to be changed. In fact, change can be dangerous, particularly starting new medications that can cause complications such as arrhythmias—" Jose said until I interrupted him.

"Jose, hold on for a moment." I thought to myself, this is not Jose speaking, this is Dr. Rostri. "Look, Jose, I like you a lot. You are a nice guy and clearly you are a dedicated clinician who deeply cares about the patients and about Dr. Rostri. I am glad your health is improving, and I welcome you back at any time you and your physicians feel it is safe to do so; however, I also need to make a couple things clear to you if we are to work well together. Dr. Rostri is my colleague, he is not my boss and I am not here to do what he wants me to do; I am here to work together with him, the rest of the current team, as well as the future team I am building so that we can evolve the care in this CICU into the twenty-first century, so I am bothered that he has asked you to meet with me to try to convince me to accept things the way they are and to stop trying to implement change, which is in fact the job I was hired to do. So, since Dr. Rostri doesn't have the courage to come discuss his concerns with me, I will ask you to tell him that I will not, as long as I am here at this hospital, stop pushing to change things for the better of the CICU. I wish you nothing but the best, Jose, and I hope we can work together soon," I said firmly as I stood up, looked him in the eyes sincerely, shook his hand and walked out the door. Justin followed me to my office as I attempted to cool down. "The nerve of Rostri to send Jose in there to try to push his agenda. The guy nearly died and his first day here he has him carrying out his psychological warfare," I said.

"Yeah, that was pretty disturbing," Justin agreed. This job was really getting to me and was getting worse by the day.

That night when I arrived home, it took me two four-fingered Scotch on the rocks to relax. I ruminated as to how I was going to move things forward in the CICU. I needed help covering the nights to prevent changes from being reverted to "the way we always do it." But how could I get others to help while the unit functioned in such a state? It was too outdated, and no junior physician was going to feel comfortable joining a program in the current state of flux and even if they did, how could I mentor them? I had exhausted all internal possibilities for help and the recruiter had been able to connect me with a few candidates, but none showed serious interest in the job. I asked Dr. Deeton to permit me to hire locum tenens help; however, he refused to commit to that idea due to the substantial cost that would be required. The only option remaining, which was pure desperation and not sustainable, was for Justin and me to pick up more night shifts, but that was crazy. We were already doing twice the workload of most CICU-attending physicians, and that did not include the massive amount of time I was spending on fulfilling my other responsibilities as the medical director. Again, even if I entertained that idea, clearly it was a short-term solution that simply wasn't sustainable, again leaving me with the feeling of being trapped.

That evening, I received a text from a well-respected colleague of mine who was the medical director of the pediatric cardiac intensive care unit at the Mayo Children's in Minnesota. The text said, "Hey Eric. Hope you are well.

Wanted to see if you would be interested in joining me here on staff. We have an opening and I thought you would be a great addition. Let me know. Dean Capner." I couldn't believe the timing of the text; it couldn't have been worse. Eight months ago, I would have accepted the position in an instant; however, here I was feeling frustrated, yet responsible for a lot of people, including the patients, which oddly left me feeling an immense amount of guilt for considering leaving the job before I had completed the construction of the CICU team. I sat with my head down and thought exhaustively about the opportunity, contemplating any scenario where I could make it work and still be able to face myself in the mirror without feeling an overwhelming sense of guilt.

I told Ana about the text, and she responded by saying, "That is awesome, sweetie; if only he would have asked sooner, huh?"

"Yeah, my thoughts exactly," I replied, as I sat reviewing all of the reasons that required me to say thanks but no thanks. I knew there was substantial risk when I accepted this position, but I told myself, if I gave it everything I had and it still didn't work out, at least I could walk away with my head held high, knowing that the end result was something that was out of my control. The truth is, I hadn't given everything I had yet, so I decided to send the text I had constructed, which said, "Hi Dean, I am honored that you would ask me to join you; however, I just accepted the position as medical director at Children's Hospital of Biloxi, and I still need some time to see how this all plays out here. Again, I truly appreciate the offer. Eric."

"Totally understand Eric. Best of luck to you. If you change your mind, please let me know," Dean responded.

As I finished my second Scotch, I stood up and walked toward my bedroom as I thought to myself, "I sure hope that was the right decision."

The next morning when I arrived at the hospital, I met up with Doris Geisinger, the junior cardiac surgeon, whom I hadn't had the opportunity to speak with for some time since she had been traveling back and forth to Alabama, receiving surgical mentorship. We talked for nearly an hour following "migration rounds." She seemed to be pleased with her new mentorship arrangement and shared that she was able to operate on several complex neonates, an opportunity which had never been offered to her by Dr. Rostri. I was happy for her, although she appeared far less connected with the staff, including me, upon her return to CHOB, although I didn't want to tell her that. I shared my frustrations with her, and she understood as she had experienced her own turmoil at the hands of Dr. Rostri and the absent CHOB leadership. I mentioned to her the text I had received from Dean Capner of Mayo Children's and shared that I had decided to turn down the opportunity. She looked at me surprised and said, "Eric, that is a great opportunity. Are you sure you want to turn that down?"

"I know you are right, but I really want to try to exhaust all options here before I consider making a move away from CHOB. I think I am going to arrange another meeting with Dr. Deeton, to ask him once again to put pressure on Dr. Rostri to let me do my job; otherwise, if I am not allowed to do my job, I am going to consider leaving," I explained to her.

"Well, good luck getting Dr. Deeton to stand up to Dr. Rostri," she said with a chuckle. "Gotta run, see you later," Doris said as she left my office.

I was able to set up a meeting with Dr. Deeton that afternoon. "Eric, how are … uh … things … going?" he asked.

"Painfully slow. I have made a little progress with early extubations, which has helped improve our overall length of stay; however, as I mentioned previously, it is impossible to implement and maintain significant change without twenty-four-hour in-house coverage because Dr. Rostri simply reverts back to his way as soon as I leave the hospital. Unless this situation changes, I am going to have to consider other job options because this is just too much clinical work for Justin and me alone, not to mention all of my other medical director responsibilities. It is simply impossible to recruit physicians into this environment with such an outdated system, which is too unfamiliar for junior attendings, making it impossible for them to thrive, not to mention the fact that it would be virtually impossible for me to mentor them in a CICU with such unabated toxicity. You need to put pressure on him and tell Dr. Rostri to back off and let me do the job I was hired to do."

Dr. Deeton's face turned firetruck red as he yelled, "You're going to give me fucking ultimatum, Eric? Is that what you're going to fucking do? That's your fucking plan? What do you want me to do, fire him? Huh?" he said without a single pause in his speech.

I shook off the surprised look on my face as his speech was once again, flawless and without a single pause, and said, "Ultimatum? You must be joking. You're the one who misled me into this environment and now, I am trapped! I can't find anyone desperate enough to join me here, while Dr. Rostri is allowed to run wild, practicing prehistoric medicine and relentlessly blocks every attempt I make at doing my job. Meanwhile, I am forced to helplessly sit and watch as babies suffer in that CICU every single day while I can't do a damn thing to help them. Do you have any idea how traumatic that is? You can call it an ultimatum or whatever word you choose; I simply call it the truth! And let's be clear, you put me into this situation, which you knew about, yet you failed to share with me during my entire recruitment process. I did not put you in any situation. You trap a rabid dog into a corner, then you are surprised that he will fight back and do whatever he needs to do to survive? Again, call it what you want, the truth is, if this situation doesn't change soon, and Dr. Rostri continues to block my ability to do my job, I will be looking elsewhere for employment," I said as I stood and walked angrily out of his office.

The following day when I returned to the hospital, I entered my office to find Justin sitting in one of the chairs and he looked as though he had just seen a ghost. "What's the problem?" I asked.

"Check your email," he said. He went on to explain to me that he had written an order for calcium chloride the previous night while on call but had accidentally based the dosing off of the recommended dosage used for calcium gluconate, which is typically about ten times the dose of calcium chloride. The nurse had identified the error and pointed it out to him, so the order was corrected and fortunately the medication was not released by pharmacy, so no harm occurred, and the patient was not placed in danger.

I explained to him, "Justin, there is a multiple verification system that hospitals have in place to help prevent errors such as this from harming patients, so in this case the system worked. Obviously, you need to be more careful and double-check your dosage, but the nurse caught it and if she wouldn't have caught it would have almost certainly been caught by pharmacy, and if pharmacy had not realized the error and delivered it to the nurse, she is required to scan it into the computer, which would have also been likely to catch it. Justin, relax, don't be so hard on yourself, the patient is fine, the mistake was caught. Be more careful. That is the take-home lesson. I am glad you have some self-reflection about the error, but you can't beat yourself up, unfortunately mistakes happen and in this instance the system caught the error at the first step of verification. Also, we are working a lot, so you need to get some rest and take care of yourself."

"Well, read your email. The nurse informed Dr. Rostri about the error and he wrote an email to hospital administration," said Justin, who was nearly in tears by this point.

"You have to be joking," I said, opening my phone to read the email. As I read Dr. Rostri's long, dramatic and heavily exaggerated email claiming how dangerous Justin is to the patients and how he shouldn't be allowed to work in the CICU any longer, I shook my head in disgust. "Relax, Justin. I will talk to Dr. Deeton about this," I said.

Before I could get to my computer to email Dr. Deeton, he had already responded with the same words I had repeated to Justin moments earlier regarding how the system of safety checks worked and prevented patient harm and that Justin clearly needs to be more careful. I walked out of my office to catch Justin, who had just left to head to the CICU, so that I could show him the message; however, he had already read the message, yet he still appeared shaken. "I just don't feel safe here. Outside of your support I feel like Dr. Rostri is out to get me, so I feel as though I might have to start looking around for other jobs. I don't want to work in an environment where I have to constantly look behind my back and make sure others aren't trying to sabotage me," he explained, as a solitary tear dripped down his cheek onto his beard.

"Believe me, Justin, I understand. I would be devastated if you left, but you need to take care of yourself, and I want you to do what is best for you. Just keep me updated along the way because that will likely alter my plans," I said to him as I gave him a big hug and pat on the back. "You're a good man, Justin, and a great doctor. Don't let him make you think any differently of yourself," I said, now holding back tears of my own. "Working the hours we are working in the environment we are forced to try to overcome has bonded us like brothers. Remember, I will always have your back! Go home and get some rest," I said as I walked him toward the exit.

When I arrived home that evening, I walked directly to the wet bar, immediately pouring myself a four-fingered Scotch on the rocks, which explains where I was mentally. I sat down and had a long talk with Ana about the day and how concerned I was about Justin, yet how torn I was about leaving. She comforted me the best she could and told me, "I will support you regardless of the decision you make because I love you and I want you to be happy, whether that is here, in Minnesota or anywhere else in the world."

"Thanks. I know I have put you and the kids through a lot, and I am struggling to understand what the correct decision is for us all, but it means a lot to me knowing that I have your support," I said, though I could see the sadness in her eyes, despite her valiant attempts to conceal it. An hour later, I decided to text Dean at Mayo Children's to see if the offer to come for an interview still existed. Based on the look I saw on Justin's face that day, I realized that it was best if I had options lined up, in case the situation unfolded where Justin decided to resign, leaving me as the sole cardiac intensivist at CHOB. "Hey Dean, I have done a lot of thinking and I would like to come check out the program if the offer is still there," I said via text.

"Absolutely Eric. Let me have my assistant call you tomorrow to set up a visit as soon as possible," he replied.

"Excellent. Talk soon," I responded. The next morning, Dean's assistant called, and we arranged my visit for the following week.

15

VISIT TO MAYO CHILDREN'S

The week leading up to my interview seemed to pass quickly. Justin had just completed an interview for an outpatient pediatric cardiology opening in Biloxi, which highlighted to me where he was mentally, as he really didn't care much for outpatient medicine; however, his family situation required that he remain in Biloxi, so I knew he was desperate and must be strongly considering leaving CHOB. Later in the week he had an interview in the CICU where he did his training, outside the state. I was concerned about him and wanted him to do what was best for him, regardless of how his decision would impact me.

Dean had asked me to prepare a presentation for the Heart Center at Mayo Children's on a topic of my choice. I decided to present a research project I had completed in Florida that I was in the process of submitting for publication, which evaluated the potential negative consequences of inadequate preoperative malnutrition on newborns undergoing congenital heart surgery. I spent most of the plane ride preparing for the presentation as I had little time to do so in Biloxi, due to my workload at the hospital. Once my plane landed, I took a taxi to the hotel where I was supposed to meet Dean in the lobby so he could drive me to dinner with one of his partners an hour later. I checked into the hotel and headed to the room to relax for a few minutes before dinner, allowing me time to call Ana and the kids, to see how they were doing. "Hey, sweetie. How are you? How was your day?" I asked Ana.

"Not bad," she said. "The girls arrived home from school about an hour ago. They are doing good. You know, still adjusting to the new school, but doing well in terms of grades. They tell me the kids are pretty nice, but they have had a little trouble finding new friends they feel close with like the ones they had in Florida," she said.

"I know it's tough, sweetie, but it will happen. They are both so sweet, they will find some good friends soon. I am headed to dinner in a little bit with Dean and a colleague of his. I may not get home before you are sleeping so I will text you when I arrive and give you a call tomorrow to let you know how the presentation and visit went," I said.

"Sounds good. Good luck. I love you," she said.

"Thanks, Ana. I love you too," I replied.

As I hung up the phone, I received a text from Dean stating, "Almost to hotel. Meet me outside."

"On my way down. See you shortly," I replied. I put my sport jacket on and headed down the elevator. As I walked out the door to the street, up pulled a beautiful Red BMW M4 and as the passenger window rolled down, I could see it was Dean driving. I opened the door and sat in the passenger seat and said, "Nice car, Dean."

"Thanks, Eric. So glad you came to check out the program. We are excited to have you here and hope we can convince you to join us."

As we drove toward the restaurant, he explained how Mayo Children's was extremely focused on research and clinical excellence but also valued the importance of balancing work and personal life. I thought to myself, "Wow, imagine that, a system that encourages balance rather than encouraging me to work more." Work and personal life balance was definitely something that was nonexistent in my current situation. Dinner was nice, and we were joined by one of the pediatric cardiologists. We discussed the Heart Center at Mayo Children's and they shared with me the hospital's plans for expansion, which included a brand-new $2 billion children's hospital that was to commence construction soon. They asked about the program at Children's Hospital of Biloxi, and I detailed the history as well as the challenges I had encountered, including the slow progress that we had made. As we ate dinner, I enjoyed hearing about the state-of-the-art facilities and amazing research infrastructure at Mayo Children's; I especially enjoyed hearing how every physician was provided a startup package, including funding that allowed them to get their research projects off the ground, easy access to biostatisticians and laboratory space for those interested in basic science research, as well as guaranteed, set-aside time to dedicate to research. As dinner finished and Dean dropped me off in front of the hotel, I thought, what a wonderful dinner and I truly looked forward to tomorrow and meeting the rest of the team. As I arrived in the room, I took off my jacket and sent a goodnight text to Ana. "Just got back from dinner. Was really nice. Excited for tomorrow. Will text you tomorrow when I am finished. Sleep tight. Love you. Tell girls I love them." I laid down in bed and fell asleep immediately without the need for a stiff drink or two, which in retrospect was telling of how much the environment can be responsible for a healthy or unhealthy sleep cycle. The relaxed feeling and some much-needed sleep were only guaranteed for one night, but I would take it and enjoy it while I could.

I woke to my alarm, which I had set for 6 a.m. I showered and dressed in my suit, tied my tie, and headed down the elevator to the hotel lobby where I asked them to call me a cab to take me to Mayo Children's. As the taxi drove me to downtown Rochester, Minnesota, I was amazed at the size of the Mayo Clinic Health system. It literally made up the entire downtown area of Rochester which, while small, appeared very clean and historic. The buildings that made up the Mayo Clinic campus were gorgeous and old but extremely well-maintained with beautiful statues carved into the top of the buildings, some of which were elegantly lined with what appeared to be bronze. The taxi pulled up under the awning housing a sign that read Mayo Children's Hospital. "Here you are, sir," said the driver. I paid for the ride and stepped out of the car. It was September and the early morning temperature was in the upper fifties, which felt incredible when compared to the ninety-degree temperature and extreme humidity of Biloxi. However, growing up in the Midwest, I knew what Mother Nature had in store and it was right around the corner. Over the next couple of months, this perfect temperature would quickly turn to freezing cold, with snow, and grey skies that would last for six months and I had to admit, I most definitely did not miss that.

As I entered the building I was overcome with the aroma of cinnamon and spotted a pastry store nearby, which was clearly the source of this magnificent smell. The lobby was filled with families and children. "Eric?" I turned as I heard someone calling my name. I looked ahead to see a woman in her mid-fifties with brown hair, wearing a brown skirt and white button-up blouse, walking toward me.

I replied, "Yes, I am Eric Philson."

"Hi, Eric, I am Laurie Stern, Dr. Capner's assistant. I will be guiding you today during your visit and I will be helping you get to all of your scheduled interviews in a timely manner. Also, just before lunch, I have scheduled thirty minutes of preparation time in the auditorium so that you may review your talk in advance of your scheduled presentation, if you would like."

"That would be wonderful," I said.

"Great. Follow me and I will take you to your first interview of the day, which is with Dr. George Twestel, chief of pediatric cardiac surgery. Would you like some coffee? We can grab a cup on the way if you would like," Laurie asked politely.

"That would be terrific. Thanks," I said. We proceeded to take the elevators up to the third floor where we stopped to get a cup of coffee and scurried down the hall to Dr. Twestel's office. George Twestel was a legend in the field of congenital heart surgery. He had joined Mayo Children's about two years earlier from Michigan. It had been said that they paid him $3 million a year to join them and in just two years, he had taken Mayo Children's Cardiac Center from a top twenty program to one considered a top-five program in the country. He was known as a technically skilled surgeon but equally as an intelligent man, an incredible leader, and an even better human being. That combination of traits, when it came to pediatric cardiac surgeons, was a true rarity and while $3 million a year is obviously a lot of money, I would say it was a wise investment on the part of Mayo Children's.

As Laurie knocked on his door, he welcomed me into his office and offered me a seat, which I graciously accepted and sat down. "Welcome, Eric," he said. George Twestel was a bald man in late fifties who on that day, wore a white button-up shirt with a red striped tie and glasses, which were clearly bifocals, as he tilted his head backward with a downward gaze of his eyes as he read over my curriculum vitae. "Looks like you have been busy publishing over your career, Eric. So, you're in Biloxi now, how is Dr. Rostri doing?" he inquired.

"Dr. Rostri is doing well. I am getting to know him a little more every day. What I have learned thus far is that he is an extremely dedicated man who cares deeply for his patients. He has been operating and performing the CICU care for twenty years and that is a massive amount of work for one individual, and I have an immense amount of respect for the pride he takes in his work," I said. I had to admit as I said those things aloud, despite Dr. Rostri and my differing opinions and struggles at times, I did admire him for these traits. The fact that he and Dr. Penton had carried this workload for twenty years was admirable. I continued telling Dr. Twestel, "Yes, I have been at Children's of Biloxi for almost five months, and it has been nice but I must say it has been a lot of work and quite a challenge for one person. The job I took on is to build the CICU from scratch in the midst of an ongoing busy cardiac surgery program while trying to make a smooth transition from a unit run by cardiac surgeons to one run by cardiac intensivists, while doing everything I can to maintain good working relationships," I explained.

"Sounds like quite the challenge. I have to ask the obvious question, why are you here after only five months?" Dr. Twestel asked.

"Good question. Well, Dean had reached out to me regarding an opening here and while at first I had to decline, the extreme amount of work and obstacles I am facing made me think, I should at least take a look and see what my best option is at this time," I replied.

"I understand," he said. Over the next twenty minutes he proceeded to explain the current state of the program as well as his vision for the future. Our interview ended as Laurie arrived to lead me on to my next interview. I thanked Dr. Twestel for his time and wished him the best.

The remaining part of the morning was filled with interviews. I had the opportunity to meet all of the cardiac intensive care unit physicians at Mayo. It seemed like a great group of individuals who were not only talented but who worked extremely well together. My last interview of the morning leading up to my scheduled time to prepare for my presentation was with Dean. We sat in his office and casually talked about my morning interviews as he validated my general observations regarding his CICU staff. "Eric, what are your thoughts so far?" he asked.

"Honestly, I am very impressed. It would be dramatically different from my current situation. I would step into an institution with a world-renowned reputation that clearly supports its employees, while also providing money and support for research and there is no doubt that I would have a much better work-life balance," I said.

"Yes. I think it's admirable what you are trying to do in Biloxi, I truly do, but it sounds like a lot for one person. I understand you would have to give up the medical director title, but honestly, in a few years you could take it over from me if you want," said Dean with sincerity.

"Dean, that is very kind of you to say and I certainly couldn't agree more that my current role is a lot for one person. I just need to finish the day and take some time to think and discuss with my family," I replied.

"I completely understand. Looks like Laurie is here to get you. Good luck with your presentation," he said, as he stood and shook my hand.

Laurie walked me to the auditorium where the information technologist for the Heart Center was waiting for me near the podium that sat in front of twenty rows of theater-style auditorium seating, which had the capacity to hold two hundred people, reminiscent of a large lecture hall seen at major universities. The tech asked if I had a flash drive, which I removed from the inside pocket of my suit jacket and handed to him. He plugged it in as I directed him to the appropriate file and within seconds my presentation was projected onto the massive screen at the front of the auditorium. He explained where I should position the microphone attached to the podium so that I would be heard best. "That's it. Any questions?" he asked.

I adjusted the microphone for my height and tested to be sure I could advance my slides. "Everything looks good. Thank you," I said.

"Alright. I will leave you to prepare and will return five minutes before the scheduled presentation to be sure you don't need anything else," he said as he walked toward the exit.

"Thank you so much for your help," I said. As he exited the door, I thought to myself, "Wow, every aspect of this institution runs like a finely tuned machine, far different from Children's Hospital of Biloxi." Over the next twenty minutes I practiced my presentation, passing through each slide. I felt slightly nervous but confident and excited to share my research with such an intelligent and accomplished group of physicians. As the time approached, the staff and trainees began filing into the seats, as the tech arrived and gave me a thumbs-up sign to make sure I didn't need anything before my talk was to begin. I returned a thumbs up signifying that I was ready to go. As the scheduled presentation time arrived, the auditorium was filled to about 50 percent capacity. Dean stood up and proceeded to give a brief introduction to the group, highlighting my background, current job, and the title of the presentation I was about to give. The presentation lasted approximately forty minutes, which was nearly identical to the time it was taking as I practiced on the plane. While naturally somewhat nervous, I felt that the presentation went smoothly and at the end, there were several comments commending my work and several questions asking if I was considering any further studies that may be developed based on the findings I had presented.

The final comment came from the chief of cardiology, Anthony Rosenthal. Dr. Rosenthal was a legend in the field of pediatric cardiology. He had joined Mayo Children's only three years earlier. Prior to his arrival he was chief at Great Ormond Street Children's Hospital in London, England. He was a short, petite British man with black but greying hair, always well-dressed in a suit and tie. He had written numerous textbooks and had published ground-breaking research in several areas of pediatric cardiology. "Dr. Philson, that was an excellent presentation. This is an area that has yet to be extensively studied in our field and there are several small tributaries from this project that could be followed to spawn further research. Well done! Have you submitted this for publication yet?" he asked with a proper English accent.

"Thank you very much, sir, for your comments. Yes, it is currently accepted, pending minor revision," I replied.

"Wonderful. Any other questions for Dr. Philson?"

Everyone applauded and started to exit the auditorium. Dean walked toward the stage and said, "Nice work, my friend."

"Thanks, Dean," I said.

Dr. Rosenthal walked to the stage and shook my hand. "Nicely done, Dr. Philson. I will be seeing you at the end of the day for our meeting," Dr. Rosenthal said as he walked toward the exit of the auditorium.

The remainder of the day moved fast. I had the opportunity to meet three of the pediatric cardiologists, two of whom were junior cardiologists who had been at Mayo for a few years, while the third was a senior cardiologist, named Tim Kowatch. Tim had dark black hair, which had actually turned grey a few years back; however, he regularly hid this aging effect by dying it black. He was in his early sixties and was the medical director of outpatient cardiology and professor of clinical pediatrics. He was very accomplished, publishing more than one hundred peer-reviewed manuscripts during his career and had practiced cardiology at Mayo Children's for the entirety of his twenty-year career. He trained at some of the top institutions in the country. I enjoyed visiting with him very much during my interview. Tim was a very personable but a notably nervous guy, as could be observed by his constant squirming as he sat in his office chair and by the notable basketball-sized armpit sweat that saturated his undershirt and his light blue button-down shirt. Tim Kowatch was easy to talk with and he shared a very interesting historical perspective of the past and how the Mayo pediatric cardiac program evolved from mediocrity to become a national powerhouse. When our time ended, I thanked him for the stimulating conversation and shook his hand, neither of us knowing that our paths would soon cross again.

Laurie walked me from Dr. Kowatch's office to my final interview with Dr. Rosenthal. As we arrived outside his office, she sat me in a chair and explained apologetically that he was finishing up another meeting and asked if I would like another cup of coffee. I was getting pretty tired by that time of the day, especially after the flight, so I graciously accepted. I sipped my coffee when suddenly his door opened and three men in suits exited his office. Dr. Rosenthal came to the door and apologized for the delay and waved his hand, signaling for me to enter. His office was massive, with large glass panes forming the two walls behind his desk, each offering a gorgeous view of Rochester. Across from his desk was a round table and four chairs. He sat in one of the chairs at the table and offered me a seat across from him. As I sat, he pointed to the blueprint that was laid out on the table. He said, "This is the reason that I unfortunately had to keep you waiting. I was meeting with administration to review the final blueprint for the brand-new children's hospital that will begin construction in the next few months. These two floors are to comprise the new state-of-the-art facilities for every aspect of the Heart Center that you could imagine. This is the brand-new pediatric cardiac intensive care unit, the step-down unit, cardiac catheterization lab, cardiac operating rooms, and more."

"Wow, that is incredible. How exciting," I said.

"We are very fortunate as a program because the institution is financially sound and understands the importance of supporting its staff and in particular it understands the value of research. Eric, the early feedback from others you have met today is overwhelmingly that you are a great guy, intelligent, maybe a bit quiet but I have no concerns about that because I can't usually shut the rest of the team up, so we have more than enough people who like to hear themselves speak," he said laughing loudly.

"That is great to hear," I said with a big grin.

"We would like you to consider joining us. I am sure you are paid well as a medical director and I am not one to waste time so tell me how much you make, and I will see what we can do to at least match that," he said.

I was taken by surprise, as I had never had anyone ask this question or be so forward with me during an interview before, but I loved it, and I respected it immensely. "I am paid well," I said as I shared my salary with him.

"Well, that is higher than I expected. We may not quite be able to get there, but I think we can at least get close," he said smiling.

"I want to thank you for my visit today. I am truly impressed by the program and have a lot to think about. I have never been somewhere where I could truly have a great work-life balance, be supported for research and be paid a generous salary. I need to get home and speak with my family, and I promise I won't delay my decision too long as I know you have other candidates you are considering. Again, thank you so much. It's truly been a pleasure," I said.

"The pleasure was ours, Eric. Safe travels," said Dr. Rosenthal.

Laurie called me a cab as she handed me my luggage, which she had been storing behind her desk for me during the day. I rode in the back seat of the taxi, on our way to Rochester International Airport, when my phone began to ring. It was Dean. "Hi, Dean. Just headed to the airport. Thanks for an incredible day, I really enjoyed meeting everyone and I feel that I was able to get a good feel for the program and the team," I said.

"Perfect. Everyone loved you. The ball is now in your court," he said. Dean went on to explain the details regarding required clinical service time and night call coverage each month and that they would be able to offer me a salary slightly less than that which I was currently making in Biloxi; however, there would be significantly less clinical time and administrative responsibility, and I would receive a starter research funding package in addition to my salary.

"That's incredible, Dean. Thank you so much. I need to discuss the opportunity with my wife and do a little thinking," I said, "but I promise to have an answer for you within one week. As I said, I won't waste your time as I know you have other candidates. Again, thanks so much for the opportunity."

"Safe travels, my friend," Dean replied.

As the taxi pulled up to the curb at the airport, I paid the driver and entered the airport, passing through security as I headed toward my gate. When I arrived at my gate, I called Ana and spoke to her in great detail about my visit. She could tell I was excited, but she could also tell I had a great deal of indecision. "You know me too well. I just feel so much responsibility to the people who have joined me and to the children of Biloxi. I don't know what I should do," I said, clearly struggling with the decision.

"Just take some time to think about it. I will support whatever you decide. Safe travels. Love you," Ana said.

"Thanks. Love you too," I said, as I hung up the phone and boarded the plane.

On the plane ride back to Biloxi, I was consumed by my own incessant introspection. I thought obsessively about the two hospitals and how drastically different they were, appearing at opposite ends of the spectrum in every aspect from finances, quality, reputation, and size to academics, work-life balance, and workplace culture. I imagined what it would be like assuming the role of CICU medical director at Mayo Children's, such an amazing and established program. I thought about the changes I would try to implement and how I would do it. Strangely, as I contemplated this scenario, I struggled to come up with what I would consider to be a single meaningful or dramatic change I could implement that would truly shift the paradigm at such an institution. As I pondered more, I asked myself what could I truly do that would make a lasting impact on the program and the community? After struggling to answer this question, I realized the real answer was that I could probably do very little, other than carry on the legacy of others, and perhaps make some small changes to fine-tune the system that was already in place. I wondered if this was the actual reality when it came to medical director positions at such well-established institutions. Don't get me wrong, I understand that all medical director positions and other leadership positions require a substantial amount of work and dedication, but when it comes to medical director positions where so much change is possible, and necessary, the results that can occur are such that they can resonate across an entire institution and even an entire state, and that is a rarity. The medical director position at Children's Hospital of Biloxi was just that, but the real question was whether that degree of change was actually attainable, and if so at what expense to the people trying to achieve it? That was the conundrum that I needed to understand. I knew that it was not possible to answer this question with certainty; however, I at least needed to understand if the sacrifice and risk associated with trying to achieve such a goal were going to be acceptable to me. As I thought about it, I remembered that it was in fact the opportunity to instill such meaningful change that had originally attracted me to CHOB, not the title. I truly had never cared about titles and accolades, I wanted to make a difference. I began to realize that I had already made my decision before the plane had even landed. I knew I had to see this through, as I hadn't given the job everything I had, but I needed Justin's help to do so. What I had in mind was absolutely insane, but it was the only option I saw that gave me a chance to succeed. I needed to call Justin as soon as I landed and see where he was at mentally and ask if he would consider staying to help me see this through. I knew I couldn't do it without him.

As the plane landed, I took my phone off airplane mode and immediately sent a text to Justin. "Hey, how are you doing? Need to talk to you. Call me when you have a minute to talk." As I exited the plane my phone rang. It was Justin. "Hey, Justin. How are you doing? Just got back from Mayo," I said. He knew about my interview. I told him I had to have a backup option since I wasn't sure if he was going to leave or not.

"Hey, Eric. I am alright. I checked out the other CICU job I told you about. I am still not sure what I should do. How was your interview?" he asked.

"It was pretty incredible. Almost too good. They offered me the job with a great package. I struggled with my decision on the plane ride back, but I came to the conclusion that I don't want to walk away at least until I have exhausted all options. I have an idea, but I can't do it without you. It is absolutely insane, but it is the only possible way I see that we can make this work," I said, likely sounding desperate.

"Let's hear it," said Justin.

"Well, the only way we can implement change is if we find a way to keep Rostri and his posse from reverting back to 'the way we always do it.' To do that we need to have in-hospital coverage by our team of cardiac intensivists, twenty-four hours a day, seven days a week. If we do that, we can implement change and push things out of the dark ages and into an era of practicing high-quality and compassionate medicine in the cardiac ICU, a quality that assimilates the standard of care represented in CICUs around the country. It is a vicious loop. One success leads to the other. Without change we can't recruit and without recruits we can't cover 24-7, which we require in order to implement change. Right? So, I suggest you and I increase our night shifts to around ten to twelve per month. Then I ask Mitch Borland to increase his night shifts to seven per month. The remaining two to four night calls per month that remain, I will beg the interventional cardiologists to help us cover. This is clearly not the smartest plan, and it reeks of desperation, yet it is the only short-term option we have at this time in order to try to make this work. I will tell Dr. Deeton that for you and me, any night call above five he needs to pay as an extra per diem shift. For the others, he needs to agree to compensate for each of the night shifts they work. I realize it's crazy and unsustainable but if we can implement enough change that results in some semblance of a 'normal' CICU that recruits are no longer terrified of, and if we can improve our CICU data even more, we just might be able to convince some candidates to join us, at which time we can reduce the number of night calls we are working. I realize it's a long shot but if it doesn't work, I feel at least I can walk away and say, I did everything I could to make it work, it is not my problem anymore. What do you think, Justin? Other than, ERIC, YOU'RE CRAZY!" I said.

"That is insane, I am in!" Justin responded so quickly it seemed as though it was a few milliseconds.

"Alright, I will speak to Dr. Deeton tomorrow and let him know that this is the short-term strategy we have decided to pursue, and I will verify that he can indeed offer per diem pay for all extra shifts. Then I will talk to Mitch about increasing to seven nights per month, and if he says yes, I will ask Kajay and Eric from the cath lab if they would be willing to pick up one to two night shifts per month each. I can't believe I am saying this, but I think this could actually work," I said excitedly.

When I arrived home, it was late, and Ana was waiting up for me. As I entered the house, she greeted me with a big hug and kiss. She saw the smile on my face and she knew I had made a decision already. "You're staying here aren't you?" she asked. I nodded my head yes. "I knew it. You are far too stubborn to walk away without fighting and exhausting every option," she said.

"You know me too well," I said, giving her another kiss. I told her my plan and that Justin had agreed. "I just need to talk to Dr. Borland and the cath doctors tomorrow," I said.

"You are absolutely insane. But I know there is no use trying to talk you out of it, so all I can do is support you," she said.

"Thanks. That's why I love you!" I said.

16

RETURNING TO THE DRAMA AT CHOB

The next day, on the way to work, I called Mitch Borland and told him my idea. He quickly replied, "No problem, happy to help."

"Thanks, Mitch," I said. As I arrived at CHOB, I walked to the cardiac catheterization lab to ask if Kajay and Eric would be willing to help. I explained to them my plan and they immediately agreed to help me cover a couple nights each month. I thanked them and explained that the final piece of the plan was talking with Dr. Deeton and getting his approval for the shift compensation. I left the cath lab with a smile on my face as I headed toward Dr. Deeton's office. As I passed by the CICU, out walked Dr. Penton into the hallway with a distressed look on his face.

"Eric, I need to talk to you. It's urgent. Can we go into the conference room?" he asked.

"Uh, sure," I said, wondering what this could be about. We entered the CICU conference room and sat across from one another. "What's going on?" I asked, confused.

"Eric, I want to be honest with you, but I don't know who I can trust," he said, rubbing his balding head repeatedly, clearly stressed.

"You can trust me," I said.

"I hope so. Well, yesterday Dr. Deeton came to me and asked me what I thought about becoming the chief of pediatric cardiac surgery," he said, as I became confused. He continued, "Look, when this all started, I was uncertain about having you become the medical director, but as time has gone on, I have been impressed with your knowledge and what you have done so far, and I have come to believe that this really might work. I have been trying to convince Dr. Rostri of the same, but he is very stubborn. Then yesterday Dr. Deeton told me that you gave him an ultimatum and said that unless he fired Dr. Rostri that you were going to leave. So, he asked if I would take over as chief. Dr. Rostri is my mentor. I can't stab him in the back like this," he said with extreme distress.

"What?" I said flailing my arms backward and landing them on my head as my fingers began obsessively combing the short, brown hair on the top of my head, repeatedly rubbing my head in distress. "This fucking guy. That is not even close to what I said to him. I did tell him that I was frustrated and that I wanted him to tell Dr. Rostri to back off and allow me to do the job I was hired to do. Otherwise, I was going to have to look for another job because this simply won't work. Not once, at any time, did I imply or tell him that he needed to get rid of Dr. Rostri. That thought never even crossed my mind. I had asked him several times before to speak with Dr. Rostri and tell him to back off and not once has he done that. So, I told him if he didn't talk to him I was going to have to leave. Those are two very different demands. Simply unbelievable," I replied shaking my head.

"Well, that's good to hear. Will you talk to Deeton?" Dr. Penton asked.

"Yes. In fact, I was headed to his office to discuss a plan I had come up with for providing 24-7 night coverage. I can't believe Dr. Deeton told you that lie. Alright, I am headed there now. I will find you after I talk to him. I am sorry you had to go through that, I really do want to try to make this work and we need to be able to trust one another," I said.

"I agree. Thanks, Eric," he said.

I walked to Dr. Deeton's office and asked his assistant if he was available. "Let me find out. Hold one second please. Dr. Deeton, Dr. Philson is here. Can he come back? OK. Sure, go on back, Dr. Philson," she said.

"Eric. Have … uh … a … seat. I … uh … spoke to … uh … Dr. Penton … and—"

I interrupted by saying, "I apologize for interrupting you, Dr. Deeton, but I never asked you to fire Dr. Rostri, I simply wanted you to tell him to back off and let me do my job and stop resisting change, that's all. I spoke to Dr. Penton already and clarified this with him, explaining that I was simply asking you again to intervene because unless I can start to make progress, this isn't going to work for me. Not once did I ever ask you to fire him; I don't know where you got that. Anyway, let's forget about that for a second. I want to discuss an idea I have because for this idea to work, I need your financial support," I said. I explained the details of my plan and outlined the compensation that would be needed to convince everyone to help me cover all of the night shifts each month. "Look, it's a huge burden on Justin, Mitch and me but it's the only chance we have right now to make meaningful change, which could allow us to recruit some candidates and break this endless cycle, which continues to resist change. I want to begin next month so I am hoping you can get the financial approval before then," I explained.

"I … uh … like the … uh … idea. I … will … uh … hopefully … get back … with … uh … approval … uh today," Dr. Denton said.

"Great. Thanks," I said as I left his office.

I headed toward the CICU to see what was happening and to find Ruth and Maddie to see how things were going and to update them on the plan. I punched in the code as the double doors opened and I entered the CICU, suddenly finding myself overcome by a wave of negativity and toxicity, which seemed to saturate my clothing and form a film on my skin, covering my entire body. It felt filthy as if I needed a shower immediately. I managed to brush that horrendous feeling off as I looked around the unit but didn't see Ruth or Maddie. I walked toward the back of the unit and asked one of the nurses if they had seen them recently. "I think I saw them walk out the back doors toward their office," she said.

As I walked out the back door I was greeted by the rancid smell of garbage. I looked left and found their office door, located directly adjacent to the morgue. As I stood outside their door, just about to knock, I could feel a breeze carrying the constant, repugnant smell of garbage down the hall. I knocked on the door thinking to myself, "I hope they are doing OK and aren't considering resigning already, and I hope they don't hate me," as I recalled my own feelings of shock when I first arrived to CHOB and subsequently uncovered the endless amount of work that lay before me. As they opened the door, I was greeted by that all too familiar look I recall seeing on my own face when I looked in the mirror each day during the first three months after starting at CHOB. It was that look of horror, lying somewhere between "just saw a ghost" and "terrified for my life." "Hey, how are you two doing?" I asked.

"Come in. Shut the door," Maddie said.

"Oh no. What's up?" I asked.

"Eric. This is so awful. It is so toxic in there. I started to ask about how they perform their central line maintenance and their dressing changes, and they told me that the hospital has care bundles in place, but Dr. Rostri tells them to disregard them and instead do what he says. Eric, the other intensive care units follow the bundles, which are the ones most children's hospitals use across the country, but they are scared to do anything outside of what

Dr. Rostri instructs. And I reviewed our line infection rate in the CICU, and it is very high. I was appalled," Maddie said.

"Yeah, we need to do something about the toxicity and negativity in this unit," said Ruth.

"I totally agree. Listen, the first couple months are tough. I can promise you that I was horrified when I arrived. I wanted to run, and I still want to run away virtually every day. It gets better. There is a ton of work and I still want to quit pretty much daily, but think of the difference we can make," I said, as I could see they weren't buying my words of reassurance. "OK, I will stop with the motivational speeches because trust me, I understand where you are at mentally. However, I do want to share with you my plan for trying to change things at a faster pace, which will hopefully prevent Dr. Rostri from constantly reverting things back to 'the way we always do it,'" I said.

"Oh my God"—they both looked at each other—"do people always say that here?" they asked, horrified.

"Unfortunately, yes they do. And they also say—"

They interrupted me by saying, "We run thin!" in complete unison.

I laughed uncontrollably. "It only gets better. Well, at least it can't get any worse, I hope," I said, half-jokingly.

I explained my plan to which they replied, "You're crazy. Are you sure?"

"Believe me, I said, it's the only way, and even then, it's still a long shot, but I have to try," I said.

"OK. I am going to start trying to convince the nurses to follow the line maintenance bundles to try to reduce the infection rate and I am going to have infection control come and help me enforce it. The other thing I noticed is that when they remove chest tubes, they are using foam tape to essentially wrap the patient like a mummy and they leave the dressing tape on for at least two days. When they go to remove it, we are seeing some major skin irritation, burns, and even tears as a result of these practices. When I left Florida, we were using an adhesive remover spray that was very effective in removing the dressings without causing skin damage, so I asked the company representative to provide us some samples. She came out today and we started trialing the product. The nurses seem to like it so far, so I am going to start ordering a limited supply for us to trial over the next few months," Maddie said.

"And I am going to start trying to weed out the negativity, which won't be easy," said Ruth.

"Both are great ideas. I am so happy you two are here and did you hear Tim is going to start helping out soon? We need to work at convincing him to join us full-time," I said.

"Yes, that's exciting. We will work at convincing him," they said.

"Alright, talk to you later," I said, as I closed their office door, held my breath and sprinted straight into a strong garbage headwind on my way back to the CICU. The double doors opened, allowing me to finally escape the dreaded trash winds, as I arrived safely in the CICU, just in time to allow me a breath of fresh air before passing out.

As I entered the unit my phone rang. "Hello. OK. That's great. Thanks for taking care of that so quickly," I said as I hung up the phone. "Yes," I said to myself. I immediately sent a text to Justin, Mitch, Kajay, and Eric. "Dr. Deeton approved the compensation for the night shifts, so we will start next month. I will send out a preliminary schedule based on your requests by tomorrow. Please get back to me with any changes ASAP. Thanks again for agreeing to help." I walked through the unit checking on the warriors. The remaining four were still fighting, and I saw Justin, so I stopped and spoke with him. "You saw my text?" I asked.

"Yep. Let's give it a shot," he said.

"Anything going on in the unit right now?" I asked.

"Not too much. There was no surgical case today, but I did just get a call from an outside hospital about a patient who had surgery four to five weeks ago who presented to their ER with concerns about a sternal wound infection. So, the patient is supposed to be arriving here in the next couple hours so Dr. Rostri can evaluate the wound," he explained.

"OK, sounds good. I am going to start working on the schedule for next month. Let me know if you need help with anything," I said as I headed out the front doors of the CICU toward my office. Now that I had confirmed everything was in place to begin 24-7 in-house coverage, I called my colleague and friend Dean at Mayo Children's, thanking him for the opportunity but sharing my decision to stay at CHOB, which he completely understood.

17

A MYSTERIOUS INFECTION AND "SPRAY-GATE"

The following morning, I arrived at the hospital with what felt like a fresh outlook on things. I arrived ten minutes early for "migration rounds" and today Dr. Rostri arrived on time and the flock formation was flawless! Things were truly looking up, so I thought to myself, "Is today the day I make the push to join Dr. Rostri at the head of the flock? Don't push it." I resisted the temptation and stayed in formation. As we walked to each patient's bedside, we came upon the patient Justin had mentioned the day prior, who was admitted with concerns for a sternal wound infection. As we looked through the patient's clinical data, Justin described the unusual presentation of the patient, specifically the timeline for which the signs of infection began to appear. Typically, a postsurgical wound infection will present within the first week, or less commonly, within two weeks of cardiac surgery, unless the child introduces something foreign into the wound by picking or excessive scratching of the incision. Some would argue that by this time, this is actually no longer a postsurgical infection, but is instead a "new" primary skin infection, unrelated to the cardiac surgery itself. Irrespective of the semantics, this particular patient presented four weeks following cardiac surgery, which was very unusual. Additional atypical features of this patient's presentation included the absence of fever, normal white blood cell count and inflammatory markers and the drainage of an unusually gelatinous material from the wound that did not resemble that of pus. Even more unusual was that when this drainage was sent to the lab for gram stain and culture, there were no organisms or white blood cells present in the gram stain, and thus far the culture was negative for the growth of bacteria. In the meantime, she was placed on broad-spectrum antibiotics to cover most organisms that could be responsible for such an infection. We completed rounds in twenty minutes flat.

As we finished, Dr. Penton stayed behind and pulled me aside. "Eric, Dr. Deeton spoke with me. Thanks for clarifying the Dr. Rostri situation with him, if we don't have trust, we have nothing," he said.

"I completely agree. If there is one thing you can be sure of with me, it's that I am an honest person and regardless of Dr. Rostri and me having different philosophies in patient care, I understand one thing, which is that we both care deeply about the patients and want what we both feel is best for them. Even if we disagree every single day, I would never want someone to lose their job. He started this program more than twenty years ago when there was nothing, I would never want to take that away from him, but I am trying to start something from zero as well, just as he did, and I am fairly certain that I am running into obstacles in much the same way he did, and like him, I intend on persevering. I can promise you that my solution for success has never included trying to get him, or anyone else for that matter, fired," I said.

"Thanks. I appreciate your honesty and what you're trying to do for the program and the children. I will continue to try to convince Dr. Rostri to support you more," he said sincerely.

"Thanks, Terry," I responded. As he walked out the door toward the operating room, I was grateful for his support. When I arrived to CHOB, it was obvious that he did not want me there, so for him to say these words to me meant so much more than simple support, it meant he was seeing that the change that was slowly occurring was actually leading to improved patient care, he saw the passion I had for my job, and I believe he was finally beginning to see how this change could positively impact his personal life, providing him more balance between his work and family life, which he had been robbed of for the last twenty years, and for these reasons, he not only wanted me to succeed, he now seemed to believe that perhaps I could actually do so. For those who have never been exposed to congenital heart surgeons before, they are truly a rare breed, extremely intelligent with advanced fine motor skills, and there is certainly no shortage of self-confidence, which is actually an essential component required for success in this complex field. However, the elite intellectual and physical skills required often come at the expense of their social skills, which are typically underdeveloped. Convincing a pediatric cardiac surgeon to alter their perspective on something is VERY difficult, some may say impossible, even if they know in their mind that they are wrong and getting them to admit it publicly is virtually unheard of. Therefore, for Dr. Penton to shift from despising my presence to supporting me to such an extent that he would try to convince his mentor Dr. Rostri to do the same was simply unheard of and highlighted for me that there may be something truly special about this guy. As I thought about how appreciative I was of his support, I walked back to my office to work on next month's schedule some more.

I worked on the schedule most of the morning as Justin took care of CICU medical rounds. After finishing rounds, he came into my office and we sat down and reviewed all the updates as well as the plan for each of the patients. As we finished, he got a call on his phone. "Uh-huh, OK, how long ago was surgery? Any fever? Any labs? Sure. No problem, we will accept the patient, I just need to speak with the charge nurse. Can I have your callback number please?" Justin asked. As he got off the phone he explained. "Very bizarre. Same story as the patient I admitted yesterday. One of our surgical cases from five weeks ago with no fever, just redness and drainage from the old sternal incision site. Labs are all normal."

"Very unusual. Nothing has grown from the wound culture of the other patient yet?" I asked.

"Nope. Not yet. I am going to head back to the CICU and let the charge nurse know about the new admission," Justin said as he exited my office. I proceeded to complete the schedule for next month and emailed it out to the group. Each person gave their final approval, so it was official, October 1 we would start 24-7 in-house coverage for the first time in any intensive care unit in the history of Children's Hospital of Biloxi.

The next morning as I arrived to the CICU early, Dr. Rostri had already started "migration rounds"; however, I was unaffected by his continued disrespect, I simply shook my head and joined the flock to complete our formation in mid-flight. We stopped at the bedside of the first patient who had been admitted with a wound infection. As we reviewed the data, the culture remained negative, and the labs remained normal. However, despite broad-spectrum antibiotics, there was no clinical improvement in the redness or drainage. The ultrasound technician had just completed an ultrasound of the wound that morning, which now suggested a fluid collection, so the surgeons had scheduled to take the patient to the OR to open the wound and drain the potential abscess. Everyone remained puzzled as we moved to the next patient who had been admitted the day before with a similar wound infection, presenting in a nearly identical fashion to that of the previous patient. Given the findings of the previous patient's ultrasound we ordered one for this patient as well. As we discussed possible etiologies for the infections, Dr. Rostri exclaimed, "These infections are occurring due to the adhesive removing spray that has started to be utilized in this unit, WITHOUT MY APPROVAL."

I looked at him with confusion and could clearly see that he was upset. "Could you please explain how a sterile adhesive removing spray that we just recently started using has caused an identical infection in two patients, who were operated on more than a month ago? Perhaps I am missing something. I was never very good at math, but that timeline doesn't seem to line up in my mind," I said, with an abundant degree of sarcasm.

"I have asked for the spray to be tested and cultured as this is most likely the source," he said.

"OK, Dr. Rostri, sounds good. It makes absolutely no logical sense in terms of the clinical timeline, but sure let's have it tested to rule it out," I said, shaking my head in utter disbelief that a man, clearly extremely intelligent, could have his entire analytic process completely disrupted by a tiny practice change, which resulted in him feeling as though he had lost even the slightest bit of control in the CICU. It was truly fascinating, yet extremely disturbing. Just then I saw Dr. Rostri holding the can of adhesive removing spray with sterile gloves, holding it ever so cautiously between his thumb and index finger, as he lowered it slowly into a plastic biohazard bag that was held open by the unit clerk, also wearing sterile gloves at his direction, as if we were watching a live filming of CSI Biloxi. I looked over at Justin and Doris with my eyes wide open and gave them a look that must have said, "Where the hell am I right now, the twilight zone?"

As we moved to the next patient, Doris whispered in my ear, "This is mycobacteria. I bet you this is related to contamination of our cardiopulmonary bypass machine (CPB)."

"This would definitely make sense given the late presentation and the lack of response to typical broad-spectrum antibiotics. Why do you think it's related to our bypass machine?" I asked quietly.

"The FDA had sent out a letter warning all cardiac programs about the possibility of such an infection as well as providing an updated cleaning protocol to help prevent colonization of bypass machines by this resistant, atypical organism, which had been responsible for outbreaks at a few cardiac centers around the world. I am certain we must have received this letter from the FDA; however, I am skeptical that our perfusion team, Dr. Rostri, or Dr.

Deeton for that matter, who is responsible for overseeing the maintenance of our CPB machine, are meticulous or organized enough to keep up, or even be aware of the importance of such a change. The identical presentation of two patients who underwent surgery around the same time is simply too usual to be unrelated," she said.

"We need to get infectious disease involved, make them aware of your concerns, and culture our CPB machine. Have you shared this with Dr. Rostri and Penton?" I asked.

After rounds Doris spoke with Dr. Rostri and Penton regarding her concern. Dr. Penton agreed it could possibly be the source and definitely required further investigation, yet Dr. Rostri was in complete denial of such a possibility and remained obsessed with the idea that it was the adhesive spray. Dr. Penton said, "We will see how the wound looks when we open it up. We need to report this to Dr. Deeton. Doris, would you do that please?"

"Sure, I will talk to him now," Doris replied. Dr. Deeton was notified and subsequently initiated an investigation into the current cleaning processes used for our CPB machine as well as the logbooks that should detail the dates the machine was cleaned. The analysis of the adhesive spray, surprising to no one with an understanding of basic math and chronology, found that it was not the source of infection; however, sarcastically among Justin, Doris, Ruth, Maddie and I, the scandal became termed "Spray-Gate" and would be a source of ongoing humor for years to come.

When Dr. Rostri and Penton returned from the OR following drainage of the fluid collection, they reported a very abnormal-appearing wound that consisted of the same gelatinous material found draining from the wound at presentation; however, they found that it was adherent to the sternal wires and therefore, they required removal and as a result, the patient returned to the CICU intubated, on mechanical ventilation, with an open chest, to be certain there were no additional areas within the chest that would require debridement. Now that the spray was conclusively ruled out as the source, Dr. Rostri's logic returned back to earth, from Mars. The ultrasound of the second patient's sternum showed no concerns for abscess and the wound appeared no worse than it did on the day of admission, so the consensus decision was made to continue broad-spectrum antibiotics and await culture results while monitoring closely for any clinical change. Two days later, the surgeons were able to successfully close the sternum of the first patient and she was subsequently liberated from mechanical ventilation upon arrival to the CICU. The rest of the week passed without any additional patients requiring admission for wound concerns, as we thought, perhaps we were all overreacting a bit and these infections were nothing more than typical wound infections.

October had arrived, which meant we were to begin implementing our 24-7 in-house coverage. Since it appeared that no further patients were requiring admission for wound infection, and the investigation of our CPB cleaning practices was still ongoing, the decision by Dr. Rostri and hospital administration was made to proceed with the scheduled cardiac surgical cases for the week. Three cases were completed that week and all three patients did well. Dr. Rostri was pleased to see that we were now providing 24-7 coverage to the patients, so he allowed us to progress the early extubation process to include two patients with more complex cardiac disease. Both did well and I felt like he was beginning to trust me a little bit more. That night, while I was on call, two new patients were admitted to the CICU with wound infections, each with an identical clinical history and presentation matching that of the first two patients. I called Dr. Rostri and Penton that night and notified them of these admissions, and we agreed to discuss the plan in greater detail the following morning; however, we developed a tentative plan to cancel all elective cardiac surgeries until we were able to gather additional information regarding the possible etiology of these bizarre infections. Strangely, not one of the cultures we sent to the lab, from any of the patients, had grown a single organism. Infectious disease had performed an extensive literature search and had found a few case series that had been published detailing mycobacteria outbreaks among other cardiac programs that had experienced contamination of their bypass machine. One such case series described the clinical histories of affected patients that resembled those of our patients, similarly, those patients had negative cultures for up to four to six weeks, which subsequently grew a nontuberculous mycobacterium, known commonly as a slow-growing organism that was often found in contaminated drinking water. Due to the similarities between the reported patients and our patients, our infectious disease team had reached out to that particular institution seeking guidance. After a conference call involving this institution, our infectious disease team, Dr. Rostri, Dr. Deeton, and Luke Leblanc, we were finally able to gain a better understanding that due to the slow-growing nature of this organism, if cultures were to become positive, it may be a month or longer before we could determine the exact organism responsible and more importantly which antibiotics the organism would respond to. This institution was kind enough to share the sensitivity profiles for the organism causing their outbreak, which showed severe resistance to multiple commonly used antibiotics, including those we were currently using to treat our patients. They also shared that due to the significant anti-biotic resistance patterns displayed, they ultimately found success utilizing a three-drug regimen for a duration of four to six weeks, some up to eight weeks, depending on the severity of the wound infection and whether or not there were foreign bodies contaminated, such as sternal wires, or permanent pacemakers, which if involved, would require surgical removal. With this information in mind and due to the lack of clinical response to our current antibiotic regimen, we changed our affected patients to the triple antibiotic regimen suggested by this institution. The second patient affected continued to have drainage from the wound, and a repeat ultrasound now suggested the development of a fluid collection.

We concluded that it was indeed vital to cancel all non-emergent cardiac surgeries for the time being. Given the new ultrasound findings, Dr. Rostri and Penton scheduled to take patient two to the operating room. When they returned, they reported similar findings to patient one, including the gelatinous exudate adherent to one of the sternal wires, which they removed and due to the fact that the bone of the sternum had already fused, there was no need to place another. The patient returned to the CICU with the sternum and skin closed, extubated and in stable condition. Over the next few days, patient two showed clinical response to removal of the contaminated wire and possibly due to the new triple antibiotic regimen we had instituted. Our relatively small yet rapidly accumulating clinical experience with these patients became invaluable, validating the importance of removing contaminated foreign material from affected patients with persistent drainage or when there appeared to be a lack of response to antibiotic therapy. While we continued to learn as we gained more experience, we understood that at this point we were guiding our therapies based completely on the experience of another institution while there was no guarantee that we were in fact dealing with the same organism. It was a very uncomfortable feeling for all of us and it was a miserable experience for these poor patients and their families. Additionally, per the advice of the other institution, we sent all of our wound cultures to a specialized lab that they had utilized during their own outbreak, which they strongly recommended, since the potential organism we were dealing with was extremely difficult to grow in typical culture mediums used by most laboratories around the country to identify organisms that we dealt with on a regular basis.

Over the next three weeks a total of twelve patients were admitted to the pediatric cardiac intensive care unit at CHOB with sternal wound infections with varying degrees of severity, but all with nearly identical clinical presentations. All patients had undergone their cardiac surgery within a four-week time period of one another. All elective cardiac surgical cases remained on hold as we cared for these patients, while Luke Leblanc and the hospital quality team investigated and performed a root cause analysis to identify how this catastrophe could have happened. By this point, the majority of patients residing in the CICU consisted of those affected by this unusual infection. The least-affected patients had superficial abscesses that responded to surgical drainage and triple antibiotic therapy. The most severely affected patient had a pacemaker in place with both the wires and the pacing system itself contaminated with the organism, requiring extensive surgical dissection to detach the wires and battery in addition to the removal of contaminated sternal wires. This patient returned to the CICU with an open chest, requiring mechanical ventilation for two weeks; however, she was able to have her chest closed one week later. Just over one month from the time the first patient was admitted, the specialized lab where we had sent our cultures called to report the organism, which was indeed the same nontuberculous mycobacterium we had suspected, which had been traced to contaminated heater/cooler mechanisms on cardiopulmonary bypass circuits. This organism was ever-present in the environment, particularly in the warm waters of the Southern United States and typically only caused infection in those who were immunocompromised. However, the skin is the body's first line of defense when it comes to preventing infection, and in these patients who had undergone opening of their sternum it provided easy access to the skin, soft tissues and potentially the organs within the chest. Fortunately, the majority of the sensitivity profiles from the patient cultures showed similar sensitivities to those reported by the other institution, so for the most part we were now on the appropriate antibiotic therapy. A couple of patients who showed resistance to the current antibiotic regimen had their therapy tailored to treat the organism appropriately. Finally having confirmation of the responsible organism, as well as reassurance that we were on the most appropriate therapy, provided some relief from anxiety; however, the effect on the patients and their families was traumatic.

This was a challenging time for the patients, their families, and for the entire team caring for these unfortunate patients who now dominated the CICU census. If I could take away one positive experience from this horrendous situation, it was that, for the first time, Dr. Rostri and I truly put our egos aside and focused 100 percent on treating the patients and their families with no ulterior motive, and it was also the first time since my arrival at Children's Hospital of Biloxi that I could see a real semblance of teamwork. It was an awful time for all involved, but after a month, every single patient survived and was eventually discharged. Unfortunately, each patient would require a minimum of four to six weeks of intravenous, triple antibiotic therapy and therefore required placement of a long-term venous catheter, including a home health provider to come to their home and administer the antibiotics daily. Additionally, each patient required regular follow-up ultrasounds, occasional CT scans of the chest, as well as surveillance labs and clinical follow-up appointments, but amazingly they would all recover and that at least made this unacceptable situation slightly more palatable, at least for the staff.

The root cause analysis performed by the hospital quality team exposed a whole new level of incompetence starting with perfusion technicians and extending to involve Dr. Rostri and even more disturbingly, Dr. Deeton, who still carried the ultimate responsibility for oversight as it pertained to the use and maintenance of the cardiopulmonary bypass circuit. The root cause analysis identified the inappropriate use of filtered tap water to run and clean the heater/cooler for the CPB machine as the underlying cause of this catastrophe. The FDA recommendation had cited the importance of using sterile water to run and clean the heater/cooler. However, the sterile water and cleaning supplies typically ordered were on back order, so while awaiting the delivery of these products, the inexcusable incompetence begun by individuals skipping one cycle of regularly scheduled cleaning, which was followed by the subsequent use of filtered tap water to run and wash the heater/cooler resulting in its contamination. Culturing of the heater/cooler as well as the filtered tap water identified the same organism on both and upon further investigation, we found multiple reports suggesting that even the most expensive water filter was unable to clear this durable and resistant organism. The other concerning problem identified, was the complete lack of an identifiable CPB circuit cleaning protocol and a complete absence of any logbook or confirmatory documentation that regular cleaning was actually performed. The details discovered were nauseating, and again the discovery of additional inconsistencies and inadequacies at CHOB continued to unfold before my eyes. Dr. Deeton, Dr. Rostri and the perfusion team each pointed fingers at one another, failing to assume any responsibility, which made it that much more intolerable, although Dr. Deeton did his best work as the veteran "good ol' boy" he was, to sweep as much as possible under the carpet, as he denied his own accountability. Fortunately, the families each received a decent payout from the hospital; however, no amount of money could possibly justify such incompetence at all levels, nor could it ever erase the morbidity and psychological turmoil that these poor patients and families endured.

18

RESUMING CARDIAC SURGERIES

It was a breath of fresh air when the CICU census dwindled, because it most importantly signified that the patients affected by the infection were well enough to be discharged home, but it also meant we were once again able to resume cardiac surgeries following the purchase of two brand-new cardiopulmonary bypass circuits and most importantly, the implementation of a standardized protocol for the use and regular maintenance of the heater/cooler and CPB circuit. One perfusionist was ultimately determined the scapegoat, and the fact that he was blamed was a clear deflection of Dr. Rostri and Dr. Deeton's involvement, nonetheless, his employment was terminated. Getting back to some semblance of normalcy was much needed for all of us. Justin and I were averaging twelve night shifts per month, which in retrospect was absolutely insane, as it was mentally and physically exhausting; however, we were surviving with the help of a LOT of caffeine. The nurses were beginning to really show their appreciation and trust as we essentially lived in the hospital and saw them at all hours of the day and night. Justin and I were basically alternating thirty-six-hour shifts every other day. We rarely slept but the progression of the patients was incredible. As I stated previously, in my opinion, the practice of pediatric cardiac intensive care medicine is not rocket science; it is simply understanding the cardiac physiology of the patients you care for and having the staffing and the ability to progress the patients during their postoperative course, twenty-four hours a day. Imagine if you were Dr. Rostri and Penton and you were in the operating room for six to twelve hours a day, or on rare occasion you may operate all night if a patient is very complex and struggling despite initial attempts at surgery. Then following a grueling surgery both in terms of physical and mental exhaustion as a consequence of the duration and complexity of the case, imagine bringing the same patient back to the CICU and being the one responsible for the minute-to-minute postoperative management, which likely entails significant hemodynamic instability, requiring regular adjustments in medical management. This extreme postoperative instability is common following complex cardiac surgery and may last twenty-four to forty-eight hours, or longer. Imagine performing the complex cardiac surgery, providing the stressful postoperative care in the CICU, and then needing to return to the operating room the following day to do it all over again. This complex situation often meant operating on minimal sleep, canceling or rescheduling the following day's surgical case, or it meant keeping the less complex patients sedated and medically paralyzed on the mechanical ventilator in order to actually get some much needed and well-deserved sleep. I understood the situation before I arrived, and it was the reason I felt the situation was fixable and was a significant portion of the reason I was pushing so hard to establish 24-7 in-house coverage. It wasn't just about pushing my agenda, it was because it was the standard of care across the country and Dr. Rostri and Dr. Penton needed help, whether they wanted to admit it or not. The point that I am making is that it is admirable that Dr. Rostri and Dr. Penton were willing and able to provide this endless circle of care, essentially alone, for twenty years. However, it is simply unreasonable, unfair and unacceptable for the institution to place such a burden on two individuals. Outdated CICU care or not, I harnessed a massive amount of unwavering respect for the passion and dedication they displayed towards patients they cared for. It was absolutely absurd that this administration had failed to deliver the necessary support for so long. I was amazed that although Dr. Rostri was still resisting major changes, he continued to allow us to progress the complexity of the patients we were extubating and the nurses began placing subtle pressure on him to buy into our changes, because they now saw the positive effects it was having on the patients they cared for.

As we attempted to move forward following the unfortunate and traumatic series of infections we encountered, I attempted to readjust my focus once again toward recruitment of CICU staff, and on that front, there continued to be some positive developments. Tim had started working some shifts with Justin and me, and the nurses absolutely adored working with him. Adam, the physician recruit from Yale that I had been speaking with, was scheduled to arrive next week for his visit, and Martha, the PA student, had finished her elective rotation in the CICU and had agreed, in principle, to join us. I was beginning to feel that things might actually work. Ruth had been working hard at improving the culture within the CICU. She began holding regular staff meetings that focused on everyone making conscious efforts to avoid using negative verbiage about the hospital or other staff members. She had also been working tirelessly, with the support of John Wozniak, the CNO, to convince the CEO to adjust the current, outdated model of nurse staffing ratios to one that was less burdensome for the nurses and safer for the patients, which meant they would care for fewer patients at one time, thereby allowing them to dedicate more time and detail to each patient, thereby improving the quality of care. They also fought to erase this decades-old, deeply ingrained institutional concept that it was acceptable for the charge nurse to carry a full patient assignment while also being responsible for delivering oversight for each of the other nurses working that shift and for their respective patients. These beliefs were all part of the "running thin" practice that CHOB had made essentially routine and acceptable. Ruth, Maddie and I had also started holding monthly CICU quality meetings to review changes, concerns, infections, poor outcomes, or anything else, utilizing it as a way for maintaining open communication lines among the CICU staff, and to air any dirty laundry that may be festering in the unit. Maddie had also made a lot of progress, particularly addressing her concerns regarding the inconsistent care of central lines and their sterile dressings. She had been able to get the support of the hospital quality team as well as the infection control team to essentially enforce the use of care bundles as mandated by the hospital, such that even Dr. Rostri was rendered incapacitated when it came to having the authority to overrule this practice. As a result, the nurses were undergoing training on the policy and they felt safe in doing so without fearing repercussions from Dr. Rostri as it was now considered a hospital mandate.

Martha had enjoyed her rotation time as a physician assistant student in the CICU, so she had agreed to join us as an APP, once she passed her board exam. After passing her board exam, she would receive her license to practice after which time her credentialing for the hospital needed to be completed and would take about one month. So realistically, she would join us in approximately two months. John Wozniak had spoken to HR in advance to be certain they wouldn't offer her an extremely low salary and offend her, thereby increasing the risk that she may pursue other employment opportunities. Sure enough, two days after Martha's verbal commitment, she called to discuss the offer from HR. "Hi, Dr. Philson, I hate to call you about this; however, I just wanted to discuss the offer I received from the hospital with you," she said.

"Of course. You can always talk to me about anything," I said, as I instinctively said, "Oh shit," to myself.

"Well, I have talked with several of my graduating classmates and most of them have accepted jobs in the outpatient setting. I had always assumed that inpatient PAs, particularly those practicing somewhere as specialized as the pediatric cardiac intensive care unit, would be paid more than the outpatient setting. Well, the offer HR gave me was $30,000 a year less than the offer most of my colleagues have received," she said hesitantly with an anxiety that was palpable through the phone, I assume feeling as though she was at risk of upsetting me.

"You have got to be joking. John Wozniak and I spoke about this in great detail, well in advance of your hiring, and I know he spoke to HR specifically about this, because I was concerned that they may act in this manner, so we hoped to remove any possibility of that in advance. I am so upset that they did this to you. I am sorry, Martha, but rest assured, I will take care of it and get back to you," I said, upset with HR yet apologetic toward her.

As I hung up, I immediately called John Wozniak's cell phone and told him about the situation. "Are you kidding me?" he said, clearly upset. "I will call you back, Eric," he said, hanging up the phone abruptly. Five minutes later he called back explaining that the issue was taken care of and that HR would be calling Martha shortly with a revised offer.

"Hi, Martha, it's Dr. Philson. I just wanted to let you know that I spoke with CNO, and he told me that the problem was addressed and that they will be calling you soon with a revised offer," I explained.

"Thank you so much, Dr. Philson, I appreciate it," she said with excitement. HR indeed called her that afternoon and gave her a more appropriate offer, which she officially accepted. In the end it worked out but this was just another example of the many unnecessary obstacles I faced on a daily basis, even when I tried to anticipate and resolve such problems in advance.

In addition to the ongoing recruitment efforts related to the CICU, Dr. Potts notified me that there was to be a national search for a new CEO, because the current CEO, Nancy Ogylview, was "stepping down," he explained with a subtle yet meaningful smile on his face. Rumor was that shortly after Dr. Potts arrived, he was campaigning for her replacement as he felt she was not qualified to run a children's hospital and appropriately felt that there could never be significant change that could occur if she were to remain in that role. So "stepping down" really meant she was being pushed out. As I said earlier, I never wish harm on anyone nor did I want anyone to lose their job; however, as I learned over time, the success or failure of a health-care institution starts at the top and if the CEO is incompetent, untrustworthy or fails to have clear objectives that elucidate the path forward, first and foremost focusing on the importance of clinic excellence, then hope for success as an organization is futile.

19

DINNER WITH CANDIDATE

Justin and I were surviving our intense night-call schedule thus far. The reward that made it tolerable was seeing the nurses continue to buy into the changes that were taking place as well as the teamwork that was continuing to develop. Our CICU data was continuing to improve despite the fact that I felt everything was moving slowly. The hospital length of stay continued to decline, far more dramatically since instituting 24-7 coverage, enough so that it began to gain the attention of hospital administration. Dr. Deeton had come by the CICU earlier in the week, for the first time since I started, to share his congratulations and comment on how impressed he was by the changes that were taking place in real time. Meanwhile, Dr. Potts had also stopped by and congratulated me and quietly chuckled as he shared that Nancy Ogylview, the CEO, voiced concern about the loss of revenue the hospital would suffer as a consequence of our reduced hospital length of stay, as they could no longer bill the insurance companies for as many inpatient critical care days as before. He explained to me that a comment such as this highlighted a complete lack of understanding of the daily workflow and financial workings of a hospital, thereby validating many people's concerns related to her ability to function as the CEO of CHOB, hence the ongoing search for a new CEO. "Financial implications on a health system, which result from the improvement in the quality of patient care, as evidenced by a shortened length of stay, requires knowledge and experience in terms of renegotiating contracts and reimbursement pay scales with insurance companies, thereby adjusting payment to compensate for the improved quality being delivered. Increased quality should always be viewed as a positive thing; in fact, the top institutions across the country strive for clinical excellence, because first and foremost, clinical excellence leads to the hospital's designation as a 'center of excellence,' which leads to more patient volume and can inevitably lead to more insurance company's seeking contracts with that institution. Any capable CEO should understand this concept," Dr. Potts said eloquently, with great wisdom.

Today was the day Adam, the cardiac intensivist candidate from Yale, was arriving for his interview, which was to take place tomorrow, and we had dinner reserved at The Emporium, one of the most historic and well-known fine dining establishments in Biloxi, with a dress code requiring gentlemen to wear a suit or sport jacket. As a goodwill gesture, I invited Dr. Rostri to join us, which he had accepted, agreeing to meet at the restaurant for a 7 p.m. reservation. I arrived ten minutes early and walked to the entrance of the restaurant where I saw Dr. Rostri waiting outside. It seemed odd to see him wear anything other than scrubs and I am certain he must have been thinking the same about me. As I greeted him with a smile and a handshake, up pulled a taxi with a young-looking guy who was rather short, with brown hair; he was well-dressed in a suit and was by himself, so I figured that he must be Adam. I walked toward him and said, "Adam?"

"Yep, you must be Dr. Philson," he said.

"Yes, please call me Eric. This is Dr. Rostri, chief of pediatric cardiac surgery," I said introducing the two of them. We all shook hands and entered the restaurant.

"Do you have a reservation?" the host asked. "Yes, it's for three under Children's Hospital of Biloxi," I said.

"Ah, yes, here it is. If you will follow me," he said. As he led us through the restaurant to our table, I was awestruck by the old, historic features of the restaurant, yet it remained in immaculate condition preserving its elegance. It appeared as though it was an old home that had been converted into a restaurant many years ago. As the host led us up the stairs, to the second level, it opened up to an area that had floor-to-ceiling glass windows that overlooked a large backyard with grand, old oak trees with serpentine branches, covered in Spanish moss. This was the perfect place to dine with a candidate, particularly one who already had a baseline love for the city of Biloxi. As we sat at our table, I could see Adam's eyes light up.

"This place is amazing. I have heard of it and always wanted to eat here, but never had the opportunity, or money," he said with a brief chuckle.

"Excellent, I am glad. How was the flight?" I asked.

"It was fine. No issues. I was on call last night, so I was a little tired and slept a bit on the plane, but overall, it was on time and was a smooth flight," he replied.

"Well, we are very excited to have you here," said Dr. Rostri. We enjoyed a drink while waiting for our food, as Adam explained how he was considering a few different programs but that he was enticed by the program here because he thought it would be a great experience and a relatively rare one at that, to help build the CICU program from scratch. "Tell me a little bit about what you're up to right now," said Dr. Rostri.

"Well, right now I am completing a two-year combined clinical CICU and research fellowship. For the last eight months I have been primarily focused on my lab research, so I have been a bit removed from the clinical aspects of the CICU; however, I am ready to get back into clinical medicine," he said.

"Great!" Dr. Rostri said. As the night went on, it seemed as though he was genuinely interested in the program.

The dinner concluded and I drove Adam back to his hotel where I wished him a good night. "It was nice meeting you in person and I enjoyed speaking with you, get some rest. I will pick you up in the morning and take you to the hospital for your interview so no need to worry about arranging an Uber or taxi," I said.

"Sounds great. Thanks. See you tomorrow," Adam said.

Morning came quick and I was off, once again driving down the pothole-filled streets of Biloxi, on my way to the hotel to pick up Adam. As I arrived at his hotel, Adam quickly recognized my vehicle and walked to the curb to meet me, hopping into the passenger seat of my Lincoln Navigator, which I had just purchased a couple of weeks prior after trading in my relatively new car due to concerns I developed for its longevity after bottoming it out numerous times in the plethora of potholes that riddled the streets of Biloxi. As we rode to the hospital, I explained to him once again that several things were going to appear different than he was used to; however, significant change had occurred and much more change was in the works. I took the time to go through his interview schedule and explain a little bit about each person he would be meeting throughout the day. As we arrived, I showed him the current condition of Children's Hospital of Biloxi and explained the extensive changes that were about to take place. I pointed to the pylons that had begun to be driven into the ground across from the hospital, marking the beginning of construction of the parking garage, the very first step of the renovation project, which would span three years in its entirety. We walked inside and I led him to Dr. Deeton's office for his first interview of the day. The day went well. Justin, Ruth, and Maddie all had a chance to meet with Adam and agreed that he would be a good fit with the rest of the team. By the end of the day, I felt that Adam had a good feel for the program, including the amount of work that would be required to succeed in building the CICU but also for the amount of potential that existed. The feedback from the staff who met with him was overall very positive, with one glaring question posed by nearly everyone who had met him: "With his training background, why the hell would he consider coming to Children's Hospital of Biloxi?"

To this I laughed and responded, "Honestly, I have the same question. I suspect the answer is twofold: First, I do truly believe he has a love for the city of Biloxi as he has visited several times in the past. Second, I think he may be a little rusty clinically since he has been focused on bench research, and I also think he is a little uncertain about his clinical ability and wants to be in a moderately sized program such as ours, while he figures out whether he wants to practice clinical medicine or if he is destined for a career in research," I said. The truth was, if I could hire someone of his caliber, at least as it related to his training background, regardless of whether or not he needed to polish up on his clinical skills, it was likely to have positive effects on my ability to recruit others. Hiring an MD, PhD with his training background would look great for the program and in particular for the CICU, likely opening the door for other recruits to join us. I was hopeful we could add Adam to our team. As the visit concluded, I told Adam that the team really enjoyed his visit. I advised him to go home and take some time to think things over and that we could speak the following week about his thoughts and decide whether he would like to come for a second visit or not. The following week, Adam and I spoke. He told me how much he enjoyed the visit and how he would love to come back for a second visit. I told him that the entire team at CHOB shared his feelings and that we would love for him to come for a second visit. I explained that someone would be reaching out to him soon to assist in arranging the visit.

Things seemed to be progressing at the hospital. There was still so much to do, and I was working so much that I was rarely home, and that obviously bothered me. My schedule essentially consisted of working a thirty-six-hour shift every other day and included covering two weekends per month, where I would work a forty-eight-hour shift straight. On average I was working one hundred hours per week in the hospital, and I was barely sleeping. When I returned home, I was exhausted and fought hard to stay awake for at least a couple of hours before the girls went to bed, so we could spend some quality time together. Working to exhaustion had at least helped curb my alcohol intake; it definitely hadn't improved it, but at least it wasn't significantly worsening. Ana remained supportive of me, but I could feel us growing apart and it appeared to be happening at a much more rapid pace. I could tell she was struggling too. She had a massive friend network in Florida that she left behind and she had found it difficult to make new friends in Biloxi. We lived in an area outside of Biloxi where the houses were much more isolated from one another, so while the neighbors here were extremely friendly, they were also much older and she had yet to find a core group of friends that she felt connected with, and I admittedly had a nonexistent social life outside of the hospital. In retrospect, as I recall this period of time, I recognized we were drifting apart, and I truly wanted to do something about it, but I was overcome with exhaustion, both mentally and physically and it took everything I had to find even an hour or two every other night in the evenings to spend some quality time with the kids, and I fully recognize and take responsibility for the fact that it was all at the expense of Ana and our relationship, which was tragic in hindsight.

Ana's family was originally from Argentina; however, she had lived in Miami since she was in her mid-twenties. Given her Latin heritage, she found it easy to make friends with those who had similar backgrounds and cultural interests while in Florida. However, in Biloxi that was not the case, so she began to take up gardening and yoga in an attempt to keep herself busy. During the one weekend each month that I actually didn't have to work or wasn't walking around like a zombie due to exhaustion, we did our best to devote this time to doing something fun as a family. We would often try to find activities that were unique to the area, ones we had never done or seen before, and it felt nice to really dedicate that time together as a family. It wasn't much time, but we maximized every second together. When the girls asked me why I wasn't able to be home for many of the holidays, school events, or during the weekends, I did my best to explain it by telling them, "Daddy imagines that if you girls were unlucky enough to be born with a heart problem, how horrible it would feel for your mom and me to have to see you sick and have to stay in the hospital, not knowing if you were going to be OK or not. Then, I imagine how much better it would make me feel to see the doctor who was there all day and all night working as hard as he could to make sure you were going to get better. Well, that's what I imagine in my mind when I am away from you at work, and for that reason, I try to treat each and every baby as if they were you and take great care of them just like it was you."

I knew it was foolish to believe that they could comprehend such a complex analogy, but it was true, or at least at the time, I felt it was true. One of the most challenging aspects of practicing medicine, particularly after having children of your own, is harnessing the emotional connection that develops between you and each of the patients you care for. The experience of managing and watching in real time the clinical evolution of a critical baby during the course of their hospitalization is something marvelous and indescribable. It begins with a baby who is so critical that they may require machines and multiple infusion pumps that deliver medications necessary for keeping the child alive, as the parents become simultaneously consumed with feelings of uncertainty, as they grasp at any sign of hope, wondering whether their baby will survive or not. Amazingly, with time, the baby slowly improves as they require fewer medications and less support from lifesaving machines to maintain stability, until eventually, they are liberated from these same machines and medications they once relied heavily upon for survival, until one day they are stable enough to tolerate being fed through a tube that enters their nose, traverses the esophagus, and terminates in the stomach. Until miraculously, the day that once appeared so distant and unreachable to the family arrives, and you see the emotions on their face, which once projected fear and despair, now displaying joy and gratefulness, as they hold their beautiful baby for the first time, void of tubes, machines and infusions, and offer a bottle to the child, as they suddenly recognize the normal baby they had dreamed of prior to delivery. The tears that now roll down their face appear of the same liquid consistency as those produced just weeks ago, yet they are dramatically different and infinitely more meaningful, as now, instead of sadness, they represent a pure joy they were unaware existed in this world. The final, and perhaps most rewarding, moment, for both the family and the care team who worked tirelessly to save the baby's life over the preceding months, occurs as you watch the parents walk out the doors of the CICU with their stable, beautiful, normal baby, strapped safely in its normal car seat, as they walk to their normal car, and drive away toward their normal home, to lay their baby to sleep in its normal crib for the very first time. It's as if they have been instantaneously regifted something they failed to even recognize had been stolen from them, and that is a sense of normalcy. Something most of us take for granted, a feeling so exquisite yet so primitive and essential, that it can't be found at the bottom of a bottle or simply replaced by swallowing a pill.

But, inevitably this same joy can just as easily be replaced with utter devastation as witnessed by the wailing tears of the parents, representative of emotional devastation, tears extruded from the same tear ducts capable of producing tears of joy, yet now incessantly resistant to doing so, as you explain to the family that there is nothing that can be done to save their child, and that their beautiful baby will never be going home with them. This is the reality of medicine. As a physician, after you have children of your own, you can't help but imagine yourself in the shoes of these parents, in both scenarios, and it is both an enlightening and mortifying experience. That is the source of the passion I felt for my job, and it is based almost exclusively on the love I felt for my children—a love so deep that it fueled the need for me to change the care that was being provided at CHOB, and to be at work to help other children, or at least at the time, that is what I believed. It was a complex concept for me to fathom, much less for two young girls. I thought that I understood it, little did I know that I would later come to question the validity of this very concept, which I used to inspire and motivate me and that helped me survive the insane hours I worked and the extreme duress I put my mind, body and family through.

The first month of providing 24-7 coverage was nearing completion, and I felt a great sense of accomplishment despite the endless amount of work that remained; however, my body was starting to feel fatigued. I was scheduled to work forty-eight hours straight the final weekend of the month and the CICU was extremely busy with all twenty beds occupied and the patient acuity was high. Four of the warriors were still alive in physicality, but they remained in their never-ending state of critical homeostatic suffering; however, now they were surrounded by sixteen other patients who were also in critical condition, whose fate remained yet undetermined. The weekend was exhausting, and I couldn't have rested my eyes, in the dungeon we called a call room, for more than an hour or two in totality, the entire forty-eight hours I remained in the hospital. Monday morning when Justin arrived, he saw the exhaustion on my face and said, "You going to be OK driving home? Crossing that bridge on the way to your house, with the rhythmic sound created as your car tires pass over the creases connecting each section of bridge, can be hypnotizing, and that is not taking into account the fact that you have taken care of twenty critical children, by yourself, and you haven't slept in two days. I am just saying … Why don't you rest in the call room for a couple hours before you drive home?"

He was right, it was rhythmic, and it was hypnotizing at times, but I was not only desperate to get home and see my family, I was also desperate to get the hell out of the hospital ASAP for my own mental well-being. However, this was the very first month that we began working one hundred hours per week and to make it worse, I was finishing with a forty-eight-hour shift with little to no real sleep. "I will be fine. I will crank the air conditioner and the radio until I get home," I said. As we finished "migration rounds," I left the hospital and got into my Lincoln Navigator and headed home. As I approached the bridge, I acknowledged to myself that I was feeling pretty good, given the circumstances and considering the fact that I had not slept in two days. There wasn't much traffic on the road, although as I entered the bridge, both lanes had a few vehicles in front of me, but they were far enough away that I felt comfortable setting my cruise control. That was the last thing I remember before awakening to the violent shaking of my driver's side seat, which was a safety feature intended to notify you if your vehicle crossed the painted lines outlining the lanes of traffic. I looked up, dazed, and noted that my vehicle appeared to be on two wheels, when suddenly I realized that I had fallen asleep at the wheel and driven the vehicle up onto the side wall of the bridge, made of concrete, which lacked any sort of railing, thereby providing direct access to the water below. I quickly tried to snap myself out of my confused state and turned the steering wheel abruptly to the left, bringing the vehicle tires back onto the bridge with a loud thud, as the vehicle swerved uncontrollably back and forth across both lanes of traffic, threatening to lose complete control, resulting in an imminent rollover accident, inevitably involving the vehicles in both lanes of the bridge that were dangerously close to me, or worse, my vehicle driving off the bridge, leading to its submersion with me inside, deep beneath the water below. I manipulated the steering wheel back and forth with a precision I had never seen, and by some miracle, I was able to regain control of my vehicle and steer it back into my lane. My heart was pounding. I couldn't believe what had just happened but even more so, I couldn't believe what didn't happen. How was I still alive? How was my car not over the side of the bride and in the water? Just one month prior, I traded in my car because I was concerned the potholes would surely destroy it due to the fact that I kept repeatedly bottoming it out. The Lincoln Navigator that I decided to buy was large enough to deal with the horrendous roads of Biloxi, but what I didn't realize at the time, was that the self-driving mechanism and warning feature that shakes the seat violently when the vehicle crosses the lines that outline the lanes of traffic would save my life. It was that shaking that woke me after I had fallen asleep at the wheel. Had I still been driving my car, I may not have awoken until I was either in the water below the bridge or until I was actively rolling down the middle of the bridge. As I got home that evening, I didn't say a word to Ana or the kids; I simply sat quietly and took some deep breaths, allowing myself time to recover from the shock of this near-death experience. I decided I needed to think about how I was going to deal with this ongoing danger because the reality was, I couldn't stop working all these night shifts, not now, not when I was finally starting to make some progress. As I went to bed that evening, I hugged Ana and the kids tightly, acknowledging that I needed to find a way to be sure I could stay awake on the ride home during this rough stretch of long hours, for a duration that was yet to be determined. Randomly, that night, without saying a word to him, my father-in-law who was staying with us for a while, told me how tired I looked. He told me that when he used to feel tired after working long hours and needed to drive long distances to see Ana's mom, he would drive without his socks and shoes on, and it worked like a charm. I was desperate, because I couldn't stop now. Not while things were finally progressing. I thanked him and told him I would give it a shot.

I was able to shake off the near-death experience, and whether it was true or not, I was able to use it as some sort of moral validation as to the importance of my existence, or at least the importance of me completing this job, because clearly God, the universe or whoever understood that there was no other human being alive on this earth stupid enough to take this job. I returned to work as if nothing had happened and I wasn't about to share my close encounter with death on the bridge with my coworkers because someone would have certainly told me I needed to back off the night calls, and while it was sheer torture mentally and physically, I knew it was the only way possible, however small the chance, that I could make progress toward my goal, and I was determined to succeed.

Adam had spoken with Dr. Potts's assistant and had officially set up his return visit, which appeared promising. In medicine, when a candidate agrees to a second visit, this typically means that they are very interested in the position, and during the second visit it is often customary that they are provided an opportunity to interview with administrators whom they have yet had the opportunity to meet. It is also an opportunity for the candidate to meet a representative from human resources who can discuss medical benefits and retirement packages. Additionally, candidates most often assume that the salary they are to be offered will also be discussed. Dr. Potts and I had discussed in advance what I considered to be a very competitive compensation package, particularly for a candidate coming directly out of training, which emphasized how essential in my mind it was that we capitalize on this opportunity. Dr. Potts had also recommended that we set him up with a realtor who could spend some time driving him around the different areas of Biloxi so that he may have an idea of the different neighborhoods he could choose to live in.

Maddie and Ruth had really begun to make progress when it came to nursing changes. The rate of line infections had noticeably dropped, and the nurses were carrying out the dressing changes per hospital protocol. The environment was also beginning to show some signs of improvement in the CICU, and now when I entered the unit, I felt less of an urge to immediately shower to try to remove the film of toxicity that once enveloped me. Dr. Rostri still held a controlling grip on most of the unit, but I made a unilateral decision and rather than ask, I informed Dr. Rostri that I intended to meet with the nephrology team on my own. Now, I didn't share that I was also going to apologize to them for the decades of disrespect they endured at his hands, but the truth was it needed to be done and I knew it wasn't going to come from him. I used our meeting time to hear the nephrology team's perspective and I spent time explaining that we were trying to usher in a new era of teamwork and collaboration in the CICU, and I promised them that we would be consulting them for all dialysis patients; in fact, I told them our ultimate goal was to involve them long before dialysis was needed, because I knew we could truly benefit from their expertise. When we cared for our first patient requiring peritoneal dialysis following this meeting, I quietly reminded Dr. Rostri when we were alone that I would be consulting nephrology and he grudgingly approved. Nephrology had been understaffed, or "ran thin" for years. That was the major frustration of the cardiac surgeons. When the CICU patients required dialysis, it was urgent and they often needed to get fluid off emergently. However, due to the "thin" staffing of the dialysis team, it often took several hours to initiate dialysis and then if the dextrose solution or the dwell time required adjustment in order to remove more fluid, it would take several more hours for the change to occur. So, I understood the frustration on the part of the cardiac surgeons; however, performing dialysis without the expertise of nephrology was simply not OK, so I was happy to reestablish even the weakest of collaborations between the two services. Again, I would take any progress I could get.

The twenty-four-hour coverage continued and while it was a lot, the nurses appreciated it immensely. After years of getting blamed for events that happened in the middle of the night, they not only enjoyed our presence and support, but they also enjoyed the teaching that we provided at the bedside during evening rounds and they began to sense the development of a more nurturing environment, particularly at nighttime when it was mostly Justin, Mitch, or me in the hospital with them. Kajay and Eric usually covered one Friday night shift each per month, which allowed Justin, Mitch, and I a brief hiatus for at least two weekend shifts per month, while it also avoided major disruptions for Kajay and Eric in terms of the cardiac catheterization laboratory schedule, when they would go home post-call the following morning.

This Friday night Eric Saltiel was scheduled to cover the night shift and I was responsible for covering the daytime CICU service that week, which meant that I was responsible for formulating the clinical plan for the patients for the entire week. Justin and I would typically alternate daytime service, every other week. We both tried to maintain the plan developed by the physician who was on service that week, unless the patient's condition deteriorated, thereby necessitating an adjustment of the plan. We did this to respect the other physicians' plan but more importantly, it was an attempt to keep things as consistent as possible while providing continuity for the families. Having a child who requires cardiac surgery, necessitating time in the CICU, was stressful enough for the families, the last thing they needed to deal with was a plan that was constantly changing, which only resulted in confusion and added to their already prevalent anxiety. The daytime physician on service would normally hand off the details of each patient to the physician covering for the evening at 5 p.m. I would usually allow the cardiac catheterization physicians a bit longer to arrive since they would occasionally have long cases in the cath lab that could drag into the early evening. That night, I waited until 6 p.m. for Dr. Eric Saltiel to arrive, but there was no sign of him, and I hadn't received a phone call or text notifying me that anything had changed. When the clock reached 6:15 p.m., I decided to send him a text message. "Hey Eric, just checking in with you. Hope you remember that you are supposed to be on call tonight."

An hour later, Eric called me. "Hey, sorry I totally forgot, and unfortunately I am unable to come in to take call tonight," he said. It was noisy in the background, and it appeared that he was at a bar or restaurant.

"Really? I am supposed to go to the movies tonight with my family, but I guess at this point I won't make it anyway. Bummer, I will call my wife and tell her that I have to stay in the hospital tonight," I said. I thought long and hard, searching desperately for a solution. Justin was on call the next two nights, Mitch was out of town and Kajay could never work a weekend without advance notice, so I was the only option. This was the reality of the situation. I made the call to Ana and the kids who pretended to understand, but I could sense their disappointment. Dr. Saltiel would forget that he was on call one other time, some months later; however, I just couldn't get upset with him. I had far too much respect for him to allow that. I knew the problem and right or wrong, I would let it go and do what needed to be done to cover the CICU. Why did I give Dr. Saltiel a pass when he didn't show up for call on two separate occasions, you may ask? The answer beyond the fact that I had no choice, is a complex one, but I will do my best to explain my reasoning a bit further along in our story! As I got to know Dr. Saltiel better over the next couple of years, I would come to understand who he was as an individual, and I would grow to admire and respect him. Eric Saltiel was a skilled and experienced interventional cardiologist in his mid-fifties, who was trained at some of the most respected institutions in the Midwest. He first began working at Children's Hospital of Biloxi in a locum tenens capacity because CHOB was in desperate need of an interventionalist, yet they had been unsuccessful at recruiting a full-time physician to fill this void. Initially,

Dr. Saltiel traveled back and forth as needed, between Biloxi and his home in Wisconsin. After a brief period of time, he fell in love with the people of Biloxi and found a way to coexist with Dr. Rostri, which was not a simple task. Most of his time was spent in the catheterization lab, so the absurdities that occurred on a regular basis in the CICU, while glaringly apparent to him, were not his concern or his expertise, and he found solace and peace in the isolation of the cath lab. Dr. Saltiel was nationally respected for his clinical skill, both in the cath lab and when it came to the everyday clinical deci-sion-making and management of complex pediatric cardiac patients. I would come to respect Dr. Saltiel as an extremely wise and gifted clinician, and we quickly developed a close friendship over a relatively short period of time. It was noticeable to me from the time of our introduction, even from afar, that Dr. Saltiel bared significant battle wounds resulting from his previous role as chief of pediatric cardiology in Wisconsin. For the most part, Eric was a guy who tended to keep to himself; however, as we became closer, he shared with me that he suffered from post-traumatic stress disorder, after a close friend and colleague working under him randomly took his own life, several years back while he was the still in the division chief role. He admitted that following this awful and traumatic event, he had become unraveled, which worsened when he suffered through a nasty divorce, and as a result, he was left yielding deep-rooted scars, which led to alcohol abuse. He was an intro-vert much like me, so I can only assume it was a coping mechanism to suppress the heinous memories tied to these horrific events. He knew drink-ing was an unhealthy way of dealing with his problems, and so did I, but I was doing the exact same thing he was. For individuals like us, it's not some-thing we plan on doing, or something we feel good about, nor do we lack the understanding of the negative consequences associated with alcohol abuse, but the reality is that the mind finds a way to cope with traumatic memories, and unfortunately sometimes the mechanism we adapt in order to cope, is not always a constructive one. However, these unprocessed feelings eventu-ally find a way of manifesting themselves, and our coping or suppressing mechanism was alcohol. I began to understand how this process works and progresses by studying the changes that were occurring in myself, in real time, and they became more prevalent each day I worked at CHOB. I also learned by observing how the process unfolded with Dr. Saltiel. While we both suffered from PTSD, and we both drank to alleviate manifesting symptoms, the truth was that at this point in our lives, we both manifested symptoms differently. I would sometimes see the persistent effects of PTSD manifest themselves as physical symptoms in Dr. Saltiel when he was involved in extremely stressful situations at work. Just two weeks prior, Dr. Saltiel was performing a cardiac catheterization on a complex patient who had undergone several cardiac surgeries and numerous cardiac catheterizations in the past, who had also spent several months, cumulatively, in the CICU over her lifespan. Treating and managing patients with this degree of complexity is often fraught with risk, and clinicians willing to take on such risk must also be willing to deal with the complications that may occur as a consequence of assuming this risk. In a patient who has undergone such a large number of surgeries and interventions, and who has spent a significant amount of time in the CICU, the assumption is that obtaining intravenous access necessary to perform a cardiac catheterization will be challenging, to say the least, due to the fact that many of the major veins and arteries are likely be thrombosed (clotted) due to their recurrent use. Therefore, when intravenous access is required and all other options have been exhausted, a transhepatic approach (accessing the veins of the liver) can be useful and is an acceptable means of obtaining venous access, but as I previously stated, because this procedure is associated with increased risk, the likelihood of complications is also increased. In this case, Dr. Saltiel had no choice but to utilize a transhepatic approach to obtain intravenous access, which he performed swiftly and without complication, therefore he proceeded with the cardiac catheterization, which was also uneventful. As the procedure concluded, the sheath (a device placed within the vein during the procedure to maintain its patency, allowing the passage and exchange of different wires and catheters into the vein) was removed. Suddenly, the patient's blood pressure rapidly dropped. Intravenous fluids and blood were quickly administered by the anesthesiologist while the surgeons and CICU team were emergently called to the cath lab to provide assistance. When I arrived, the cardiac surgeons had already agreed that there must be internal bleeding involving the hepatic vein, because the patient had remained stable the entire case prior to sheath removal. They had already opened the patient's chest and extended the incision into the abdomen as they searched for the source of bleeding, as anesthesia continued to push packed red blood cells. I entered the cath lab to find Dr. Saltiel, who appeared somewhat pale as he sat quietly on a chair in the command room, still wearing his sterile gown from the case. "What's going on, Eric?" I asked. He tried his best to explain the clinical situation evolving rapidly before our eyes; however, his speech was muffled, almost incoherent, as he sat in the chair rocking back and forth repeatedly. I tried to say something comforting; however, in my career, when involved in life-or-death situations, I have yet to find someone capable of saying anything that is truly comforting, so I ultimately decided to leave him alone. Let me attempt to explain such a situation to you as best I can. In scenarios such as this, the pressure and stress associated with trying to save a patient's life, while they are actively attempting to die, right before your very eyes, is so severe it is unmeasurable. In nearly every aspect of congenital heart care, whether it's cardiac surgery, cardiac catheterization, cardiac intensive care, or cardiac anesthesia, life-or-death events are far from uncommon. The reality is that the lives of the smallest patients are in our hands, and their clinical condition can change in an instant. No matter how many times you are involved in situations such as this, the physical stress and anxiety as well as the emotional and psychological effects of being immersed in that environment are dramatic and lasting on the human body, mind, and central nervous system. These effects are severe, and I firmly believe that they are cumulative over your lifetime. Don't let anyone tell you that there isn't cumulative damage to your nervous system as a result of experiencing repetitive trauma, because anyone who has experienced it on a regular basis, would be unable to deny that there are long-term detrimental effects. I felt awful seeing Dr. Saltiel in such a state and felt helpless knowing that there was nothing I could do to help him, outside of assist-

ing in saving his patient's life in any way that I could. The reality was that he had done nothing wrong, in fact he did everything perfectly; however, this was the nature of the beast, and in this instance, risk showed up to the cath lab that morning driving a Maserati at high speed and complication was riding shotgun and urging risk to go faster. As physicians, we care deeply about our patients, but when something such as this happens, you have to rely on your teammates to perform their job while you sit and watch, and it is extremely uncomfortable to have zero control over the outcome, but you have to believe, and in this case, the surgeons found the source of bleeding, they sutured the lacerated vessel, which ended up being the hepatic vein, and were able to close the chest after stabilizing the patient. The patient recovered in the CICU overnight, in stable condition, was extubated the following morning, and discharged home one day after that. The reality of my job in the CICU is that when the situation evolves quickly from one of stability to one that is life or death, you have to be able to function under these stressful circumstances, or the positive outcome described above can instead easily turn into a traumatic death. Those involved in life-or-death situations experience the same amount of stress in the heat of the moment, regardless of whether the patient survives or not; however, when a patient sadly dies, the trauma and stress experienced do not simply end as they do when the patient survives. Instead, it continues beyond the event itself, because we often obsess about whether we could have or should have done something differently, which may or may not have changed the outcome at all, but nonetheless we go through the process. Depending on the type of person you are, the process of self-reflection in my opinion is a healthy practice, in theory. It allows time for processing complex feelings and emotions resulting from the stressful event; however, self-reflection that persists, can lead to a period of self-ridicule and self-doubt, which may transpire into verbal or emotional abuse as you blame yourself for failing to save the patient's life, which can then lead to unhealthy feelings of guilt and shame. This cascade of thoughts and feelings is complex, and morbidly I find it fascinating, but it can be unhealthy,

especially for people like Dr. Saltiel and me, who are introverted and tend to avoid processing feelings and emotions, which only exacerbates the problem.

People manifest symptoms differently, though all stem from traumatic memories and the emotions connected to them. I firmly believe that PTSD is not solely the result of physical, mental or sexual abuse occurring outside the workplace, as previously stated. I feel that in high-stress professions, such as ours, the repeated exposure to stress is cumulative and will lead to PTSD if the individual is not provided healthy avenues for processing these emotions. As I witnessed the symptoms manifested in Dr. Saltiel as a consequence of PTSD, I wondered how others interpreted my clinical manifestations as they occurred in real time during life-or-death situations in the CICU. I have always been able to maintain a calm demeanor exteriorly and I believe that I am gifted with an excellent "poker face." However, inside my mind, in that moment, it is anything but "calm"; instead, it is straight-up wildfire or a Category 5 hurricane, take your pick, but when the event is over, particularly if the patient doesn't survive, that is when the traumatic event affects me most and results in the subclinical manifestation of symptoms. If the outcome is negative, I tend to bypass the self-reflective state and jump right into the self-critical phase. I obsessively replay every detail of the event in my mind, beginning with the events leading up to the life-or-death situation, followed by the obsessive dissection of the minutia occurring during the actual event itself, desperately searching for ways I could have done things differently and potentially saved the life of the patient. The unhealthy part is that every theory you develop in your mind is merely hypothetical; therefore, it is implausible to suggest that changing any intervention in the moment would have conclusively led to a better outcome, yet that's my process and it is unhealthy. I realize you may think I am rambling, and perhaps I am, as there is no scientific proof validating anything that I have just suggested; however, this is my belief and it is based on the extensive study of myself and many colleagues working in high-stress fields over the years, and the extremely high rate of physician burnout among these specialties suggests there is something there that warrants scientific attention if we are to break this cycle.

After all the trauma Dr. Saltiel had experienced in his career and personal life, I wondered if the manifestations I saw that day would inevitably become my manifestations further down the road. Perhaps the symptoms manifested by individuals are directly proportional to the degree of exposure to repeated stressful events. Meaning, for example, what if experiencing a few traumatic events over one's career and lifetime result in the manifestation of milder symptoms, such as mood swings, nervousness, restless legs, or mild sleep disturbance, while perhaps someone experiencing twenty or more life-or-death situations during the span of their career may be more susceptible to manifesting symptoms that are life-altering or even so severe that they cripple one's ability to function in society, such as social anxiety disorder, insomnia, impulse control or even severe depression, or catatonia? In such cases, I suspect that the body is left with no choice but to revert to relying on its involuntary yet powerful instinct to survive, which unknowingly leads the affected individual to seek out coping mechanisms, whether healthy or destructive, to get them through the difficult time. I believe that individuals who use alcohol or drugs to cope, are, in fact, guided by an involuntary instinct to survive. Speaking from my own experience, I wasn't drinking to get drunk, I was drinking so that I could have a mere hour or two where I didn't feel overwhelmed with stress and anxiety. This type of drinking, at least in its primitive stages, felt very different from habitual drinking to get "drunk," although admittedly, one may eventually lead to the other. My point is, I hesitate to believe that we understand the long-term repercussions of stress, so I make a point to avoid jumping to conclusions or rushing to judgment when I encounter someone who is drinking simply so they can get through each day. I didn't wake up one morning with the epiphany "You know what, today is the day I am going to drink every day with the goal of becoming a raging alcoholic!" It just happened without any forethought! That leads me to believe that this survival instinct inside us directs us toward a coping mechanism that helps ensure our survival, while maintaining our ability to function in society, and the coping mechanism that it has chosen to direct us toward, is merely one that is based on our current state of mind and the severity of our clinical manifestations at that point in time. I believe our basic survival instincts work tirelessly to find any way possible to deal with trauma, with the primary goal of helping us to survive at any cost. I assume the algorithm guiding us toward our coping mechanism is extremely complex and may change regularly based on the factors I just mentioned. Your instincts will lead you toward the exact coping mechanism that you need, are ready for, or that is available to you at that exact point in time in your life, carrying the philosophy of "Let's do whatever we have to do, in order to survive until tomorrow, where we can find a healthier, more sustainable coping mechanism." Obviously, I don't condone the use of alcohol to suppress your emotions, and clearly long-term alcohol use is an awful strategy for dealing with ANYTHING, I am simply trying to understand why we do the things we do.

Life is hard and because I believe a life of repeated traumas can have long-term repercussions, I try my best to avoid judgment of others who drink alcohol or take drugs to provide even momentary relief from endless anxiety that may be crippling. I think it is important to understand that things such as alcohol abuse are rarely as simple or as black and white as they may appear. To truly understand someone's behavior you have to get to know them and get a feel for what they have been through; without learning this, it is simply impossible to root out the source responsible for these manifestations. I do not believe you can simply say, "You have an alcohol problem, stop drinking." Because doing so without finding the source of the issue, and without offering a healthier coping mechanism to replace it, could leave them alone with uncontrolled manifestations, so intolerable that they could resort to drastic measures to stop them, such as suicide, which is scarily prevalent among burned out physicians who must feel helpless. So, I try to be cautious not to judge anyone because as the saying goes, "Everyone is suffering in silence with something, and you could be the one person who helps stop that suffering by listening and remaining unbiased." I know you're probably thinking, who does this guy think he is, Confucius? No, I do not. I am simply sharing some anecdotal observations I have observed as they pertain to myself and other colleagues. And no, I don't condone the use of alcohol as a means of treating anything; instead, I emphasize the importance of maintaining an open mind while refraining from the judgment of others who may do so. I also suggest, instead of wasting our energy on inappropriately labeling them as useless alcoholics, that it is far more useful to spend our time helping them find a healthier way to cope.

Again, I want to emphasize that there is zero scientific basis for any of my theory; nonetheless, it makes sense to me, and I truly believe it, and I am hoping that perhaps someone may read this and find comfort in what I am saying, perhaps providing some momentary hope in their time of despair, which they may be suffering from in silence. I also hope this will be an area of focus for future research, particularly as it relates to the repeated exposure to traumatic events and the long-term effects it may have on physical and mental health, and to what extent such factors could play in physician burnout.

As you have read thus far, it is clear that some administrators may lack the understanding or may simply lack empathy for those vulnerable individuals living this reality on a daily basis, because they are blinded by their own selfish goals. I feel it is important to delineate these concepts a bit further, because as you will see later in our story, a new generation of administrators appear more aware of "burnout" and the long-term effects of working excessive hours; however, BEWARE, because what may appear on the surface as "understanding" or "empathy" displayed by such administrators, may be nothing more than the repetitive use of these buzzwords, which are actually nothing more than an illusory smokescreen, void of their respective true meaning. Institutions that show they will not only withhold necessary resources in order to save money but will also go so far as to pressure employees into working unhealthy hours in high-stress environments, are likely using you for their own personal gain, with zero concern for your well-being. I will go so far as to suggest that perhaps new legislation is necessary to protect physicians and others in such high-stress positions, mandating a limit to the number of hours one may work, with the passage of additional strict laws aimed at holding greedy and selfish hospital administrators accountable for such malicious behavior and utter disregard for the safety of their employees; however, I digress. Luckily, in this particular scenario, my good friend and role model Dr. Saltiel shook off this traumatic event, and was back to his usual self, at least on the surface, both in appearance and in behavior, by the following week.

Let me be clear, Dr. Saltiel NEVER drank on the job, nor did I, but when we were off, we did. Dr. Saltiel unknowingly led me to a greater understanding of this concept, even more so as he continued to help me cover some nights in the CICU. I will always be grateful that he helped me cover nights in the CICU, but I am eternally grateful that he helped me understand myself and my behaviors as I struggled in this role. I knew that when Dr. Saltiel was not at the hospital, he was likely at the bar. Tonight, he forgot that he was on call, therefore he followed his usual routine and went to the bar, so I at least respected that he didn't say, "Sorry, I forgot, I will be right there and put patients at risk by coming to the hospital under the influence." Nor did he attempt to lie to me or avoid my phone call, instead, Eric Saltiel, an honest man, did what honest men do and that was tell the truth. Eric would turn out to be the most talented non-ICU clinician I had ever had the pleasure of working with, and I would learn a lot from him during my time in Biloxi, medically and personally. He often had a difficult time communicating what was going on in his mind to others, but I understood him when others did not, and I arrived at the conclusion that he may actually be a genius, who struggled to dumb things down to a level that the rest of us could understand, because sometimes he appeared to be on a different level, and most times, when he could find the words to help us understand, he was right! Dr. Saltiel always supported me during my time at CHOB and while I was disappointing my family by missing the movie that night, I understood that his forgetting was not intentional or malicious, so I had no choice but to do the night shift myself and move on.

20

SEALING THE DEAL WITH THE CANDIDATE

Time passed and Adam's second visit was upon us. I had arranged to pick him up from the airport. I was excited but felt the pressure of landing this candidate as it was likely to have major repercussions on my ability to recruit additional intensivists in the future. As I arrived at the airport, I saw Adam waiting at the curb in casual attire, as his actual interview was the following day. I pulled up next to him and waved to get his attention as he opened the door and sat in the passenger seat. "Hey, Adam. Good flight?" I asked.

"Yeah. It was smooth, on time and I got to rest some, so overall, I can't complain," he responded.

"Great. Well, I am really excited that you are back for a second visit. Things continue to progress here, slowly, but progress nonetheless. We are providing 24-7 coverage, which is a lot of work, but the patients are benefiting and so are the nurses, who are really beginning to enjoy it. If you decide to join us, I want you to know that I don't expect you to do what we are doing, in terms of the number of nights Justin and I are covering. The expectation will be five nights per month. If you want to work more than that, that is great, you will be compensated for that, if not, that is fine too. The first month, I think you should stick to the five required night calls, that way you can get used to the system, but we can talk about all that later," I explained. We talked very informally as we drove toward his hotel. I could sense his interest. I shared with him the proposed salary offer that I had arranged through the university, as I felt that may help increase the likelihood that he would deliver his verbal agreement to join us prior to his departure back home. As I shared the proposed salary we were offering him, I purposefully watched for any changes in his facial expression, in hopes that it may provide me a hint as to his feelings about the number, and as I watched his expression, indeed it put my mind at ease as it was easily interpreted as one suggesting pleasure with our offer. I wanted to get that out of the way before the second interview actually began, because I knew from experience that most people at this stage, including me, would be wondering about the salary and there was no sense in making him wait in anticipation any longer. As I dropped him off, we said our goodbyes as I said, "See you tomorrow. Have a good night."

"Thanks, Eric. Same to you," he replied.

Meanwhile, in the background, the recruitment for CEO was progressing. Dr. Deeton had interviewed for the position; however, he had been eliminated as a potential candidate, and I was relieved and grateful for that. Dr. Potts was part of the search committee involved in the recruitment and interview process, evaluating potential candidates for the position. Dr. Potts had communicated to us at the division directors' meeting that they believed that after reviewing and interviewing several qualified applicants, they had narrowed it down to a single candidate and were close to making an offer. The candidate's name was Antoine Boykins. Antoine was an African American man who functioned as the current COO at D.C. Children's Hospital in Washington D.C. He was said to be adored and respected at D.C. Children's and the consensus among his colleagues there was that he was next in line to become CEO. He was reportedly an energetic and intelligent leader who was known for his creativity and his quirky ideas as they pertained to his ability to engage the staff and the community. The day of Adam's arrival to Biloxi, the news was released that Mr. Boykins had indeed accepted the job, which was another selling point I could use to convince Adam to join us.

The next morning, I picked up Adam at the hotel. As we exchanged greetings, I shared with him the news of the new CEO, making every effort to cement the concept in his mind that the institution was committed to continuous change for the better, with the promise of a new day at Children's Hospital of Biloxi. "Wow seems like a lot of great change going on here," he said. I could see his excitement and it appeared sincere. We exited my vehicle and walked toward the hospital. "Looks like they have progressed on the parking garage," he said.

"Yes, it seems to be progressing quite fast. They say that the new CICU will be ready in less than two years. A lofty goal, which I will believe when I see it, but I have to admit that I am excited," I explained.

Adam's day of interviews went without a hitch. We treated him to a catered lunch where he had the opportunity to meet several of the CICU nurses, Tim my PA friend, who happened to be working that week, and Martha, the PA student, was also able to meet him. Ruth and Maddie each had thirty minutes to meet with him, and both enjoyed the visit and were impressed by some suggestions Adam had made for engaging and educating the nursing staff including teaching during medical rounds and developing a formalized lecture series. We arranged dinner at another one of Biloxi's most beloved restaurants. Dr. Potts, Adam and I attended dinner, where we initially chatted informally, eventually leading us to the formal discussion of salary, benefits, and expected clinical time he would serve each month. Dr. Potts explained that if Adam decided to commit to joining us, he could have an offer letter sent overnight so that he could have it in his hands within a week. Adam said he was likely to commit; however, he needed a day or two to review and think about the offer after arriving home. We understood and dinner concluded as Dr. Potts thanked him for the visit, and I drove him back to his hotel to rest before an early morning departure. "Eric, I wanted to mention that I have a colleague who may be a good candidate to consider for one of your other cardiac intensivist vacancies. Her name is Astrid Slovak. She is completing her fellowship at the same time as me, she is very intelligent and easy to work with; however, she is Russian, and would need a visa and I am not sure if the university supports J-1 visas or not," Adam explained.

"To be honest with you, I am not sure either; however, I appreciate the recommendation and I will definitely investigate the possibility. Could you text me her contact information and I will look into it and once I have the answer, I will reach out to her. Have a good night. Let's touch base in a couple days after you have had an opportunity to think over the offer, and then if you're interested, I will keep you updated on the progress of the offer letter. Please don't hesitate to contact me with any questions. Safe travels," I said, shaking his hand as he exited my vehicle and walked to the hotel. I felt good about the visit and was relatively confident that Adam would say yes. I was equally excited about the potential candidate, Astrid, whom he had mentioned. Another candidate that came highly recommended, would be incredible. Next week I planned to speak with Dr. Potts about the feasibility of the university sponsoring her visa. Things definitely appeared to be looking up.

Monday arrived and I was off again, driving down the pothole-filled streets of Biloxi. Admittedly, driving across the bridge each day had new meaning for me as I now noticed a newfound involuntary state of alertness that occurred the minute my vehicle tires made contact with the bridge. As I arrived at the hospital, I walked to Dr. Potts's office and sat down to discuss whether or not the university was willing or able to offer visa support for Astrid. Dr. Potts explained that unfortunately, the University of Southeastern Mississippi did not sponsor visa waivers; however, in the past Children's Hospital of Biloxi had done so under certain circumstances. He suggested that I speak with Dr. Deeton. After speaking with Dr. Deeton he confirmed that indeed, they would consider sponsoring the visa if Dr. Slovak was felt to be a good candidate; however, he wanted to be clear that the process was lengthy and could take more than a year. "It is unfortunate about the time-line I said, but at this point it may be our best option. Adam already shared her contact information with me, so I will reach out to her today," I said. That afternoon I spent thirty minutes speaking with Dr. Slovak. She seemed very nice, fluent in English with minimal to no accent, and appeared very intelli-gent and clearly interested in knowing more about the program. At that point we mutually agreed to set up an in-person visit, and I explained that someone would be in communication with her soon to schedule it.

Two days later, I received a call from Adam and after two days of salary negotiation, he verbally accepted the position. "Wonderful, Adam, I am very excited to have you join us. Also, I spoke with Astrid, and she seems lovely. She has agreed to come for a visit. Thank you so much for the refer-ral. I will let Dr. Potts know that you have accepted the job and I will keep you updated regarding the progress of your offer letter," I said, hardly able to curtail my excitement.

"Sounds great, Eric. Thanks for everything," he replied.

21

DR. ROSTRI'S MIND GAMES AND AN ATTEMPTED COUP

Word of the CEO's acceptance became widespread at CHOB. I wasn't sure if there was more excitement regarding Antoine Boykins's acceptance of the CEO position or for the imminent departure of Nancy Ogylview. Either way, you could feel the anticipation of change among the staff. I was the service attending so I was performing medical rounds for the week. There was no surgical case that day, Dr. Rostri was supposed to return from a one-week vacation in St. Petersburg, Russia the previous night; however, he did not show up for "migration rounds," which was odd for him, and it was far too late to chalk his absence up to his usual mind games. In his absence, Dr. Penton had been leading migration rounds for the preceding week, which was a nice change of pace. It was refreshing because Dr. Penton would actually listen to suggestions from others, although not always agreeing with them. It became clear to me, and understandably so, that he had been mentored by Dr. Rostri since the time that he completed his pediatric cardiac surgical fellowship nearly twenty years ago. As a result, his CICU management style was very similar to Dr. Rostri's, which was not surprising, as the reality is that we are all a product of our medical training. We learn what we are taught, until we become independent or in a leadership position, after which time most successful clinicians modify their style over the years by adding new tools to their arsenal that they have learned from others over time. The painful truth was that Dr. Rostri had not allowed Dr. Penton to function independently, as they always operated together, usually alternating who would function as the "primary" surgeon for each case, but Dr. Rostri always had veto power and was still critical of Dr. Penton though his criticism was rarely warranted. Dr. Rostri's mistrust in Dr. Penton, or perhaps not mistrust, but inability to relinquish control, was never more apparent than when he would leave town to go on vacation. When this occurred, there would either be no surgical cases scheduled for the week he was away, which was intentional on his part, or alternatively, there may be one or two simpler cases scheduled. As an example, while Dr. Rostri was away this time, he had only scheduled one simple case for the entire week. A major problem with controlling behavior such as this was that it stunts the growth and arrests the necessary development and confidence of the junior staff, which is essential for becoming a confident, efficient, and autonomous clinician, capable of making quick, life-saving decisions under pressure and in the blink of an eye. So, when junior clinicians are deprived of the nurturing environment required to develop as a clinician, when faced with a scenario requiring rapid critical analysis and decision-making, they are overcome with fear and panic due to the perceived consequences of a poor decision, instead of strengthening the necessary skills needed to rapidly process differential diagnoses and potential treatment algorithms in their mind in a matter of seconds. This is further exacerbated by the fact that the nurses are left waiting in anticipation for direction from the young physician, yet instead there is silence as their first thought is, "Oh shit, let me call Dr. Rostri (or whomever the controlling leader may be) to ask what he wants me to do," instead of the instinctual vocalization of orders such as, "Give IV fluid, get a dose of epinephrine, call for ECMO, start CPR, etcetera." Not only does this process arrest the development of the young clinician, it also inevitably fertilizes the seed of doubt inherent in all CICU nurses as it relates to junior staff. Lack of confidence is something that must be managed and overcome by every young physician, with each clinical success functioning as a repeated application of pesticide leading to the eventual eradication of this budding mistrust. Overcoming this natural process is vital in the CICU and is challenging in isolation; however, when combined with a toxic environment that discourages self-thought and critical analysis, it can irreversibly damage a young physician beyond repair. This scenario is a medical director's worst nightmare, as it leads to an insurmountable burden placed on his or her shoulders, because it leads to a unit staffed by individuals who fail to trust one another, thereby destroying the concept of "a team." This was a danger I was fully cognizant of and was one of my greatest concerns as I began recruiting inexperienced cardiac intensivists, straight out of fellowship.

Dr. Penton was very intelligent, and from what I had observed, he was a more technically skilled surgeon than Dr. Rostri, which was probably the reason Dr. Rostri felt threatened by him, and he was far from "junior." When it came to controlling leaders I had encountered over my career, my experience suggested that when their trainees began to display skills that exceeded their own, their will to suppress them became even greater. It is such a fascinating yet disturbing paradigm. True to this point, and even more fascinating (yet disturbing) is that when Dr. Rostri would return from vacation, he spent most of his time criticizing the surgeries Dr. Penton had performed in his absence, and even more so, he would publicly ridicule his management of the patients in the CICU in front of the staff during "migration rounds." In fact, the only time Dr. Penton joined "migration rounds" at the same time as the rest of the group, was while Dr. Rostri was away, and in the first few days following his return. What I came to realize is that the only reason Dr. Penton joined "migration rounds" following Dr. Rostri's return from vacation, was to defend his decisions from the criticism of Dr. Rostri. It was sad yet fascinating to witness such an interpersonal dynamic. It was equally intriguing to watch Dr. Penton's behavior during a typical week when Dr. Rostri was around, where he would arrive to the CICU about an hour after "migration rounds" had finished, at which time he would walk around to the patients he had operated on and perform his own rounds, in isolation. He would review the data, speak with the bedside nurse, and review the orders that had been placed at the direction of Dr. Rostri, and if he disagreed, which was often, he would proceed to rip the order sheet out of the chart, crumple the paper into a ball and throw it across the unit until it as it bounced across the floor, finally coming to rest in front of the nursing station to ensure maximum theatrics. I am not joking! Or, on occasion, he would draw a stick figure with a sad face or a thumbs down, next to Dr. Rostri's order that he had scribbled out, and replaced with his own order. I was dismayed by their dysfunctional relationship, but I was more awestruck by Dr. Penton's ability to adapt and survive the controlling grip of Dr. Rostri for such a long period of time. I was barely hanging on by a thread and it had been less than a year, while he had survived twenty years of psychological warfare. It was quite an admirable feat. However, in life and in medicine, much like nature, to endure and survive, we must adapt and evolve, or we risk extinction. This concept would become true for many of us at Children's Hospital of Biloxi, including Dr. Penton and me; however, it simply wasn't evident to either of us at this stage. The unusual circumstance that morning was that Dr. Rostri, who always arrived at the hospital early the morning following his return from vacation, which I sarcastically assumed was to ensure extra time for criticism of Dr. Penton, was absent. It was unusual, and his nurse scheduler confirmed that morning that he had indeed arrived the night before. "Where could he be?" I thought to myself.

Approximately one hour after Dr. Penton completed "migration rounds" with us in the CICU, Dr. Rostri arrived. I was preparing to start medical CICU rounds when he called my name. "Eric. Can I speak with you for a moment?" he said.

I turned to find Dr. Rostri and Dr. Penton standing together, both displaying a look of concern on their face. "Sure," I said, with a confused look.

"Let's meet in the conference room." Dr. Rostri said.

"Shit. I hate that damn room. I wonder what I did now?" I said to myself.

We opened the door and sat in the CICU conference room, which was dark and freezing, as usual. Dr. Rostri and Penton sat side by side at the table, directly across from me in their now patented interrogative fashion. Dr. Rostri looked distressed. "Eric. I was called to a surprise meeting this morning by Gene Forester, CEO of the entire Mississippi hospital health system. He informed me that due to your and my deteriorating relationship in the CICU that he was going to terminate my employment. What have you told him?" he yelled angrily.

I was in absolute shock. "First of all, who the hell is Gene Forester? I have never heard that name and I have most certainly never met him in my life, much less tell him that you and I weren't getting along," I replied.

"I explained to him that you and I were getting along wonderfully and that we weren't having any problems. So, you need to go meet with him immediately and tell him that we are working together without issue," he demanded.

"Look, Dr. Rostri, they are clearly using me as an excuse to try to terminate you. I have never spoken to this man; in fact, I haven't spoken to anyone about you at all, much less in a negative manner. However, I am certainly not going to seek out Mr. Forester to tell him things are perfect between us, because quite frankly, they are not. You refuse most of my changes and disregard most of my suggestions. Yes, I would say our relationship is better, but it is far from perfect. You can tell him that, but I refuse to run to someone's office, whom I have never met, to contradict something I didn't say. If he truly wishes to speak to me, he should call me, or email me to set up a meeting like most professionals do! Doing so third person is not the way anyone, particularly the CEO of a large organization, should conduct business," I responded.

"Eric. This is urgent. I need you to meet with him immediately," he repeated.

"I get your concern, trust me I do, but they are using me as a pawn in their game, attempting to distract from their true motive. This absolutely has to be a request from the new CEO, Antoine Boykins, which he must have placed as a condition of his employment. The timing is suspicious, and I cannot think of anything else that could explain such a random maneuver," I said, as I thought to myself, "I will bet he negotiated in his agreement with the hospital that they would be responsible for terminating Dr. Rostri prior to his start date. Why else would they do this now and without any advance warning to anyone?"

"I am not sure what is going on, Dr. Rostri, and I am sorry you are dealing with this, but it has nothing to do with me. I refuse to allow Mr. Forester to use me as his excuse for terminating you. If he seeks my input, he will need to reach out to me in a far more professional manner, starting with a simple introduction, before he tries to throw me under the bus," I said, as I left the room in anger. "The nerve of this guy who has never introduced himself and who has never asked me a single question as it relates to my relationship with Dr. Rostri, while he attempts to use me as an excuse to justify his spineless attempt at terminating Dr. Rostri," I thought to myself. The next several days were met with repeated attempts by Dr. Rostri to bully and pressure me into speaking with Gene Forester; however, I heard nothing from Gene Forester himself. I spoke to Dr. Potts regarding the details of this absurd situation. He relayed his support for me and agreed that the act appeared cowardly and reinforced that I had no obligation to speak with Gene Forrester. In fact, Dr. Potts called Gene directly and told him that if he wished to speak with me that Dr. Potts would need to be present. After a week of pestering by Dr. Rostri and complete silence from Gene Forrester, the whole thing disappeared and Dr. Rostri remained employed and as controlling as ever. I was later informed by Dr. Potts that Dr. Rostri had flexed his power by speaking with the board of directors of Children's Hospital of Biloxi, who had all but muzzled Gene Forrester and crushed his attempted coup d'état.

22

MORE RECRUITS

Another month passed and the slow progress continued. Adam had officially signed his offer letter and Dr. Slovak had completed her first interview and it was clear that there was mutual interest by both parties, and given the complexities of the visa process, we decided to offer her a position so that we could proceed with the lengthy application process. So far, we had recruited two cardiac intensivists, one full-time APP, one part-time APP, and we had recently received three applicants for the cardiac pharmacy opening. At the same time, 24-7 coverage of the CICU was going well besides the extreme fatigue, excessive caffeine intake during the day, followed by excessive alcohol intake in the evening when at home, which continued to serve its short-term purpose, allowing me a brief period of relaxation and a few hours of continuous sleep, and I continued to fight hard to maximize what little free time I had with Ana and the kids. Our CICU data, primarily our hospital length of stay, continued to improve despite Dr. Rostri's tight control of major changes. We had now improved from the worst length of stay among participating institutions to performing within the top 35 percent. This was truly incredible given where we had started, the lack of staff, and the mountain of work that remained ahead, but it was an accomplishment that validated our efforts and it was something we could use to show the staff what an amazing job they were doing, while also utilizing it as a recruiting tool for potential candidates.

Finally, we had received some applicants for the CICU clinical pharmacy opening, three in total, and this time the applications did not sit unacknowledged in human resources. All three applicants were reasonably well qualified; however, one was completing specialized pediatric cardiac pharmacy training at Stanford University. He was fresh out of training; however, once we met him, we quickly realized that he was extremely motivated and passionate about his job. The fact that his wife was a neonatology-trained clinical pharmacist, which was another need for the hospital, he immediately became our primary focus of recruitment. After his wife completed her interview at CHOB, we sat down with the neonatal intensive care unit team to discuss our desire to make an offer to George Macklin, the cardiac pharmacist. Fortunately, they equally wished to make an offer to Mary Macklin, the neonatal pharmacist. An offer was extended to both candidates and following some negotiation due to the typical lowball offer from the CHOB HR department, we were able to come to an agreement for both. It was truly an exciting addition. These two would become the first fellowship-trained, dedicated inpatient pharmacists in the history of the entire hospital. They were both looking to start working within the next two months.

A new development on the recruiting front included receiving an application from a nurse practitioner who was born and raised in Mississippi her whole life. She had studied at Northern Alabama University to obtain her degree, which was a hybrid online program. As you can recall, the acute care nurse practitioner program at University of Southeastern Mississippi was just beginning, and prior to that, there were no options for those wishing to pursue such a degree in the state; therefore, this program was the best option for residents of the state who simply could not relocate to study. The applicant's name was Brenda Paige. She was a young woman in her early thirties with red hair who had worked as a bedside nurse in the children's emergency room for approximately five years at a hospital ninety minutes north of Biloxi, prior to pursuing her acute care nurse practitioner degree. She had four kids, two of her own and two who belonged to her long-term boyfriend, from his previous marriage. She lived in a small town, which was a seventy-minute drive from Biloxi. She spoke well during her interview and appeared confident and intelligent. When asked about her feelings related to traveling such a distance, roundtrip, four days a week, she explained that she didn't mind, in fact she drove to Biloxi regularly to visit family and consequently, it was not a concern for her. After a period of salary negotiation following a patented lowball offer from CHOB HR, she became the most recent addition to the team and hoped to start working within the next two months, as she had already obtained a Mississippi license and only required credentialing at Children's Hospital of Biloxi. With two full-time APPs on board, I felt like it was a good time to start working on convincing Tim to join the team full-time.

Tim had been working three twelve-hour shifts, twice a month. It was a huge help having him around and the nurses loved working with him. Several of the staff had shared how much they enjoyed working with him. He was friendly, funny, easy-going, calm under pressure and was an experienced cardiac advanced practice provider. Not to mention, he was always good for some inappropriate humor, which while that had become taboo in healthcare, was always welcomed in stressful situations to help keep the mood loose. Not inappropriate in a creepy, sexual harassment type of way, but more like inappropriate in the occasional R-rated joke type of way. Each time I heard a nurse speak about how much they enjoyed working with Tim, I responded by saying, "Next time he is here working, start gently suggesting that he should consider joining us full-time. Mention about how you enjoy living here in Biloxi and how great it is for families, etcetera."

Since Ruth and Maddie both knew Tim from their time working with him in Florida, I asked them to work on convincing him as well. Over the course of the next three months, we all did our best to do so, although I knew it was going to take more than some verbal convincing to get him and his family to move to Biloxi. Tim was paid handsomely in the ER where he worked in Florida; however, the two aspects of the job that he didn't care for were the fact that he didn't feel clinically challenged in his current role and most importantly, he missed working with pediatric patients as he dealt almost exclusively with adults. Tim was a father of three and admitted to me when he started covering shifts in Biloxi that he missed working with children and he missed the challenge and excitement inherent to the CICU. Before making the final push to convince Tim to join us, I would need to have another sit-down meeting with John Wozniak, CNO, to discuss a strategy that would make our offer competitive financially, thereby providing us the best opportunity to add him to the team full-time. During his previous stretch of shifts, I asked him how much he was paid monthly in the ER. After getting a solid idea of how much he made, I sat down with John Wozniak. Tim made a lot of money for an APP, more than any other APP I had worked with. John, being the amazing leader he was, got creative. We talked about offering Tim the director position, responsible for overseeing all CICU advanced practice providers, and John found additional compensation for assuming that role. Ultimately, after a couple of weeks, John was able to come up with a salary matching that which he made in the ER. Plus, we were able to offer him reimbursement of moving expenses and the potential for an annual salary increase by achieving certain benchmarks. When I discussed our offer with Tim, it was relevant enough for him to stop and consider. I told him, "I know your wife doesn't want to move, but just let it simmer and digest a little before you answer. You can make your own schedule, you can mentor Martha, Brenda and the future APPs. I want to have you all learn to manage the patients and not just function as scribes." After three weeks of contemplation, Tim accepted the position, and we had our first experienced APP and our new director of CICU APPs. It was a huge win for us. It was agreed that one month later he would start full-time, and his family would move at the end of the school year. Meanwhile, Martha received her license while she and Brenda both received their necessary credentialing, and both were set to officially start the following month. Things finally seemed to be falling into place.

23

ARRIVAL OF THE NEW ADMINISTRATORS

The time was upon us, Antoine Boykins, the long-awaited CEO who had joined Children's Hospital of Biloxi from D.C. Children's, was starting. In the months leading up to his arrival, there had been appearances by different members of his presumed staff who had performed walk-by visits to the CICU, all unannounced and in relative secrecy. Also, during this time there was speculation regarding Dr. Deeton's future at CHOB. It became crystal clear Mr. Boykins had no intention of keeping any of the administrative staff onboard except John Wozniak, chief nursing officer, and Luke Leblanc, chief quality officer. Rumor was that Dr. Deeton as a result of his "good ol' boy" connections, would not only land himself a new job, but he was to receive a promotion and would now assume the newly developed role as CMO of the entire Mississippi Health System, which consisted of CHOB and four other adult hospitals throughout the state.

The team Mr. Boykins brought with him had all been part of the D.C. Children's health system. Some worked directly at D.C. Children's, while others worked at affiliated institutions. Only one of his incoming staff had any previous administrative experience, though they all boasted distinguished academic careers. Michael Stringer, the new chief operating officer, had functioned previously as the chief operating officer at Washington D.C. Methodist Hospital, a sister hospital of the D.C. Children's system. While it was primarily an adult hospital it had a children's wing, allowing him some exposure to pediatric patient care. Michael was a younger guy for a COO, in his early forties with curly brownish-blond hair. He was about five foot ten and was always sharply dressed in a suit and tie. He was clearly intelligent and displayed confidence, but also carried himself as a down-to-earth man of the people who was able to relate and had the natural ability to read people and situations with ease.

The new chief medical officer's name was Gerry Blount. Gerry was a short, moderately overweight man who was completely bald. He was extremely friendly, and very accomplished academically. He was clinical professor of pediatric radiology at D.C. Children's where he practiced for the last fifteen years. Though he primarily practiced radiology, he was triple boarded in pediatric radiology, pediatric nephrology, and pediatric endocrinology. As stated previously, Dr. Blount was a kind man, but when assuming the role as CMO, particularly at an institution in need of such dramatic change and investment, it is vital to have a strong understanding of the hospital workflow and a dynamic vision of the evolving needs required by each specialty in order to ensure success. Let me say again, nice guy; however, as I came to understand, expecting a radiologist to understand the flow or needs of anything outside of sitting inside a dark room and looking at a screen all day, without additional leadership training or experience, is a recipe for disaster. Another red flag when it came to Dr. Blount's assumption of this role was the fact that he was triple boarded. The term "triple boarded" describes an individual who underwent fellowship training and board certification in three different subspecialties. While it is clearly a major accomplishment, particularly on paper, as I gained experience throughout my career in medicine, you quickly realize that those who choose such a path have one thing in common: They aren't typically very good at any of the three specialties they trained in! And even more so, if you ultimately settle on radiology as your final chosen specialty, that says it all! Sitting in a room all day long, staring at images on a monitor with minimal social interaction, is unlikely to provide the necessary experience required to understand the interworking and workflow of a hospital necessary to function as a CMO. During his brief time as CMO, Dr. Blount would struggle in his leadership position, validating this preconceived notion of mine.

The new chief surgical officer's name was Edward Arnold. Edward, or Eddie as he would be known, was a short, brown-haired man, who was always well-dressed. He was a general pediatric surgeon, who was an MD, PhD, and had a very distinguished career where he had trained and practiced at some of the most well-known institutions around the country. Eddie was a very intelligent and emotionally mature man who was distinguished and well-spoken. He would prove to be a great leader during his tenure at CHOB and would go on to do great things for the institution.

The final administrator hired by Mr. Boykins was the new chief financial officer, Hector Ramirez. Hector was a real piece of work. While in my experience, no CFO in the history of humankind had ever been liked by the hospital staff, I could honestly say that in my previous experience, most CFOs were simply unknown to the hospital staff. But not Hector, he was a Hispanic man in his early sixties, who felt he was God's gift to women. Unlike most CFOs, he made no excuses for cutting budgets nor did he try to conceal the fact that he was doing so. Make no mistake about it, this was a business to him, it was not a children's hospital, and his motivation was his own selfish financial bonuses that would be paid out based on the amount of money he would save the hospital. He found the highest-paid physicians in the hospital and made it his goal to cut their salary or frustrate them to the point that they would leave on their own accord. A real parasite, who would greet you with a phony smile as he conspired behind the scenes for ways to deplete your division of the funds necessary to provide patient care representative of the national standard. He was excessively compensated as would be later validated after reading the mandatory online posting of executive leader salaries for all nonprofit organizations. He would be compensated nearly $1 million a year as he progressively slashed the salaries of vital physicians and refused to fill vacancies of those who resigned as a result of his predatory behaviors.

These were the traits I would come to learn about these administrators over a period of years. If only I had the ability to foresee these characteristics at the time of their arrival, it would have allowed me the ability to predict just how it would affect all of us at CHOB, both positively and negatively. But as I learned over time, we are all held at the mercy of the administration that runs the hospital—a sad but true reality that we all face as health-care providers. The vision outlined or portrayed by these leaders has an everlasting effect on every employee and patient in the hospital and if that vision drifts from one that focuses on supporting the staff and the overall goal of providing exceptional patient care to one primarily focused on financial gain, then the effects can be catastrophic. Even more unfavorable is when an elaborate web of deception is weaved over a period time, rendering the staff powerlessly entangled in these lies, leaving you with no choice but to submit to their cultish beliefs or to cut yourself loose and run for dear life.

Their arrival resulted in an overall feeling of excitement by the staff, myself included, as it appeared to signify a new day. Mr. Boykins was a man of the people and while he came from the North, his roots were in the South, as he was born and raised in Alabama. The first time I met Antoine Boykins was as he walked through the CICU one night when I was working a thirty-six-hour shift. The unit was cold, as usual, and I had come to be known by the nurses for wearing a navy-blue wool jacket over my scrubs with a "Children's Hospital of Biloxi" logo on it, which I of course was wearing that evening. As Mr. Boykins showed his wife and another Hispanic man through the unit, he passed by me, having no idea who I was. As he walked by, we met one another's glance. "Hello, Mr. Boykins," I said, extending my hand in introduction. "My name is Eric Philson, pleasure to meet you."

"Oh, hello, Dr. Philson. I have heard that you have been working hard to bring change to the CICU. This is my wife, Nancy Boykins, and this is Hector Ramirez, our new chief financial officer," he introduced, as he proceeded to look me up and down with his eyes as he scowled, as if analyzing me and ultimately arriving at a disappointing conclusion, as if saying to himself, "This is our choice for medical director of the CICU?"

"Very nice to meet you both," I replied.

"We are just passing through each department so that I can show these two all the great work you guys are doing. Can you explain to us a little bit of what y'all are doing?" Mr. Boykins asked, with a Southern drawl that appeared fabricated, as if attempting to display some sort of connection with the staff of CHOB.

"Well, to be honest, it has been a real challenge to recruit the staff necessary to provide 24-7 in-house coverage; however, so far, we have recruited two cardiac intensivists from Yale, a dedicated cardiac pharmacist and three advanced practice providers. Despite our staffing deficiencies, we have still managed to provide 24-7 coverage for the first time in the history of the hospital, and as a result we have reduced our median hospital length of stay from the worst in the country to one performing within the top 35 percent nationally, all in just under a year. It has been a lot of work, but I am proud of what we have done and I am excited for the future," I said with enthusiasm.

"That is fantastic, Dr. Philson. Keep up the great work. You and I should sit down and talk next week. I will have my assistant reach out to you," he replied, shaking my hand.

"Thank you. I would love the opportunity to sit down and talk with you. It was a pleasure meeting you all. Enjoy your tour," I said. As they walked out the doors of the CICU, I was left with the feeling that Antoine Boykins was a sincere man who valued what we were doing; however, I couldn't help but sense an underlying skepticism on his behalf as to my qualifications as medical director. Perhaps I was being paranoid, as I was definitely sleep-deprived, but the truth was I had no choice but to dismiss these feelings of uncertainty and see what would transpire over the coming months.

The following morning, I received a text from Luke Leblanc, chief quality officer. "Hey Eric, I have been meaning to reach out to you. I have heard the great things you have been doing in the CICU in a short period of time. I want to introduce you to the new COO, Michael Stringer. I know you were on call last night, but do you have time to stop by my office on the fourth floor to meet him?"

"Hey Luke. Good to hear from you. I can stop by after medical rounds, around lunchtime, if that works?" I replied.

"Sounds good. See you then!" he responded.

"See you then," I texted.

Medical rounds proceeded uneventfully and after handing off to Justin, who was going to cover the unit while I was gone, I headed to the elevator and pushed the button for the fourth floor. As the doors opened, I walked down the hall to the C-suite and headed toward Luke's office. As I approached Luke's office, I saw him standing outside the door, speaking with another man as he said loudly, "Hey, Eric, how was your night shift?"

I arrived at Luke's office door and extended my hand in greeting, shaking his hand as I said, "Hey, Luke, good to see you. My night was fine. I am tired but no major issues overnight."

"Great. Eric! I want to introduce you to Michael Stringer, the new chief operating officer," Luke said.

"Hi, Eric, great to meet you. I have heard great things about you, from Luke and several other people," Michael said.

"Thanks, Michael, nice to meet you too," I said shaking his hand.

After exchanging pleasantries, Michael said, "Eric, do you have some time tomorrow for you and me to sit down and chat. I can come to your office. Just let me know a time that works best for you."

"Sure, Michael, that would be great. How about tomorrow around 11 a.m., that will allow me adequate time to finish CICU medical rounds?" I replied.

"Great. See you then," he said. As I exited the hospital and drove home after removing my socks and shoes, I had a good feeling about Michael. There were only a couple of things in life that I gave myself credit for, one was that I was a pretty self-motivated guy. When I said I was going to do something, there was a high likelihood that I was going to complete the task, or at minimum, I was going to exhaust every option until I was convinced my original goal was actually unachievable. Hence the whole working one hundred hours per week thing that was happening in real time. The other skill I gave myself credit for was my refined ability to read people and situations. I believe this ability contributed to my success as a cardiac intensivist over the years because it allowed me to identify early shifts in data trends or subtle clinical changes, which if left unaddressed, may lead to patient deterioration, thereby permitting early intervention and prevention of adverse events such as cardiac arrest. Equally, I felt skilled at assessing an individual's character, and in the case of Michael Stringer, our new COO, I sensed he was a kind and genuine person, but I relished the opportunity to meet with him one-on-one to further support my gut feeling.

I managed to arrive home safely to find Ana outside working in the garden. She greeted my arrival with a kiss, which felt unusually cold. I asked, "Everything OK?"

"Yep, just working in the garden," she replied as she turned away and returned to focusing on her tomato plants. I could tell things were not OK; however, I was too exhausted to inquire further, and in retrospect, this was one of several opportunities I was provided by her to push for a greater understanding of her unhappiness, but I didn't. Instead, I went inside and tried to rest for a bit before the girls arrived from school, so I could have enough energy to spend some time with them before bedtime.

The next day following CICU medical rounds, Michael arrived promptly at my office door with a knock at 10:58 a.m. That type of punctuality tells you a lot about a person, and as a result I began to develop a picture in my mind about Michael, one that pointed toward a man who was organized and respectful. As he entered my dimly lit office, I offered him a seat. I kept my office intentionally dark, so I could use the room as a retreat to escape the loud and stressful environment of the CICU, and as I entered, I would often play ambient music to help calm my mind and allow me to think more clearly. As Michael sat, I asked, "Would you like me to turn the lights on, I enjoy it dark, it helps me to relax and remain focused," I explained.

"No. Actually, I like it like this," he replied. We sat together, conversing as if old friends, as we shared our backgrounds, education, and details about our families. I explained how it was that I came to accept the job as medical director, as well as the obstacles I had encountered and the approach I had used to overcome some of those challenges. I immediately felt comfortable with Michael, and I trusted him, though I barely knew him. I shared with him that I had been close to leaving and had considered joining the team at Mayo Children's but that I ultimately stayed because I didn't feel like I had given everything I had to the job yet. I also shared that I felt a great deal of responsibility for improving the care that was being provided to the children of Mississippi because I thought they deserved better. While this was a massive burden for one individual to shoulder, I did my best to vaguely explain the situation to Michael, without placing blame on others, describing that it was impossible to unsee what I had now seen, and this blaring gap in the quality of patient care that existed, when compared to our colleagues around the country, fueled my drive to succeed. I also shared the hours Justin and I were working in order to ensure progress. He appeared amazed at our accomplishments over such a short period of time, although admittedly it felt like an eternity for me.

He asked me questions directly related to my relationship with Dr. Rostri. "Michael, that is a complicated question. I would be lying if I told you everything was perfect; however, Gerald and I have found a way to coexist, and we maintain a professional relationship. We respect one another and the fact we have different philosophies or approaches to patient care in the CICU. I respect all he has done for Children's Hospital of Biloxi. He built this program and he and Dr. Penton have relentlessly dedicated their time and lives to care for these patients with little to no resources, and I have an immense amount of respect for that. Individually, I wish I had more autonomy in the CICU, which would allow me to implement change at a much faster pace; however, I have nothing negative to say about Dr. Rostri," I said. And that was the truth, I respected both cardiac surgeons; however, I wished they would let me do my job, but I wasn't about to spend my time with Mr. Stringer speaking negatively about either one. Instead, I chose to focus on the positive work we had done. I recognized that he was fishing for information about Dr. Rostri, most likely at the direction of Mr. Boykins, but they would have to gather that information on their own, or from someone other than me. I refused to knowingly take part in any negative scheme to remove Dr. Rostri, although based on the events that had transpired recently between Gene Forester, CEO of the entire Mississippi hospital system, and Dr. Rostri, I became suspicious that such a campaign was indeed in the works.

"Eric, I want to thank you for taking the time to sit and speak with me today." He quickly followed this gracious statement by asking a question that validated my initial sense of who Michael Stringer was as a human being—a simple yet profound question that resonates with me to this day as one that defines a true leader and a caring individual. "What can I do to help you succeed?" he asked.

I was taken aback. In life, too often we become obsessed with the question, "What can you do for me?" Or as an administrator, this question could easily be replaced by the statement, "This is what I need you to do for me." Living life in a manner that places others ahead of ourselves, defines selflessness. Regardless of the religion, spiritual teaching, or life philosophy you choose to follow, the fundamental belief consists of living a life with the goal of helping others, without concern for personal benefit. Yes, I know, perhaps I am diving a bit deep here by attributing such meaning to a simple question, but quite honestly, I don't think so, even as I reflect on the incident in hindsight. However, living a selfless life should come with a warning or disclaimer, of which I was incapable of understanding at the time, one that would inevitably hit me like a ton of bricks in the future. After speaking with Michael, I came to believe he was given a gift, he was kind enough to share with me that it was a health-related tragedy affecting a young child in his family, which had led him away from a career in mechanical engineering and into a career as a health-care administrator. That personal tragedy fueled a motivation that made the job personal for him. He was blessed with the ability to understand that it took investment and support to provide the staff and resources required to provide exceptional medical care, while also building necessary trust between the staff and hospital leaders. He understood that he must first provide the necessary resources that had been neglected for decades so we could provide the care needed to become a top children's hospital and by doing so, it would attract patients and referrals from throughout the region, while also allowing the growth and development of money-making specialties, which would provide consistent revenue leading to the financial success of the institution. Financial support leading to exceptional clinical care that would lead to financial success, seemed complex, and had been interpreted as such by his predecessors, yet he presented it with such simplicity. Rather than merely viewing the hospital as a business that cared for patients on the side, Michael Stringer displayed an advanced understanding, as if he held the long-lost recipe for success and had combined it with an instinctual and forthright passion for helping children and for making the world a better place, a gift that I would come to admire and respect him for. "Michael, I don't have any immediate needs right now, but hearing you say these words puts my mind at ease and assures me that there are no ulterior motives behind our conversation, and that gives me the peace of mind necessary to do my job, and right now, that is plenty. But I promise you, if something arises, I will let you know."

I thanked him for his visit and as we shook hands and I looked him in the eyes, I could feel the mutual respect. We exchanged cell phone numbers and as he walked toward the door of my office, he said, "I bought a house near yours, and our kids are around the same age, our families should get together sometime."

"That would be wonderful," I replied, as he walked out the door and down the hallway.

Two days later, I received a text message from Michael, again thanking me for the meeting and describing how he would like for me to meet with Mr. Boykins. I agreed and the meeting was scheduled for the following day. When I arrived at Mr. Boykins's office, his assistant knocked on the door, which he quickly opened, welcoming me inside and offering me a seat. His office was huge with a large desk, a sofa, and a large circular table surrounded by four chairs. The wall directly across from his door was made of floor-to-ceiling glass, overlooking a beautiful park. On the wall hung his degrees from Princeton and Georgetown University. I sat in a chair directly across from his at the circular table in front of his desk. We shook hands. His handshake appeared superficial and cold, while still maintaining professionalism, different than the one offered by Michael Stringer, his COO. We sat in silence as he skimmed my curriculum vitae that had been handed to him by his assistant. "Michael told me he met with you this week and speaks very highly of you," he said.

"That's good to hear I said. I enjoyed meeting him very much," I replied.

"Do you know Peter Nuremberg, chief of pediatric cardiac intensive care at D.C. Children's?" he asked.

"Yes, he is a legend in the field of pediatric cardiac intensive care. I have met him once before, briefly, at a conference; however, I don't know him well on a personal level," I replied.

"Well, I know Peter well. I would like you to reach out to him and see what his thoughts are on your approach to building the CICU. I need to make sure we have the right people in leadership positions here at Children's Hospital of Biloxi. You know, I would just like for him to hear what you are doing to develop the unit and to give his input," Mr. Boykins replied in a condescending and elitist manner. He coldly ended the meeting by sharing Peter's cell phone and instructed me to call him when I had the opportunity.

I left the meeting feeling insulted as I thought to myself, "Does this guy realize what I have sacrificed for this institution and does he realize the amount of progress we have accomplished in a relatively short period of time, and under such awful circumstances?" I felt nauseated and in hindsight, I should have recognized his behavior toward me as a prelude for things to come. Instead, I called Michael, the COO, and told him about my interaction with Mr. Boykins. He explained to me that Mr. Boykins was simply validating my approach and offering Peter Nuremberg as a resource to help ensure my success. He told me not to worry and that he had explained everything to Mr. Boykins, and they were both fully supportive of me as the leader of the CICU. He managed to reassure me and after speaking with Peter that day, he validated my approach and was impressed with the work that I had done, particularly given the obstacles I had encountered. By the end of the day, I felt much better about having the support I needed to succeed.

24

DRAMA IN THE PATIENT AND FAMILY WAITING ROOM

Following my meeting with Michael Stringer, I felt good about my support from the COO, which allowed me to refocus my attention on continuing to push things forward in the CICU. There were two things that I was currently focused on changing in the CICU, which I felt would be both advantageous to unit progress and more importantly, to improving patient care. The first change focused on the cardiac intensivists assuming responsibility for performing all necessary procedures for the patients in the CICU, which were currently being performed by the cardiac surgeons. These procedures included the placement of central venous lines, arterial lines, and chest tubes. Historically speaking, when a patient required a procedure, the cardiac surgeons would move these patients to the operating room so cardiac anesthesia could provide sedation. This process was cumbersome for the patient, OR staff and the CICU staff. At CHOB, because the patient was undergoing a procedure in the OR, this implied that they would then require a period of recovery in the post-anesthesia care unit (PACU) before returning to the CICU. This process was problematic for the nursing staff working in each of the areas involved, while also placing an unnecessary burden on already limited hospital resources and exposing the patient to the inherent risk associated with transporting a critical patient, in this case, three separate times. I was trained in procedural sedation and performing bedside procedures and had done so with regularity prior to arriving at CHOB. Justin had undergone the same training during his fellowship, so there was no reason to burden the staff or to place the patients at unnecessary risk by transporting them elsewhere. With Justin and I both willing and capable, one could provide sedation while the other performed the procedure. Additionally, all patient intubations in the CICU had been historically performed by anesthesia, even though we were now providing in-house coverage every night. While having in-house anesthesia was a nice safety net to have as a backup, I had been performing my own intubations for my entire career and was well aware of my limitations, plus it was a skill I simply did not wish to relinquish. In the field of pediatric cardiac intensive care, there are times when our patients are born with airway anomalies that make intubation challenging, and when such a scenario occurred, I would always ask anesthesia to perform the intubation or at least to be there at bedside should an issue arise. I grudgingly convinced myself that these particular scenarios were best addressed one-on-one with Dr. Rostri and Dr. Penton in private, which unfortunately meant meeting in the dreaded, arctic cold of the CICU conference room. So, I arranged a meeting that same day following completion of the scheduled cardiac surgery. Following arrival to the CICU, we settled the patient in and made sure they were stable and then an hour later, the three of us proceeded to the conference room to meet. As usual, we all arrived with our defenses up to begin the meeting, with the assumption that one was about to put the other in some sort of uncomfortable situation. Today, it was me leading the meeting rather than assuming my typical role as the suspect awaiting interrogation. "Dr. Rostri, I wanted to suggest something that I feel can help the patients and staff, while also helping to relieve one of the many responsibilities you two have been burdened by over the years. I would like to offer my help by assuming responsibility for providing sedation and performing procedures required for our patients in the CICU. The transportation and the need for anesthesia to provide sedation is unnecessary and expose the patients unnecessarily to the added risk involved with transporting a critical patient, followed by recovery in the PACU. I have been trained in this and have performed sedation and bedside procedures for my entire career and think it would be much more efficient and safer for the patient to perform these in the CICU. In addition, this is the expectation of the staff that I am hiring and those we continue to recruit. This is the model of care that many small-to-medium-sized programs around the country practice, particularly those with limited resources such as us, and it is essential in order for me to keep my staff proficient at these skills, not to mention it is something that our nurses should be skilled at as well," I explained.

A fifteen-minute period followed consisting of the usual, "Who do you think you are? I have been doing this for twenty years; how dare you think that you are more proficient at performing procedures than me." None of which I said, by the way. These psychologic warfare tactics were followed by Dr. Rostri storming out the conference room and slamming the door as Dr. Penton and I simultaneously stared down at our watches, as if counting down the thirty seconds we both knew it would take before he would reenter the room and reengage in the conversation. We both stared at our watches and proceeded to count down in our minds in unison, five … four … three … two … one, and right on cue, the door opened. "OK, I will allow it, but Justin cannot do procedures," he exclaimed.

"OK for starters, but let's revisit that after a period of time?" I asked.

"OK. Fine," he said, in a tone reminiscent of my daughters following a temper tantrum, who realized they had lost the battle but helplessly grasped to retain the appearance of control.

As we exited the room, Dr. Penton looked at me and smiled as he whispered, "You are starting to understand him now!" It was true! Over the next few weeks, Dr. Rostri would supervise every procedure I performed, as if I was a first-year critical care fellow in training once again. I swallowed my pride and kept my mouth shut, hell, I even sought his input on occasion, acknowledging that indeed he did have a substantial amount of experience that I could learn from, but also admittedly to feed his starving ego a bit and to gain his trust, which would be required to eventually allow Justin and my future hires to perform procedures as well. And it worked. Over time, Justin was allowed to perform procedures and I ended up performing all of my intubations outside of a few patients who were said to have difficult airways. I recommended to Justin that he practice conservatively when it came to intubations and if there was any question, call anesthesia who was always in-house, which he did. I viewed this as a major success for the CICU team and for patient safety and resource utilization.

The second area where I felt I could intervene and help improve patient care, while also helping relieve some burden from the cardiac surgeons, would prove to be a much greater challenge, so let me provide a little background. Performing pediatric cardiac surgery is difficult; however, when it came to performing cardiac surgery on newborns, this level of difficulty was on a whole different level. For the majority of complex newborns requiring cardiac surgery, these patients often return to the CICU with their sternum left open. This means that the incision created at the beginning of the surgery, necessary to provide the surgeon access to the heart and structures within the chest, remained open, now covered by an opaque material sutured in a lens-shaped manner, which connected the edges of the skin surrounding the opening, thereby providing a window, allowing visualization of the beating heart, while also functioning as an artificial barrier to help prevent infection, a task normally provided by the overlying skin. On top of this barrier, another sterile, transparent yellow, adherent bandage was placed, providing yet another layer of protection against infection. The idea behind this practice was that edema or swelling that occurs as a result of cutting into the heart muscle would occupy much of the space within the chest cavity, which was already limited. When combined with expectant bleeding that occurs after surgery, this edema results in a very small cavity for the heart muscle to function in, which can restrict and impair its ability to relax and contract inside the chest. In addition, if any blood accumulates in this small cavity, then the heart has virtually no space to relax and contract in, which can compromise the function of the heart and cause the baby to have low blood pressure, among other problems. By leaving the chest open for a couple of days, it allows time for the swelling to regress, the bleeding to cease, the heart function to improve and time for the baby's overall condition to stabilize. In babies with very complex heart disease there is still some degree of instability, even after a few days; as a result, the process of chest closure can be tenuous and a significant stressor for the baby. The process I became familiar with in Florida, involved either the cardiac intensive care physician or cardiac anesthesiologist giving the baby sedation and pain medication leading up to the procedure, which was then followed by the minute-to-minute management required to respond to hemodynamic changes including blood pressure, heart rate, and management of the mechanical ventilator that occurred during the process of chest closure. Oftentimes this process was lengthy, requiring additional sedation, administration of intravenous fluids or blood products as well as administration or titration of medications such as epinephrine in order to stabilize the baby. Sometimes, the baby didn't tolerate closure and would require reopening of the sternum in order to prevent cardiac arrest. Due to the complexity of this procedure, it requires a team, because the surgeons needed to be focused on performing the procedure while also directing the OR team, while the nurses and cardiac intensivist or anesthesiologist monitor changes in vital signs and clinical stability, responding accordingly when necessary with lifesaving interventions, all the while keeping the cardiac surgeon aware of clinical changes and the patient's overall condition.

Well, at Children's Hospital of Biloxi, this delicate procedure was performed in its entirety, by the cardiac surgeons, which in my eyes, was a nearly impossible task. At CHOB, the cardiac surgeons would perform the chest closure while titrating the sedative and narcotic infusions as well as the epinephrine infusions up and down while also directing the nurses to administer intravenous fluids or any other intervention needed to counteract low blood pressure that may develop during the procedure. Watching this process from outside the room was painful. In CICU medicine, early recognition and reaction to shifts in data trends or subtle changes in vital signs that occur are essential in order to prevent major problems from developing, because if they go unrecognized, they will inevitably result in catastrophe. If the surgeons both have their attention directed toward surgically closing the chest, they cannot possibly recognize and react to early clinical changes until the monitor alarm is triggered, which in many instances, is far too late to intervene and thereby prevent a correctable patient deterioration. In my time at CHOB, I observed several patients who failed chest closure, many of which I could confidently say resulted from late identification and intervention. Not because the cardiac surgeons were incapable of recognizing the trend, but merely because it is IMPOSSIBLE to do both simultaneously with great success. On several occasions, I had asked both Dr. Rostri and Dr. Penton, "Why doesn't anesthesia assist you during chest closure?"

To which Dr. Rostri replied, "We don't need them, we have done it this way for years."

"Of course he was going to say that," I thought as I chuckled to myself. "Well, why don't you let me help you?" I asked.

"No need, Eric, we have done this for years," he said again. Finally, one day, when the plan was to close the chest of a very complicated newborn in the CICU, I decided it was time to force my way into the procedure. That morning, I asked the bedside nurse in advance to set up a push line, which is the addition of extension tubing to the central venous line, allowing it to extend across the bed, and to reach beyond the length of the sterile drape they would place for the chest closure. Then I asked them to draw up intravenous fluid boluses into premeasured syringes and to draw up several bolus doses of sedation, pain medications, epinephrine, and calcium so we could be prepared to respond to any instability that was likely to occur during chest closure. Next, I asked the nurse to administer a sedative, an analgesic medication, and a dose of a paralytic medication to the baby, just as Dr. Rostri and Penton walked toward the room to begin the procedure. When Dr. Rostri entered the room, he directed the nurse, "Increase the fentanyl drip and give the baby a dose of paralytic."

"I already gave the baby some fentanyl and a dose of vecuronium (a paralytic), Dr. Rostri," I said.

"Oh, OK," he said, with a surprised look. I stood at the foot of the bed with the push line in hand and a table before me containing the fluids and medications I had requested, arranged neatly, as they started the procedure. As the case went on and the alarm would sound, Dr. Rostri would say, "Give …," and I would respond by saying, "I already gave …," as I explained whatever the intervention was I had just delivered. The chest closure was rocky, but the baby successfully tolerated the procedure, with a lot of interventions, and both cardiac surgeons were happy and thanked me for my assistance with the case. That was the last day the cardiac surgeons had the impossible duty of performing both tasks. From that day forward, Dr. Rostri would ask if I was available to assist with the chest closure. For the next several chest closures I had Justin observe and assist me, with the intention of teaching him to perform the procedure, but even more so to be sure Dr. Rostri witnessed me instructing him, hoping that this action would build confidence in Justin's ability to perform the task, just as it had with bedside procedures over time. Justin picked up the skill quickly, as I knew he would, honestly, it really was nothing more than typical cardiac intensive care unit postoperative management. These were activities we performed on a daily basis when patients were unstable upon arrival from the operating room. As I watched Justin pick up this skill quickly, I thought to myself, what a fantastic job he was doing. I always knew he was a skilled doctor who had been trained well; however, to excel in this unit, under such pressure, and in such a toxic environment, was admirable. He had come so far; I could hardly recall the beat-down man I saw when I first arrived at CHOB. When I first met him, Justin used to ride his skateboard to the hospital each day and the nurses would frequently tell me stories about him doing pull-ups in the doorway of patient rooms or of him riding office chairs on wheels around the CICU at nighttime while on call. The same guy who had built a home gym in the ten-feet-by-ten-feet call room we essentially called home the last several months. The same Justin who once strung a hammock to sleep in from the rafters of the ceiling of that same call room. I came to know Justin well over that time period, perhaps too well. Although admittedly, not only did I come to really care for him as a friend, but I continued to be impressed at the cardiac intensivist he had become in such a short period of time. I made it a point to share my observations related to his development with him. I also shared with him my belief that professional experience occurrs with each night call and with each unstable patient or complication he was forced to deal with, and due to the excessive number of night shifts we were working, his development was occurring at an acceler-ated rate, meaning that one year of experience may be closer to two to three years in his particular circumstance. I was grateful to have him there to help me develop and build the ICU, but I was also very worried about his risk of burnout, and quite frankly, I was equally worried about the same for me.

At Children's Hospital of Biloxi, directly across from the CICU and adjacent to the CICU conference room, was the "Family Waiting Room." This was a space designed for the families of our patients so that they may sit and wait for updates while their child was in surgery or while they were admitted to the CICU. There was also a table and chairs that provided a small space to eat. Directly behind the waiting room was a sleeping area that contained several chairs capable of fully reclining to become a single-occu-pancy bed, for family members to sleep in if their child required overnight or longer stays in the CICU. Other family members would occasionally bring sleeping bags and pillows to sleep on the floor. At any one time there could be up to ten different people sleeping in this room. While I knew that this room existed, I had no idea of the activities that took place within this whole different world outside the CICU. My first true introduction to this room came the same month that the new administrator arrived. While performing evening rounds, while on call in the CICU that evening, the parent of one of the patients who had been admitted to the CICU rushed into the unit yelling, "We need to call security immediately, there is a physical altercation in the family sleeping room!" Security was called and arrived promptly to find the father of a different patient in the CICU, bleeding profusely from a laceration of the skin above his left eye. Our social worker gathered information detailing the events and found that the father, in the middle of the night, while the mother had gone home to get some fresh clothes and to check on their other children that were being watched by the grandmother, was having sex with another patient's mother in the family room while the others in the room were asleep. When the mother returned and used the flashlight on her cell phone to find her sleeping spot, she realized it was empty and called her spouse's phone. When she followed the sound of the ringing cell phone, the noise led to her discovery that he was hiding under the covers with another patient's mother, naked. She proceeded to grab her tennis shoe and beat the father in the head with it until she eventually caused the laceration above his eye, resulting in the bleeding witnessed and the ensuing chaos in the room, which woke everyone. The mother was taken into custody but eventually released as details emerged and the father decided not to press charges; however, they were both removed from hospital property and only the mother was eventually allowed to visit but not to sleep overnight. This was one of several such sex, theft, or violent activities that I became aware of, which occurred over the two-and-a-half-year existence of this room, up until the new CICU and family waiting room was opened. The next most memorable case involved two young parents whose baby had been in the CICU for his entire life, which at that point was just over four months. The baby had horrendous heart disease and had been unfortunate enough to encounter nearly every complication that you could imagine during his hospital stay. The father had an extensive history of drug use and was frequently reported to social work by the nurses for being "stoned" when he came to visit his child. He and the mother had been warned twice before because they had been caught having sex in the patient and family room, once in the middle of the day, with the lights on as other families entered and exited the room to gather their belongings. The father wore the same long T-shirt, which read "Purple Drank," virtually every day, for more than a month. If you're not familiar with "Purple Drank," let me explain because I didn't know either until the social worker educated me on it. "Purple Drank" is the name used to describe a street drug made by mixing large amounts of prescription cough syrup, most commonly promethazine and codeine, with a carbonated soft drink and hard candy, giving it the characteristic purple appearance, hence the name "Purple Drank." Well, after being warned for being stoned and having sex in the room in broad daylight in the sleeping room of a children's hospital, Mom decided to make a trip home to get some clean clothes. You see where this is going right? Well, either Dad had been discretely harnessing his best Casanova moves in secret, for some time now, while Mom was there in the hospital, or he very quickly made successful advances on another patient's mother, but you guessed it, he proceeded to have sex with another one of the patient's mothers. When Mom returned, she didn't catch him in the act but one of the other family members, who had walked in on them in the act, reported what she saw to the mother. And just as though it was an episode straight out of Gerry Springer, the mother started pounding on the father until security removed them both. After cooling down, the mother was allowed to return, and the father was only allowed to visit his child while being accompanied by security.

25

MR. BOYKINS, MEET DR. ROSTRI

Rumors started to swirl that Dr. Rostri had made it his mission to influence Antoine Boykins upon his arrival to Children's Hospital of Biloxi, just as he had succeeded in doing with the hospital board members and university leaders. He made an appointment to meet with Mr. Boykins immediately following his arrival. Based on the recent actions of Gene Forester and probably following my suggestion to him as to the reason for such actions, Dr. Rostri likely suspected that Mr. Boykins, at minimum, was keeping a watchful eye over his actions and behaviors. Following my frigid interaction with Mr. Boykins, I couldn't help but think Dr. Rostri's "qualifications" or his suitability as the leader of the largest money-making specialty in pediatrics would be inspected closely under the microscope by our new leader. Dr. Potts would later validate the rumor that Dr. Rostri was attempting to influence Mr. Boykins, by explaining how he was the helpless victim and how he was never provided the resources he required to succeed. While there was certainly some truth to what Dr. Rostri was saying, it became clear that Mr. Boykins had been provided a thorough briefing, detailing the longstanding history of controlling behavior displayed by Dr. Rostri, including his unrelenting resistance to change, as well as the previous failed attempts by administration to terminate his employment. It was also believed that due to these previous failed attempts, Antoine Boykins had negotiated in his contract that he held the full authority to terminate Dr. Rostri without the requirement for approval from the university or hospital board members. Upon their first meeting, Mr. Boykins outlined a clear list of expectations that Dr. Rostri was to follow. He was given a timeline of six months to achieve these goals or at least he was given this timeline to change his controlling ways, and while the details outlined between the two of them were never made public, the timeline laid out was crystal clear. Dr. Rostri did not have a great track record when it came to change. During the previous administration, prior to their failed attempts to terminate his employment, they hired a life coach for him. The coach and he would meet weekly to review behavior challenges and the coach would suggest new ways to approach addressing the behavior. The coach lasted a total of two weeks before he actually quit. Life coaches are trained specialists who have extensive experience in dealing with difficult people. I have known many physicians who have electively utilized or been forced to utilize a life coach; however, Gerald Rostri was the first I had ever encountered that actually caused a life coach to quit! Given this knowledge pertaining to his past experience related to behavior intervention, I was skeptical that Mr. Boykins would succeed with his proposed interventions, although perhaps he never wanted Dr. Rostri to succeed and merely wanted to say that he provided him ample opportunity to change before terminating his employment. I believed this was likely the case based on the recent failed attempts by Gene Forester to randomly terminate him.

Meanwhile, for the first time, I felt as though Dr. Rostri and my relationship was improving. He was actually allowing some changes to occur in the CICU and he was starting to show some trust in Justin, which was wonderful to see. I hoped to have Adam, the new cardiac intensivist, join me on staff within the next month and Tim, my PA friend, was starting full-time soon. I was feeling very positive about the momentum I was experiencing in terms of our staff recruitment, and meanwhile, it was reassuring to see our CICU outcome data continue to improve, reflecting the progress we were observing in real time. Our hospital length of stay had improved to where we were consistently among the top 25 percent when compared to other top institutions and our median length of stay was now the same as our colleagues around the country, when previously our patients stayed in the hospital three days longer when compared to others performing the same surgery. While I was proud of the work we had done, I was exhausted, and I know Justin was too. We were literally counting the days until Adam and Astrid would join us, providing some relief from the extreme number of night shifts we were working.

Four months passed and state licensing delays occurred with Adam, which meant that he not only didn't have a medical license to practice in the state, but he could not even begin the credentialing process by Children's Hospital until his licensing was completed. Therefore, best-case scenario was that it would be at least one month before he could start working. Meanwhile, Justin and I were struggling. The lack of sleep was really getting to us both, whether I wanted to acknowledge it or not, my nighttime alcohol consumption, which in the short term calmed my nerves, allowing me to relax momentarily, and fall asleep, in the longer term was wreaking havoc on my ability to have any meaningful REM sleep. For anyone who has consumed more than a drink at nighttime, you understand that while alcohol may help you fall asleep, it does not provide you with quality REM sleep, in fact, it frequently causes you to awaken in the middle of the night. As a result, on the nights I slept at home, I found myself awakening at 3 or 4 a.m., unable to fall back asleep as my mind raced to review the multitude of tasks that lay ahead the following day. Usually, I would toss and turn for an hour or so, until I would finally give up, get out of bed and shower. I was exhausted in the morning, so my caffeine consumption had become outrageous. I was drinking a quadruple espresso in the morning before leaving the house, followed by another quadruple espresso after arriving to the hospital. During the week Justin and I would buy growlers of cold brew coffee, essentially a large glass jug of cold brew coffee, which we would finish within a day or two. We would order Uber Eats from a local coffee brewer, who would deliver the quad espresso, a growler of cold brew, and whatever drink each of the nurses wanted. Justin and I would alternate days where each of us took a turn paying for the delivery. We were at the hospital so much that year, that by the time the year ended, I had spent approximately $10,000 on coffee for us all, and I would assume Justin spent close to the same. It was absolutely insane. The more we worked, the more stress I felt, the more alcohol I drank at home, the more tired I became in the morning, the more coffee I drank throughout the day. It was a truly vicious cycle I wanted to end.

Eventually Dr. Potts notified us that the reason Adam's license had been delayed was due to the fact that his background check revealed that he had run a red light in another state resulting in a ticket, which he had not paid, thereby resulting in a bench warrant that had been served for his arrest. So, when he underwent the mandatory fingerprinting and background check required for a Mississippi State medical license, his application was flagged. On the application, he had checked the box that stated he had never been cited or convicted of a crime; therefore the board of medicine was flagging his application because it perceived that he was dishonest when he filled it out. It was an innocent error on his behalf; however, as a result, he had to go to court in the state of the violation, which was Texas, in order to pay the fine, then he needed to resubmit his application with the change stating that he had been cited for an offense, after which time he would need to await the board's decision. I was so nervous. After all this time to consider that he may not be able to join us was truly devastating. I didn't know how much longer I could work one hundred hours per week, not without at least seeing a light at the end of the tunnel. Fortunately, Dr. Deeton, the "good ol' boy" he was, knew someone at the state board who was able to get his licensing completed. I was relieved because it was a near catastrophe that could have sabotaged everything because Astrid may have changed her mind to join us as well had Adam not received his license, but fortunately this crisis was averted. However, the entire process would take an additional two months, plus an additional one month for credentialing. Meanwhile, Astrid's visa paperwork was moving along and with Adam's delays it looked as though she would be able to begin shortly after him.

I was on call the night I was notified that Adam's whole licensing debacle was finally resolved. The next morning I received a text message from Dr. Potts at 7 a.m. saying, "Eric, I need to talk with you. Please come to my office as soon as possible."

This was very odd. I had never seen or heard from Dr. Potts that early in the morning. I wondered what I could have done to be summoned to his office this early. Dr. Rostri also happened to be late for migration rounds that morning, so I told Justin, "I need to run across the street to Dr. Potts's office. He wants me to come by right away. I'm not sure what I have done, but it sounds urgent. You can join Dr. Rostri for 'migration rounds,' right?" I asked.

"Sure. No problem. Hope everything is alright," he said.

"Yeah. Me too," I responded. As I walked across the street, a thousand different thoughts raced through my mind as I contemplated things I could have done or said to get me into this type of trouble.

I arrived at Dr. Potts's office where he was waiting in the doorway to greet me. "Come in, Eric, and have a seat," he said urgently. I sat across from him at the circular table across from his desk as he said, "I need to inform you that right now Dr. Rostri is in the office of Antoine Boykins, where he is being told that his employment is being terminated, effective immediately. He will then be escorted to his vehicle by security and required to leave the premises." I was in utter shock and disbelief. I couldn't believe this was happening and I certainly couldn't believe it was happening like this. "Do you have any questions?" Dr. Potts asked.

I attempted to shake off what must have been a look of disbelief, as I stuttered, "Uh. No … I … uh … don't think so … uh right now, anyways," I said, feeling as if I was doing my best Dr. Deeton impersonation. I stood up and walked out of his office and out the doors of the building, heading back toward the hospital. As I approached the hospital, still in shock, I suddenly saw the large African American security guard, who was the head of security for the hospital, walking Dr. Rostri to his car as two administrators trailed in the background. As Dr. Rostri got into his car I could see him talking on his cell phone as he backed his car out of its parking space and prepared to leave. I froze as Dr. Rostri looked my way; I am not sure why, perhaps I thought he would think I was somehow involved with his dismissal; I don't know. I only know that I involuntarily pointed my head and eyes toward the ground and walked in the opposite direction, I guess I hoped that he would not see me. I simply walked in the opposite direction, astonished not only that they had terminated Dr. Rostri but had done so in such a despicable manner. It was ruthless and cold to treat a man who dedicated his life to building this program at a time when the hospital had nothing. He grew the program's surgical volume over the years and had surgical outcomes that were comparable with the rest of the country. Yes, there was significant morbidity, but as I said, this was primarily due to a lack of resources and the devastating effects of Hurricane Kelly. I couldn't believe what was taking place; they at least could have forced his retirement, given him a generous severance package, and thrown him a celebratory gala, even perhaps allowing him to be involved in the selection or recruitment of his replacement?

As Dr. Rostri drove away, I turned around, again redirecting my gait toward the main entrance of the hospital. At the entrance, there stood the large African American security guard and the two administrators, whom I did not know, staring down the street as Dr. Rostri's car disappeared out of sight. As I entered the hospital one of the administrators whom I would later find out was the head of hospital development and responsible for the construction project asked, "Are you OK, Dr. Philson?"

I looked at him puzzled and said, "A little shocked at what just happened, but I am OK." I walked directly to my office and sent a text to Justin. "Meet me in my office. I can't believe what just happened."

Justin arrived quickly and shut the office door. "What's going on?" he asked.

"Dr. Rostri was just fired! Dr. Potts called me to his office to notify me and as I was walking back toward the hospital, I saw Dr. Rostri being escorted to his car by security and two administrators. It was awful and so surreal to see it unfold before my eyes. I will never forget that sight. The only thing I could think of is that one day you are king of your domain, and the next day you are being escorted to your car by security. Really, I mean it, that is a reality check right there, we are all at the mercy of the hospital administration, and whether or not we fit their plan. Or perhaps we fit their plan until they use us to complete their agenda, and then they replace you," I said, as my hands were still shaking involuntarily from the shock of what I had just witnessed. Justin shared his disbelief at what had happened. I understood the positive cascade of events Dr. Rostri's termination would have on me personally as well as the CICU, but my mind couldn't get beyond the disgusting treatment of a man who was so passionate and dedicated to his patients. I knew that this likely meant that I could finally have true ownership of the CICU and push progress at a much faster pace; however, it was impossible for me to even entertain basking in any such glory at the time. In retrospect, the fact that I was unable to find happiness in this moment, a moment which carried such significance, as it instantly granted me the autonomy I so deeply desired, was actually an instinctual understanding that this administration held little regard for the dedication displayed by a man who had devoted his entire life to caring for the children of Mississippi. If Mr. Boykins could act in such a way toward a man who had done so much for the organization, it meant no one, including me, would ever truly be safe. As I attempted to process these complex feelings, it was impossible to celebrate my gain, particularly in the face of Dr. Rostri's demise. I failed to realize at the time, but this action by Mr. Boykins was a red flag, one that we all overlooked, but nonetheless, it was a sign, warning us of what was to come. It was attempting to teach us that behaviors displayed by leaders at the very top (i.e., the CEO) don't change, and the consequences of ruthless behaviors, such as those displayed on that day, trickle down through the entire organization, affecting us all, while delivering a message of fear and instability that reads "I do not care about the number of years you have worked, or patients whose lives you have saved, or how your dedication has benefited the hospital, you will do as I say or you will be escorted to your car by security, because you are all replaceable." If I knew then what I know now, I would have resigned that day, and my lack of awareness, as it relates to this dark message, would come back to haunt me in the future.

The news of Dr. Rostri's termination spread like wildfire. There was a mixture of panic, sadness, shock, and admittedly there were many who quietly celebrated his departure. But regardless of the emotion felt, there was one consistent underlying theme that resonated, and that was the shock that was felt due to the unmitigated disrespect displayed by Antoine Boykins and the manner in which he terminated Dr. Rostri. The lingering question on the minds of the CICU staff was, who would be the new chief of pediatric cardiac surgery? Would it be Dr. Penton? If so, would it be an interim title or permanent? Shortly after arriving to my office and explaining the details of what had just occurred, I received a text from Dr. Penton, asking if we could meet in the conference room. "Sure. I will be right there," I replied.

I entered the ice-cold conference room and sat directly across from Dr. Penton, who was already seated. Admittedly, it felt odd to be sitting there without Dr. Rostri directly beside him. Dr. Penton held his head in his hands, rubbing his balding head repeatedly in a distressed manner. He looked pale as if he had seen a ghost. "Eric, I don't know what to say. I am in shock. I don't know who I can trust. I just finished speaking to Antoine Boykins and he has asked me to function in an interim role as the chief of pediatric cardiac surgery. I had no choice but to accept. But honestly, I don't know if I will be the next to be terminated. I know they need me right now and they asked if I felt I was capable of functioning in that role. I told them I was, but honestly, I feel disloyal. Dr. Rostri has been calling me and telling me I should resign, then they would have to reconsider their decision to terminate him; however, I can't quit, I need this job, I can't take that risk and I feel guilty saying this, but part of me really wants this position and I am not sure if Dr. Rostri would have ever given me the opportunity. Who knows, but what I need to know is can I trust you?" he asked as tears began to emerge.

"Look, Terry, as I told you before, you can trust me. As I have always said, I have never been out to get Dr. Rostri or anyone else for that matter. This institution has been attempting to use me as their pawn to carry out their shady plans from the moment I arrived here in Biloxi. I had nothing to do with the firing of Dr. Rostri. I am absolutely appalled by the manner in which they have done it, but here we are. Yes, you and I need to trust one another, and I believe in you and feel that you can do great things as our leader," I explained emotionally.

"Thanks. I am going to need a month or so to transition into this new role, but I am going to hand the CICU over to you; however, I still want to be involved," he said.

"That means a lot to me to have your trust. I won't let you down and yes, I most certainly want you to remain involved. I will also need a little time to transition myself, but I would like to modify our morning surgical rounds to be more collaborative. I will run my idea by you once I have the format more firmly established in my mind," I said.

"Sounds good, Eric. Thanks," he replied. We gave each other a big man hug, and both dried our eyes before we exited the conference room. I met with Justin, Ruth, and Maddie and discussed everything that had happened as well as the plans moving forward in regard to changes affecting the CICU. We would have many meetings over the next month to discuss these plans, including prioritizing the implementation of clinical management protocols we had been developing. The events that had just transpired uncovered a mixture of emotions for me. I felt sad for Dr. Rostri, and I became somewhat skeptical regarding my ability to trust the CEO, but admittedly I was excited about the prospect of finally moving the CICU forward at a faster pace. One of my top priorities consisted of reaching out to Adam and Astrid to be sure they were aware of the change in surgical leadership that had taken place and to be certain that I reassured them that everything was fine, as a change such as this could always scare candidates away. I reached out to both of them and explained what had happened and that while sad and shocking, it would allow the CICU to progress more rapidly and allow us greater autonomy. I also explained that I had faith in Dr. Penton as our new chief of pediatric cardiac surgery, and I promised to keep them updated weekly as to how things were progressing. They were both in agreement that while surprised by the events that occurred, they still had every intention of joining me as colleagues in the CICU, which helped put my mind at ease.

Over the next few days, several more disturbing details emerged regarding the great lengths to which Mr. Boykins and his team had gone to undermine Dr. Rostri with the excuse that they were ensuring "protection of the hospital." In advance of implementing the brutal measures they used to terminate Dr. Rostri, Mr. Boykins had reached out to many of the more prestigious law firms throughout the city of Biloxi and had offered compensation to each of them in return for guaranteeing that they would refuse to represent Dr. Rostri, attempting to avoid any potential litigation against Children's Hospital of Biloxi. Signs displaying Dr. Rostri's photo, as if mug shots of an escaped felon, were placed at every entrance to the hospital, at the direction of Mr. Boykins, which instructed security to prevent him from entering the hospital at all costs. The final, and perhaps most disturbing, aspect detailing the lengths to which Mr. Boykins would go to "protect the hospital" was that he interfered with Dr. Rostri's ability to obtain employment anywhere in the state of Mississippi. Following his termination, Dr. Rostri's connections at the University of Southeastern Mississippi had allowed him to obtain employment as an adult cardiac surgeon, which in no way represented competition for CHOB. However, despite this arrangement being in place, one-week later Dr. Rostri was notified that the university was unable to offer him the position anymore. I was simply amazed and nauseated after discovering the lengths to which this administration would go to not only terminate a man who had dedicated his life to building the congenital surgery program at CHOB, but the measures they would use to ensure that he had no hopes of obtaining employment in the state at all. While I ultimately came to understand that the decision to appoint a new chief of pediatric cardiac surgery was necessary to advance the entire congenital heart program, the manner by which it was done was disrespectful and appalling and quite frankly unnecessary. But I would have to mentally digest this situation and move forward.

26

SEARCH FOR THE NEW CHIEF OF PEDIATRIC CARDIOLOGY AND MEETING THE REFERRING CARDIOLOGISTS

From the time of my hiring at Children's Hospital of Biloxi, I was told that the same recruiting firm responsible for my hiring had also been hired to lead the national search for a chief of pediatric cardiology, a search that had been ongoing for two years. The previous chief and his wife, who was also a pediatric cardiologist, were terminated a few months prior to my arrival at the request of Dr. Rostri. Apparently there had been long-standing friction between the surgeons and the husband-wife combination that was affecting patient care, so Dr. Rostri had convinced the previous administration to part ways with the two of them. Since that time, two candidates had interviewed approximately a month prior to my start date; however, both candidates had turned down the position. Since that time, the candidate pool had dried up. Approximately two months prior to the arrival of the new administration, Dr. Potts had asked Dr. Eric Saltiel, interventional cardiologist, if he would fill the vacancy as the interim division chief of pediatric cardiology. As I mentioned earlier, Dr. Saltiel had substantial experience as a leader, and he agreed to do so to provide some direction and leadership for the cardiology department; however, given his experience in such a role in the past, he understandably agreed to do so in an interim role only, and emphasized that he had no interest in being a long-term candidate for the job. Dr. Saltiel served in this role masterfully and displayed his natural ability as a leader. He was soft-spoken, but vocal when needed, he was extremely intelligent, and was well respected and admired by everyone throughout the congenital heart program.

A month after Dr. Rostri's termination, as promised, Dr. Penton turned the CICU over to me and my team. Tim, my PA friend, had officially accepted our offer and was now working full-time as an APP. Adam was a month or two from finally starting as a staff cardiac intensivist and Astrid was only three to four months from having her visa situation taken care of, after which she would be able to begin working. It was just in time too, as Justin and I were really struggling from the one-hundred-hour workweeks, which had now been ongoing for a full year. I had started feeling extremely fatigued and for some reason was having hot flashes where my face would turn red for no reason. I had been trying to use Justin's pseudo-gym he had set up in the call room because I felt extremely out of shape and had noticed that I was beginning to become short of breath easily with minimal activity, most likely from lack of sleep and a not so healthy diet of caffeine and snack food while at the hospital. Despite feeling exhausted, our CICU length of stay and infection rate continued to improve. Our length of stay over the next month would fall into the top five among all programs participating in the database. This was a major accomplishment. Word of mouth reached the administration, and Michael Stringer, COO, had come down to the CICU to speak with the team and congratulate us all on this major accomplishment and had communicated this feat with leaders all the way to the top, including Mr. Boykins.

After a month's time, you could really see a team beginning to develop. Dr. Penton was doing an exceptional job at both operating and leading us all. He trusted me, I trusted him, and we both trusted Dr. Saltiel. I had begun incorporating the cardiology team members into CICU medical rounds in order to engage them and to get their input on the management of the patients we were caring for in the unit. Cardiology's past relationship with Dr. Rostri was less than ideal, especially following the forced departure of the previous cardiology division chief and his wife due to his insistence. They didn't feel welcomed in the CICU and for the most part, Dr. Rostri did not seek their input outside of the weekly presurgical conference, where patients in need of surgery were discussed, and even then, it was primarily Dr. Saltiel's opinion that was sought. As a result, they mostly felt excluded, and I did feel that this had a negative impact on patient care. So, incorporating them into CICU medical rounds was not just a kind gesture, it was truly needed in order to have a multidisciplinary approach to patient care. Another major change that we were able to implement was the concept of family-centered care. This national movement started to take place when I was still completing my fellowship training several years ago. In the past, intensive care units had visitation hours, where families could come see their child who was admitted to the unit, during predetermined times. Then many units progressed toward twenty-four-hour visitation, but still required families to leave the unit if any child was undergoing a medical procedure or if a cardiac arrest occurred. Then the concept of family center care began to take hold, which allowed families to remain in the unit while a sterile procedure took place, just not directly at the bedside in order to maintain sterility. That continued to evolve until it included allowing families to stay in the unit at all times, including during episodes of decompensation requiring cardiopulmonary resuscitation (CPR), so that the families could see that the team was doing everything they could to save their child's life. The other part of this evolutionary process was to encourage the families to be present at the bedside during medical rounds each morning, so that they could listen to the team present the data from the previous twenty-four hours, hear the discussion by the team, and ultimately be included in the plan and some of the decision-making process, while also offering a time for the family to ask questions pertaining to the care plan outlined. This process had been adopted by most institutions around the country for some time. However, upon my arrival to Children's Hospital of Biloxi, this concept was not only foreign, it was also heavily discouraged. The unit would still completely shut down during procedures, so all families were required to leave the unit and families were not allowed to join "migration rounds" in the morning and in fact, they were asked to leave during that time. Families were definitely not allowed to enter the unit or were asked to leave if their child decompensated or required CPR. Since we implemented CICU medical rounds, we had started encouraging families to join, which was very well received by all except the cardiac surgeons. Since Dr. Rostri's unfortunate departure, Dr. Penton had allowed, although somewhat grudgingly at first, families to stay in the unit during procedures and even gave in to allowing families to be present during code-blue situations. This was amazing progress, and the families were ecstatic about these changes. Families who had children that required more than one cardiac surgery were simply astonished at the changes that had occurred when they returned for their next staged operation. Due to the fact that Mississippi was one of the poorest states in the country, many of the patients we cared for had Medicaid insurance. But what I came to find out, shortly after my arrival, was that many patients with traditional health insurance either sought referral independently or were intentionally referred to top programs outside the state, such as Boston Children's and Stanford University, as directed by their private cardiologists. However, now as word of mouth traveled among the families of children with complex heart disease, we were beginning to see some patients who chose to come to Children's of Biloxi for their care, rather than return to Boston or Stanford. This was a great sign that our changes were starting to influence some referral patterns. But still many patients were being referred outside the state by private cardiologists around Mississippi. This was a major focus of the new administration and for the cardiac team at CHOB. We felt like the care we were offering was now comparable with that provided by many top programs around the country, but we needed to convince some of the referring cardiologists that this was the case.

In an attempt to share our progress within the institution and throughout Mississippi, Michael Stringer had suggested that first Dr. Penton, Dr. Saltiel, and myself deliver a presentation named "The Current State of the Heart Center," which was to include data detailing our CICU outcomes, surgical outcomes, and data related to the expansion of our cardiology clinics as well as data related to the increase in clinic volume. We were scheduled to present these data to the hospital board and hospital administration. Michael Stringer felt it would be meaningful to show these positive changes to them because as I came to understand, the board had been skeptical about the termination of Dr. Rostri. I understood this was Mr. Boykins's attempt at convincing the board that he was "right," and I certainly didn't feel great about validating the inexplicable treatment of Dr. Rostri; however, it was at least an opportunity for the board members to see our incredible progress, which was really due to the accomplishments of the team, rather than the dismissal of Dr. Rostri. The three of us presented our data and the board members appeared delighted, and a couple of board members at the end of the presentation actually gave one another high-fives at the end saying, "See we did make the right decision to let Dr. Rostri go." It was sad to hear such nonsense, but at least they got to hear the progress we had all made. I realized that they could try to reconcile the demons in their own mind regarding his departure, if that's what they needed to do in order to sleep at night, but I knew this was far from the truth.

Following completion of the board presentation, the next stop on the "Heart Center tour" was dinner with the private cardiology group in Jackson, Mississippi. This group consisted of three cardiologists and boasted the largest pediatric cardiology practice in the state. The founder of the practice, Dr. Morgan Lorthrap, was a native of Mississippi; however, he had undergone his medical training at Stanford University, and it was believed that he and his group referred the largest number of patients outside the state of Missis-sippi. Dr. Lorthrap was a man in his early sixties. He had grey hair and was known to be somewhat emotionally unstable. His relationship with Chil-dren's Hospital of Biloxi was fragile at best, and his referrals over the years were inconsistent and primarily consisted of Medicaid patients who had no other choice but to receive their care at CHOB. Dr. Penton and Dr. Saltiel had known Dr. Lorthrap for many years. Dr. Saltiel spoke to him with some regularity in order to update him on his patients following cardiac catheter-izations he would perform on them. While Dr. Penton knew him and would speak with him on occasion, Dr. Rostri was typically the point person who spoke with Dr. Lorthrap, from a surgical perspective, while I was yet to make his acquaintance. The three of us met Dr. Lorthrap at the finest restaurant in Jackson. We all sat at a table in the middle of this highly touted Italian restau-rant. Dr. Penton started things off by introducing me to Dr. Lorthrap. He shook my hand and then proceeded to go off on a ten-minute tangent about Dr. Borland, who had previously been a partner in his practice. "This fucking guy. This fucking piece of shit. I can't fucking believe Children's would employ this motherfucker," Dr. Lorthrap virtually screamed at the top of his lungs in the middle of this fine establishment, as he continued to drop F-bombs, for what seemed like an eternity. I was so embarrassed, as we sat in the middle of this restaurant with every other patron staring at us as he cursed in the most vulgar manner you could imagine.

"Morgan, please," Dr. Penton said, urging him to at least lower his voice. As the cursing finally stopped, I could see everyone start to relax. I never have and never would understand why he despised Dr. Borland so much, but the evening finished with each of us presenting a short spiel about the current state of the Heart Center, which included sharing of our CICU outcome data.

At the end, Dr. Lorthrap acknowledged my existence for a brief moment and said, "Dr. Philson, thank you for coming to Mississippi. I know it hasn't been easy for you but the long stays in the CICU, experienced by many of my patients, have been a concern of mine as well as a concern of my partners for some time now. We are happy that you are here."

As we walked to our cars, Dr. Penton stopped and looked at me and said, "I told you he was an interesting character."

"That's putting it lightly," I said. "Safe drive home."

"You too," he replied.

The following week, the next stop on the tour was to be at the practice of Dr. Alan Glinton, which was in Hattiesburg, Mississippi. For this trip, we rode together in a van; however, this time, along with Dr. Penton, Dr. Saltiel, and me, came Michael Stringer, COO of Children's Hospital of Biloxi. Again, Dr. Penton and Dr. Saltiel both knew Dr. Glinton well. He was notoriously difficult to work with. Dr. Saltiel's interaction was again primarily to update him following cardiac catheterizations he performed on his patients, and similar to Dr. Lorthrap, Dr. Rostri did most of the direct communication with Dr. Glinton, so while he knew Dr. Penton well, he viewed him as more of the "second cardiac surgeon." Dr. Glinton was a short, overweight man who was notoriously difficult to deal with from an interpersonal perspective. He had an inconsistent history, at best, of referring patients to Children's Hospital of Biloxi. To make matters more complicated, he was a relatively incompetent pediatric cardiologist and rumor was he would inappropriately schedule multiple follow-up visits for patients found to have a simple patent foramen ovale, which is a small communication found as a normal variant between the two upper chambers of the heart and is something that many of us may find we have if we were we to all undergo echocardiograms. However, in the absence of any other abnormalities, this does not typically warrant follow-up. Reportedly, he would have these patients follow up at least one or two times and perform an echocardiogram at each visit and bill the patient for this expensive test. In addition to a difficult personality, and some shady clinical practices, he was known to use patient referrals to negotiate something that benefited him, whether it be financial or something else he found beneficial for himself, such as attempting to get his daughter admitted to medical school at the University of Southeastern Mississippi. He was constantly attempting to get Children's Hospital administration to do something for him, whether it be to buy his practice for an astronomical amount or some other extreme ask. To make matters worse, in the rare instance he did refer a patient, again it was typically a Medicaid patient, and while we obviously had no issue with caring for any patient, regardless of their insurance, his referral simply meant that he was sending the patient to us because he had no other choice. He was known for owning expensive cars and luxury properties while also being smug and passive aggressive. He and Dr. Rostri got along very well, so his perceived problem when it came to Children's Hospital was usually with the hospital administration. Michael Stringer had mentioned to us on the drive there that Dr. Glinton was very upset with the termination of Dr. Rostri and questioned what our team had to offer as he appeared to have little faith in Dr. Penton's ability as the chief of pediatric cardiac surgery and as the leader of the Heart Center. As the van pulled up in front of Dr. Glinton's clinic, Michael Stringer quickly reviewed the goals of our visit. Mr. Stringer was to begin with an introduction of himself, followed by a review of the changes that had occurred since Dr. Rostri's departure. Michael was to be followed by Dr. Penton, then by me, and lastly, Dr. Saltiel. We would each give a brief review outlining the current state, including recent data, and accomplishments within our respective divisions. Michael also told us that Dr. Glinton had a partner who also saw patients in his clinic, although he was pretty quiet and didn't talk much. It was believed that his partner was likely to be departing the practice in the next several months because Dr. Glinton treated him so poorly, paid him very little, and rarely sought his input regarding decisions related to the office. As we exited the van and entered the office building, which Dr. Glinton owned, the lobby of the office appeared elegantly decorated, and in the waiting area were two patients with their respective family, waiting to be seen. As we entered, we were met by Rita, Dr. Glinton's clinic manager, who was reported to be even more rude and passive-aggressive than he was. She greeted us with a fake smile and explained to us how busy Dr. Glinton was, and as a result, we would need to wait in his office for him to see us. We followed Rita through a door revealing a hallway lined on both sides with doors, which inside, housed the individual clinic exam rooms. Hung on the wall of the hallway, leading to the clinic area, was a massive sign that read "Alan Glinton, MD," while humorously, or to be more precise, pathetically, below his name, hung a much smaller sign, reading, "Joseph Toth, MD," although you may have had to squint to read it with certainty. The sign was no more than half the size of Dr. Glinton's and was clearly metaphoric for the amount of respect he held for his "colleague." As Rita led us to Dr. Glinton's office she repeated again, "Dr. Glinton is extremely busy and he won't compromise patient care, so you may have to wait a little while." Gleaming her fake smile toward us once again, as she sat us each in chairs that had been arranged to assimilate theater-style seating, consisting of two rows of chairs lined up in front of his massive mahogany desk containing elegant carvings, behind which was an oversized, padded office chair with elevated armrests, which coincidently, I am sure, resembled a throne.

I glanced at Dr. Penton with my eyes wide open, saying to myself, "Where the hell am I right now?" as I felt that this may actually be another planet.

After waiting for approximately fifteen minutes, in strolled Dr. Glinton, short and fat, just as advertised, repeating the same spiel as Rita, "Alright guys, I don't have much time so let's hear what you have to say," as he sat in his chair, immediately dwarfed by its size and that of the giant desk he sat behind, as if a child playing grown-up at their parent's desk. As Michael Stringer shook off his disbelief at what was occurring, he gave a well-spoken and direct presentation of the current state of affairs at CHOB, which was met with Dr. Glinton's astounding delivery of the wise words, "Oh … OK …," in what can best be described as a smug and almost feminine voice that came attached to a fake smile, so vile it caused us each to cringe in our theater-style seats. He sat unenthusiastically on his throne, I mean chair, waiting for the next person to speak, as if a king unamused by the first gesture's performance as he voiced his displeasure by saying the words, "Awful, who's next?" Dr. Penton also shook off his shock at the disrespect that was occurring at that very moment, but he managed to move on and explain his sadness with the release of his friend and mentor, Dr. Rostri. However, he explained that he was fully capable of filling the void as the division chief of pediatric cardiac surgery and the leader of the Heart Center and went on to detail the complex cases he had undertaken and the excellent outcomes that had occurred since the change in surgical leadership had occurred. Dr. Glinton, unamused, said, "OK. Next!" It was my turn. I went on to deliver the dramatic shift in data we had seen during a short period of time and how we had shifted to a family-centered— "Uh, sorry, where did you train?" he asked, rudely interrupting me mid-sentence.

I stuttered a bit, surprised by the rudeness he had displayed. I began to explain, "I completed my critical care fellowship at—"

"Uh, well I trained at Columbia University." Which was actually not true, as his training certificate hanging on the wall directly behind his desk clearly showed, he trained at one of the smaller New York programs. I had heard that he frequently boasted that he studied at an Ivy League training program that he actually did not attend. As he finished name-dropping a university he didn't attend, I said, OK. I think that's all I have. I was done with this guy.

Dr. Saltiel jumped in and continued to boast about all the work my team and I had done in the CICU and how the reduction in hospital length of stay was astronomical and he asked Dr. Glinton confidently, "Wasn't that the major complaint and reason you have stated in the past for not referring patients consistently? Well, that no longer exists." Dr. Saltiel went on to present the progress that he had achieved in the cardiology department.

Upon completion of the entire talk by the group, King Glinton said, smugly, again in a rather feminine voice and with a fake smile, "OK, guys. Well, I am sorry, I am just not feeling confident about what you as a group have to offer me or my patients. I guess we will have to see what happens over time. Thanks so much for your time. Rita, please show them out," as if summoning the guards to remove us from the castle.

We all stood up as Michael Stringer said, "Thank you for your time, Dr. Glinton, but I just want to finish by saying that we feel pretty good about the group we have and care that they provide, and we hope you will keep an open mind as we continue to communicate with you and share our fantastic clinical results." The two of them shook hands and we all walked out to the van, feeling quite offended and as though we all needed a shower to wash the disgusting feeling of negativity and toxicity that overwhelmed the room, which now felt as though it was stuck to our skin. As we drove back toward Biloxi, we were all disgusted but relieved that it was over. Michael Stringer thanked us for going through the painful process and noted that he was notoriously difficult to deal with and that all further dialogue between Dr. Glinton and Children's Hospital of Biloxi would be via Mr. Boykins. He repeated that we should all be proud of our accomplishments and that this interaction with Dr. Glinton was not unexpected and was a reflection of who he was individually and not who we were collectively. I appreciated his words. They were the words of a true leader and team builder, but I couldn't help but be amazed at what an awful human being Dr. Glinton was and how I felt for the patients that he cared for.

Our final stop on the Mississippi statewide Heart Center promotional tour would take place the following week, involving the city of Starkville, Mississippi, and the office of Dr. Steven Kleinburg. Dr. Kleinburg was a German-born pediatric cardiologist, who completed his training in Ohio. He moved to Mississippi following his training for visa purposes and had resided in Starkville for the duration of his career, building a successful practice over the last fifteen-plus years. His referrals to Children's Hospital of Biloxi were inconsistent and had actually dwindled to single digits over the previous five years, prior to my arrival in Biloxi. The reason for this was uncertain but it was felt that he had established a relationship with the University of Alabama, which was actually closer in terms of distance for his patients. The few referrals that CHOB did receive from him were critical newborns who were likely refused by the program in Alabama, so they were typically ones unlikely to survive due to severe forms of complex congenital heart disease.

During the two brief conversations I had encountered with Dr. Kleinburg, he seemed as though he was a kind man, a bit on the anxious side, but intelligent, nonetheless. As we arrived in the van to his office, following a long four-hour journey, it felt good to get out and stretch our legs. Michael Stringer again joined us on this journey and had laid out the same approach for our presentation of data and progress to Dr. Kleinburg. As we entered the front doors leading inside the beautiful office building, Dr. Kleinburg graciously welcomed us in the family waiting room of his clinic. For this visit, we had arranged the meeting time to be after clinic hours, as not to waste his valuable time. He met us all with a friendly handshake and thanked us for the visit. We each delivered our portion of the presentation effectively and Dr. Kleinburg showed particular interest in our CICU data as well as our transition from a surgeon-run CICU toward a model where cardiac intensivists staffed the unit and provide 24-7 in-house coverage, which was the model he was familiar with during his fellowship training in Ohio. He was very excited about these changes and laid out a very honest explanation detailing the reasons that his patient referral numbers had declined in recent years. At the top of his list was the prolonged hospital length of stay his patients had experienced in the CICU following their cardiac surgery, hence his excitement with the changes we had made. The other concern of his was the multiple steps that he would encounter while trying to transfer a patient to Children's Hospital of Biloxi. "Being completely honest, I want to pick up the phone, speak with one person, and know that the process of transferring a patient is being taken care of and that the team will arrive as soon as is feasible. In the past I have been asked to call many different people to set up the transfer and this process becomes too cumbersome and time-consuming because I am alone here in this practice and cannot afford to spend my day on the phone when I have many patients to see in clinic. In all honesty, I have established this type of relationship with the University of Alabama and quite simply, the distance is closer for my patients. So, if Children's Hospital of Biloxi was able to address this issue and simplify this process, I would gladly consider increasing the number of patients that I refer to you," he stated with sincere honesty.

I thought to myself, "This is a reasonable guy with reasonable expectations. These are issues of patient quality and when a physician is not referring patients because he can ensure better quality for his patients elsewhere, I cannot fault them for that."

"I completely understand, Dr. Kleinburg, these are valid concerns. I definitely feel like we can address them in a short period of time for you. I promise to work on developing a system that we feel will work best for your patients and you and get back with you regarding the details of our proposal very soon," explained Michael Stringer, appearing equally sincere. Dr. Kleinburg appeared pleased, and we thanked one another as we headed to dinner, which we had arranged at the finest restaurant in Starkville, Mississippi. Dinner was excellent and I had an opportunity to talk in great detail with him. He told me about his family and about the challenges he faced in finding employment after completion of his pediatric cardiology fellowship, due to his visa restrictions. He was proud of the practice that he had built and was now officially a U.S. citizen, and I told him that he indeed had much to be proud of. He again expressed his excitement for the work we had done to improve and update the CICU, and agreed with the importance of achieving our goal, which was to provide medical care equaling the standard of care already provided to most children around the country, care that the children of Mississippi so desperately deserved. He told me of his house on a lake nearby, not far from his practice and he invited me to join him sometime for fishing on the lake. I thanked him and told him that I would happily consider. As we drove the long four hours back to Biloxi, I reflected on how impressed I was with Dr. Kleinburg as a kind and reasonable human being and for all he had achieved while building his practice. Admittedly, I felt the complete opposite about him as a person when compared to the feelings I harnessed for Dr. Glinton, when we left his office just one week ago. I also realized the realness this tour was relaying to the referring cardiologists, whether they chose to acknowledge it or not. It highlighted the vision, teamwork, and personal touch Michael Stringer was having us portray to the private cardiologists, which again spoke volumes about his elite skill as a leader and as a kind and caring individual. I could see that he believed in Dr. Penton, Dr. Saltiel and me as leaders, even if others did not. Perhaps to outsiders or those unwilling to look beyond the paper, the three of us were nobodies or misfits, but somehow, we found a way to mesh and work together as a team, and as a result, we were now providing specialized patient care at a level that exceeded anything delivered to the children of Mississippi before, and just as Michael, I felt proud about that.

27

HEART CENTER TEAM PROGRESS

With our statewide tour now complete, we were back to work. Justin and I continued to work one-hundred-hour workweeks. I continued to feel fatigued and somewhat short of breath with mild exertion, while still experiencing unexplained periods where my face would turn red. I decided to schedule an appointment with an internal medicine physician. I had not undergone a medical exam in more than a decade, so it was clear that something felt off for me to consider doing so. Given the persistence of these new onset symptoms, my physician decided to order some laboratory work and a chest X-ray, neither of which revealed any abnormalities, so we both attributed my symptoms to stress and a lack of sleep; therefore, I carried on with my current work schedule, while I desperately awaited the arrival of Adam and Astrid. My nighttime alcohol consumption when at home, continued to escalate, and I was now averaging two to three three-fingered Scotches each night, just to achieve that momentary relaxation my body and mind craved, which again, allowed me to initiate sleep, but only lasted a few hours before I would awaken, unable to fall back asleep. I knew it was a problem, and I knew it was worsening, but it is what I had at that moment in time, and it was helping me get by.

At this point the hospital had begun utilizing electronic medical records, and despite a rocky transition, it felt incredible to finally do away with paper charting and to remove the volumes of medical records that had occupied the majority of space atop the medical carts and bedside tables at many of the patient's bedside. By this time, all five of the warriors had passed. It was a relief to know that their suffering had ended; it was also a huge emotional relief for the staff to know the same. This simultaneous passing of the warriors and the implementation of electronic medical records appeared strangely symbolic, as if announcing the changing of the guard and the arrival of a new day in the CICU, an end to the tumultuous but admirable legacy of Dr. Rostri, with the dawn of a new era, whose story was yet to be told or written, uncertain, yet filled with hope and potential.

Dr. Penton was thriving as the new chief of pediatric cardiac surgery. He had verbally committed to mentoring Doris Geisinger and allowing her to perform more complex cardiac surgeries. She continued operating with her mentor in Alabama, and she appeared pleased with the new opportunity that existed at CHOB. Now that Dr. Rostri had been terminated, he was no longer able to restrict the number and complexity of the cardiac surgeries she could perform. However, as we spoke, she appeared distanced and less engaged with the rest of the team, which was a noticeable change that had occurred since she had begun operating with her mentor in Alabama. I could sense her lack of confidence in our new administrators' ability to recruit a top pediatric cardiac surgeon to lead our program. While Dr. Penton had been arranging more cases for her to perform, their relationship was severely damaged as a consequence of her mistreatment at the hands of Dr. Rostri, and I remained skeptical that it was reparable. Equally, I could sense that she was unsure that she wanted to be trained by Dr. Penton as he was a disciple of Dr. Rostri. Her outside mentoring had immersed her in a system that was familiar to her, awakening memories of her time in Boston, where she thrived. Each of these factors when analyzed in summation, led me to believe that her remaining days in Biloxi were likely to be numbered. It was a difficult situation for Dr. Penton as well, because he was learning how to be a leader, while he himself was learning to operate independently for complex cases, something that he and Dr. Rostri had always done together. Remember, Dr. Rostri barely allowed Dr. Penton to operate in his absence, and when he did, he only allowed him to do so with less complex cases. From what I could ascertain from afar, for Dr. Penton, the challenge was less about the technical aspects associated with complex surgeries; instead, it was gaining real-time, invaluable decision-making experience on the fly and in the moment, experience he simply hadn't been permitted to acquire during his career, due to the controlling nature of Dr. Rostri. Experience only comes with exposure and time, and obviously time cannot be rushed. The process of developing critical thinking experience can only occur when there is repeated exposure to stressful situations, thereby demanding immediate thought and action. When leaders are controlling, they neglect their understudies' exposure to such stressful yet necessary clinical scenarios. Such exposure is essential if a clinician is to gain the experience required to master critical decision-making under stressful conditions. Summarized more simply, if a physician is not allowed the opportunity to experience stressful clinical scenarios where he/she is the one who must make an instantaneous decision, right or wrong, then this lack of exposure will inevitably lead to a lack of experience. This conundrum leads us back to my previous concern regarding the environment present in the CICU, one lacking support and dominated by toxicity, which created the potential for rendering young clinicians psychologically paralyzed and unable to make critical decisions under stressful conditions, because they would learn to fear the repercussions of a wrong decision, leading to the impulsive thought, "What would my mentor want me to do?" rather than, "This is what I should do based on the information provided to me in this moment." This process is even more complicated when the person neglected of this experience is a pediatric cardiac surgeon with twenty years of clinical experience but little to no independent critical decision-making experience, in particular one who has been thrust into a surgical and programmatic leadership position at the expense of his mentor. I can't imagine the stress Dr. Penton must have been experiencing; however, at least on the surface, he appeared to be handling it masterfully. The ideal scenario is when you find yourself in one of these situations as your mentor says to you, "What do you think we should do?" and after taking the time to hear your answer, they respond by saying, "That is a great idea. There are many ways to deal with this situation but let me share with you what I would do. I would begin by trying … for this reason … and if that doesn't work my next approach would be to consider this … because …" That is how a great mentor assures maximum exposure to critical decision-making situations, not only are they taking advantage of the opportunity by pushing you to assess the situation and provide your own solution, but they are also sharing their approach to solving the problem while explaining the reason for doing so, which actually doubles the trainee's exposure. I was fortunate enough during my training to have a mentor who provided me with such exposure and insight. Unfortunately for Dr. Penton, he was forced to acquire this skill in isolation, without a mentor, but let me tell you, he would prove to be one of the most adaptable individuals I have ever encountered, who was also gifted with innate clinical instincts, a skill that simply cannot be taught. It turns out he and I were both blessed with this gift, which we recognized in one another, and as a result we learned not only to trust one another, but to seek one another's input during difficult situations.

When Dr. Penton turned over the responsibility of the CICU to me and the team I had built, the pace of progress accelerated quickly. We were extubating complex patients on the same day as surgery. At this point we continued to perform all early extubations in the CICU. While the anesthesia group was exceptional, we hadn't yet evolved this process to include early extubations in the OR. I enjoyed our current process due to the fact that we were able to do so under relatively controlled conditions, which helped to ensure success while minimizing risk of complications. Doing it our way, on our timeline, permitted us the opportunity to adjust sedative and analgesic dosages to a level where we felt confident that the patient was free of pain, but awake enough to take adequate-sized breaths, while also allowing us sufficient time to assess hemodynamic stability and to be sure postoperative bleeding was well controlled and would not become problematic. With such rapid clinical progress occurring and with Dr. Penton's trust ever apparent to the entire CICU team, the environment began to noticeably change from one dominated by toxicity to one of support and collegiality, and for these reasons, I once again looked forward to coming to work every day. It was truly gratifying to see the nurses smiling and laughing at work. The staff who predated my arrival to the CICU couldn't believe how different Dr. Penton was, he was always smiling and joking around with the staff, and he dedicated a significant amount of his time to teaching the nurses, APPs and cardiology fellows at the bedside, and quite honestly, I was stunned at the transformation as well. It was a glaring example of how we are all a product of our environment and equally how the emotional maturity and optimism or pessimism displayed by the leader is contagious and sets the tone for the environment. In a toxic environment, people function based on fear. Fear of making a mistake, fear of not fitting in, fear of not knowing the answer, and even fear for your job, and when fear dominates, staff members hesitate to share their true selves because they fear being criticized or disliked. As much as I despised the manner in which Dr. Rostri was terminated, his removal proved to be the perfect example of how quickly an environment can change, not by forcing such change, but instead by encouraging everyone to be themselves. I remain a firm believer that people are inherently good, so once the team witnessed Dr. Penton and me not only working exceptionally well together but actually becoming close friends, that trust they observed spread through the CICU like the bubonic plague! Dr. Penton was now showing his true self because he no longer lived in fear, and he was now the product of a new environment, one that he was helping to build. Nurses who had worked in the CICU for many years, the same nurses who refused to share their thoughts and opinions with me when I first arrived, now began volunteering to champion hospital committees and began sharing their incredible ideas for unit development, completely unprovoked. It was truly inspirational to observe, and while I was extremely proud of the clinical changes that had occurred and the improved quality of the care we were providing to the patients, the supportive environment that was rapidly developing, validated by the smiles displayed on the nurses' faces, was by far our greatest accomplishment as a team.

Tim had now joined us full-time as an advanced practice provider in the CICU and his personality was a key factor responsible for creating this positive work environment. Martha and Brenda had both started working and Tim's mentoring was having a dramatic impact on their development. Adam and Astrid had officially started but I was not yet having them take night call, as they were still getting accustomed to the new system, but my plan was for them to start covering some night shifts following month. Finally, things at the hospital were moving at a consistent pace and everyone seemed happy with the team that was developing.

Unfortunately, I couldn't say the same about my home situation. While Ana and I had never been a couple who argued, I continued to feel that she appeared more removed and isolated emotionally. For a man as emotionally underdeveloped as me, to recognize that my wife appeared emotionally cold and distant must have meant that her emotional state was tenuous and dire. Ana was the first woman in my life capable of tearing down the fortress that had imprisoned my emotions, shielding them from the light of the outside world and those closest to me. I don't know why, but her ability to do so made me realize that she was the one for me. I often felt that I may be somewhere on the autistic spectrum, or perhaps I suffered from mild Asperger's. No, I am most certainly not the type of Asperger's or autism where the affected individual is blessed with mind-blowing intelligence. Instead, I am admittedly more the type who is unable to understand how their actions might negatively affect another person's feelings or emotions. I often find myself asking, "Did I do something wrong?" being absolutely mystified as to what I might have said to offend someone. I knew it was a weakness of mine, but she saw through that. When we dated, there were periods where I felt vulnerable and instinctively, I would attempt to recede behind the walls of the fortress that had protected me my entire life, but she refused to let me hide. Her insistence on knowing me inside and out, left me feeling vulnerable and more uncomfortable than I had ever felt in any situation in my entire life, and she became the first and only woman to actually succeed at getting me to open up and share my feelings. I sat on the couch and watched Ana as she lay curled up in a ball, her body language screamed that her guard was up and that she was unwilling, or perhaps unable at the time, to share her feelings with me, yet her body language was strangely familiar, reminiscent of a time when it was me who resisted sharing my feelings, instead of her. I felt sad and guilty to see her in such a state. Even I, the emotional illiterate, required no additional information to understand what it was that I had done to hurt her this time, it was obvious, I had neglected her since we arrived in Biloxi. Not only had I moved her and the kids away from the place they knew and loved, but I had also stripped them of their closest friends, whom they adored. I had abandoned Ana and the kids in a place they never wanted to be. I began to feel that I had emotionally regressed, if such a feat was actually possible, so for me to be the one who needed to reach out and offer emotional support to Ana was definitely unchartered territory for me. I still obsessively think about my failures as a husband and as a father nearly every day when I reflect on my time in Biloxi. Each of us identify things in life that we are skilled at, and equally, we all have things that we characterize as weaknesses. Emotions and feelings are admittedly my kryptonite, I look upon them as if they were hieroglyphics, which I try so hard to decipher, desperately attempting to uncover their deeper meaning and significance; however, they are so foreign to me, that I eventually give up because I find the process of interpreting their meaning stressful and morally defeating. If only I had tried, she needed me and I wasn't there, absent physically and emotionally. I now understand—hell, who am I fooling? I understood for some time; I just had no clue what to do, and quite honestly, after all the work I had put into this job, I was too dedicated, or perhaps more accurately, I was too stubborn to stop. I had tunnel vision, and these characteristics wouldn't allow me to stop, though my body and my family were silently pleading with me to do so. No matter how exhausted I was, I always managed to find time for my daughters, even if only for an hour or two at night. I made every attempt to practice my philosophy of "high-yield dad time." I found time to play basketball, board games or time to simply sit down and talk or watch a movie with them. And while I acknowledge I had developed a progressively worsening alcohol problem, I never drank in front of the girls, I at least waited until they went to bed. But mistakenly, I failed to set aside dedicated time for Ana and while I never drank in front of the kids, I did drink in front of her. In hindsight, I now realize the perception I was relaying to her, which was that I was more committed to Great Uncle Scotty than I was to Ana. The reason I was drinking was irrelevant in this matter, I chose alcohol over her and that was a grave mistake, one of many I would come to regret when it came to our deteriorating relationship.

I continued to feel physically unwell, despite a normal physical exam and labs. The shortness of breath I was experiencing had worsened, to the point where I had to stop midway through lovemaking with Ana because I felt as though I was going to pass out. I wish I could chalk these symptoms up to my passionate lovemaking skills; however, I had collected enough data over the years to know that this was certainly not the case. Over the past few weeks, I began experiencing drenching night sweats at least once or twice per week. That weekend marked the last weekend of the calendar month. Next month Adam and Astrid would begin taking night call and I would finally be able to reduce the number of nights I was working down to seven for the month, which happened to be half the number I was working at the time. However, even seven night calls per month was twice the workload considered the "standard" or "average" when it came to the typical number of night shifts covered per month by cardiac intensivists around the country. It had now been just over a year since Justin and I began working one hundred hours per week. This weekend was my only full weekend off, although my home schedule already appeared pretty full, as Ana had asked for my help doing some chores around the house and the girls had already planned a morning fishing expedition in the pond in our front yard, as well as an afternoon swimming adventure in the pool, later in the day. On Saturday, Ana and the girls decided to head to the grocery store. "Sweetie, would you please spread those pine needles around the trees in the front yard? I bought them from the landscaper, but rather than pay him to place them I told him we would do it, since I knew you were going to be home this weekend," Ana said.

"Sure, no problem," I replied. As they pulled away, I put my tennis shoes on and headed outside. I was still feeling unwell, but no worse than I had been feeling earlier in the week; however, admittedly, I felt more short of breath as I slowly walked toward the front yard. I stopped and picked up a bundle of pine needles, which couldn't have weighed more than five to ten pounds and proceeded to place them on the ground next to the large oak tree in the front yard. I reached and grabbed ahold of the garden rake that was leaned up against the tree, when suddenly I felt my heart begin to race and I began to feel dizzy as my visual field became black. That is the last thing I recall before awakening to find myself lying on the ground in the front yard, with the handle of the rake resting on my chest. I looked around, confused as I slowly sat myself up and looked at my watch. "I couldn't have lost consciousness for more than a couple minutes," I said while I attempted to gather myself, using the rake as a crutch to lift myself up off the ground. "I must have experienced an arrhythmia, and if I had syncope associated with it, it must have been ventricular tachycardia! But why? What was going on?" I said to myself as I attempted to process what had just occurred. I had never experienced an arrhythmia before, so I knew something was wrong, something more than just stress and fatigue. I walked back into the house to lay down on the couch. Ana and the kids arrived home minutes later, and Ana asked if I could help carry the groceries inside the house. Stupidly, I said, "Sure!" As I got up from the couch, she could see that I was short of breath.

"Are you OK? You look pale," she said. The kids went into the other room and I quietly whispered to Ana that something was wrong and that I wasn't feeling well. She already knew something wasn't right after I had to stop our lovemaking session just a day earlier because I felt as though I was going to pass out. I minimized the event in the front yard, telling her that I simply felt dizzy, intentionally withholding the details of my collapse, which in my mind almost certainly resulted from a near-fatal arrhythmia, likely ventricular tachycardia. I am not sure why I didn't tell her the entire truth; I guess part of me thought if she knew that she would make me stop working such crazy hours, and the truth is, I was so damn stubborn, I couldn't possibly stop now that we were finally making significant progress and the future was actually beginning to look bright. Especially now that help had finally arrived. Ana insisted that I be seen by a physician on Monday morning since I had immediately vetoed her suggestion of going to the emergency room. That day I reached out to my internal medicine physician who was able to get me an appointment Monday morning, to be seen by a well-respected cardiologist at the University of Southeastern Mississippi. Ana was worried, and quite honestly, so was I. The weekend came and went without further issue, and I was still able to enjoy my time with my daughters and they had no idea that I wasn't feeling well, because I didn't want to worry them.

Monday morning I arrived bright and early at the cardiologist's office as I explained to him the details of everything that had been occurring over the preceding months since the development of my symptoms. He performed an echocardiogram in his office and found that my cardiac function was mild to moderately depressed. The electrocardiogram at the time was normal; however, he placed an event monitor that I would wear for the next seven days, which would continuously monitor my heart rate and rhythm. I was instructed to push the button on the device if I experienced dizziness or the feeling that my heart was racing. Ultimately the results of the event monitor would reveal several short runs of ventricular tachycardia, which was exactly what I had predicted, as it was the arrhythmia that was most likely to result in a syncopal episode such as the one I had experienced in my front yard. After hearing the details and chronology of my symptoms as well as my medical history, the physician directed the diagnostic workup toward an autoimmune myocarditis. He referred me for urgent cardiac magnetic resonance imaging (MRI) and PET scan, which confirmed the diagnosis of cardiac sarcoidosis.

Sarcoidosis is believed to be an autoimmune disorder of uncertain etiology, which can affect virtually any organ system in the body. Like most autoimmune disorders, a conclusive cause is rarely identified; however, some cases may be inherited, and any factor that results in the disruption of immune homeostasis may contribute to the development of an autoimmune disorder. In my circumstance, the excessive work hours, extreme stress, sleep deprivation and the excessive consumption of alcohol were all well-understood lifestyle factors that were known to adversely affect the immune system, and in my case the extreme nature of these lifestyle factors almost certainly contributed to the development of the disease. Sarcoidosis oftentimes may regress and disappear on its own over a period of several years when it involves virtually any organ system in the body, EXCEPT when it affects the heart or the brain, and in these circumstances the disease rarely regresses, and can be fatal. Cardiac sarcoidosis was once considered nearly universally fatal, just five to ten years earlier, with a very high incidence of mortality within the five-year period following diagnosis. However, due to the evolution of cardiac MRI and PET scan, diagnosis was now occurring earlier and with aggressive immunosuppressive therapy, limited data now suggested people may survive ten years or more. I was obviously devastated by my newfound diagnosis, but I was glad there were treatment options and even more so, I was glad to finally understand why I was feeling so poorly. I was immediately started on high-dose steroids (prednisone) following my cardiac MRI. Over the next few months three additional immunosuppressive medications would be added to the prednisone I was already taking, in hopes that these medications would allow me the wean off of the prednisone, or at least allow me to decrease the dosage in order to minimize the morbid side effects that inevitably occur with the long-term use. Within a week of starting prednisone, my cardiac function normalized, my shortness of breath resolved as did my red-face episodes, night sweats and arrhythmia; however, I began experiencing significant side effects from the steroids. I am not one to complain in general; however, after a few months of prednisone, the side effects that resulted became intolerable and life-altering, as I began to experience horrendous abdominal pain, worsening insomnia, and severe mood swings that led me to the harsh realization that "roid rage" was in fact a real phenomenon. I endured unimaginable mood swings, which became a real problem for me. On the surface, I was known by friends and colleagues for my "laid-back" persona, and I took great pride in my ability to maintain a calm demeanor and an expressionless face, in even the most stressful of situations, so for me to feel as though I had lost complete control over my emotions, let's just say it left me feeling vulnerable and unsettled. I couldn't predict when it would happen, or who it was going to be directed at, but suddenly, out of the blue, often for no identifiable reason, I would simply "snap" and find myself barking comments aggressively at some poor soul, who much like me, had no idea what it was that set me off. By the time I realized it was happening, it was too late, the filter that normally protected my mouth from verbalizing something I intended to keep quietly in my mind would fail, and I would instantly feel like the biggest asshole in the universe. Sometimes, I would find myself snapping at the kids or Ana for the most ridiculous reason and it left me feeling remorseful, like I was a different person, and an awful father and husband. I didn't recognize this person who appeared so angry all the time, often for no valid reason, but I really didn't like him; in fact, he was a prick! I could go from zero to pissed off in less than 0.5 seconds. Pre-steroid Eric was masterful at hiding his emotions and boasted a poker face rivaling that displayed by the top players in the world competing on the final table at the World Series of Poker. However, I began to notice colleagues at work, both inside and outside of the CICU, who began to tiptoe around me, asking questions in an unusually timid manner, as to avoid getting their heads bitten off by me. It became bad enough at work that after a while, I had no choice but to bring it out in the open and try to make a humorous situation out of it. I would warn my colleagues when my dose of prednisone would reach twenty milligrams or more, because at that dose, my side effects were severe. "Good morning everyone, I am just giving you a heads-up, that I am on twenty milligrams of prednisone at this time, so you may want to steer clear of me until I can wean it down," I would say jokingly. The joke spiraled a bit and before long my colleagues developed the acronym D.I.R.R.E (dire), and would say, "Look out everyone, the steroid situation looks D.I.R.R.E.," which stood for "drug-induced roid raging Eric"! I was glad to try to ease the tension with humor because I knew my colleagues genuinely felt bad for me, but I was also making them uncomfortable with my mood swings. Over time, I began to be able to sense that things were about to become D.I.R.R.E. I knew it was coming because I began to feel this intense energy rising from inside me, and then the slightest comment by anyone regarding something I didn't necessarily agree with, or equally likely, for no reason at all, something would lead to me aggressively exclaim exactly what was on my mind. In the year 2017 B.R. (before roids), I would obsessively overanalyze what I wanted to say, to be certain I wouldn't upset anyone while trying to deliver my point clearly. I saw this as a real strength of mine, which helped me survive the Rostri years. Whether or not he and I disagreed, which occurred regularly, we also managed to treat one another with respect, at least in public. That was the only way I knew. Yeah, well that skill disappeared in an instant and it was very unfamiliar to me and I didn't like the fact that I had no control over it; in fact I hated it, but I couldn't help but laugh to myself as I wondered how D.I.R.R.E. things would have been if I had lost control over my emotions and was left with a dysfunctional filter back when I had to work with Dr. Rostri on a daily basis, it certainly would have been entertaining.

As I shared the news of my illness with the team, many were devastated because as physicians, when we don't understand something well, we naturally turn to the National Institute of Health, National Library of Medicine website, pubmed.gov. It is here where physicians and health-care professionals seek answers by querying this massive online database in search of answers in the form of research publications and other medical literature that has been published to help answer our medical questions. If you performed a literature search on "cardiac sarcoidosis," some of the articles from five or more years ago provide a dismal prognosis. So many of my colleagues assumed that my life clock was ticking and that I wasn't going to be around for very long. Quite honestly, at first, that's what I thought as well. However, after reading more recent publications and after speaking with my physician, and given how good I felt, I began to feel confident that I would be around for at least a few years. My physician shared a very informative, updated review of the literature on the current state of cardiac sarcoidosis with me, saying that while still uncertain, many individuals appear to be surviving up to ten years following diagnosis, especially if their cardiac function remained normal, which mine now was. So, I shared this review with Dr. Penton and Dr. Saltiel and encouraged them to pass it along to anyone else who may have questions pertaining to my diagnosis. I became less worried about dying from cardiac sarcoidosis, but as time went on, I was left with an unanswerable question, which was, would it be the disease itself that would kill me, or would I succumb to the adverse effects resulting from the need for long-term, higher-dose steroids? My colleagues were thankful for the review and emphasized their unwavering support, offering whatever help I may need. "More than anything, I need to back off the number of night calls I am working," I said, and the timing of Adam and Astrid's arrival couldn't have been more ideal. Both were ready to start taking night call and had offered to pick up as many shifts as needed in order to offload some of my clinical work. It was great to finally have a team that was so supportive, and it couldn't have come at a better time because I literally wouldn't have been capable of carrying on with the one-hundred-hour workweek, not even for a single week longer, and this would have resulted in our inability to provide 24-7 coverage, putting all of our progress at risk. While I was devastated by the diagnosis and felt uncertain as to my future, I couldn't help but sense that someone or something was indeed looking out for me. Between the near-death episode with my vehicle on the bridge and the near-death collapse in my yard, for me to still be here, alive and standing, while suddenly, after months of waiting in anticipation, the staff I desperately needed to fill the gaps in the night schedule arrived at the exact moment where the situation had become dire, was too incredible to explain as mere coincidence.

I completed the following month's CICU schedule and was able to reduce my night call number to seven, which was again, a 50 percent reduction. It was still a lot, but it was a big step in the right direction. Adam and Astrid did well covering the CICU in their first month. I made myself available to them at all times by phone. In the beginning I received a lot of phone calls, at all hours of the night, but I didn't mind, as it was much better than being in the hospital. The prednisone worsened my insomnia, and now even the usual two to three three-fingered Scotches I drank in the evening failed to deliver the momentary relaxation and couple of hours of sleep it once did. After speaking with my internal medicine physician, I tried taking Ambien, which didn't work, until eventually he prescribed me Lunesta, which finally allowed me to get three to four hours of continuous sleep, which felt incredible. Now that I could actually sleep, I was able to wean myself off of the nightly Scotches, and I instead transitioned to having a single Scotch on occasion. I was happy about that because I failed to envision a viable exit strategy, particularly when the dose of alcohol continued to escalate, and as I tried to look forward, I foresaw a future consisting of alcohol dependence, and honestly, I wanted no part of that. I thanked Great Uncle Scotty for his assistance during a time when I had nowhere else to turn. He had served his purpose admirably, but things were different now, I was different now, and regardless of what lie ahead for me, I failed to see a consistent place for him in my life.

28

NEW CHIEF OF CARDIOLOGY CANDIDATE

Our CICU outcomes continued to improve. Establishing complete autonomy in the CICU had allowed us to develop and run the unit as we saw fit. The quality of the patient care we were now providing continued to be validated by our data, which showed that we were consistently performing in the top five in terms of our risk-adjusted hospital length of stay, when compared with our colleagues around the country. Again, this is by no means representative of a true ranking of cardiac programs, as larger programs typically assume far more risk by operating on a larger number of patients with a greater degree of complexity, when compared to small-to-medium-sized programs. While the ranking was risk-adjusted, the algorithm was far from perfect. For our institution, since its inception, or at least from the time we began participating in the national CICU database, we could only compare our current data to our data from the past, simply because our data was so far skewed from the mean when compared to many of the other participating institutions around the country, it made it impossible to compare our data to that of virtually any other program, without appearing foolish. However, for the last year or so, the care we were providing in the CICU was beginning to result in outcomes that finally appeared to be at a stage that would allow us to loosely compare our data with those of most participating institutions. The fact that we were now able to perform such a comparison, for us as a program, was actually a huge feat of its own, and a major accomplishment for the team, one that I can honestly say, I never imagined would be possible. So, when I speak of outcomes, I am not attempting to portray an idea that I truly believed that we were ranked number four in the nation in terms of hospital length of stay, nor am I attempting to boast such results. I am, however, using our data to validate what we were seeing take place clinically in our CICU, in real time, at the bedside. And my repeated mention of such metrics simply functioned to provide something measurable that I could share with my team, as a means of complimenting their efforts and validating the hard work they were displaying on a daily basis. The staff took great pride in what they were doing rather than complaining about their lack of resources, which was what was occurring at the time of my arrival to CHOB. Additionally, these data were invaluable to me individually, and the database provided me a timeline that allowed me to map our progress over time, and that alone was a vital reason I was able to recruit anyone to join my team in the CICU at CHOB. As time went on, word of mouth continued to spread throughout the institution regarding our rapidly improving outcomes in the CICU, until eventually, the hospital administration began to grasp on to these data and use them as a recruitment tool to attract candidates for leadership positions both within and outside of the Heart Center. Most notably, they had shared our outcome data with a new recruit who had recently been identified as a potential candidate for the chief of pediatric cardiology, and co-director of the Heart Center, a position that had remained vacant for more than three years.

In all honesty, the two applicants who had previously interviewed for the chief of pediatric cardiology position, whom I had met upon my arrival to CHOB, appeared average. Their curriculum vitae was not something that jumped out at me as memorable, but then again, who was I to make such judgments? I didn't know them personally, nor did I have a solid understanding of their ability as clinicians. The truth is, my CV was not all that impressive either. While submitting a CV is an essential part of the application process, I viewed its review as nothing more than a primary screening tool for determining if the applicant warranted further evaluation as a potential candidate. I am a believer that in order to truly evaluate an individual's candidacy, particularly for a leadership position, you must look well beyond the multitude of pages that make up their CV. I am also a firm believer that stating an individual is "top trained" based solely on the program that they trained at is nothing more than a superficial assessment of their true capabilities. In my experience, gauging an individual's qualifications based on the institution they have typed on their CV under the section "Education and Training" does two things, the first of which is that it places an unnecessary emphasis on the institution where they trained, thereby insinuating that if the words typed beneath the aforementioned heading, read Boston, Stanford, etcetera, or some other well-known institution, this infers that the individual is in fact, an exceptional physician, which is obviously not always the case. If you believe that this statement is in fact true, that training does in fact infer the quality of a physician, then you are supporting my second belief when it comes to placing unwarranted emphasis on the program that the candidate trained at. This second point actually builds off the first and is rather simple. If you are the individual responsible for recruiting candidates, and you are in fact the one who is placing unnecessary and unwarranted emphasis on the institution that they trained at, and you fail to further investigate whether or not the candidate is a skilled clinician, a hardworking individual, who is also a team player, then I believe you CAN actually infer that you are unqualified to lead such a recruitment, because you are incapable of recognizing the importance of hiring an individual who not only fits the system but more importantly is the appropriate fit for the team. Now, back to my first point, yes, it is true, training at elite institutions will most certainly increase the likelihood that an individual is indeed well trained, due to the environment that surrounds them during their training. However, training at such an institution and being surrounded by greatness does nothing to clarify whether they are hardworking, a team player, or if they have the innate ability to take what is learned from a book, a course, or from the greatness that surrounds them and translate that information into actual clinical excellence. These simple yet indispensable characteristics will not be found on an applicant's CV but are in fact fundamental attributes that are paramount for the success of the individual and of the team. As you will see later in our story, these invaluable traits are frequently overlooked by administrators with inadequate experience, with no medical background, who prematurely make impulsive decisions based unnecessarily on where the individual trained, believing the fallacy that "top training" infers clinical excellence, which unfortunately is far from the truth and may lead to the hiring of the wrong individual, who may then go on to cause irreversible damage to the team. As dramatic as this may seem, I believe every word of this to be true.

For example, I am a firm believer that my unique skill set simply cannot be understood solely by reading the words I have typed to fill the sixteen pages that make up my humble CV. Instead, I pride myself on being an exceptionally skilled clinician who is equally skilled at being a kind, honest, and caring individual who also understands the importance of a team. I challenge anyone who may consider my hiring to call, at random, any colleague or employee, from the janitor to the CEO, from any of the institutions where I have previously trained or worked and ask them to describe me as a physician and a human being. If the hiring institution is able to find a single person who is willing to speak negatively about me as a physician or a person, then they should pass on the opportunity to hire me; in fact, I will voluntarily withdraw my application from consideration. I challenge anyone to find another applicant willing and able to say the same. Such a statement is far more powerful than a CV that is seventy pages in length and details one hundred plus publications. I don't believe myself to be an arrogant person, but I am confident in my ability, and I know my character and I would put that up against anyone. So, as you can see, Children's Hospital of Biloxi and the University of Southeastern Alabama showed that they were exceptionally gifted and displayed elite recruiting skills throughout my recruitment process. The rare ability they displayed during my recruitment allowed them to veer beyond the superficial layer represented by my CV, to dive deeper, allowing them to recognize that I indeed held the necessary tools required to succeed in this role. Ha ha ha ha! I am sorry, I could barely keep a straight face as I typed such BULLSHIT! Let's be realistic, Dr. Deeton and Dr. Potts were not a couple of geniuses, who masterminded my recruitment; let's tell it like it is, they were desperate, and I was the only one stupid enough to consider the job, and ultimately, they got lucky by hiring me because otherwise, they would never have found someone stubborn enough to not only take the job but also to see it through. Ha ha ha! Masterminds? Now that's funny!

I was living proof that quality clinicians can actually come from training programs that were not Boston or Stanford. Was I successful? I am not sure, because the definition of success can vary significantly, and each different definition comes tied to some degree of subjective emotional ambiguity, which is to say that success is in the eye of the beholder. For example, if I have a job I love and work with phenomenal colleagues, and we take excellent care of the patients, am I successful? I would answer, "Hell yeah, I am successful. That sounds incredible. Where do I sign up?" On the other hand, some may say success is defined by the number or publications you have authored or by the number of pages that make up your CV. So, to these individuals the previous example may not actually represent success, and vice versa.

"Eric, did you hear that the administration has reached out to a new candidate for the chief of cardiology position, to gauge his interest? I don't recognize the name, but apparently the CMO, Gerry Blount, worked with him years ago at Mayo Children's. I heard that he has been at Mayo for twenty years and he is the current medical director of outpatient cardiology. You interviewed there; do you remember him?" Doris Geisinger asked as we assembled in the CICU, awaiting the start of the new morning "surgical rounds" we had developed to replace "migration rounds." The concept was the same; however, we now rolled the computer on wheels to each patient's bedside and pulled their chest X-ray while the intensivist provided a brief history, details of the previous night's events, and the proposed plan for the day, which then led to discussion by the Heart Center team members. We constructed these rounds with the goal of developing a collaborative team approach rather than the old model of following Dr. Rostri around the unit as he told us what to do.

"That's great news! I think I remember the man you are talking about; I recall he looked kind of like 'Ken Doll,' but with dark hair. You know, Ken, as in Ken and Barbie!" I explained to Doris as I laughed quietly to myself. "Let's go look him up on the Mayo website in my office after surgical rounds," I replied. I was admittedly excited and hoped it was the friendly guy I recalled having a stimulating conversation with during my visit to Mayo Children's. As surgical rounds came to an end, Doris and I ran, I mean we quite literally sprinted like children racing for the last cookie, as we arrived simultaneously at my office door. As I sat in my office chair, I navigated to the Mayo Children's pediatric cardiology website and confirmed, indeed it was Tim Kowatch, the same pediatric cardiologist I had met during my visit. "Yep, that's him," I said with a big smile on my face. "He has been there forever and apparently, he was also being considered as a candidate for the division chief position at Mayo, but ultimately he was passed up and they hired Anthony Rosenthal. That had to hurt to be passed up for that job after dedicating twenty years of your life to the institution, but they passed him up for a legend in the field, so I understand their decision," I said.

"Apparently, there is mutual interest, and he has agreed to come for a visit. Can you ask around and see if anyone knows him? I will do the same," Doris said.

"Yes, I will ask around. Obviously, I can't ask my connection Dean, who is the CICU director at Mayo Children's because I am certain Dr. Kowatch wants to keep his visit discrete, but I will ask around to others," I replied.

After a couple of weeks, Dr. Kowatch's visit to Children's Hospital of Biloxi was confirmed and I was scheduled to interview him. Doris and I dedicated a significant amount of time trying to gather any information we could about Dr. Kowatch's clinical ability, his interaction with the team at Mayo Children's, as well as any information we could dig up regarding why he was passed over for the division chief job at his current institution. Oddly, nobody really seemed to know who he was, despite working at such a prestigious institution for so long and despite the fact that he was the medical director of their outpatient cardiology program. I did have one of my friends who is an echocardiography guru say he knew the name back from his echocardiography training days, fifteen years ago, but hadn't heard much about him since then. Doris reported similar findings. None of the most-recognized cardiologists from Boston knew who Dr. Kowatch was, but in my eyes, he was medical director at Mayo Children's, and even if it was only a title overseeing the outpatient cardiology department, the title combined with the fact that he had twenty years of experience at such a prestigious program were characteristics of a candidate that we had not seen before at CHOB. When I sought the wisdom of Dr. Saltiel, he agreed, he had not heard of Dr. Kowatch but his forty-page CV was impressive, at least in regard to his medical director title, his experience, and the seventy-five publications and multiple book chapters he had authored over his career. He clearly looked VERY qualified, on paper that is, though I will admit, deep down, I was a little concerned about his clinical ability because first of all, he was an outpatient cardiologist who was virtually unknown among our small community, but much like my other Heart Center teammates, I chose to disregard my gut instinct, which was telling me something was off, and instead I focused on the fact that we were interviewing a candidate of his caliber, which appeared to be from a much finer pedigree when compared to our past candidates, on paper that is.

The date of Dr. Kowatch's visit had arrived, and he was given a red-carpet welcome, which included a limousine that escorted him from the airport to his hotel and then to Children's Hospital of Biloxi. I was scheduled as the third person on his interview itinerary, and was to follow Antoine Boykins, the CEO, and Gerry Blount, the COO. His interview took place in the newly renovated C-suite administrative conference room. As my time approached that morning, I took the elevator up to the fourth floor and walked toward the administrative office suite, arriving at the new conference room. I was impressed, the conference room was gorgeous, it appeared brightly lit, inside sat a large rectangular table, surrounded by chairs that could comfortably seat thirty people, and the room was equipped with state-of-the-art audio-visual equipment. This was the first time I had seen this room since its renovation. I thought to myself, "Having Dr. Kowatch interview in this beautiful new conference room was truly a great recruiting tactic by the hospital administration, as was the construction map that was sprawled out on the table, detailing the $300-million construction transformation that was currently underway, which was clearly on display by intention rather than mere coincidence. Showing him the conference room as an example of the first bright, shiny new project to be completed would provide him a sample tasting of what was to come, and perhaps increase his craving for the delicacy of a new children's hospital that would be served as the main entree in the near future." As I entered the room, we met one another with massive smiles, as if old friends reunited, acknowledging the irony of the current situation, without saying a word. "Hi, Tim. It is great to see you again. Who would have thought after our meeting in Minnesota that we would find ourselves in opposite seats during the interview process, and in a different state?" I said.

"Yes, who would have thought? I still can't believe I am here, and a big part of that reason is because of the work you and your team have done. Mr. Boykins shared with me the incredible progress you have made in the CICU; honestly, without that, I wouldn't be here," Dr. Kowatch said.

"I remember being in the identical position you are in right now when I first interviewed here. I recall thinking to myself, what are you doing considering this job, and being blatantly honest, I am surprised to still be here, but I can tell you that I am glad that I am. Seeing someone of your caliber consider this position seems surreal to me and highlights the change that has occurred and continues to occur, whether you decide to join us or not," I explained.

"Eric, Gerry Blount shared with me your CICU data and what you and your team have done is incredible and you should be proud. He also shared with me that you have recruited some 'top trained' cardiac intensivists to join you. In all honesty, though I know Gerry Blount well, I wouldn't even consider this position if it weren't for the work you and your team have done to improve things," he explained, again repeating the same point.

"It's been a lot but thank you so much for saying that. It has been a team effort; it was most certainly not just me who put the work in. Quite honestly, the fact that you are here today is all the reward I need. As we recruit more and more talent, in my opinion, the potential here is limitless," I replied.

Dr. Kowatch's first interview was limited to meeting with hospital administration, Dr. Penton, Doris Geisinger, Dr. Saltiel and me. Following the visit, the word from Michael Stringer, COO, was that Dr. Kowatch enjoyed his visit and had requested some time to process the information he acquired and to discuss the opportunity with his wife, after which time he would determine if he was interested in returning for a second visit. After a couple of weeks of deliberation, Dr. Kowatch agreed to visit Biloxi for a second time, which was huge, because as I said earlier, second visits typically mean there is serious interest by both parties. During the second visit, spouses typically accompany the candidate, and it is understood that things such as salary and details of employment will be discussed, and often activities such as touring the city and meeting with a realtor are arranged. The entire team was ecstatic about the opportunity to have a candidate with Dr. Kowatch's background seriously consider joining us, and as a result, the excitement in the air was palpable.

For his second visit, all four cardiac intensivists were scheduled to join Dr. Kowatch for an informal lunch, again in the administrative conference room. The four of us sat dispersed around the conference room table near Dr. Kowatch's seat. The three others introduced themselves and gave Dr. Kowatch some background information as to their upbringing as well as their medical training. He was clearly impressed by the team we had assembled and how well we worked together. We shared with him that we were currently interviewing candidates as we looked to add a fifth member to our growing team. I explained to Dr. Kowatch that we were selectively reaching out to some experienced candidates who I knew personally and explained my desire to reserve this position for someone with at least five years of CICU experience, so that I could offload some of my responsibilities due to some recent health issues I had developed. I explained that I hoped to hire this person as the associate medical director of the CICU, to share some of my administrative and mentoring responsibilities as well.

Lunch went well, and Justin, as a native of Biloxi, took the time to share some historical aspects of the city with Dr. Kowatch, including the multiple stories of haunted homes and supposed child ghost sightings that had occurred at CHOB. Just as Justin began detailing these ghost sightings, the hands of the clock, which was hung on the wall of the conference room, began spinning rapidly clockwise in repeating circles, advancing by an hour every ten seconds. I was the first to notice it, and as the others subsequently began staring at this bizarre and creepy phenomenon that I brought it to their attention, Dr. Kowatch laughed and said, "Stop, guys. Real funny! Is this some sort of Biloxi recruiting gimmick? Alright, you have had your fun, you can stop now," he said, assuming we had staged this oddity on purpose.

"Honestly, Dr. Kowatch, this is real!" I said as I continued to stare at the clock, completely mesmerized. The four of us were equally awestruck.

The clock continued to spin until Justin said jokingly, "OK, no more ghost stories." Suddenly, seconds after those words had departed his mouth, the hands of the clock stopped spinning. It was unbelievable and the fact that it occurred in unison with Justin's stories was nothing short of eerie and too much to be explained as coincidence.

As our scheduled lunch concluded and the clock returned to a normal state of functioning, the four of us stood up and thanked Dr. Kowatch for his visit and for the stimulating conversation. Dr. Kowatch said, "It was great meeting you guys and congratulations on all the work you have done."

"Thanks!" we replied.

"Hey, Eric, can you stay behind for a minute? I want to ask you a question," Dr. Kowatch asked.

"Sure," I replied.

I stayed behind as the others filtered out of the room as Dr. Kowatch asked, "How is your health? And has your health altered your plans regarding your future here at CHOB, because that would definitely decrease the likelihood of me committing to this job?" he said.

"I am good. I feel good, my cardiac function is normal, and I am not experiencing any arrhythmias at this time. I am not sure about my long-term prognosis, but I hope to be around for a long time, and I am hoping to be here at Children's Hospital of Biloxi for the foreseeable future," I said. He thanked me and wished me good health.

After his second visit had concluded, there was a prolonged gap in communication between Dr. Kowatch and hospital administration, despite confirmation that he had received his offer letter from the university following a brief period of salary negotiation. I could sense he was having second thoughts about leaving the comforts of such an elite institution, where he had worked and grown professionally for his entire career. Plus, given the fact that he would be departing the comfy confines of such a castle, to join a program with no reputation whatsoever, or at least no positive reputation, which happened to exist in the Deep South, in a city still recovering from the destruction caused by Hurricane Kelly more than a decade ago, I knew he was torn, and I completely understood his reservations, as I went through a similar process in my mind, and I wasn't leaving the ivory tower that he would be. Understanding that he was struggling with the decision that was before him, I suddenly came up with an idea based on the fact that nearly all pediatricians struggle when it comes to saying no to children. It is our weakness, so being the opportunist I was, I immediately put my daughters to work and asked them to create and decorate a sign that read, "Dr. Kowatch, please say yes! My dad and the children of Mississippi need your help!" Once they completed the sign, Ana took a picture of my daughters, Heather and Erica standing next to me as they held the sign they had just masterfully created. I then proceeded to text the picture to Dr. Kowatch. Two days later he accepted the position, later sharing with me that the picture had helped inch him toward making this difficult decision, although I was certain he was just being kind. Regardless of the reason he chose to join us, this was an unprecedented hire for the Heart Center and for CHOB, which definitely appeared to open the door widely, increasing our recruiting potential for the future.

Within a month of his official hiring, Dr. Kowatch forwarded the CVs of two candidates that he had trained at Mayo Children's, whom he wished to hire at CHOB. One candidate was a transplant cardiologist, who had been practicing in Arizona for the last five years following completion of her training. Her name was Tricia Cranton, and she had studied and trained at some of the most prestigious programs across the country, including Mayo Children's, where she completed her training in pediatric cardiology and heart failure/transplant medicine. The second candidate was named Sherry Monroe. She was just completing her advanced imaging fellowship at Mayo Children's, with a focus on fetal echocardiography, and this would be her first job post-training. Dr. Kowatch and his two recommended hires would all ultimately agree to join CHOB. While all three were notably "top trained," we would soon be reminded of my earlier words and the harsh reality that what appears impressive on paper does not always translate into clinical acumen.

29

IMMUNOSUPPRESSION AND ARRIVAL OF THE NEW HIRES

Three months passed and things appeared stable, a word I never imagined I would use to describe Children's Hospital of Biloxi. From a health perspective, I was feeling great, and I remained asymptomatic on the same treatment regimen. I had begun slowly tapering my dose of prednisone and remained hopeful that I would be able to come off this medication completely at some point. In addition to prednisone, I was administering weekly subcutaneous injections of methotrexate, a medication often used for chemotherapy, which had accumulated years of data and experience that continued to highlight its effectiveness and long-term tolerance as an immunosuppressant. In addition, I was also taking injections of adalimumab, which was considered a biologic immune suppressant, known as a TNF-alpha blocker. TNF-alpha is an inflammatory cytokine that is also involved in a complicated network of cell signaling pathways, which can lead to cell death. It has been implicated

in the pathophysiology of many autoimmune disorders. As a result, its usage
had increased over the years, particularly in certain autoimmune diseases
such as Crohn's disease and rheumatoid arthritis. The use of adalimumab in
patients with sarcoidosis had been limited to those with pulmonary sarcoidosis (affecting the lungs); however, its use in cardiac sarcoidosis (affecting
the heart) was relatively new and scarcely researched. The fourth medication
I was taking was called hydroxyurea, known as an antiproliferative medication, which had been used for many years as an anticancer treatment as well
as a treatment for autoimmune diseases. It is believed to function more as
a means of preventing cell proliferation, rather than as a typical "immune
suppressant." Again, its use in cardiac sarcoidosis was unproven; however, I
was in agreement with the plan to use these other medications aggressively
in an attempt to try to taper off steroids altogether. I was feeling great from
a heart standpoint, although I was still currently on twenty milligrams of
prednisone, which is a high enough dose to produce significant side effects,
but I remained hopeful that the continued weaning plan would be successful. The side effects related to prednisone were many, and new side effects
continued to develop and accumulate, all equally unbearable in their own
respects. Despite their severity, none of the side effects hailed in comparison
to the symptoms I felt when the disease was active and at its worse. The side
effects I experienced from prednisone were many, and the longer I used this
medication, the more that showed their ugly face and the worse the severity. What I mean is the side effects were annoying at the beginning, such as
gastritis, weight gain, abdominal pain, insomnia, fluid retention, and mood
swings, but for patients requiring years of continuous prednisone therapy
the side effects became much worse, many of which can be debilitating and
life-shortening, such as diabetes, cataracts, glaucoma, bone demineralization
leading to fractures and severe back issues, muscle atrophy, tendon rupture,
adrenal insufficiency, and many, many more. If you looked at any pharmaceutical references related to prednisone, you could read through the long
list of potential side effects and in my case, you could quite literally check
them off one at a time, because I was experiencing nearly all of them. To make

matters worse, prednisone was considered the gold standard medical therapy for cardiac sarcoidosis, and the only medication studied and proven to improve heart inflammation; however, it was NOT a "cure" for the disease, as it simply functioned to keep the inflammation from progressing, in fact there was no cure. Most literature suggested that patients with cardiac sarcoidosis, more often than not, require lifelong steroids, even if at low dose. Despite this understanding, I was still hopeful to be able to wean off this drug, which I would come to term "the lifesaving poison," as it truly was keeping me alive, but it was also wreaking havoc on my body in the meantime. During my years of intensive care practice, I had seen many patients with systemic lupus erythematosus (an autoimmune disorder) requiring long-term prednisone or transplant recipients who would often cycle on and off prednisone to treat or prevent graft rejection, and many of these patients were debilitated to varying extents, as a result of the long-term effects of prednisone. So, the question in my mind as a physician remained, if I was unable to be weaned from prednisone, and my disease severity remained stable, what would my life look like in five to ten years? This uncertainty ate away at my psyche, but I tried to focus on the positive, and that was the fact that from a disease standpoint, I felt good, and at least for the time being, the disease was yet to issue an impending death sentence. The other medications that made up my treatment regimen were not without side effects of their own, and if you read the possible side effects found in any pharmaceutical reference, they were enough to cause some anxiety. Methotrexate's major risk was liver failure, and fortunately I had already significantly reduced my alcohol intake, which helped to decrease this risk. Adalimumab contained a black box warning, which was intended to raise awareness of the risk of developing serious infections and malignancy, specifically the increased risk of developing lymphoma, while hydroxyurea carried a risk of liver toxicity, diarrhea, weight loss, visual problems, bone marrow suppression, and possible hair loss, to name a few. Clearly none of these medications were associated with side effects that I would consider "benign," and while I recognized these were potential side effects, rather than guaranteed, they were scary to read nonetheless, even for a critical care physician. The side effects of prednisone were nearly assured, so as with everything in life and in medicine, it is important to evaluate the risk-to-benefit ratio of the therapies used in your individual treatment regimen. In this scenario, I accepted the risk of the other side effects because in my mind, the proposed benefit of coming off prednisone far outweighed the potential risk presented by the other medications, and as I said, the other side effects were theoretical at this point, while those resulting from prednisone use were a certainty.

It took approximately three months for Dr. Kowatch to receive his medical license and to complete his hospital credentialing. In the meantime, I sought his opinion via telephone regarding a couple of complex patients we were dealing with in the CICU, or when there was indecision among the team, regarding the surgical plan or timing of surgery for these complex patients. It wasn't apparent to me at the time, but in retrospect, I now realize that Dr. Kowatch frequently responded to my questions regarding his clinical opinion with a question of his own, such as, "Sounds like a tough case, Eric, what do you think should be done?" After giving my clinical opinion, he would always say, "I agree with you." First, in his defense, it is difficult to get a true understanding of a patient's clinical condition by telephone, without the opportunity to perform an examination or at least to see them in person with your own eyes, regardless of how detailed the explanation may be. The second part is, I guess I felt reassured that someone with his background agreed with me because outside of Dr. Saltiel and Dr. Borland, the pediatric cardiology group was rather hesitant to give a confident clinical opinion, a likely aftereffect of the years of control exhibited by Dr. Rostri. However, I would learn over time that in the case of Dr. Kowatch, his avoidance of offering his medical opinion had far greater meaning.

Dr. Kowatch's arrival to Children's Hospital of Biloxi was met with great excitement. By the time he started, the construction of the new atrium, which was the name given to the side entrance of the hospital, had been completed, as was the parking garage, which included a covered walkway elevated above the street, providing a direct, covered connection between the garage and the interior of the hospital. The atrium was gorgeous, the walls were floor-to-ceiling glass and the staircase leading down from the second floor where the covered walkway entered the hospital was elegant and was illuminated on both sides by colorful neon lights. On the wall opposite the glass hung a massive television monitor that displayed the message "Welcome to Children's Hospital of Biloxi," which also allowed the message displayed to be changed at any time. The ground floor consisted of a large welcome area and information desk, elaborately lit with neon colors that alternated every five minutes between green and pink. This desk consisted of five private stations, each staffed with a different employee who could answer general questions while also having the ability to provide admitting or outpatient services for incoming patients. Interspersed among the open area in front of the information desk were a plethora of children's games and colorful seating arrangements for patients and families to sit and wait or to rest. It was a spectacular site to see, and the timing of its completion was impeccable as it aligned in unison with Dr. Kowatch's arrival. Strangely, the progress of the ongoing construction project appeared to coincide in perfect unison with the continued development and progress of the CICU and that of the Heart Center, for in both instances, so much work had been completed with magnificent results, yet so much work remained to be done. The completion of the atrium construction had literally been no more than two weeks prior to Dr. Kowatch's arrival at CHOB. The administration had arranged for a Mardi Gras-style band and had encouraged all employees to gather in the atrium to greet Dr. Kowatch upon his arrival to Children's Hospital of Biloxi. As he walked through the doors into the new atrium, the crowd of approximately twenty people cheered and the band commenced playing "For He's a Jolly Good Fellow." Mr. Boykins instructed his administrative team to dance, which actually meant he delivered a "serious stare" in their vicinity, reminiscent of an angry father delivering such a stare containing subliminal meaning to his children, as if to say, "Get your ass dancing to the music, now!" and eventually he even coerced Dr. Kowatch to join in dance. It was awkward and extremely painful to watch them all dance, if that is what you could call it; however, I had to give them an A for effort as the entire celebration was very thoughtful. It was truly a momentous day for CHOB. As I said before, hiring someone of his caliber was something that would not have occurred just one year earlier. Similarly, I had recently been involved in the recruitment interviews for the new chief of pediatric gastroenterology and for the new chief of general surgery, who had been recruited by the chief surgical officer, Eddie Arnold. I presume that they included me in the recruitment of these leaders because they witnessed my recruiting success in the CICU and likely for the motivational spiel I had learned to effectively deliver during my time at CHOB, which I used to help recruit my team. Both of these candidates eventually accepted the leadership positions and started at CHOB a few months after Dr. Kowatch began. As the celebration went on, in my mind I began to plead for the music to stop as I watched Mr. Boykins dance like an alcoholic uncle who had one too many drinks at the family Christmas party and Dr. Kowatch, who danced like an awkward and insecure seventh grader, dancing for the first time at a middle school dance. The celebration was magnificent, yet I couldn't rid myself of the scarring images of the dancing, and when the music finally stopped, I had never been so grateful to see a celebration come to an end. As I struggled to erase these traumatic dancing images from my mind, I grabbed Dr. Kowatch and explained that I was going to lead him to the CICU so that he could join the rest of the team for morning surgical rounds. When we arrived in the CICU, I provided a brief introduction of Dr. Kowatch to the team and explained how we were truly blessed to have him join us as a leader. We then proceeded as if it was any other day, advancing to each subsequent bedside, reviewing each patient's X-ray, labs, and pertinent medical history while attempting to engage Dr. Kowatch, seeking his input regarding patient management, whenever the opportunity presented itself. Again, he remained somewhat elusive when it came to providing firm recommendations; however, I simply attributed this to the fact that he had just arrived and needed time to adjust.

Approximately two months after Dr. Kowatch's arrival, his new recruits also began to arrive at Children's Hospital of Biloxi. Tricia Cranton, the transplant cardiologist, was the first to arrive. She moved to Biloxi with her husband and her arrival was highly anticipated by the team and hospital administration. Not only had she trained at Mayo Children's, but she had trained under Dr. Kowatch and the two were very close friends, which for some reason, led to this preconceived notion that her clinical competence and collegiality were thereby guaranteed, or so we thought. Her arrival also felt as though it represented the future direction of the program, which was to include pediatric heart transplantation, and the narrative repeatedly delivered by hospital administration appeared to suggest that Dr. Kowatch and Tricia's arrival marked the beginning of a new era, one where the institution was finally able to recruit "top trained" physicians, as if to imply that those of us who had been at CHOB prior to their arrival were merely scrubs who were needed to fill the gaps until the real doctors arrived. It didn't feel right, but I simply chalked it up to clueless administrative hearsay and blew it off as false perception. However, as I once again reflect on this time, I realize that it was true, the arrival of our new teammates did mark the beginning of a new day; however, this time actually represented the birth of the terminology "top trained," rather than marking a day where we would suddenly see a dramatic improvement in the patient care we were providing. The entire belief was insulting to many of us, but nonetheless, the term "top trained," which would come to be regurgitated with great regularity by hospital administration and by Dr. Kowatch, would eventually evolve to become what I would describe as an unhealthy infatuation, one that I now understand represented the developing disconnect between the majority of the Heart Center team and hospital administration, which would ultimately have detrimental effects on the program, which would become visible to all in the near future.

Tricia Cranton's title was medical director of pediatric heart failure. Tricia's arrival was closely followed by that of Sherry Monroe, Dr. Kowatch's other new hire, who specialized in fetal echocardiography. There were already three other pediatric cardiologists within the Heart Center who practiced fetal echocardiography at CHOB and had been doing so for many years. Two of them did not undergo advanced training in the field; however, they had substantial experience and each of them was quite proficient with fetal echo-cardiography, in particular Dr. Borland, who had well-established relation-ships with the majority of maternal fetal medicine, ob-gyn physicians across the state of Mississippi. Despite the fact that Sherry had just completed her fetal fellowship training only weeks earlier, and had no real-world experi-ence, within a month of her arrival, she was named medical director of fetal echocardiography by Dr. Kowatch, as he also simultaneously announced that four cardiologists, two of whom were identified as him and Sherry Monroe, would be dedicated to performing the official reads for all echocardiograms from that point moving forward. These two changes were met with great controversy by several of the cardiologists who had been reading echos and performing fetal echocardiography for years.

After two months on the job, I started to get a sense that not only was Dr. Kowatch experiencing a difficult transition from Mayo Children's to CHOB, but he also seemed to display significant discomfort when it came to making confident clinical decisions pertaining to inpatient cardiology and cardiac intensive care. He struggled to deliver confident cardiology recommendations during our weekly case management conference where we presented upcoming patients who would be requiring surgery in the near future. There were clear knowledge gaps that began to show, and I wasn't the only one to notice, both surgeons, all of my CICU colleagues, and several cardiologists brought these same concerns to my attention. The other concern that had developed was the display of sheer favoritism when it came to the treatment of Tricia Cranton and Sherry Monroe, when compared to what he displayed toward the rest of the cardiology team. Beyond the clear knowledge gaps and the favoritism displayed by Dr. Kowatch, he began to show that his defense mechanism when someone would question or expose his knowledge gaps was to respond with an authoritarian disposition, essentially doubling down on his mistake or knowledge gap by repeating his same words, only more aggressively, as if saying the same thing louder and aggressively would suddenly make others see his words differently. It was obviously a sad attempt to shut down any questioning on behalf of the rest of the team, as if they required scolding for their display of disobedience—a leadership style I had unfortunately become all too familiar with, and one that I fully understood to be dangerous and a team destroyer.

Dr. Kowatch, Tricia, and Sherry interacted as if they were the popular kids who made up a high school clique, despite the fact that Dr. Kowatch was in his sixties and Tricia was in her early forties. Sherry was in her mid-thirties and fit the classic stereotype of the rich Valley girl who was a high school bully and actually spoke with a voice and vocabulary that fit the stereotype to perfection. When the three were together, Dr. Kowatch appeared to regress to what I would most closely describe as a twenty-year-old girl, where he would use frequent and rather flamboyant, feminine hand gestures, as the three would exchange the patented phrases "Oh my God" and "OMG" as if they were openly criticizing the unpopular kids at school, in plain sight, and without fear of reprimand. It was clear they projected an elitist, superiority complex as they looked down on those that had been at CHOB for years with judgment and without a morsel of respect—a disturbing sight to see, and clearly a defense mechanism that they had developed over the years to disguise their own weaknesses and insecurities. To make matters worse, they would go on to display a toxic disposition, speaking nice when face-to-face with their colleagues; however, behind the scenes they were ruthless and talked negatively about everyone. In fact, Tricia and Sherry would even speak poorly of one another when in the presence of others. This behavior was immature and very concerning, as we had just battled hard to eradicate the toxic environment that once ruled CHOB for decades.

While there was cause for concern given the clear lack of clinical knowledge and insight as well as some clear leadership flaws displayed by Dr. Kowatch, I could see the "deer in headlights" when I looked into his eyes. I recalled that same look in my eyes, and those of so many others who were new to Children's Hospital of Biloxi—the look that I came to interpret over time as the "Oh shit, I made a huge mistake by accepting this job" look, a look I knew all too well. I decided rather than lowering myself to the level of immaturity displayed by my new colleagues, I would reject my impulse to propagate my discovery of Dr. Kowatch's underlying fear to my other team-mates as such an action would be counterproductive. Instead, due to the amassing concerns related to his clinical weakness and the toxic behavior he was displaying, I felt the best approach was to sit down with him, and have an open and honest conversation, and offer any assistance in any way that I could. So, I arranged a meeting in his office. I sat at the table aside his desk and asked half-jokingly, "How are you doing with the transition from such a finely tuned machine like Mayo Children's to the rusty, piecemeal, jerry-rigged, barely functioning jalopy of a system here at CHOB?"

Dr. Kowatch stuttered anxiously as he tried to relay a message of posi-tivity and confidence but failed miserably at doing so. His long-sleeved, button-down shirt appeared battle-tested with weathered armpit stains the size of a Greyhound bus on each side, as he squirmed uncontrollably in his office chair as if he had just shit his pants and anxiously awaited the right moment to escape the room so that he could rid himself of his diarrhea-satu-rated briefs. He muttered buzzwords such as "happy to be here" and "getting used to the system," all the typical gibberish we often say to maintain an appearance that everything is wonderful.

"Tim, you need to relax, I know exactly what you are thinking. You're thinking, Oh shit. I just gave up my job of twenty years where I was esteemed, respected and comfortable to take on a job in a system that is dysfunctional, under-resourced, with inadequate subspecialty support and now I am stuck here without a viable exit strategy. Am I wrong?" I asked.

He revealed a slight smile and responded, "You are not wrong."

"I know exactly how you feel. I regretted my decision and told myself what an idiot I was for accepting this job for more than a year. I dreaded coming to work every day, but all that changed about six months ago. Once the patient care began to improve and once the individuals here bought into the concept of a team, everything changed, most importantly the culture. Everyone began taking pride in what they were doing and in the quality of care that they were providing. They felt nurtured and it showed, families were happier because the staff was happier, which became contagious. It is extremely important that you understand any feelings of uncertainty you are experiencing are completely normal here. Every new person I have witnessed join this hospital has gone through this same transition and everyone who has chosen to stick it out has moved beyond the shock phase and has now adequately adjusted. Here, we aren't pretending to be one of the best, hell, we know we aren't even close to that yet, but that is certainly the goal, and once you buy into the idea of making a difference and learn to let go of the fact that you once worked at one of the best, you can begin to relax and truly enjoy the challenge of this job. It is far too much pressure to place on yourself to say that you need to make this program the best, you need to build off of each success and develop an attainable, long-term goal, which for me, is to make things better every day and to ultimately provide care to the children of this state that is equivalent to that already being provided to the rest of the children around the country. Trust me, don't swing for the fences, take a bunt for a base hit. Hell, I would even take an intentional walk or a hit by pitch, they both lead to the same destination," I explained as I laughed aloud. "The other aspect, in my humble opinion, is that it is vitally important that we protect the collegiality and nurturing environment that exists within the CICU and Heart Center. These are very new concepts here at CHOB. This institution was riddled with negativity and toxicity when I arrived, and it was intolerable. Allowing such an environment to reappear and reestablish dominance could be devastating and could sabotage our current trajectory and negatively impact our growth and progress as a team," I continued. I sensed Dr. Kowatch's distaste for Dr. Penton, so I decided this may be the most appropriate time to discuss this sensitive topic. Dr. Penton had remained relatively unknown in the world of pediatric cardiac surgery due to the program's isolation, which resulted from the lack of resources, the devastation caused by Hurricane Kelly, and the controlling practices of Dr. Rostri. For Dr. Kowatch, the quality of a congenital cardiac program was defined by the national reputation of the cardiac surgeon tasked with leading the team. Dr. Penton was a blue-collar guy, he wore scrubs to work every day, he rarely wore a tie, much less a suit, and had always carried a heavy clinical workload throughout his career. He was never the beneficiary of "set-aside time" or "research time," which could have allowed him ample opportunity to publish research and present at national conferences, thereby gaining him national recognition, or at least the perception of national recognition. As a result, he did not boast a thirty- or fifty-page CV; however, I had worked with him long enough to know that his true value was far greater than anything that could be summarized by some words typed on a few pieces of paper. It was hard to fault such a hardworking, caring and dedicated individual who was never provided the opportunity to present or publish, which had resulted in his inability to pad his CV, and as I said earlier, it is impossible to understand someone's qualifications or their clinical competence by simply reading a piece of paper. Dr. Kowatch had not had ample opportunity to work with Dr. Penton to understand his value, nor did he display the slightest desire to search deeper for the presence of the many qualities that make up a great congenital heart surgeon. By Dr. Kowatch's accord, Dr. Penton didn't dress like a "director of pediatric cardiac surgery" nor was his CV plastered with the multitude of publications, exhibited by many of the top congenital heart surgeons, which led to his simplistic inference that he was therefore unworthy and unqualified to serve as the leader of this program, the same program he had helped develop for more than twenty years. It was blatantly obvious that Dr. Kowatch did not respect Dr. Penton, and he often attempted to disregard his suggestions, frequently in a disrespectful and unprofessional manner, in front of the other members of the Heart Center. Dr. Kowatch went on to discuss with me that he indeed didn't feel that Dr. Penton was the right choice for the role of division chief of pediatric cardiac surgery. "Tim, to be honest with you, six months ago I would have agreed with you 100 percent. When I arrived here, I thought Dr. Penton would be nothing more than a thorn in my side, who would obstruct my ability to carry out my job. However, over the last six months, I am amazed at his adaptability and how much he has bought into the concept of team. He trusts me to the extent that he voluntarily handed over control of the CICU to me, which is incredible, particularly considering he is a congenital heart surgeon. He has been performing some very complex cases with fantastic outcomes. Even more so, he has started to blossom into an incredible leader who supports collaboration and has even taken an active role in the education of my CICU team," I explained.

"Eric, I think I am going to ask administration to approve my request to begin a nationwide search for a new chief of pediatric cardiac surgery," he replied, appearing to ignore every word I had just spoken.

"Oh, I thought Dr. Penton told me yesterday that they had named him the permanent chief, which to my understanding was to be formally announced tomorrow," I said, confused.

"Yes, well technically, I already spoke to Mr. Boykins about the search, and he said he agreed, and that he will tell Dr. Penton of this decision and explain to him that it was an oversight on his behalf," he explained, with a fake smile, and a look on his face that screamed "guilty."

Once again, I shook my head in astonishment at the disrespect displayed by our hospital administration. After all of the emotional trauma Dr. Penton and I had been through over the preceding year, in addition to the dedication and success that Dr. Penton had demonstrated, they were going to retract this decision? What kind of person would do such a thing? I quickly moved past the shock I had experienced and was now visibly disturbed that this administration would do that to him or anyone for that matter. I shook my head and told Dr. Kowatch, "This decision will need to be your own, because I support the hiring of Dr. Penton. I hope you and the administration know what you are doing, because you are playing with people's lives and their emotions, and that is not OK."

"Dr. Penton will be among the candidate pool," he exclaimed, trying to regain my support for his plan, but I knew his words represented nothing more than theatrics, especially now.

The following day, Dr. Penton pulled me aside after surgical rounds to detail the events that had transpired, including his promotion and subsequent demotion, without apology, in less than twenty-four hours. I played stupid, but I was pissed, and I truly felt for him as my friend. "What else could I have done?" he asked, clearly distraught.

"My friend, there is nothing more you could have done, in my opinion. You are speaking to a man whom you converted from a nonbeliever to a believer, and who has now grown to become a strong proponent of yours. It is appalling to know that they would do such a thing to you. Terry, it's not over, you are still a strong candidate for the position, and I will continue to be your biggest supporter," I said, as I did my best to appear sincere, but I knew the truth, and that was that Dr. Penton would never be considered a viable candidate, at least in the eyes of Dr. Kowatch and Antoine Boykins, and sadly it was becoming clear that those were the only eyes that mattered. This was another example of the changing times, as the administration intensified their obsession with hiring "top trained" candidates, based solely on the training documented on their CV. The truth was, the program desperately needed to increase its bandwidth by adding clinically sound physicians, as we were at a stage of development where it was essential to convince local families and private cardiologists that we were capable of providing high-quality, comprehensive cardiac care, and until we did so, it would be nearly impossible to increase our cardiac surgical volume and referrals, while erasing the negative historical stigma that had been attached to the institution for so long. Only then could we progress to the second stage of program development, which would require the recruitment of researchers and scholars to add that vital component to our repertoire. I felt that it would be a critical mistake if we were to overlook the importance of establishing clinical excellence, first and foremost. Attempting to bypass this first stage and proceed directly to the second would be a grave error in my opinion. Without several strong clinicians, there was no path forward for the program because it would place an additional burden on the few individuals who had displayed clinical excellence, thus far, and it would ultimately place them at increased risk of physician burnout. There appeared to be two distinctly different programmatic paths that were diverging before our eyes, one focusing on clinical quality first, the other focusing on blindly hiring individuals based on their pedigree, without prior assurance of their clinical ability; unfortunately, the latter path was being promoted by the individuals with power, and that was going to be difficult to change.

As I departed Dr. Kowatch's office, I couldn't help but feel deflated and defeated as I pondered the deeper meaning of everything I had just heard. I thought about how we as human beings, often unknowingly, walk down the same path, in the same direction, every single day, unaware of our surroundings, staring at our feet as they move across the ground without thought, involuntarily, in a repetitive manner. Meanwhile, a few inches aside the walking path exist wildflowers, growing in silence, right in front of our face, unobscured yet hidden from our sight. For years they thrived, unacknowledged by us, yet they return annually, boasting a more durable stem, with petals exhibiting more profound color variations, more attractive than the year prior, yet we hastily walk past, oblivious to their existence, much less their natural beauty which screams for our attention, as we rush to the store to purchase an artificial flower to place in the windowsill of our home because we crave something beautiful to look at each day, though it is lifeless. Despite our unawareness and neglect, the wildflower continues to thrive, until one day, by chance, you suddenly become aware of the plant's existence. The learned individual cannot believe they have bypassed and neglected such natural beauty for so long, and resultantly, they feel remorse for their lack of awareness, which has forced the plant to grow unassisted and in isolation. This same individual self-reflects and learns from their mistake, promising to be more aware and to treasure all of the amazing aspects of the flower, which had been there all along. Alternatively, the unaware individual one day trips over their feet, and as they stumble off the path, they come to acknowledge the plant's presence; however, while the plant appears superficially attractive, its pedigree is of uncertain origin, and therefore it becomes labeled as foreign, leading to the inference that it cannot be of the highest quality, and is thereby labeled as a weed and determined to be a nuisance, until one day it is plucked from the earth, leading to its demise. I pondered these two vastly different viewpoints, which detail the exact same plant. I realized that this differing perception of the same plant by separate individuals is precisely analogous to the drastically differing viewpoints Dr. Kowatch and I held for Dr. Penton. While I initially failed to recognize Dr. Penton's kindness, clinical skill, and his ability to adapt and evolve with ongoing change, these characteristics had actually been present all along, I had simply failed to notice them, or more accurately, I failed to take the time to notice them. I don't recall the event that led to my awakening as it relates to Dr. Penton's ability as a surgeon and a leader; however, I do remember the moment it occurred because it was as if a light switch had flipped. The skill, dedication, and the leadership ability he harnessed became blatantly obvious to me. I felt remorseful that I had neglected him the fair, unbiased assessment of his clinical and leadership ability, that he deserved. The moment I recognized these skills, I was certain they were not newly acquired; instead, they had been present all along. He had been surviving alone, unsupported, and in isolation, yet somehow, he adapted, and thrived, and sought no reward other than witnessing the smile on the face of his patients and their respective families as they walked out the door to go home. If these qualities don't describe a leader, I don't know what does, and these attributes were simply not going to be found on his CV. Conversely, Dr. Kowatch viewed Dr. Penton as different, or atypical, from the very beginning, because through his eyes, Dr. Penton was not constructed from the same mold as that of the prototypical congenital cardiac surgeon, and therefore he couldn't possibly be of the highest pedigree. And for these reasons, it was inferred that he couldn't possibly be a highly skilled cardiac surgeon, which rendered a superficial and biased opinion concluding that he was unqualified to function as the director of pediatric cardiac surgery. As they say, beauty is in the eye of the beholder, and in this circumstance, the only eyes with an opinion that mattered happened to belong to two individuals who had predetermined Dr. Penton's fate and were unwilling to dedicate the time necessary to recognize the skill and attributes of a great surgeon and leader, which had been silently displayed by Dr. Penton for the last twenty years.

The following day after my meeting with Dr. Kowatch, Michael Stringer called an urgent meeting that was to include Dr. Penton, Dr. Kowatch, Michael, and me. Michael was so intelligent and given his uncanny ability to read people and situations, I assumed that he was calling this meeting to address the recanting of the leadership promotion that had occurred at the expense of Dr. Penton. Michael began the meeting by apologizing for his promotion and subsequent demotion as the chief of pediatric cardiac surgery. He relayed his unrelenting support for Dr. Penton and proceeded to pass on the supposed support of the entire administration. He promised that Dr. Penton was to be given fair consideration as one of the top candidates for the position. Michael admirably delivered a passionate speech, and had I not already understood the secret underworking and underlying bias that existed, I would have believed the words he was saying. I could see in Michael's face that he truly believed what he was saying, but the truth was, it was out of his control. Mr. Boykins had become obsessed with the concept of "top trained" physicians. However, the glaring deficiency in his recruitment philosophy, which was actually void of logical reasoning, was the fact that he was a nonphysician for starters, and in particular one that came from a high-functioning institution capable of attracting candidates from across the globe. He appeared oblivious to the fact that it was not infrequent to encounter physicians with fifty-page CVs who were quite frankly clinically incompetent. In fact, I was becoming more convinced that we had recently hired one by the name of Dr. Tim Kowatch. Dr. Kowatch, like most weak clinicians, tend to take the approach of keeping silent and fading quietly into the background due to a constant fear of being exposed for their inadequacies. I had encountered such individuals during my career who had practiced at large, highly resourced institutions, where things were so specialized and the staff was so large, that it was easy to shield clinical inadequacies from public knowledge simply by fading quietly into the background, while allowing the numerous individuals with clinical competence to absorb their workload and hide their weakness. Such a process is enabling and naturally exacerbates such incompetence by limiting their clinical exposure. Therefore, it becomes a perpetuating cycle that tends to get worse over time. For example, in a large system such as Mayo Children's, it was possible to place a clinically weak individual, such as Dr. Kowatch, in the outpatient setting, where he could cause little to no harm, and even give him a leadership title with some administrative tasks that he could complete with ease, while never allowing him or pushing him to become familiar or competent at managing sick children in an inpatient setting. As a result, he would have plenty of time to achieve academic success, which was good for him and for the institution. Now, imagine such a scenario that has been ongoing for a twenty-year period, and naturally you can begin to understand how someone who may have begun their career as a clinically weak individual, has now helplessly regressed to a stage of irreparable clinical incompetence because they have now had zero exposure to caring for sick children for many years. Yet, due to a plethora of academic time, this individual hopefully will now boast a multitude of publications that they have authored over this extended period of time. As a result, they most likely will have been promoted to professor. Now, when this individual applies for a leadership position, you find yourself reading a very impressive CV, which lists buzzwords such as medical director, professor, twenty years experience at a prestigious institution, and one hundred publications. Impressive right? I hope you are beginning to understand my point. Indeed, these are impressive accolades; however, nowhere on their CV does it list "clinically incompetent" or "warning, danger to patients." If you give credence to these achievements alone, you may find yourself stuck with an individual who is incapable of managing patients safely, who will literally stop at nothing to hide such incompetence. Now imagine thrusting such an individual into a leadership position, much less as the co-director of a complex specialty responsible for overseeing and directing the medical and surgical care of the some of the most fragile and complex patients in medicine. Scary! Once you work with such an individual, you tend to become hypervigilant and question everything about future applicants, while believing nothing, as you obsessively attempt to avoid finding yourself in such a scenario again. As a result of my prior experience with such a scenario, I tend to view the CV as nothing more than a primary screening tool, to determine if I wish to proceed with a phone interview or not. I try to avoid making judgments one way or another, based solely on their CV, until I have had adequate time to develop a better feel for the candidate's integrity by speaking with them. Then, if they pass this stage of the screening, I proceed to performing a detailed investigation into their interpersonal skills as well as their ability as a clinician, which in my opinion, can only be determined by speaking with several of their current and past colleagues. This method is far from foolproof, but it is much safer than placing too much emphasis on an individual's training background alone. Such scenarios of hiding weak individuals in the background at large institutions do not merely apply to clinically weak individuals, it also applies to physicians with extensive behavioral issues, which may border on personality disorders, making them nightmare colleagues to work with while also making them a nightmare for families and patients to deal with, thereby making them a liability from a risk management standpoint.

Mr. Boykins ultimately became so obsessed with recruiting "top trained" physicians that he, as a nonphysician who had never been stuck in a scary situation such as the one I previously outlined, failed to recognize the importance of putting in the time to appropriately vet candidates, to be as certain as was humanly possible that they displayed a personality that was complementary to the current team, while also vetting that they had an established history of clinical competence. Instead, he continued to behave like the high school girl, infatuated with pursuing "top trained" physicians, as if they were celebrities whose autograph he simply must have, despite repeated press coverage suggesting that they were people of deception and of poor moral character. It appeared he had lost his way and perhaps he had forgotten that his job was to build a team that can work together to provide exceptional care to children, rather than to see how many "top trained" physicians he could hire, while disregarding important details such as whether they could safely care for children or whether they had the interpersonal skills to work together as a team. I truly tried to remain as objective as possible and my analysis of Dr. Kowatch and the situation at hand was not personal, it was all about the patients and the staff. Sadly, as a person, I liked Dr. Kowatch, but I was terrified of the repercussions the dangerous combination of clinical weakness, an authoritative approach to questioning, leadership flaws, and the ultimate power to dictate care, could have on the children and the nurturing culture we had fought so hard to develop.

Following our last meeting where we discussed what had happened to Dr. Penton, I began to notice Michael Stringer's glowing personality and leadership were beginning to wane. I felt as though he couldn't hide his growing mistrust in Mr. Boykins, and I couldn't help but sense a developing dissension between the two of them. The truth was, Michael was the heart and soul of the hospital, everything flowed through and from him, including ideas, communication between physicians and the CEO, news, and plans. Michael recognized the glaring leadership flaws displayed by Dr. Kowatch immediately. He regularly scheduled team-building meetings and coached each of us on how to be the best leader we could be. Well, I suppose coach is the wrong word. Michael had the gift of teaching you when you didn't realize that you were being taught. I always walked away feeling as though I had grown a bit more as a leader and as a person after our interactions. I could see the look on Dr. Kowatch's face after these meetings, which were clearly mostly directed at him, and he was not amused in the slightest. In fact, Dr. Kowatch displayed some of the same classic behaviors that I had observed in others coming from "top trained" programs where they had been able to mask their clinical incompetence by hiding among the masses, that is until they decided to accept a position at a smaller, less-resourced institution, where it became impossible to hide. Somehow, these individuals had learned survival tactics throughout their career, such as developing alliances with powerful people immediately upon arrival to a new job or position. This observation of forming high-powered alliances was consistent and reproducible and was executed by many individuals from elite institutions. Most were not incompetent, yet most seemed to do it; however, those who had established credibility on their own, did not appear to rely on such alliances unless it became necessary for some reason. Of course, there are many truly "top trained"

BURNED OUT

physicians who are exceptional clinicians. However, you can quickly identify the "sham" doctors who train at these same "top institutions," because when they arrive at a new job or position, they immediately scurry like rats to flatter and form friendships with others in positions of power, in order to provide protection for that dreadful yet certain day when they are exposed for their incompetence. I had witnessed many weak clinicians do this over my career and Dr. Kowatch and his two new hires had immediately formed alliances with the administrators upon their arrival, particularly Mr. Boykins, who appeared vulnerable to some good old ass-kissing!

Dr. Penton appeared to be struggling mightily following the retraction of his promotion, and understandably so. After a week or so, he incredibly appeared to shake it off, or at least on the surface. The holidays were upon us, and Dr. Penton somehow appeared able to direct his attention toward his family. Christmas Eve came, and I was working a twenty-four-hour shift in the CICU. There are times in this field when you get the sense that the universe aligns in such a way that it brings the necessary people together at a specific point in time, in order to save a life. Well, on this particular Christmas Eve, such a perfect alignment of the universe appeared to occur. Jody Myers was one of the most experienced nurses in the CICU. She had worked at CHOB for nearly twenty years. Unfortunately, she had recently been diagnosed with breast cancer and was resigning so that she could undergo a bilateral mastectomy and chemotherapy. Christmas Eve happened to be her last shift. I was walking around the CICU to check on the patients and I stopped at the bedside of the patient Jody was caring for. She and I were talking just outside the doorway of her patient's room. Her patient was a teenage girl who had recently undergone cardiac surgery and was extubated and sitting up in bed. As we stood there talking, the patient started to violently hiccup, and following three loud hiccups, her chest tube began filling with fresh blood. This same chest tube had not been draining anything the entire day and we were planning on removing it the following day. Suddenly, in a matter of seconds, there was 500 milliliters of blood that had filled the chest tube chamber. I looked at Jody and said call the blood bank and have them release

353

emergency blood STAT, meanwhile grab some liter bags of normal saline and bring the airway cart. The patient's blood pressure began to drop rapidly as we pushed saline. As I prepared to intubate her, I directed the nurses to push fluid and blood as fast as possible. I laid my cell phone on the bed and called Dr. Penton via speakerphone. I said, "Terry, I need you to get here ASAP, the patient is hemorrhaging, and we are having a hard time keeping up with the output and maintaining an adequate blood pressure."

"Eric, I am actually walking down the hall and am right outside the CICU," Dr. Penton replied.

"Get the open chest cart and call the ECMO team," I said as I intubated the patient. Dr. Penton walked through the doors of the CICU as if he was an angel delivered instantly from above, just as the open chest cart was delivered to the bedside. We pushed emergency blood as Dr. Penton opened her chest at the bedside and quickly identified the source of bleeding, placing a clamp at the site that temporarily stopped the bleeding, allowing us an opportunity to stabilize her blood pressure. He found that when the patient had hiccupped, the end of the chest tube had lacerated the inferior vena cava, a major vein in the body. As it turns out, Dr. Penton had bought his housekeeper a gift certificate for a massage as her Christmas present, but for some reason, his printer at home had randomly stopped working that day. He happened to be at the hospital at that exact time because he was going to use the printer in his office to print the gift certificate. The patient quickly stabilized, the laceration was repaired, and the bleeding resolved. The following morning, less than fifteen hours after the event, she was successfully extubated and discharged home two days later, in perfect condition. It was one of the most memorable emergencies I have faced in the CICU that resulted in such a rapid turnaround and a positive outcome. Not only does this example show how dramatically a patient's condition can change in the CICU in an instant, but it also suggests that there are situations that are simply unexplainable, and sometimes extraordinary circumstances must occur at a precise moment in time in order to be able to save a patient's life. I couldn't help but reflect on this event and analyze what could have happened had things not aligned in the manner that they did that day. For example, what if Jody had been at lunch and I had already passed by the bedside fifteen minutes earlier, or what if Dr. Penton's printer had been working at home, or what if we failed to recognize the severity of the bleeding and we couldn't get emergency blood from the blood bank? Regardless of the scenario I contrived in my mind, all other avenues appeared to lead to the demise or the neurologic devastation of this beautiful little girl, on Christmas Eve. The one factor that became clear to me was that her survival universally depended on the near instantaneous arrival of Dr. Penton to her bedside. Without that, she wasn't leaving the hospital as the normal little girl she was. It is experiencing situations such as this that makes me question the meaning of life and consider the possibility that on rare occasions there may be connections between people that seemingly lead to some sort of brief yet perfect universal alignment, resulting in something so incredible that it simply cannot be attributed to coincidence. If Dr. Penton had arrived even fifteen minutes later, we wouldn't have been able to continue to keep up with that degree of blood loss and the patient would have died or at a minimum she would have suffered significant neurological injury, perhaps leading to brain death. Fate brought Jody, Dr. Penton, and me together on that Christmas Eve at the only time that mattered. The teamwork we displayed was flawless and we saved a patient's life, but I truly believe her survival had a divine component to it. It was an incredible gift for Jody to leave the hospital on her last day knowing that she helped save this beautiful little girl and for the family of this little girl, as they would still be able to celebrate Christmas with their daughter. In the back of my mind, I couldn't help but wonder if this event was intended as some sort of sign or message for Dr. Penton, due to the mental struggle that he must have been enduring. Perhaps it was a reminder that he had been given a gift, and that gift just saved a little girl's life, and while things may seem dark in his life at the moment, he was still needed on this earth to help save other children.

30

TROUBLE AT HOME

With all the changes ongoing at the hospital, the situation at home continued to deteriorate. Despite making some friends in Biloxi, Ana continued to have a hard time. She and the kids missed their friends in Florida badly and Ana subtly voiced her displeasure with Mississippi several times and had mentioned in passing, that someday she would like to go back to Florida. Meanwhile, Erica, my youngest daughter, began to have trouble at school, where she was being bullied by some kids in her class. Erica was very sweet and intelligent, but she was also shy and quiet. Ana and I began to notice that Erica started to isolate herself in her room at home, and despite repeated attempts by both of us, to talk with her and ask what was wrong, she didn't want to share what was happening to her. I would later find out that she was scared to tell me about being bullied because she didn't want me to feel bad that I had moved them to Mississippi, away from their friends. However, when she finally spoke with Ana about the details of the bullying that was occurring at school, Ana shared them with me. I was devastated, the guilt I felt for moving my family, against their will, began to intensify.

I was torn, I knew my family supported me, but they were doing so at the expense of their own happiness. At the same time, my confidence in the direction of the program once again began to dwindle. Dr. Kowatch continued to display bizarre behavior, and I simply didn't trust him as a leader, and most certainly as a clinician, and when you can't trust the co-director of the entire program, where do you possibly go from there? Equally concerning was the recent behavior of the CEO, Antoine Boykins, who now seemed willing to unabashedly share his obsession with hiring "top trained" individuals with all employees at CHOB. Once I had the time to sit down and mentally dissect and analyze all of the events that had occurred over preceding months, I felt the public message Mr. Boykins was portraying to all employees, when analyzed in in more detail, spoke a subtle, perhaps more subliminal message that may not be apparent to everyone. The general message was "A new day is here, and we can now recruit 'top trained' talent to Children's Hospital of Biloxi"; however, the deeper message appeared to say "A new day is here where we can finally attract real doctors to Biloxi, so from this point forward I will work with the real doctors to develop a plan and that plan may or may not include many of you." Yes, this was my subjective interpretation, but let's quickly rehash the events leading to such a conclusion. First, Mr. Boykins questioning my qualifications while ignoring Dr. Penton and my hard work. Second, promoting Dr. Penton to chief of pediatric cardiac surgery, only to retract it the same day without explanation or apology after secretly developing a plan to recruit a new chief, while falsely reassuring Dr. Penton that he was a viable candidate, because they needed him to operate until they found his replacement. Third, publicly endorsing his plan to acquire "top talent," which was messaged in a way that minimized the value and impact of the employees who had been at CHOB for many years. Fourth, throwing his unwavering support behind Dr. Kowatch, who was brand new to the institution and who had displayed concerning behaviors recognized by several other employees, including Michael Stringer, COO. These may seem small, but to a rapidly evolving program with PTSD from the past, they are not. As I learned earlier, here at CHOB, trust means EVERYTHING, and he was beginning to lose it. While it remained unspoken, I couldn't help but sense a developing uncertainty among the staff of the CICU, and perhaps elsewhere throughout the hospital, which was leading to the development of an ugly, unanswerable question in their minds, "Is the program moving backward toward the same environment we were in before when Dr. Rostri was here?" And that was a frightening thought for all of us!

I was also becoming increasingly concerned with Michaels Stringer's longevity as his displeasure with Mr. Boykins and his lack of faith in Dr. Kowatch mounted. There were so many ongoing factors in my life that seemed to be pulling me simultaneously in different directions. Yes, things had been progressing at work but the uncertainty I felt about Mr. Boykins and Dr. Kowatch as leaders was real, and the repercussions of poor leadership could not only halt our progress, but it also held the potential to destroy it. After transcending the worst of times since joining Children's Hospital of Biloxi, admittedly, the momentum for change appeared to stall as if a sailboat that had been moving with a swift tailwind that suddenly shifted into a strong headwind. It was frustrating to be thrust back into the once familiar feeling of uncertainty, after so much sacrifice, and I worried that if I was forced to push aggressively once again for change, it may have a lasting negative impact on my family and my health. Was this the universe trying to tell me that I had accomplished all that I could and now it was time to move on and focus on my health and my family? But how could I possibly walk away now, after we had accomplished so much, and while there was still so much work to be done? I felt disappointed and couldn't believe I was reexperiencing the same uncertainty I felt when I first arrived to CHOB. I decided I needed to consider all my options.

After much deliberation, I decided that I would discretely do some searching to see if there were any job openings back in Florida. Coincidentally, a colleague of mine, Elanor Roth, who worked with me in Fort Myers called me to catch up. She proceeded to explain to me how the Children's

Hospital of Tampa was looking to restart its congenital heart program. Three years earlier, their congenital heart program had been shut down following a media scandal that exposed suboptimal surgical outcomes. My colleague explained to me that the program had recently hired Dr. Joseph Zalenski, a nationally recognized surgeon, known for his expertise in neonatal cardiac surgery and equally renowned as a being a wonderful man and a great leader. Dr. Roth said, "They are searching for a division chief to rebuild the cardiac intensive care unit. You should apply. I know Dr. Zalenski, he is an extremely talented surgeon and very easy to work with. I will talk to him about you if you are interested." In all honesty, I had no idea what I should do, but I felt the need to at least investigate the opportunity.

The following week I was put in contact with Dr. Zalenski. We spoke for nearly an hour on the phone. Dr. Zalenski had a clear vision for rebuilding the program. Two cardiac intensivists remained from the previous program along with four advanced practice providers. The job would require a rebuild of the entire CICU, which I obviously had experience in doing, and while this position would require a lot of work, it was clearly not to the extent of that required at CHOB. I knew I was mentally capable of carrying out the job; however, I had concerns regarding my body's ability to keep up with my mind. After my experience in Biloxi, I now understood and acknowledged that the biggest risk to myself was actually me. My stubbornness had achieved newfound highs in Biloxi, and I knew when I committed to something, that I was all in until the very end, and that terrified me.

I decided to formally interview for the position. My first visit was scheduled for the following week. Once the interview was officially arranged, I had to tell Ana. She was excited but appropriately cautious with her feelings so as not to be disappointed if the job didn't work out. We both decided that it was best not to share the possibility of moving back to Florida with the girls, at least until it appeared like a more distinct possibility.

My plane touched down at Tampa International Airport and I took an Uber to the hotel. I hadn't visited Tampa for more than three years and as a result, I had forgotten how beautiful the area was. The sky was clear and sunny, and the palm trees blew beautifully with each gust of wind. I thought of how happy my family would be if we were to move back to the gorgeous state of Florida, perhaps I would be happier as well? Was I already happy in Biloxi? The truth was, I had no idea, I couldn't even define what happiness meant to me anymore. I was so focused on building the CICU and advancing the program that I had forgotten about the things that made me feel happy and grateful, such as spending time with my family and friends, golfing, and traveling. Perhaps a new job and a change of scenery would reinvigorate me mentally, which may lead to improved physical health, increasing the likelihood of weaning off prednisone. Or would I be putting myself right back into the same situation in a different CICU?

The next day was filled with interviews. I had friends who worked at Tampa Children's, so it was nice to catch up with them. They all spoke highly of the hospital and were excited at the possibility of me joining them. The cardiac program rebuild was being directed by a legend in the field of pediatric cardiac intensive care named Winston Greenburg. He was a cardiac anesthesiologist who had practiced cardiac intensive care and had authored the textbook that was considered the "bible" for pediatric cardiac ICU care. It was an honor to meet him. During our interview, Dr. Greenburg shared with me his own experience building the CICU from scratch at North Carolina Children's twenty years earlier and the challenges he needed to overcome in order to succeed, which immediately provided a connection between us. While I already had immense respect for his remarkable career, our shared experience made his legacy more real for me and gave me confidence that the rebuild of the Tampa Children's Cardiac program was in good hands. Meeting with Dr. Zalenski, the pediatric cardiac surgeon, was equally reassuring, his vision was clear and calculated. He envisioned a stepwise approach for staffing, training, and executing the program rebuild. He was very soft-spoken, yet his aura emitted confidence and respect. The visit concluded with dinner that evening where specifics were discussed about the second phase of interviews for the CICU division chief opening. As the evening ended, Dr.

Zalenski and Dr. Greenburg thanked me for the visit and were honest about the fact that they had two other candidates scheduled for interviews over the next month, after which time they would contact me regarding who would be chosen for second visits. The following morning, I was back on the plane to Biloxi. I felt good about the visit and the plan that had been laid out for the rebuild. My only concern was related to my body's ability to endure another CICU rebuild. I had much to consider. My health was obviously a major concern as was the time that would be required to perform the job up to my standard, which would certainly detract valuable time from away my family.

When I arrived back in Biloxi, I shared my thoughts with Ana regarding the possibility, who was appropriately skeptical. "Let's see what happens. If they call you back for a second interview, then we will discuss the option further. Until then, I won't get my hopes up," Ana said.

"I agree. Sounds fair," I replied.

A month had passed, and I sensed neither Ana nor I wanted to discuss the possibility of moving back to Florida for differing reasons. Clearly she didn't want to get her or the girls' hopes up only to have them crushed if the opportunity was not right, and honestly, I wasn't sure what I wanted. My feelings were constantly changing. I no longer felt the extreme commitment I had for CHOB, I had already built a substantial part of the CICU, and I had been responsible, in large part, for recruiting Dr. Kowatch. More than anything, I felt uncertain regarding the current direction of the cardiac program, and worst of all, I felt I no longer had the ability to influence the direction the program was headed. Michael Stringer's future also appeared uncertain to me, as did Doris Geisinger's, and I simply didn't trust Antoine Boykins after the way he treated and misled Dr. Penton. Nor did I have faith in Dr. Kowatch or his recruits as collaborative colleagues or as quality clinicians. I think subconsciously I hoped for the easy way out of this difficult decision, wishing desperately that Dr. Greenburg would take the decision off my hands by deciding to go with another candidate for the position. However, just as I hoped I wouldn't have to make another difficult decision, my phone rang. I answered the phone, hearing Dr. Greenburg's voice, saying, "Eric, we completed the last of our candidate interviews, Dr. Zelenski, myself and the rest of the team truly enjoyed your visit, and we would love to invite you and your family to come for a second visit." I was unsure whether I should be excited or pissed! I felt happy for the opportunity because they had interviewed candidates who were clearly more qualified on paper than I was, which told me that either those candidates had said no already, or that they were a team that felt that personality fit, dedication, and clinical ability are attributes that were most important, and perhaps they had done the work required to determine that I held such qualities, and if they had, I respected that. The team felt like a good fit for me and clearly Ana and the kids would be happier back in Florida. The uncertainty for me pertained to my body's ability to keep up with my mind and its desire to give everything I had to building a CICU once again, granted, in a much more supported and established system when compared to CHOB. I decided that I needed to at least see the details of the offer and allow Ana an opportunity to be involved in the decision to move or not. That evening I shared the news with her, including my concern regarding the potential stress on my body and my immune system and the likely substantial number of hours I would again need to work. She acknowledged understanding and said that she didn't need to go along with me on the visit as we had visited Tampa many times and we would need to take the kids out of school to do so, because we didn't have any friends or family to watch them in Biloxi, while we traveled. Ana reinforced her support regarding my ability to make the decision, and that she would love nothing more than to go back to Florida, but not at the expense of my health. I was happy to hear her say that, although I knew how badly she wanted to move. That evening I called Dr. Greenburg and notified him of my interest in returning for a second visit.

The following week I was back on the plane headed to Tampa. I hadn't shared the possibility of leaving with anyone. I knew others' knowledge of the situation would cause major panic. My arrival to Tampa Children's felt different this time. Everyone I had met with during the first visit appeared excited about the possibility of me functioning as the new leader of the CICU. Dr. Greenburg spoke to me in detail regarding the specifics of the package they were to offer, including salary, benefits, the work schedule, and the number of intensivists they had already hired, as well as the total number of cardiac intensivists and advanced practice providers I would be allowed to hire, were I to accept the position. It was obvious Dr. Greenburg was very focused on providing a staffing model that ensured longevity and a good work-life balance, something CHOB completely disregarded. Additionally, Dr. Greenburg was very focused on research and outlined to me that he would dedicate set-aside time for clinical research, provide biostatistical support, and even lab space and funding for bench research for those interested. The difference in terms of understanding the importance of these resources and for the necessary time allocation to carry out these duties were lightyears ahead when comparing the program he was developing versus the one developed by the leaders at CHOB. The salary offered was nearly identical when I factored in the absence of state taxes in Florida. I felt positive about the opportunity and the commitment displayed by Dr. Greenburg and his team toward staffing the CICU in a manner that assured a healthier lifestyle while also pledging to support research. I began to feel that this could really work for me and certainly for Ana and the girls. The visit ended with dinner that evening as Dr. Greenburg and one other current CICU colleague treated me to an excellent seafood restaurant in St. Petersburg. At the end of dinner, the CICU colleague, Jordan Cunningham, who was only a few years less experienced than me, offered to drive me back to my hotel. Jordan was in his early forties. He had joined the Tampa Children's program about two years prior to the events leading to the shutdown of the cardiac program. He had described to me the awful situation he was forced to endure prior to the demise of the program. He had been named the interim associate director of the CICU initially, then one month later had been promoted to the position of interim medical director of the CICU. Earlier in the day, when I interviewed with him, I asked him, "Jordan, I have to ask, why haven't you put your name in the pool of candidates for this position, or why haven't they asked you to do so?"

"That is a great question. I made my interest in the position known; however, Dr. Greenburg and the team felt that the program needed a fresh start from every aspect, so they chose to pursue outside candidates," he replied. Trying to understand this dynamic situation led me to believe that there were likely two distinct possibilities, one is that he was planning his imminent departure and was in the process of finding another job, or two that he was hoping that the candidate who accepted the position of division chief would ultimately ask him to assume the role as medical director. I happened to be thinking that the latter option was something that could potentially benefit us both. As we drove in his Mercedes sport utility vehicle toward the hotel, I asked him bluntly, "So are you going to stick around or are you planning on leaving?"

He smiled and replied, "Great question. I have been offered the position of medical director at another program here in Florida, but I am waiting to see what is going to happen here."

"I figured as much. I am strongly considering this position but, in all honesty, given my health issues, I would need to name someone like you as medical director upon my acceptance in order to offload some of the workload. I am clinically feeling good now, but I know how quickly that can change and I would need to lean on you a lot in order to make this work," I said.

"I will stick around if you accept the job," he replied.

"That is helpful to know. Let me go home and speak with my wife and family and I promise I will let you know soon, even before I let Dr. Greenburg know, that way you can make your decision regarding your other offer," I said. We shook hands and I exited his vehicle and entered the hotel lobby and took the elevator to the fourth floor, leading to my room. It was late so I sent a text to Ana telling her goodnight and that I would call her in the morning to discuss everything. As I shut my eyes, I fell asleep feeling good about the opportunity and I felt that I was likely to accept the offer to become the division chief of the CICU at Tampa Children's.

I awoke early, dressed and quickly packed my bag as I spoke with Ana on the phone. I explained I was likely to accept the position but that I needed to speak with Michael Stringer, COO at CHOB, and I needed to speak with Dr. Penton and Dr. Kowatch as well. Ana seemed skeptical; she could always read me like a book. "OK, well I won't say anything to the girls until you have an opportunity to talk with the team here in Biloxi. I know you, and I don't believe you feel you are finished achieving the goals you set out to achieve here, and I just don't envision you abandoning all of the people who came here for you, much less abandoning the Children here in Mississippi, even though I know that you have done more than enough for this program, especially after seeing the effects it has had on your health. You need to do what's right for you. I will support your decision," she said.

"Thanks, I appreciate the support even though I know how badly you want to leave. Let's see what they say when I get back," I replied. Part of me wanted to accept the position immediately, thereby avoiding any possibility that the team in Biloxi would try to convince me to remain, but, as usual, Ana was right. Clearly I was uncertain, obviated by the fact that I was leaving the door of possibility open, which allowed for further discussion with the team back at CHOB. I don't know why, but I felt so much guilt when I considered the repercussions of leaving. Ruth, Maddie, Tim, the new cardiac intensivists and APPs we had hired, our new pharmacist, Dr. Kowatch, Dr. Penton, Justin, Mitch, and all the nurses who pledged their support for me—the truth was I felt responsible for all of them, whether perception or reality, it really didn't matter, that's how I felt. At the time I didn't realize it, though it was staring me right in the face, for some reason I had allowed it to become acceptable to put the program's success and the well-being of my colleagues ahead of my own family's happiness and well-being. In hindsight, I was a fool, because I would come to realize that the institution was clearly unwilling to put my own well-being ahead of theirs or the programs, an important yet hard life lesson I would come to understand later.

When I arrived at the airport, I sent Michael Stringer a text. "Hey Michael, I need to speak with you today if you have a few moments."

Michael immediately called me. "Hey, Eric, what's up? Sounds important," he said.

"Yes, it is. Let me explain," I replied. I proceeded to explain everything regarding the opportunity in Tampa, including the resources being offered to me, as well as the details of my family's long-standing desire to return to Florida and my concerns regarding certain leaders at CHOB, in particular Dr. Kowatch and his interaction with Dr. Penton.

"Before you make any decisions, let me do a little research into what we can do to convince you to stay," he said.

"Look, Michael, that is not what I am trying to do here. I am not trying to leverage this opportunity to get more for me or my team, I am just being open and honest with you about the real possibility of me leaving and the reasons I would do so," I replied.

"Let me see what I can do and let's meet later today after you arrive at the hospital," Michael said.

"Sure, I will text you when I land. I would really like the opportunity to sit down with you, Dr. Penton, and Dr. Kowatch. I am a straightforward, honest and to-the-point guy and I would like to get my concerns regarding Dr. Kowatch's leadership style and his interaction with Dr. Penton out in the open. If I am going to consider staying at CHOB, I need to feel that we are all on the same page when it comes to culture and collegiality," I said.

As my plane touched down, I hopped in an Uber and headed toward Children's Hospital of Biloxi. "On my way to hospital," I texted Michael Stringer.

"Great, I set up a meeting with Dr. Kowatch and Dr. Penton for this afternoon," he replied.

"Wow, that was quick, this guy doesn't mess around," I thought to myself. On my Uber ride to the hospital, I made notes regarding the important points I wished to address; the topics for discussion were sensitive ones, but I needed to be honest and quite blunt, because I needed to make a decision and I didn't want to continue to put myself and my family through the same stress and work hours if it was for something that was inevitably going to fail so I didn't want to sugarcoat anything.

I arrived at CHOB and dropped my bag off in my office where I found Michael Stringer literally waiting for my arrival. "I spoke to Mr. Boykins about your situation and relayed how vital you are to this program and as a leader for the Heart Center. I think we can adjust our current staffing model in the CICU to hire for eight cardiac intensivists instead of six, to match that offered by Tampa Children's as well as providing you with dedicated administrative and research time, which is something I know you were promised but have yet to see delivered. How does that sound?" he asked.

"Thank you, Michael, that sounds great; however, again, that was not the purpose of me telling you about the opportunity in Tampa," I responded.

"I know, Eric, but I want you to understand your importance to this program and this is one way that I can personally show you that. Is there anything else you need?" he asked.

"No, I don't need anything for me individually, but I do need to feel more confident in the direction of program, because currently I feel skeptical about Dr. Kowatch's vision and plans for the future, not to mention I am concerned about his ability and integrity to act as our leader, and I feel that my voice no longer carries influence here, which gives me the perception that the future is completely out of my control, and I am not OK with that, after all we have committed and suffered through to achieve some success," I said.

"Let's head to the CICU conference room, I have arranged a meeting with Dr. Penton and Dr. Kowatch," Michael replied.

When Michael and I arrived to the conference room, Dr. Penton and Dr. Kowatch were already seated inside. It was clear that they were confused as to the purpose of the meeting and Dr. Penton looked concerned. As Michael and I each took a seat at the conference room table, Michael took the initiative to explain that I had been harboring some concerns that I needed to express so that we could openly discuss them together, which would help me make a difficult decision at hand, that would ultimately affect everyone. I went on to explain the opportunity presented to me while also detailing the desire my family had to return to Florida. I did not detail the specifics of my offer from Tampa Children's; however, I elaborated in great detail the behaviors I had witnessed, specifically the recent deterioration in teamwork and dissent I was observing within the Heart Center since Dr. Kowatch and his team had started. I outlined the lack of respect and collegiality I had observed between Dr. Kowatch and Dr. Penton and that regardless of who we would recruit as the chief of pediatric cardiac surgery that it was absolutely essential for the two of them to portray a strong and collegial relationship when in the presence of the other team members. Dr. Kowatch refused to accept responsibility or acknowledge such behaviors were occurring, which was deeply concerning. The fact was, he was either being dishonest or perhaps he was truly that clueless that he was behaving in such a manner, regardless of the explanation, both possibilities were problematic. Michael Stringer and Dr. Penton both acknowledged their observation of this behavior by Dr. Kowatch. Dr. Penton agreed that he had responded to the behavior inappropriately and unprofessionally at times and accepted responsibility for his part in this negative interaction and promised he would actively work at modifying his own behavior. "Eric, I will do anything you want, just please, don't leave! If you leave, the CICU will collapse and this will lead to the destruction of the entire program," he said with sincerity.

This was the first time I had heard these words spoken aloud by anyone. I repeated these words daily in my mind, and this was the major reason I felt so much guilt at the thought of leaving CHOB and Dr. Penton's words, for the first time, validated a more widespread understanding of the potential cascade of events that could transpire, leading to the potential collapse of the program. I was torn, this burden was intolerable and unfair to place on a single individual's shoulders. I tried, but I could no longer fight back my tears and I began to cry, as I proceeded to lay all of my feelings and concerns out on the table, in the open. Dr. Kowatch also became emotional and began to cry as he said, "I have been struggling with the transition from Mayo Children's to CHOB, and if you leave, Eric, I think that would be it for me."

The three of us were all in various stages of crying as Michael Stringer said, "I think this is great that we have brought these sensitive thoughts and feelings out into the open. I am going to do my part to make it impossible for Eric to leave. Eric, if I can deliver on the things we discussed earlier regarding the CICU and if Dr. Penton and Dr. Kowatch agree to focus on working together collaboratively as leaders, do I have your commitment to stay?"

I was put on the spot, and I felt the shift in my decision happening in real time. I should have said I needed time to think but we were all emotional at the time and if they were committing to providing me a better work-life balance, then perhaps things would get better, and I still felt that I couldn't possibly abandon everyone who had been loyal to me, and I definitely wasn't ready to watch the fruits of our labor disappear and cause the potential collapse of the program. "Sure. I will stay," I said reluctantly. Dr. Penton and Dr. Kowatch let out sighs of relief as I internally felt nauseous and disappointed in myself.

The next morning, Mr. Boykins texted me and asked if he could meet me in my office. He arrived at 8 a.m. and explained that Michael had relayed the details of my offer in Tampa and emphasized that Michael felt that I was vital to the success of the program, so as a result, he would approve the request to increase the number of cardiac intensivists we were to employ. I picked up on every subtlety in his words and immediately recognized that he never once stated that he saw the value I provided to the program, instead, he said that Michael saw my value. He finished our brief talk by saying among the oddest and most ethically borderline comments I have experienced in my professional career. "Eric, Michael explained that your wife is not happy here. You need to make her happy, if that means you have to have sex with her more frequently, then you should do that, whatever it takes. Hopefully when you have more people you can manage your time better to deliver that," he said.

"Uh, I am quite sure that is not what she is unhappy about, but I appreciate the concern," I said with a baffled look on my face. I resisted the overwhelming urge to tell him to mind his own business and that it had nothing to do with sex. I considered whether I should report him to human resources, but I was skeptical that doing so would result in any sort of disciplinary action, since he was the boss. It was not the response I would ever expect from the CEO of a children's hospital. I ultimately agreed to stay; however, this encounter left me feeling more disturbed regarding Mr. Boykins's ability to lead, and quite frankly, how creepy he was becoming as a person. I was too overwhelmed at the time to understand that having approval for more cardiac intensivists was a great start; however, I had apparently developed amnesia when it came to remembering how difficult it had been to fill the openings I already had approval for, and I had no idea how much more difficult it was about to become. Having the approval for eight cardiac intensivists was great, but how long would it take for me it fill these vacancies?

31

RECRUITMENT OF A NEW CARDIAC INTENSIVIST AND A NEW PEDIATRIC CARDIAC SURGEON

Dr. Kowatch had been hard at work solidifying his alliance with the CEO, Antoine Boykins, and the CFO, Hector Ramirez, both very powerful allies, and both clearly the most susceptible to his obvious "ass-kissing" tactics. They both equally saw that they could use him as a secret mole within the Heart Center, capable of gathering sensitive information, but more importantly someone who could be easily manipulated as their puppet to carry out their plans while maintaining the appearance that they were actually coming from Dr. Kowatch himself. Michael Stringer, COO, was too savvy and intelligent and saw the entire pathetic display unfolding before him. His disgust and growing frustration with the situation that was developing and his distaste for the culture that Mr. Boykins and Hector Ramirez were enabling became increasingly visible, though he tried to hide it. While Dr. Kowatch was busy developing his protection, he and Mr. Boykins were convinced that a new chief of pediatric cardiac surgery was essential. He printed out a copy of the U.S. News & World Report's top 50 pediatric cardiology and congenital heart surgery programs and had begun cold calling both the chief and the junior cardiac surgeon from each ranked program on this list. After two weeks of phone calls, he had compiled a list of three pediatric cardiac surgeons who had agreed to interview for the opening. A fourth candidate, whose program was not on the top fifty list, was also being considered after he responded to the online job posting that they had placed.

At the same time, I had recruited a colleague of mine that I trained with during my critical care fellowship by the name of Lorraine McMaster. Lorraine was one year junior to me during our fellowship and had completed her CICU training in South Carolina and had several years of clinical experience. Lorraine was a kind and gifted intensivist who was a great teammate. I had struggled to find an experienced intensivist to function as the associate director and I was excited that she had agreed to join me because I already knew I could trust her clinically and I considered her a good friend so I knew she would work well with the rest of the team. It was going to be a huge addition since she could help to offload some of my administrative responsibilities as well. She hit the ground running and was immediately loved and admired by the nursing staff. She was able to take over the CICU schedule, which was also a huge help to me.

Following Lorraine's arrival, we had begun the search for a sixth cardiac intensivist and had narrowed our search down to two candidates. One had trained at the University of Michigan and completed her CICU training in Colorado. We worked hard at recruiting her but in the end, it became clear that she was uncomfortable accepting the position while we were in limbo as to who would be named the future chief of pediatric cardiac surgery. She had met Dr. Penton during her visits and felt comfortable with his surgical outcomes but even more so, she saw the strength of our working relationship as leaders, and understood the importance of such a relationship, particularly the trust, and that without this, there could be consequences that could trickle down and affect the entire CICU team. Therefore, the fact that the administration and Dr. Kowatch had independently decided to open a nationwide search for a new surgical leader, left the candidate, and all of us, wondering who would fill that role and how that individual's relationship would be with the CICU team. As a result, this candidate said no to our offer, so we proceeded with making an offer to our second choice, Rebecca Holbein, who had completed her CICU training at the Children's Hospital of Chicago. She ultimately accepted the position as the sixth cardiac intensivist at CHOB.

At the same time, we had successfully recruited two additional physician assistants who were new graduates with no experience but who came highly recommended by Martha Sandister, the PA student we had recently hired. Martha was showing great potential and had established herself as a wonderful person, which gave me the confidence I needed to hire the two new PA graduates she recommended. The two new hires resulted in a net gain of one advanced practice provider, as we ultimately had to let Brenda Paige, the nurse practitioner we had hired, go. Brenda was clearly an intelligent NP with a lot of potential, but we had been dealing with two major problems, well actually three. The first problem we encountered was that Brenda failed to buy into our team approach when it came to working in the CICU. We had a lot of young nurses on staff, and we had all worked hard to develop the nurturing environment that currently existed, so that these young nurses would feel empowered to share their concerns and feel comfortable asking questions, no matter how silly they may seem. Well, Brenda frequently snapped at the nurses, calling them stupid, either to their face or behind their back and even more concerning, when they would ask her questions that she didn't know the answer to, she would make up an answer and say it confidently to the nurses who would listen to her, at least in the beginning. In a very specialized field like pediatric cardiac intensive care, there is nothing more dangerous than inexperience or incompetence that is combined with an individual's inappropriate self-confidence. That can lead to errors, which in our field can lead to death. Despite several conversations with her during which I provided specific examples, she denied such events. The second problem that began occurring was that she regularly showed up to work one to two hours late and then at least two to three days per week she had an excuse as to why she needed to leave early. At first, I was extremely understanding of her situation given the long drive she had, and given her home situation as it pertained to childcare for her kids. However, after a couple of months of complaints from the nursing staff and the other advanced practice providers who were required to pick up her workload and, due to her lack of accountability, it was clear it needed to be addressed. The third issue, which I refused to believe initially, was a bit odd and far more delicate. Justin and Tim had both reported to me that Brenda, who was as I can best describe in a professional manner, top-heavy or big-bosomed, had on multiple occasions rubbed her breasts persistently against their hand or arm while in tight quarters at the beside of patients while carrying out procedures. Justin was noticeably uncomfortable to the point that he and Tim had discussed this in great detail privately before bringing it to my attention. After hearing their description, I initially labeled it as an accidental brush of the breast, which I will admit, was based on preconceived notions I had developed in my mind. However, when it happened to me, I saw that it was much more than a single, coincidental brush against the arm. Following my own encounter, I would more accurately describe it as a rhythmic, pendulous smacking of her entire breast back and forth against my arm, which continued unabated until I moved my arm away. Any question regarding the intention of this action was answered when I placed my arm back in front of me, as I felt the miraculous return of her breast as it pounded the back of my arm relentlessly in a synchronized, swinging motion resembling the second hand of a grandfather clock. I had never experienced such a situation, and it was extremely uncomfortable. This same behavior was observed by Martha and by several nurses, so it was something that needed to be addressed. I sat down with Brenda and proceeded to discuss my concerns regarding her regular tardiness and her regular need to leave early, in addition to my concerns regarding her interactions with the nurses. I explained to her that I felt perhaps this was not the right job for her, as she sought more independence and that is something that develops over a longer period of time, often several years in this specialty. I also told her that the commute was problematic for her and for me. Before I ventured toward addressing the third concern regarding the involuntary contact between her mammary glands and the male staff, I asked if she felt like this was the right job for her? She said she needed to think on it overnight. As a result, I decided to wait for her answer before I addressed the third concern, more due to my own discomfort discussing the situation than hers. The next day she called to notify me that she was resigning, which I believe was the best outcome for both of us, while also thankfully freeing me of the burden associated with dealing with the third issue.

Meanwhile, the four pediatric cardiac surgeons who displayed some interest in being considered for the role of division chief were beginning to be scheduled for their respective visits. The administration had arranged for their visits to be discrete and would include only the administrators, Dr. Kowatch and myself. I was to receive a "secret folder" delivered to my office the morning of their interview, which contained pertinent details about each of the candidates, including a copy of their CV. Two of the candidates were currently the division chief at their respective programs, while the other two were the junior surgeon but who had substantial experience and were clearly surgeons that would be sought as division chief candidates in the near future. I was instructed that I was not to discuss these candidates with anyone internally or externally and that following my interview I was to fill out an evaluation form and return it to Edward Arnold, chief surgical officer via email.

The first candidate to interview was Phil Porter. As you may recall, Phil was the chief of pediatric cardiac surgery at Children's Hospital of Pennsylvania for over ten years, followed by a brief stint in Idaho. At the time of the interview, he served as the division chief of pediatric cardiac surgery in North Dakota and had done so for the last two years. The administrators were excited by the fact that someone "top trained" and of his surgical caliber would even give them the time of day, as the previous administrators had struck out miserably, and multiple times, when it came to recruiting a new pediatric cardiac surgeon. However, now between the changes in the CICU and the outcomes that we had achieved with our changes, plus the fact that we had recruited Dr. Kowatch, things were different. While I understood their excitement that someone of his surgical skill would consider joining us, I felt their giddy school-girl behavior, chasing the "top trained" celebrities, was premature, as much more investigation would be required to vet his true candidacy, in my opinion. I admit, I was equally proud that things had changed to the degree that we could now recruit high-caliber surgeons, but the behavior displayed by the hospital administrators screamed desperation, which any experienced pediatric cardiac surgeon would smell as weakness, using it as leverage to obtain a lopsided contract filled with excessive salary or lengthy time commitments, making an amicable separation nearly impossible, should things not work out. Dr. Porter was picked up by a limousine from the airport to take him to his hotel. I thought perhaps this was a little bit of overkill for the first visit; however, who was I? I had no experience with the process of recruiting a congenital heart surgeon, so I went along with it. When I met Dr. Porter for the first time, it was clear he was very accomplished and confident in his ability. His curriculum vitae consisted of seventy-five pages highlighting his "top training" and outlined more than one hundred peer-reviewed publications he had authored over his career. However, what his CV did not display was his notorious history of behavior problems and toxicity. It became quickly apparent during the interview, by the awkward nature of our interaction, that social skills were not his forte, nor were they of any particular interest to him. He wanted to focus our time discussing how great of a surgeon he was. It was clear that he had little respect for the concept of team and felt that all that was needed to have a successful congenital heart program was to have a great cardiac surgeon. Since leaving Pennsylvania he had yet to be part of a program with an established and dedicated CICU. During his brief stint in Idaho, the ICU revolted against his behavior. His response to my inquiry regarding what happened in Idaho was to deflect his own accountability and divert attention toward the hospital administration at that institution, whom he said had failed to deliver on the promise of providing him a dedicated CICU. Instead, he said they merely had a pediatric intensive care unit that had experience dealing with cardiac patients; however, he viewed that as inadequate, which may or may not have been true. At the conclusion of our interview, I was left unconvinced that he was the right fit for the program at that time. While clearly a gifted and accomplished pediatric cardiac surgeon, I did not view him as the right leader for a program that had just fought to exit a bubble that had arrested its clinical progress, resulting in clinical care that was stuck in the 1990s and plagued by toxicity as well as a complete lack of collaboration and teamwork. After executing the impossible and moving the program forward at least a decade and after working tirelessly to rid the CICU and Heart Center of toxicity, the wrong hire could be catastrophic for the program and the entire institution. When I filled out Dr. Porter's interview evaluation, these are the precise words that I wrote, and were the reason that I felt he was not the right fit for us, which I proceeded to email to the chief surgical officer, Edward Arnold.

The second candidate to interview at Children's Hospital of Biloxi was the junior surgeon from Dallas Children's Hospital, a man by the name of Prescott Charlton. Prescott was in his early fifties and was previously the junior surgeon at Phoenix Children's Hospital where he spent a brief stint as the interim division chief after they decided to fire the division chief at the time. During his brief year as the interim director, the program thrived under his leadership with the best year of surgical outcomes that the program had produced in its existence. When he was not chosen as the permanent division chief, he decided to move to Dallas where he had also been thriving as the second surgeon. He had taken that position with the understanding that he would be made division chief in the near future upon the retirement of the current director. Prescott was also known to be a good technical surgeon and had a reputation as a nice man; however, like many pediatric cardiac surgeons, social interaction was not his strength. As we sat at the conference room table, the awkwardness of our conversation made it crystal clear that socialization was indeed a weakness. During the interview I asked, "This is potentially a real scenario, so please don't take offense to this question, but how would you deal with becoming the division chief and overseeing Dr. Penton who has been here for twenty years, has more clinical experience, and has the support of most of the OR staff? I only ask because I can tell you that while I am not a cardiac surgeon, I experienced a similar scenario when I first arrived. So, while you may not have the answer now, it is one that you should think about if you are truly interested in this position, because I can tell you it is not a situation with an easy solution or one that is commonly dealt with."

Prescott was not pleased with this question and replied, "Well, if that's how the situation turns out, he will need to understand that I am the leader and he will need to fall into place accordingly," as if we were talking about the military. After he realized he snapped at me and may have overreacted, he gave a somewhat more empathetic response, but it was too late for me, he had shown his cards and I could see he was bluffing. He didn't have the type of leadership skills that our program needed at that time. They may have been ideal for another program or another situation, but we needed a skilled surgeon with confidence in his own skill, both as a surgeon and a leader—someone with a frictionless personality who could take adversity in stride without snapping at others.

The third pediatric cardiac surgical candidate was Constantinos Christoforou, the chief of cardiac surgery at Indiana Children's Hospital. Dr. Christoforou was of Greek origin and had completed his pediatric cardiothoracic fellowship at the University of Michigan. He was also known as a technically skilled surgeon while also having a reputation for being a kind man who supported his teammates who each spoke highly of his leadership skills. I happened to be leaving the following morning to go out of town with my family, so our scheduled meeting time was brief. Therefore, we met for a drink at the bar in his hotel. He was being dropped off in his limousine as I arrived at the hotel. We greeted one another and shared the commonality that we both trained in Michigan and spoke of our favorite outdoor activities in the Great Lakes State. I was impressed by his personality and his insight, and I appreciated the fact that he was direct and to the point while always maintaining professionalism, just like me. He asked me quite bluntly about my early experience at CHOB. He applauded me for the work we had done to move the program forward. I asked him, "Why would you come here to be chief when you already built a quality program in Indiana?"

"Honestly, it would be either for higher surgical volume or for more money," he replied.

"I appreciate the honesty," I said.

"Eric, I need your help. I know people throw around a lot of numbers when it comes to surgical volume. Of course, administrators will try to pad the statistics a little when you come for a visit, but for me to strongly consider this position, I need to know what the true surgical volume is and I need to know how many total cardiac surgeries and how many Norwood procedures Dr. Penton and Dr. Geisinger have performed over the last year," he stated bluntly, which I again sincerely appreciated.

The Norwood procedure is among the most complicated pediatric cardiac surgeries and really defines the skill of a pediatric cardiac surgeon and the outcome of these complex surgeries defines the success of a congenital heart program. Dr. Christoforou was clearly seeing if the other two surgeons were performing enough surgeries to maintain their board certification and quite intelligently, he also sought to understand how his arrival as the chief of the division would affect both his and their surgical volume. He understood that through the cardiac critical care database that we participated in, that data was easily retrievable. "Sure, Constantinos, I can obtain that information for you. It may take me a couple days, but I can get it for you," I said. In my mind this was not only an extremely intelligent question to ask, but honestly, it was data he deserved to know before considering such a decision. He made it clear that higher surgical volume was a top priority in order for him to truly consider this job. I respected the fact that he was upfront about what it would take for him to join us. As expected, Dr. Christoforou withdrew his name from candidacy following his interview, stating that though he was impressed by the developments that were taking place in Biloxi, the surgical volume was not adequate for him to leave the program he had worked so hard to build. While I was disappointed, I appreciated his character and the fact that he held true to the word by withdrawing his name from consideration and did not string the program along. I felt discouraged because I felt he was the perfect candidate and even more so, I didn't feel the other two candidates were the right fit for our stage of development. However, then I met the fourth candidate who was named Bill Callahan.

Dr. Callahan was a Stanford-trained pediatric cardiac surgeon who was the junior cardiac surgeon at Children's Hospital of California. He was in his early fifties. He had been operating at the Children's Hospital of California since he completed his training and had taken the program from being unranked to a top-twenty-five ranking, all while functioning in the shadow of well-established program like Los Angeles Children's Hospital. I knew very little about Dr. Callahan other than what was revealed in his top-secret file from administration, which was delivered to my office in a sealed envelope reading "confidential" that morning. When I sat down in the administrative conference room to meet with Dr. Callahan, I was immediately impressed. He was a tall, thin man, probably around six foot two who was in the early stages of balding. He greeted me with a firm handshake and a sincere smile while making eye contact, which is no small feat for a congenital heart surgeon. As we sat across from one another, we carried on a conversation that flowed as if we were best friends who hadn't seen one another for years and had picked up right where we left off during our last meeting. Before I could even think about asking interview-related questions, there was a knock on the conference room door notifying us that our thirty-minute meeting time had come to an end. We both couldn't believe it and wished there was more time to continue our conversation. We shook hands and sincerely thanked one another for the enjoyable conversation that certainly didn't resemble an interview. I left the room feeling that he was the right fit. He was clearly intelligent, and checked Mr. Boykins's extensive list of criteria, meaning he was considered "top trained," but more than anything he saw the vision of what we were trying to accomplish at CHOB. He appeared to have the uncanny ability to understand which stage of program development we were currently at and seemed to have the skill that would allow him to jump right in and continue on with development toward the next stage, without a hiccup or setback, because he had experience developing his current program, which was once unrecognized, and now found itself in the national spotlight. He had the perfect combination of surgical skill, temperament, experience, and motivation to want to make things better. I was reinvigorated with the idea that he was the perfect candidate and relayed that in my evaluation that I emailed to the chief surgical officer. After each of the evaluations that I sent to Edward Arnold, CSO, I failed to get a response acknowledging receipt or review of my comments. Over the next week, I saw Dr. Arnold and Dr. Kowatch in the hospital, and I took the time to reiterate my thoughts regarding the candidates. The response I heard from both was "We are looking at all the candidates, but we are looking for 'top trained' individuals and if Dr. Porter remains interested, it would be difficult to not pursue his hiring." There it was, the dangerous evolution of a single idea that had been planted in the mind of the CEO, which had now sprouted and grown to maturity, spreading seeds of its own throughout the chain of administration, all the way down to the Heart Center leadership. This idea that "top trained" can be simply defined as someone coming from an elite institution alone, infuriated me because it was too simplistic, and lacked critical, unbiased evaluation of each candidate, and I fully understood the risk associated with such an approach and more importantly the consequences that could follow if we were wrong.

The second visits for the chief of pediatric cardiac surgery candidates had been arranged. Unfortunately, due to the rapid spread of coronavirus at the time, travel was becoming significantly restricted or at least ill-advised. As a result, Dr. Callahan and his wife decided that the timing was not right for them to entertain a move to another state. Despite the fact that he was willing to revisit at a later date, Dr. Kowatch and the administration felt an urgent need to fill the vacancy, despite the fact that Dr. Penton continued to excel in his interim role; nonetheless, those whose opinion mattered, decided to proceed with second interviews of the remaining two candidates, both of whom I felt were the wrong fit for our program at the time. While my opinion was clearly not being heard, I hoped that during the second round of interviews, more people would have the opportunity to meet the candidates and give their own opinions. However, I came to understand that it would have been more accurate to describe Dr. Kowatch and Mr. Boykins's view of the need to hire a new chief of pediatric cardiac surgery as "desperate" rather than "urgent." Dr. Penton was automatically granted inclusion in the second round of interviews, which gave the appearance of his strong candidacy, but I wasn't fooled by Mr. Boykins and his illusory methods for hiding his true intentions.

The second visit for Prescott Charlton was even more convincing than his first visit that he was not the right fit for CHOB at this point in time. His interview was even more socially awkward the second go round. This visit he was much more assertive about his involvement in the CICU care of his surgical patients, and he communicated how he had independently constructed and implemented a feeding protocol at his current institution that he required his cardiac intensivists to follow, thereby making it clear that he was a micromanager, something I had been very familiar with during the Rostri years. Dr. Kowatch was pushing hard for us to support his hiring, saying he knew someone at his old institution who spoke very highly of him as a surgeon and a leader. However, between my own digging into his background as well as that done by others within the Heart Center, Dr. Kowatch was the only person who was privy to positive feedback regarding his leadership and social skills.

The second visit for Dr. Porter had a bit of an interesting twist to it. Since his first visit, Dr. Porter had not contacted Dr. Kowatch or Mr. Boykins, despite their repeated follow-up attempts at reaching him. It had been months and it was assumed that there was no interest on his part. However, a few days before the decision was made to proceed with second interviews, Dr. Porter had finally returned Dr. Kowatch's call and he asked if there was still interest on the part of CHOB for him to consider the position. I am assuming there was a desperate "yes" that was relayed to him on behalf of Dr. Kowatch and Mr. Boykins. By the time he arrived for his second visit, the Heart Center team had pushed back hard on the idea of hiring Dr. Charlton. Hence, in stepped the perception of "desperation." Dr. Kowatch and Mr. Boykins had already made their mind up privately that Dr. Penton was not a real candidate for the position, despite the fact that he was "the final candidate to be interviewed." As a result, Dr. Porter had played them all right into his bluff. Children's Hospital held three of a kind, while Dr. Porter merely held a king-high hand that represented nothing but a bluff, and he definitely had an elite poker face. So, after the staged interview with Dr. Penton, after ignoring my blatant warnings about Dr. Porter being the wrong hire, and without asking the input of any other member of the Heart Center, Mr. Boykins and Dr. Kowatch extended Dr. Porter an offer. Not only did they extend him an offer, but he bluffed his way to a victory without ever showing his hand. The truth would later be revealed that his program in North Dakota was tiring of his behavioral issues and his surgical outcomes were less than ideal. However, he bluffed CHOB not only into paying him $2 million a year when he was on the verge of losing his current job, but he also suckered them into guaranteeing a multi-year contract, which meant if the hospital determined that things were not working out and wished to terminate the agreement, they would be stuck paying the bill for the entirety of his contract duration, which in this case would equal $10 million. These actions were desperate, incompletely thought through and held the potential for drastic ramifications, made by bush league, first-time leaders who were more interested in chasing celebrities than they were in building a team. Not only that but they had just drastically overpaid a man who was about to be fired from his current job and whom no one else in the country was willing to hire. I couldn't believe what had just happened!

Dr. Penton appeared to be struggling with the recruitment process and with the final decision to hire Dr. Porter, and for good reason. He became detached and I was concerned about his well-being as his friend. He had been through so much already between Dr. Rostri's traumatic departure, him being promoted and demoted as division chief within a single day, and despite doing a phenomenal job at leading the program, he was put through a sham interview process, only to have the administration pass him over and overpay a surgeon with a national reputation of behavioral problems. It was too much for any individual to endure without being affected psychologically and emotionally. Dr. Penton and I had become pretty good friends, so for the most part we knew where each of us was mentally at any given point, and his recent change in affect began to worry me. I became especially concerned when he sent me a text message containing a link to a newspaper article from the late 1990s that described a pediatric cardiac surgeon who was passed up for the job of division chief at the institution where he had practiced for many years. The article detailed how the surgeon went on to commit suicide and not a single person in his life knew he was suffering.

I immediately texted him and said, "Let's meet for a drink tonight! I need one badly!"

He responded, "Sure, how about 6 p.m. at University Grill?"

"See you then," I replied.

I met him there and we talked casually about life and work. Then as we both neared completion of our first drink, I said, "Terry, I am worried about you. You have been through so much over the last year or two and there is no chance that you sent me that article by mere coincidence. I just want you to know that no matter what the message was that you intended to send with that article, I have been where you at right now, previously in my life, and I know just how dark and lonely that place is. And while it may seem like an impossible dungeon to escape, I am here to tell you that it can be done and I know you will find a way to get through this, but this is not the time to try to do it alone. These are the times when you need to rely on the love and support of your friends and family, we can help you get out of that dark place and bring you back to the light and it is our job to help you remember how amazing you are and all the incredible things you have done and continue to do for everyone around you, including CHOB, whether those idiots want to recognize our work or not. I know all you have done for the children of this state. As I told you, when I arrived in Biloxi, I thought you were the biggest asshole in the world! It's true. However, as time went on, it became impossible not to love everything that there is to know about you, believe me, I tried! You are an amazing pediatric cardiac surgeon, you care so deeply about your patients, and that is something I respect immensely. You have adapted like no one I have ever seen before, and you deserve to be the chief. I heavily supported you, but it didn't happen, and I am sorry. But I know the father you are, and you need to fight through this so you can be there for your kids and for me. So please, cut yourself some slack and look at the amazing accomplishments you have achieved." Barely holding back my tears, I raised my drink and clanked his glass and said, "Fuck the past because it's in the past, and here is to the future, and who the hell knows what that will bring, but we will deal with it when it gets here, together! Regardless of what happens with the program, I will always be there for you. Remember that!"

As I left that evening, I felt empathy for Dr. Penton. He had dealt with so much and handled it like a professional, but for the ultimate introverts such as Dr. Penton, Dr. Saltiel and I, "handling it" on the surface, really means pushing it down deeper, into the subconscious and after a while, that takes a toll. Not getting a job is a disappointment to most. Now imagine being awarded the job, then having it taken away, but you are reassured that you are definitely a candidate when in reality, you are not, and then being passed over for the position only to hire someone with a known history of behavioral problems. That is brutal! The psychological toll that mind games such as these take on a human being is infinite and timeless; anyone who believes differently doesn't understand the field of medicine. When the goal becomes hiring a list of "top trained" physicians, as classified by words on a piece of paper, and you lose sight of what really matters, meaning the patients, and you lose sight of what it was that got you where you are right now, meaning the work of physicians like Dr. Penton and me, then your purpose is no longer to help others, instead it becomes personal accomplishments rather than team victories. The despicable behavior displayed by Mr. Boykins and Dr. Kowatch was evolving rapidly, it no longer appeared to consist merely of poor decisions based on meaningless titles or name recognition, their actions were now leading to malignant results that were causing mental and physical damage to dedicated employees who had delivered everything to them on a silver platter, yet they chose to snatch the platter claiming it as their own, while spitting in the faces of those who delivered it. Meanwhile they projected a sense of entitlement that was most certainly unearned. This was not a game; these were people's lives and mental health that they were playing with as if it was a toy. The behavior they displayed toward Dr. Penton was inexcusable and after witnessing the detrimental effects it was having on his mental health, it made me angry and it made me realize that we were no more than temporary employees to them, who in their eyes, were easily replaceable, but not before they had the opportunity to squeeze every last ounce of passion and hope from our body and soul. Fortunately, over the next few weeks Dr. Penton was able to work his way through these complicated feelings and continue leading the team with great success, at least until Dr. Porter arrived.

32

"TOP TRAINED"

Early on I felt perhaps I had the wrong understanding of what it takes to build a successful team. According to Antoine Boykins, I did not meet the qualification for consideration as "top trained," yet the physicians and staff we were able to recruit had all stated that they were joining or considering joining due to the work that we had done to build the CICU, which had led to outcomes comparable with some of the top programs around the country, not because of the training program that was listed on our CV, but because of the teamwork that we had displayed. I had come from a small-to-medium-sized program in Fort Myers. When I joined that program more than ten years ago, I didn't understand it, but with time, it became clear that while the number of staff was small in comparison to major institutions, the physicians who led each division within the Heart Center were indeed exceptional physicians, yet based on Mr. Boykins's definition, they were not all "top trained." How could that be? (Insert sarcasm.) However, I came to understand this term to have a much different definition. What I observed was that, yes, many of these physicians were trained at "top institutions"; however, they were more than what was on paper. First of all, none of them wasted time telling you where they trained. Instead, they spent time telling you about the great team that they were part of and how collectively they each trusted one another to carry out their respective jobs with great skill and expertise. They had done the unimaginable—while the world had been busy publishing papers and presenting at conferences, showing data that suggested large volume programs have superior outcomes when compared to small-to-medium-sized programs, thereby inferring that in order to be a proficient program you needed to have a high surgical volume. However, over the ten-year period I spent in Fort Myers, I came to understand that it was indeed possible to have an elite, high-quality congenital heart program that was not high volume, leading me to the realization that the essential factor that resulted in excellent outcomes was not volume, it was instead patient complexity and teamwork. Fort Myers Children's performed an average of 150 cardiac surgical cases each year that required cardiopulmonary bypass. This was the metric that most institutions use to accurately depict their "cardiac surgical volume." However, while the overall surgical volume was classified as "small-to-medium-sized," the reality was that the program on average, performed between ten to twenty Norwood procedures annually, accounting for approximately 10 percent of its overall volume. As I said earlier, the quality of each program is evaluated by outcomes for all ranges of surgical complexity; however, many assess a program's performance based on its outcomes following the Norwood procedure. When you add the other single ventricle, aortopulmonary shunted patients who were operated on each year in Fort Myers, you realized that more than 20 percent of the program's surgical volume consisted of patients who required the most complex congenital cardiac surgeries known to man. So how was a program of this size ranked annually among the top fifty in the U.S. News & World Report, when they did not have a cardiac transplant program and when they were merely a "small- to medium-volume" program? And how did they have a mortality rate well below the national average when it came to the most complex surgeries? I came to understand that the answer was teamwork and trust. When I finished my critical care fellowship and interviewed for the cardiac intensivist opening at Fort Myers Children's, they continuously repeated that they were extremely selective in who they hired. Yes, training at a center with plenty of exposure to cardiac pathology was vital; however, interpersonal skills were equally, if not more essential to the success of the team. Understanding the importance of trust and knowing that you can lean on your teammates was a concept that they imprinted in my subconscious, and it became a reflex for me. I knew it was the right fit for me the minute I interviewed there. Ana had insisted that we move to warmer weather after she had delivered our first daughter in the middle of one of the most brutal Midwestern winters on record. She was essentially confined to our condominium due to the weather and the fact that she was caring for a newborn while I was working extreme hours, and it tested her mental toughness. She missed socialization and when her best friend moved to Fort Myers because her husband had joined Fort Myers General as a robotic adult gastrointestinal surgeon, and a job opened up at the children's hospital, she begged me to at least apply. I didn't have a desire to live in Fort Myers, but I said I would at least inquire about the position at her request. Well, the minute I stepped into the hospital, I knew it was the right position for me. Each member of the team I met reinforced the idea of quality patient care, teamwork, trust, and elite outcomes. They were proud of what they had built and for good reason and I was sold, immediately. When asked about joining the group now, I always repeat that I underwent a ten-year pediatric cardiology/congenital heart fellowship, training under some of the brightest minds and best human beings in the field and I thrived and succeeded because of them. Real "top talent" I came to understand is defined by your training, your interpersonal skills, your passion, your empathy, your willingness to learn, and your ability to incorporate these skills for the betterment of the team. Defining "top training" as the line of print on your CV that highlights the program where you trained is simplistic and naive. But as I would come to see, it is impossible for someone without a medical background to understand this complex philosophy, particularly if your only experience occurred at a "top training" institution that likely regurgitated the same buzzwords.

Naturally, I came to understand that when physicians change jobs or when they move on to undertake leadership roles, they have a tendency to transplant the model of practice that they were exposed to during their training or from the institution they practiced post-training to the new program or institution they are joining. It is what we are familiar with, and we have seen it succeed, so it is common to use these past experiences as a blueprint to help construct or invoke change at a new program or a new institution. I can say with sincere honesty, I used my past experience in Fort Myers as the vision to construct the CICU at Children's Hospital of Biloxi and over time the staff bought into this approach, and with a lot of work, it became successful, and we developed a team. Equally, when Dr. Kowatch and Antoine Boykins started at CHOB, it became clear that they too were using this same approach to construct what they visualized as a model of success from their previous institutions. At first, I thought, they came from well-respected institutions, their plan is certain to ensure success. However, as time went on, Dr. Kowatch began to implement changes that resembled the model utilized at Mayo Children's, yet I began to notice a glaring difference, the Mayo Children's blueprint, which was clearly successful, didn't appear to fit the model at CHOB, simply because the staff at CHOB consisted of far fewer pediatric cardiologists and the patient volume we cared for was much less. For example, the entire division of pediatric cardiology at CHOB consisted of nine members and Dr. Kowatch decided to invoke a new model where only four of the pediatric cardiologists were allowed to officially read echocardiograms, despite the fact that most had been doing so for more than ten years. This not only relied on four individuals to read all of the echocardiograms, but it also decreased their availability to help cover cardiology clinic with regularity, which placed an additional burden on the remaining cardiologists, who were forced to pick up the extra workload. This was not a popular maneuver, and it simply didn't maximize efficiency when it came to utilizing the small number of pediatric cardiologists at CHOB.

His next move, equally unpopular, included naming Sherry Monroe, fresh out of fellowship training, with zero clinical experience, the director of fetal echocardiography. This messaged the idea that "top training" as defined by him, superseded experience and relationships that had been carefully built with maternal fetal medicine physicians within the state of Mississippi for many years. Dr. Borland and others had spent many years establishing these important relationships, which had generated referrals. It was painfully apparent from the time of his arrival that Dr. Kowatch despised Dr. Borland and after a period of time I came to understand that he actually felt this way because he felt threatened by Dr. Borland's clinical acumen and how respected he was in the community and within the Heart Center. He would later complain that Dr. Borland was seeing too many patients in his clinic and that he needed to distribute the patients and "stop hoarding them for himself." I repeatedly expressed my opinion, and asked, "Why would we harness Dr. Borland's cultlike following within the community? Instead, we should empower him and promote his popularity and unleash his skill set." However, neither Dr. Borland nor I fit the criteria as "top trained," so Mr. Boykins ignored our opinion and followed the direction of Dr. Kowatch. Additionally, Sherry Monroe now dedicated most of her clinical time to fetal clinic, which also removed her from the pool of cardiologists available to cover the many outpatient clinics around the state, again placing an additional burden on the other cardiologists.

Another unpopular provision implemented by Dr. Kowatch was ensuring that Tricia Cranton's only clinical responsibility was heart failure clinic. This meant that she had clinic one afternoon per week to start, which would eventually be increased to two afternoons per week. She was given an advanced practice provider to help her see on average one to two patients per afternoon. And while other cardiologists were traveling around the state to cover several clinics, which were booked to capacity, she was strolling into the hospital around 11 a.m. to see her two patients without any additional responsibilities. Keep in mind, the hospital had not committed to building a transplant program, so that process was a minimum of two years away.

Meanwhile, Tricia would openly admit how she was enjoying so much free time and liked the fact that there was no transplant program. Dr. Cranton was also responsible for carrying out inpatient heart failure consults sought within CHOB. These were relatively infrequent; however, her disinterest became apparent when a consult was placed. Over the years I had come to observe that physicians who are not passionate about their profession, or who are simply lazy or incompetent, tend to develop repetitive behaviors or safeguards to hide these inadequacies. Dr. Cranton mastered such behavior, and when called for a consult, she repeatedly expressed that her time was limited by her busy clinical schedule and that it may be a while before she was physically able to come evaluate the patient. When she did eventually show up to evaluate the patient, it was typically somewhere between one to three days after the consult was requested, depending on whether the request fell on a weekend or if it interfered with her personal training appointment. When she eventually arrived, she had a pre-orchestrated consult template that was void of even the most minuscule evidence of critical thought. The perfect example of this was displayed nearly two years following her arrival to CHOB. A newborn had been admitted to the pediatric intensive care unit with myocarditis, a viral infection of the heart, which in this case resulted in the baby presenting in a state of cardiogenic shock. The CICU was at capacity so the pediatric ICU accepted the patient with the idea that Dr. Cranton would assist in managing the patient by consulting and providing recommendations until a bed became available in the CICU. When I arrived that evening to take night call, Dr. Slovak, who was the service attending that week, handed off to me that the patient was deteriorating in the PICU so we were exchanging a less critical patient with them so that we could free up a bed and assume the management of this patient. When the patient arrived to the CICU, he was in critical condition, he had florid pulmonary edema (fluid in the lungs) and had poor cardiac function and severe mitral valve regurgitation (leaking valve). The patient was on no inotropic medications or afterload reduction (drugs to help with heart function and leaking valve) and no diuretics (drugs to help remove excess fluid from heart failure). Dr.

Slovak and I were utterly confused by the mismanagement of this patient. When we looked at the PICU admission note, they commented on recommendations that had been provided by Dr. Cranton. As we checked her consult note, we realized it was her patented pre-completed note that we had seen many times before, stating the patient didn't need IV inotropic therapy or diuretics, and that the PICU should consider starting oral diuretics and oral medicine for heart failure, prior to discharge and that she would follow up in heart failure clinic two weeks after discharge. WTF? This patient was in such a critical state that there was no guarantee that he would ever make it out of the hospital, and it was possible that he may require ECMO or transfer to a center that was capable of providing a ventricular assist device, or possibly even heart transplantation. He had been completely mismanaged. She had used the same skeleton note that was used on all her patients so she could minimize the need for her to reevaluate the patient, allowing her to see the patient once, and then follow up as an outpatient, or it was a glaring sign of her clinical incompetence, either way it was unacceptable. I immediately called her to ask her about these recommendations. I explained to her the condition of the patient and that the delay in implementing diuretic therapy and IV milrinone had likely led to further deterioration of the patient's clinical condition. She denied that she wrote those recommendations and blamed it on the cardiology fellow. As I hung up the phone, Dr. Slovak and I checked her consult note again; however, it had mysteriously been deleted. Fortunately, the patient responded well to therapy and had a full recovery and was discharged home. But this is the "top trained" concept that we began to become inundated with. Clinical incompetence combined with deceptiveness and lack of passion for our vulnerable patients—a tragic and disturbing quality noted in our new colleagues.

Prior to Dr. Kowatch's arrival, I had discussed at great lengths with him my desire to develop a step-down unit where patients who were no longer in critical condition could continue to be cared for by the cardiologists. The model when I arrived was that all patients with a "cardiac problem" were admitted to the CICU whether they were critical or not. Equally, patients admitted in critical condition following cardiac surgery would stay under the CICU service even after they had recovered and were no longer critical. This placed an unnecessary burden on the staff of the CICU. So, when Dr. Kowatch started, we set up a model where simpler cases would be transferred to the "step-down" unit where the cardiologists would assume the care until discharge. Dr. Kowatch proceeded to promote Dr. Canton to medical director of the step-down unit and then subsequently promoted Dr. Monroe to the role of associate director. As you can imagine, this was not received well by the group. By this point there were questions regarding their clinical competence and even more so the poor attitude and lack of teamwork they displayed were blatantly obvious. They often refused to accept patients with central venous lines in place, or those requiring low-dose heparin drips, and patients who were on more than three liters per minute of flow by nasal cannula. Yet, based on these criteria, these patients would have been accepted to the general pediatric floor under the general pediatric service, without question. At first, the CICU team was accommodating, giving them the benefit of the doubt that they simply needed time to become comfortable with things that we viewed as trivial. However, when things failed to progress over the first year, particularly when the CICU was at capacity and they refused to help by accepting such patients, we became discouraged. The final criteria developed at the hands of the two step-down leaders and ultimately enforced by the clique leader himself, Dr. Kowatch, was the rule that all patients must be transferred and handed off to the step-down team before 1 p.m. or they would refuse transfer. That was it, the final act of laziness, an act in direct opposition to the concept of team. What had transpired since the inception of the step-down unit was rapid-fire medical rounds that occurred in the morning by the staff cardiologist on service with the pediatric resident and cardiology fellow, after which time some of the attending physicians would disappear for the rest of the day. Dr. Cranton was seen many times leaving the hospital at 11 a.m. while she was on service. By modifying the rule to require hand off before 1 p.m. they were ensuring that they would not have to return to the hospital to see a patient who may be transferred later in the afternoon. It was a pathetic display of laziness and entitlement! Not only was it a disgusting lack of teamwork, but Tricia and Sherry used their influence on Dr. Kowatch to ensure he would support such a nonsensical rule before they implemented it. I immediately told Dr. Kowatch when I took over service, don't worry, we will keep all the patients under the CICU service because it is clear that the cardiology team is unwilling to help, as the criteria that have been developed are actually obstructive; therefore, we will stop transferring patients altogether to ensure that they are cared for properly. After discussion with the other pediatric cardiologists who were also not "top trained," they agreed on the absurdity of this rule and proceeded to ignore it, thereby making this trio seem evermore petty until the rule finally dissolved and became obsolete. It became utterly apparent that Dr. Kowatch's recruits not only felt entitled, but they felt untouchable. In addition to their laziness, they began displaying toxic behavior that can only be accurately described as high school bullying. Shortly after Rebecca Holbein, the newest cardiac intensivist, had started and was covering the CICU service, I was in my office and heard yelling coming from her office, which was across the hall from mine. Concerned for her well-being, I knocked on the door and opened it to find her crying as Dr. Cranton and Dr. Monroe stood there next to her. I asked, "Is everything OK, Rebecca?"

The duo responded, "We were just clarifying some of the processes for stepping down a patient with Dr. Holbein."

"Rebecca?" I asked again.

"It's fine, I am just a bit emotional and stressed with the transition," she replied.

"OK, well I am right across the hall if you need something," I said with a concerned look on my face. I left the room and once I heard the duo leave, I went back to Rebecca's office to talk with her. She explained to me how the CICU was extremely busy, and she tried to transfer a patient who was no longer critical to help offload some of the clinical burden from the CICU but they had refused to accept the patient. Rebecca had spoken directly to

Dr. Kowatch who advised his recruits to help the CICU by accepting the patient transfer. As a result, the duo had come to her office and proceeded to retaliate by threatening her and telling her that she had better not go to Dr. Kowatch again to tell him that they weren't being cooperative or that she would regret it. I was astonished, where the hell was I? Dr. Cranton was in her forties and Dr. Monroe was in her thirties. This was high school nonsense. I was irate! Rebecca begged me not to go to Dr. Kowatch and inform him of this pathetic display of unprofessional behavior. I reluctantly agreed; however, I made her promise to make me aware if such behavior returned at any point. From that point forward, I now recognized that these two were nothing more than imposters, disguised as "top trained" physicians who were questionable clinicians with the maturity level of a high schooler, and probably a freshman at best!

While this may all seem as though I am being petty and merely criticizing everything about my new colleagues, and admittedly, there is some truth to that, all of this information is leading to my point. Attempting to change the model at a small-to-medium-sized program to a model based on the philosophy of a large-volume program, without significantly adding additional staff to the team, quite simply does not translate into success. The two models rely heavily on entirely different concepts. The small-to-medium-sized program must rely heavily on strong clinicians whose success depends on trust of their teammates and demands that each individual be armed with a solid understanding of all aspects related to the field of pediatric cardiology, rather than each being specialized in one specific area. This concept is analogous to that of a chain, with each individual representing a separate link in the chain, yet the chain is only as durable as its weakest link. Conversely, a large-volume program with a national reputation can easily attract "top trained" individuals, most of who are skilled clinicians and team players. Because there are many team members, it allows for individuals to become specialized in certain areas of cardiology rather than requiring each individual to have a general knowledge of everything, because there are other teammates who specialize in each of the other areas, whom they can rely on.

However, intermixed among these clinicians are the "pseudo top trained" individuals who were indeed trained at top programs, but who are in reality clinically weak, some of whom are actually incompetent; however, they are able to hide themselves among the many competent colleagues that surround them. When these individuals are transplanted from a large program to a small-to-medium-sized program, camouflaging such weakness becomes extremely difficult, and typically leads to exposure of their facade. When exposed, these individuals have no choice but to rely on their defense mechanisms, which consist of undermining others and labeling them as not "top trained," to distract from their incompetence, a disturbing yet real phenomenon. This problem is amplified a thousand-fold when administrative leadership is not only incapable of understanding this concept, but actually act to positively reinforce this perpetuating cycle by believing in the identical philosophy, thereby leading to their biased support of the "top trained" physicians. I realize that I am belaboring this concept, but I am trying to drive home its importance because such behavior was actively destroying everything we had worked for. Instead of adding additional strong links to the chain that made up our team, we had added three new links that were rusty and weak, and it was resulting in a fragile chain that could break at any moment, and in a small-to-medium-sized program, team is everything!

My frustration was mounting as I bore witness to the cringeworthy behavior displayed by Dr. Kowatch and his new hires, and Mr. Boykins's blatant disregard for the continued feedback provided by several members of the Heart Center, who were becoming fed up with the behavior of these three. Later that same day, I was notified by Michael Stringer that he was leaving CHOB to assume the role as CEO at a children's hospital in Nebraska, and shortly after Doris Geisinger told me of her impending departure, as she had accepted a position at Yale. Doris had expressed her concerns regarding Dr. Kowatch's lack of clinical knowledge, his inadequate leadership and pointed out the fact that after twenty years at Mayo Children's, the only people he was able to recruit were two inexperienced, clinically weak, and toxic employees who only functioned to negatively impact the progress we had made. She was right. She also pointed out that this administration failed miserably at recruiting a cardiac surgeon prior to the work we had done to invoke change in the CICU, and now they were acting in desperation as they overpaid for someone who, while skilled, was a notorious culture destroyer. Michael Stringer to this day still denies that he left for any reason other than to accept an opportunity that he couldn't refuse, although those who know him understood that his faith in Mr. Boykins and Dr. Kowatch had dwindled to an extent beyond repair and therefore, he appropriately understood that it was time to move on. One month later Kajay Swami, one of the interventional cardiologists and one of our best non-invasive cardiologists would resign, citing the deterioration in the workplace culture and Dr. Kowatch's poor leadership as the reason for their departure.

33

VALUES TRAINING, NEW CICU, AND ARRIVAL OF THE NEW CHIEF OF PEDIATRIC CARDIAC SURGERY

Shortly after arriving to Children's Hospital of Biloxi, Antoine Boykins hired a nationally recognized author and values coach named Jerry Hyde. Jerry Hyde was the author of a motivational book about positive attitude and its impact in the workplace. Following publication, he began touring and offering consultation services to health-care organizations including "values training" for the entire institution, although for a hefty fee. Mr. Boykins paid more than a million dollars to have this guy come teach people how not to be an asshole! Absolutely mind-blowing! However, once again, I was too naive to understand at the time, but I was soon to be rudely awakened to the fact that this was nothing more than typical Boykins theatrics. When I had first arrived at Children's Hospital of Biloxi, the hospital had begun administering an annual physician burnout survey, focused on asking CHOB physicians specifically how many hours per week they worked, if they felt less interested in their job, if they found themselves more easily frustrated at work, if they felt unsupported and so forth. Meanwhile, the second time I took the survey, I had been working one hundred hours per week for more than a year. The administration and university congratulated themselves because the results of the survey suggested, or at least they interpreted the results as such, that they were taking amazing care of the physicians and that most physicians no longer felt overworked or unappreciated. The results of the survey also showed a much lower percentage of physicians who felt at risk for burnout. Everyone celebrated, while both the hospital administration and the university leadership knew exactly what I was doing and the hours I was working. They saw my timesheets; in fact, they were required to sign my timesheet each month after they were submitted. I realize that while the survey was intended to be anonymous, in this particular circumstance there was one individual who definitely reported working in excess of one hundred hours per week, and of course they knew that individual was me, yet they chose to say nothing, which alone was an unforgivable act in my eyes. The fact that they still found a way to congratulate themselves for somehow doing a better job at caring for their physicians, which actually meant they may have done a better job at caring for every single physician, except me. This was my first real-life encounter dealing with the administrative smoke-screen and propaganda designed to distract you from reality and to fool you into believing that the administration actually cares about you. It took me some time to truly realize the deception taking place. I was deeply offended by the fact that Dr. Potts and Dr. Deeton said nothing and of all people, Dr. Potts was the one presenting these data to the medical staff. I was there in the audience, and he said nothing, not during, not after, not ever, not a single word. The fact was I never wanted or needed to be thanked, but for the love of God, I am still a human being. They could have said something as simple as, "While this year's scores are much improved, there still appear to be an individual or two who are working excessive hours, so we still have some things to address." That would have been plenty for me; instead, they not only showed that they couldn't care less about my well-being, but they also failed to even acknowledge that I existed. By then I should have had a better understanding of the fact that I was being used, but I was too focused to believe that people would do such a thing to another human being, without an ounce of gratitude or guilt.

After nearly three years, the medical tower, which housed the new twenty-five-bed CICU on the third floor, was finally complete. Once again, the completion of this stage of construction appeared to coincide with the stage of progress occurring within the CICU at the time. The new CICU was now complete and simultaneously, we had reached our initial staffing goal in the CICU, hiring six cardiac intensivists, five advanced practice providers, a dedicated cardiac pharmacist, nutritionist, and social worker. While staff training and education were ongoing, so was the remaining renovation and construction of the rest of the hospital. As we transported each of the CICU patients from the old unit to the new one, the hallways of the hospital were lined with staff members cheering in celebration of the grand opening, but also celebrating the amazing accomplishments that the entire CICU team and the Heart Center had achieved. I had to admit it was a nice touch by the hospital administration, which was definitely a final touch orchestrated by Michael Stringer, the only one insightful enough to plan and carry out such an act. The new unit was astonishing. The walls were a lime green, which was a bit loud, but I had to admit it was nice and bright. Many staff and family members commented on the bright green color, which was officially named smashed lime green. I wasn't sure about the color to start with, but it grew on me over time. There were twenty-five private CICU rooms. The rooms had to be close to double the size of the private rooms in the old CICU. They were each equipped with a private bathroom, a shower and a brightly colored couch that converted into a foldout bed so that family members could sleep in the room with their child. Seeing the amount of space available for medical equipment in the new rooms gave me a newfound appreciation for how we were able to make do with the facilities and equipment that we had in the old CICU. We had previously been functioning in a twenty-bed CICU; however, only about half of the rooms were private rooms with a door that could be closed, but they didn't have a private bathroom or shower. The remaining beds were configured in what is referred to as a pod distribution. This means that they were essentially spread out as evenly as possible in a centralized open space in the middle of the CICU. The only available privacy was a curtain that could be pulled around the bed space, that is assuming that the curtains actually worked. However, even when they worked as designed, there was no actual privacy. In the old unit, even the private rooms lacked a space for families to sleep, hence the family orgy room, sorry I mean sleeping room, across the hall! I felt blessed to be moving into such a beautiful space to care for our complex children and their families. It legitimately seemed a fitting reward for everyone's hard work in developing the CICU and for enduring some traumatic times along the way. Moving into the new unit felt as though we were stepping out of a time warp that had lasted for nearly three years and we had finally been returned to the present. Two weeks later our permanent existence in the present was secured as the portal to the past was permanently closed, represented by the demolition of the old CICU. I stared out the window as I watched the construction crew pummel the old unit. I was amazed at the ease with which the excavator converted the old CICU to rubble, beams and dust. I had mixed feelings watching it happen before my eyes. My first thought was, thank God that phase of this job is over. While the fall of the old CICU closed the door to the past, it also caused a lot of traumatic memories to resurface, as well as thoughts related to the amount of work Dr. Rostri had put into building the cardiac program and the CICU. I felt that he deserved to be here to witness this moment and wondered what memories would flash before his eyes as he watched the destruction take place. I am certain they would be different from mine, probably much more emotional than mine, but the truth was, he had dedicated his life to this program and regardless of the thoughts that would enter his mind, whether good or bad, they were his, and I felt he deserved to be there to experience whatever memories this historic feat for the hospital would trigger. My final thought, admittedly somewhat sarcastic, as I watched the formation of a massive cloud of dust and debris as the last wall of the CICU crumbled to the ground, was, "Wow, I sure hope those construction workers are wearing masks because some of the most resistant gram-negative bacteria and fungi in the history of humankind have now become airborne."

Six months passed and we had comfortably settled into our new space in the CICU. The Heart Center staff continued to grow and evolve. The new cardiac intensivists and advanced practice providers were being incorporated into the team flawlessly. You could feel a sense of pride and ownership in what had been built, and the final piece seemed to be the arrival in our new home. Not only had I spent a significant amount of time congratulating and reinforcing the great work the CICU team had been providing but now I was bolstering a new aspect of their achievement and that was performing care that was recognizable on a national level. No longer did I need to show our individual progress as it pertained to our own CICU outcomes, now we could compare ourselves to our nationally recognized colleagues around the country. Our new home seemed to be the final vote of confidence the staff needed to own the realization that not only was the care we were providing comparable, in some areas it appeared that we were actually performing better than the standard around the country, and now we had a facility that rivaled that of any top cardiac intensive care unit around the country. It was fascinating to watch and quite frankly, it made me feel proud, as if watching my daughters graduate high school with honors, witnessing their hard work finally come to fruition. Michael Stringer and Doris Geisinger had officially departed. Michael Stringer was replaced by Joseph Bergeron as the new COO. Joseph was a lawyer who had started working at Children's Hospital of Biloxi around the same time that I arrived. He had functioned previously as part of the hospital's legal team, and I suppose they felt after watching how things worked that he was suddenly qualified for the role. It was a bizarre hire in my opinion; however, prior to the departure of Michael Stringer, in his usual professional and positive manner, he met with the Heart Center leadership and relayed his vote of confidence on behalf of Joseph. But I wasn't buying it. I could tell that upon Michael's departure from CHOB, that he didn't feel good about the state of the hospital leadership.

Joseph Bergeron was average height. He always dressed in a suit although he looked as though he was sixteen years old and appeared awkward as if he was wearing his dad's suit for the first time on his way to the high school prom. I had met Joseph several times previously. He always seemed pleasant; however, he communicated as a lawyer, which meant there were typically a lot of smiles, handshakes, and verbose fluff delivered when he spoke. Nevertheless, it was void of anything substantive. He met with the Heart Center leadership after taking over as COO to relay his support. With the administrative staffing changes taking place, the highly anticipated arrival of Dr. Porter, as well as the concerns related to the clinical ability and behavioral problems displayed by our newest colleagues, you couldn't help but feel a sense of uncertainty related to the future. The CICU team, who consisted of individuals who had endured so much psychological trauma and toxicity over the years, now found themselves thriving in a gorgeous new CICU, yet for some reason, you could cut the tension with a knife. Michael Stringer's departure resonated throughout the institution and given Dr. Porter's past history of behavioral issues, there was an unspoken, or at least quietly spoken, anxiety regarding the direction of the program from this point forward. Quite honestly this uncertainty hovered in everyone's mind, including mine. I felt clinically well and symptom-free from my autoimmune disease but had failed weaning from prednisone several times. I felt stuck in this repeating cycle where I had severe insomnia due to the high-dose steroids that were required to control my disease. As a result, I needed to take Lunesta to help me sleep; however, obviously I could not take a sedating medication while I worked nights at the hospital. As a result, each night I was on call in the hospital, meant I was awake the entire night, while typically there is a period in the night where the on-call physician may be able to rest for two to three hours, although there were certainly nights where there was no sleep. As a result, that translated into seven nights per month where I would be awake for thirty-six hours straight. In the past my body could endure those hours, or at least at the time I felt that it could; however, now it would routinely take my body several days to feel recovered after a night shift. The consequence was that the lack of sleep had major repercussions on my immune system, and I believed that was limiting my ability to wean the prednisone, which led back to the insomnia I was just describing. I saw this as a recurring loop that I needed to eventually break, for my own well-being. For this reason, I scheduled a meeting with Dr. Kowatch and Joseph Bergeron, the new COO, to discuss my plans for Dr. Porter's arrival as well as my intentions for the future, so that we could discuss potential avenues for arriving where I felt I needed to be, for my own health, and so that I could be clear what my long-term plan consisted of. "While Dr. Porter was not my first choice to function as our chief of pediatric cardiac surgery, I am a professional and I believe in giving everyone a chance. I am going to disregard the behavior problems that have reportedly plagued his past. I believe in forming my own opinion and that everyone deserves a fresh start and should begin without prior judgment based on their past history. I plan on welcoming Dr. Porter with open arms to Children's Hospital of Biloxi; however, I want to be clear about my approach to dealing with him individually and I would also like to discuss possible avenues for my future after he has had time to settle in. First, I want to be clear that after everything I have been through personally and professionally here, I have no intention of sticking around for a repeat of the Dr. Rostri years, so if things began to trend in that direction, I wanted you both to be cognizant of the fact that I will likely resign and ultimately leave CHOB. That is not intended to be a threat or ultimatum, it is simply the truth and you both know that is who I am, honest and direct. I also want you to know that I am going to push myself clinically when Dr. Porter arrives and ask my CICU team to do the same, so that we are performing at our very best to be sure that he knows that he made the correct decision to join us. However, after three to six months, I want to consider starting the process of recruiting for my replacement. I was hoping that the hospital would support my continued employment in some other capacity. As you both have heard me say repeatedly, since my arrival, I have sincere concerns, due to the team I have built and the loyalty we feel for one another as a group, that if I were to resign or develop worsening health that resulted in my inability to work, that I fear there could be a mass exodus of CICU staff. For this reason, I have felt trapped here for years. Therefore, I would like you to consider the scenario where I help CHOB recruit my replacement while I stay on in another role, one which includes me mentoring my replacement, as well as helping them navigate systemic or interpersonal challenges they are likely to encounter upon their arrival," I explained.

"I like that idea … So do I," Mr. Bergeron and Dr. Kowatch responded in unison.

"Great. Let's revisit this idea in the near future," I said excitedly.

January 2021, the new year welcomed the addition of Dr. Porter as the new chief of pediatric cardiac surgery at CHOB. In classic Boykinsesque fashion, a welcome party including a marching band ensued in the hospital atrium, which led to Mr. Boykins, Dr. Kowatch, and eventually Dr. Porter, all dancing like Muppets or possibly having a seizure, I can't be sure which, but given the fact that no one was rushing to assist them, I had to assume it was some sort of secret "top trained" dance ritual, or perhaps mating ritual, which I was simply not privy to. Whatever it was, I prayed it would stop and soon and, fortunately for everyone, it did. As they appeared somewhat post-ictal, Mr. Boykins walked over to me and stated, "Dr. Porter will be giving a lunchtime lecture in the administrative conference room on the fourth floor today, it would be wonderful if you could join us."

"I will be there. I am on service so I may be a few minutes late, but I will be there," I replied.

Noontime arrived promptly and fortunately I was able to finish CICU medical rounds and make my way up to the fourth floor on time. As I walked into the conference room, there were approximately twenty people standing and conversing in the room. The attendees consisted mostly of administrators and hospital board members. Dr. Porter, Dr. Kowatch and I were the only members of the Heart Center who were present. Mr. Boykins saw me walk through the door and immediately walked toward me and shook my hand as he said, "You came from Fort Myers Children's, correct? That is a great program."

"Yes, I did. Uh yes, it is a solid group of individuals who make up an outstanding team that delivers high-quality care to extremely complex patients," I replied, somewhat confused by his sudden interest in my background and by his gracious interaction with me.

"Oh great," he responded, insincerely, as he walked away to assume his position at the top of the rectangular conference room table. This was a very odd statement from Mr. Boykins. In the years leading up to this point, not once had he asked me where I trained, outside of making me feel unworthy as he stared at my CV, unimpressed, when we first met in his office, following his arrival to CHOB. To ask me this and state that Fort Myers was a "great program" at this point in time really left me dumbfounded. I attempted to shake the bewildered look from my face as I grabbed a plate of food and took my seat as Dr. Porter took his position at the podium just as Mr. Boykins announced, "Can I have your attention please? I would like to take the opportunity to introduce Dr. Phil Porter who was previously the division chief at Children's Hospital of Pennsylvania for ten years (neglecting to mention his brief stints at two other institutions) and is now our new division chief of pediatric cardiac surgery. As you can see, due to the changes we have made since my team and I have arrived, we are now able to recruit 'top trained' physicians to Children's Hospital of Biloxi. The key to achieving our goal of becoming a top twenty-five children's hospital is our ability to recruit such 'top trained' individuals, so please join me in welcoming Dr. Porter." The room erupted with applause. As I looked to my right, seated directly next to Mr. Boykins, in the seat which might just as well have had a sign attached to the back of it saying "Ass-Kisser of the Month," was Dr. Kowatch. His eyes aggressively searched around the clapping hands of others seated at the table, until he was able to visualize the expression on my face in response to

Mr. Boykins's words, as if a child waiting to see if he had gotten away with a mischievous behavior that he knew was inappropriate. It was one of the most nauseating experiences of my life and left me squirming in my chair. It was as though someone had snuck me into some secret society meeting so they could study how a physician who wasn't "top trained" would behave when he was exposed to such greatness. The fact that Mr. Boykins thought he was responsible for recruiting anyone in the Heart Center was laughable, but I truly couldn't care less. It felt desperate and validated my analogy of the high school girl chasing celebrities for their autograph. I listened to Dr. Porter's mediocre lecture and upon its completion made my way to the exit and back to the CICU. In retrospect, this was a sign of what was to come as it signified a shift in focus from strengthening the Heart Center "chain" by filling each deficient "link" with strong clinicians, to instead focusing on which program a candidate trained at or how many publications filled the pages of their CV.

The following day, Dr. Porter joined the rest of the Heart Center at surgical rounds in the new CICU conference room at 7:30 a.m. The new conference room consisted of a projector screen at the front of the room, lined on each side by rectangular tables positioned parallel to one another, in a straight line with approximately twenty chairs on each side. In the back of the room was a table covered with state-of-the-art audio-visual equipment with four additional chairs, where the cardiac intensivist who had been on call the night before would sit. This individual was responsible for pulling up the chest X-ray and labs for each patient, while providing a brief background history as well as any pertinent clinical events that may have occurred over-night. As Dr. Slovak went through the patients, Dr. Porter was silent; however, he appeared extremely uncomfortable, constantly shifting and squirming in his chair as he would intermittently rub his head in what appeared to be an anxious manner. It was odd and I was unsure what it was all about. I attempted to engage him in discussion thinking maybe he felt troubled by being an outsider. He declined to contribute his opinion that day; however, on subsequent days, the etiology of his apparent anxiety would become blatantly obvious. Each day as the intensivist would present the patients for surgical rounds, his distressed body language progressively worsened until it gradually turned into agitated vocalizations and eventually over a period of two months, it revealed his loathing disdain for cardiac intensivists. "Did we replace that low potassium? Why does that say arterial blood gas when it is a venous blood gas? Can we just stop the sedation? I want this patient extubated," he would ask or state rudely often interrupting the intensivist without providing an opportunity for them to explain.

His track record for despising intensivists eventually became clear, and his anxious body language represented his failed attempt at withholding verbalization of the criticisms that were consuming his conscious mind. I made several attempts in private to understand the source of this rage, seeing if there was some remedy I could offer to put his mind at ease; however, there was no clear reason. Dr. Kowatch spent about a week in total, stuttering nervously, as he failed miserably at corralling Dr. Porter's rude interaction with the CICU team, which bared no resemblance to collaboration on this planet or any other in this solar system. "Phil, this is surgical rounds, it is intended to be a quick review of the patients in order to update and engage our cardiology and cardiac surgery colleagues in a manner that seeks your input as it relates to your specialty. We really don't need help with potassium or sedation," I would say to him in private.

"I don't understand what you mean, Eric. In Pennsylvania we called this collaboration, people here are too sensitive. I think I should just stop coming to surgical rounds. I can simply meet the cardiac intensivist on service and walk to each patient's bedside and I can just tell them the plan for the day," he replied.

"Phil, you're missing the point, we don't need you to tell us what to do. We are seeking your surgical input," I said.

"These are my patients, I want to be involved," he snapped at me angrily.

"We want you involved; that is why we are attempting to discuss the overall plan as a team," I explained.

"I just won't come to surgical rounds anymore," he said like a spoiled child throwing a temper tantrum.

"OK, well that is your choice, but I hope you will reconsider since we have developed surgical rounds specifically to get input from the surgeons and the cardiologists," I said calmly.

"We will see," he responded. As expected, Dr. Porter continued to join and "participate," although it would be more accurate to describe his behavior as heckling.

After taking the first couple of weeks to settle in and adjust to the new system, Dr. Porter performed his first cardiac surgical case. As I said earlier, Dr. Porter had two qualities for which he was nationally renowned, the first was operating with great precision on even the tiniest of newborn babies with complex heart disease and the second was for being a world-class asshole to nearly everyone he encountered. We had already witnessed the latter; it was now time to hopefully witness the first. His first case was extremely complex and involved operating on a tiny baby less than 2 kilogram (approximately 3.5 pounds) with multiple congenital anomalies and complex heart disease. The operation went well, and the patient returned in stable condition to the CICU; however, the chest was left open, as is often the case for newborns, in particular tiny newborns with several other congenital problems. On postoperative day number three, Dr. Porter felt that the baby's chest was ready to be closed, so the team prepared for the procedure, which meant the entire operating room team would wheel carts of equipment from the operating room to the CICU. The OR team would prepare the room in sterile fashion, which meant that everyone who would be involved in the procedure would require a cap to cover their hair and a surgical mask. The surgical technician would prepare a table with all the surgical equipment that would be required to carry out the procedure, including all surgical tools that were required by the cardiac surgeon, such as sutures to close the skin, wires to close the sternum, new chest tubes in cases they needed to be added or replaced, antibiotic irrigation for the open chest, sterile gowns and gloves for the teammates involved, as well as Dr. Porter's surgical loops (magnifying glasses) and cauterizing equipment, to name a few. While the OR team prepared for the cardiac surgeon, the CICU nurse would simultaneously prepare the necessary medications and equipment for the cardiac intensivist to assist during the procedure. This included placing an infusion of epinephrine inline in case the blood pressure decreased during sternal closure; however, in this instance the baby was already on an epinephrine infusion. The other medications would be neatly arranged on a table, which were divided into groups by medication name including "spritzer" doses of epinephrine (mini boluses of diluted epinephrine which are smaller than doses used during code-blue events) as well as bolus doses or calcium chloride, which are both used to counteract episodes of hypotension. Additionally, the nurse would prepare doses of other resuscitation medications as well as doses of fentanyl, midazolam, and vecuronium to ensure the patient was sedated and medically paralyzed for the procedure. Packed red blood cells were prepared and at the bedside in a cooler as was 5 percent albumin, which could be administered intravenously as fluid boluses, again to counteract episodes of hypotension. The team appeared prepared as the surgeon and his assistant walked to the bedside, holding their hands upright as water dripped from their hands to the floor, after scrubbing them in preparation for the procedure. They were each met at the bedside by the surgical technician who presented them with their sterile gown, and assisted them with dressing and tying the gown, followed by helping them to place their sterile gloves. By this point the sternal dressing had been removed and the first assistant had exposed, cleaned and sterilized the entire sternum with large amounts of betadine. After Dr. Porter was dressed in sterile fashion, a sterile drape was handed to him and his assistant as they proceeded to lay it on the patient, starting with the window-like opening that was placed over the sternum permitting easy visualization during the procedure. After positioning the window, the massive drape was unfolded, covering the entire patient and crib. In preparation, the CICU nurse had prepared a push line for administering medications and fluid by attaching extension tubing to the central venous line and feeding it through the prison-like openings on the side of the crib and under the drape, finally resting it on the table near the foot of the bed, where the intensivist would stand during the procedure. The final process signifying the start of the procedure is referred to as the "time out." This was a nationwide safety measure implemented prior to a procedure that consisted of a staff member, typically the OR or bedside nurse, who would announce the words "time out," after which all involved staff stopped what they were doing, as the nurse read aloud the name of the procedure to be performed, the patient's name, medical record number, while also verifying informed consent had been obtained and that the patient had been NPO (nothing per oral; i.e., no food had been given enterally).

Dr. Porter commenced the procedure by silently holding his outstretched arm to his side while maintaining his gaze on the patient's chest, as the surgical technician knowingly placed the suction device he sought firmly in his hand. Dr. Porter aggressively inserted the sucker into the open chest, removing old blood and fluid, notably more aggressively than I had witnessed other cardiac surgeons maneuver. He manipulated the sucker throughout the mediastinum, completely void of finesse, an odd and unexpected characteristic for a surgeon nationally recognized for technical precision. After removing small amounts of old blood from the chest and rinsing the mediastinum with antibiotic irrigation, the next step was to remove the tourniquets that were intentionally left in place at their aortic and venous origins, in case the patient were to deteriorate, requiring ECMO prior to chest closure. Dr. Porter removed the aortic tourniquet and pushed his pointed index finger slowly down the suture while the tech squirted water on his hand to provide lubrication, attempting to bring the knot he had tied together, thereby closing the hole. Suddenly, his hand jerked, and you could hear a snapping noise as the suture broke. Blood began to fill the mediastinum as Dr. Porter and his assistant urgently applied suction. I began to push packed red blood cells just as Dr. Porter yelled anxiously, "We are losing some blood here."

"Yep, I am pushing blood as we speak," I replied.

Abruptly, Dr. Porter's demeanor changed from anxious to distressed as blood began to accumulate, eventually overflowing from the mediastinum and spilling onto the sterile drape, as if a swimming pool overflowing onto the patio following a torrential rain. "I think the right atrial line became dislodged by the sucker as I was trying to control the bleeding," Dr. Porter screamed loudly. This signified that we had lost our source of intravenous access and I now had no way to deliver blood products as the patient actively hemorrhaged.

"Phil, I am going to have to use the arterial line to push blood products because I have no other option for access. Activate the ECMO team," I said aloud.

Typically, it is ill-advised to use an arterial line for anything more than continuous monitoring of hemodynamics or for lab draws. We are taught early on in our intensive care unit training that medications should never be delivered through an arterial line; however, in previous emergent situations I have been forced to use the arterial line as a means for pushing fluid. The downside was that we could no longer continuously monitor the blood pressure. "Do what you need to do, Eric. Yes, call ECMO team," Dr. Porter repeated anxiously. As he searched for the source of the bleeding, Dr. Porter realized that there was a tear in the aorta that required he take the patient to the operating room for repair; however, we both agreed that the safest way to do so was to first place the patient on ECMO. I pushed blood as fast as the arterial catheter allowed me, while attempting not to push too hard, which could put the catheter at risk of infiltration. Dr. Porter was able to slow the bleeding, allowing me an opportunity to replace the deficit in hemoglobin that had rapidly developed due to the hemorrhage. The patient stabilized and was successfully placed on ECMO and was taken to the operating room for repair of the aortic tear. The baby returned three hours later to the CICU in stable condition; however, he remained on ECMO for another thirty-six hours. The following day we weaned the ECMO flow to determine if the baby was ready to come off. The baby remained hemodynamically stable while undergoing a circuit clamping trial, which is a process of placing a surgical clamp across both ECMO cannulas, stopping the artificial flow of blood to and from the body, thereby requiring the baby's heart to assume 100 percent of the work. This trial is a crude maneuver used to help determine if the baby's heart appears ready to tolerate the full workload on its own. The patient tolerated the fifteen-minute clamp trial; however, he required a moderate amount of medical support to do so. As a result, we decided to allow an additional twenty-four hours for continued patient recovery with plans to electively decannulate the baby from ECMO the following day. However, that evening the plan drastically changed. At approximately 2 a.m. the ECMO circuit suddenly stopped. The circuit is continuously plugged into an electrical outlet. In fact, it is plugged into the emergency reserve outlet, which is intended to maintain functionality via emergency generator power in the event a primary power failure occurs. The circuit is also equipped with a backup battery that serves as a second layer of protection in the event of a primary power failure. In this instance, the emergency outlet power failed, the generator power failed, and so did the backup battery—a truly unheard-of sequence of events. As a result, the ECMO circuit ceased functioning and therefore, no blood was flowing to support the patient. "Grab the crank. Call the doc quickly!" yelled the perfusion technician sitting at the bedside, who was responsible for managing the ECMO machine. As they called Justin, the CICU physician on call, they hooked the emergency crank to the ECMO circuit and began hand cranking the pump in an attempt to maintain some blood flow to the patient.

Justin arrived and yelled, "I need some volume and an epinephrine bolus. Increase the epi drip to 0.1 micrograms per kilogram a minute and activate the emergency ECMO page." The nurse followed the orders as the patient's blood pressure stabilized in response to Justin's interventions. The emergency page was activated; however, the circuit remained without power despite trying other outlets in the room and troubleshooting the backup battery failure. The ECMO cannulas were again clamped, and the patient was able to maintain stability without the support of the lifesaving machine.

The ECMO team and Dr. Porter arrived to the patient's room within fifteen minutes. "What the fuck happened?" Dr. Porter yelled. As Justin and the perfusion technician attempted to detail the sequence of events, Dr. Porter cut them off by yelling, "Enough! Stop talking. Explain to me how three levels of backup power fail in a brand-new CICU?" Justin struggled to give an explanation, as did the others, because quite simply, they were all shocked by this unheard-of turn of events. After trying several different outlets, they were able to reestablish power to the circuit; however, by this time it was clear that the baby was capable of maintaining his own cardiac output without ECMO and given the uncertainty as to the etiology of what had just occurred, it was decided that it was safest to decannulate the patient from ECMO. As the surgical team prepared for cannula removal, Dr. Porter walked over to the perfusion technician and said, "How did you let this happen? I have never seen a situation such as this in my twenty-five years of practice."

"Neither have I," responded the seasoned perfusion technician.

"Well, maybe that's the problem," Dr. Porter replied as he walked by the perfusion tech, nudging him aggressively with the side of his shoulder, sending him flailing backward, as he narrowly escaped falling to the floor. The staff in the room looked on in awe. Dr. Porter walked to the side of the machine as he suddenly noticed a sticky note attached to the side of the circuit that read "Check heater/cooler." He snatched the sticker from the ECMO circuit and slammed the sticky note on the perfusion technicians back resulting in a loud *smack* that was heard throughout the room. "What the fuck is this?" screamed Dr. Porter.

"The perfusion technician covering yesterday noted that the heater/cooler appeared to be inaccurately regulating patient temperature. We were going to have it investigated after this patient was either removed from the circuit or when the circuit required changing. Since the baby's temperature remained stable, we didn't feel it was necessary to change the circuit immediately," the perfusion technician explained.

"Why would we choose not to investigate the malfunction now? Who services and maintains the circuit? When was it last evaluated by biomedical services?" asked Dr. Porter, in an aggressive tone.

"I am not sure, you would have to ask Donald Henderson, the ECMO director," said the perfusion technician. The reality was that Dr. Porter was correct, why would we continue to use an ECMO circuit with a presumed malfunction involving any portion of the circuit and his questions pertaining to the last time the circuit had been serviced and who was responsible for certifying that it underwent regular quality testing were valid. Ultimately, a root cause analysis was performed, which found that it had been two years since there was formal testing of the backup battery by biomedical engineering and in terms of preventive care and maintenance of the ECMO circuit, there was no ownership or protocol in place for such care. It was also determined during the root cause analysis that the outlets in the room had lost power due to a circuitry malfunction. While there was clear reason for Dr. Porter to be upset regarding the events that had transpired, it was equally apparent that there were indeed two different issues that needed to be addressed separately. The first involved the mechanical and electrical failure that occurred as well as the lack of protocol in place pertaining to ECMO maintenance and repair that were identified during the root cause analysis. The second issue was related to the verbal and physical abuse endured by the staff at the hands of Dr. Porter. Following this event, Donald Henderson, the ECMO director constructed an email alluding to the inappropriate behavior displayed by Dr. Porter. In particular he highlighted Dr. Porter's verbal and physical abuse of the staff. This email was addressed to me, Dr. Penton, Dr. Arnold (chief surgical officer), and Dr. Kowatch (chief of cardiology). As I read the email, I felt unsettled by the fact that Dr. Porter was left out of this group email correspondence. I was immediately taken back in time to 2017, during the first few days of my employment at Children's Hospital of Biloxi. I remembered how poorly I was treated and how alone I felt because I was the outsider, the one trying to disrupt the ideology "this is the way we have always done it." I felt empathy toward Dr. Porter and while I did not support his hiring and I certainly did not support his behavior toward the staff, I understood how upset he was at the situation, it was unacceptable. I made a commitment to giving him a chance and I felt that any discussion regarding repercussions for his behavior should involve him. As a result, I responded to the email. "Donald, thank you for your email outlining your concerns regarding the events of last night related to the ECMO circuit failure and the treatment of our fellow Heart Center staff members. Let me start by saying, I agree with you that we could have reacted to this unfortunate situation in a more collegial and professional manner; however, I also want to ensure that we are not distracting from the primary problem that occurred, which is that the failure of our ECMO circuit nearly resulted in the death of one of our patients. While I agree that the behavior displayed needs to be addressed, I feel it is best that we are transparent with our colleagues and in my opinion, Dr. Porter should be included in your email because as a team we should feel that each of us is empowered to discuss, in a professional manner, our mistakes and shortcomings openly. If we do so without including those directly involved in the event, we create silos and as a result mistrust will develop and it ultimately leads to fractures in the 'chain,' which will weaken us as a team. Thank you for your concern and leadership." Sounds great, right? Wrong! Boy, was I stupid. During my tenure at Children's Hospital of Biloxi, I learned countless lessons. Unfortunately, almost zero of these lessons actually pertained to medicine. Instead, I learned numerous lessons about myself, both positive and negative, as well as those pertaining to life. In this particular case, I learned that individuals who have a history of displaying major behavior problems, at least in health care, don't tend to be amenable to change.

In fact, I sat down with Dr. Porter in my office, the day after Donald Henderson sent the email, and he and I had a very direct and honest conversation that I respected very much. I asked him about the events, and he said to me, quite honestly and calmly, "Eric, I am nearly sixty years old. I am who I am, and I am not going to change." The reality is, I knew this prior to his arrival. This pattern of behavior had been displayed throughout Dr.

Porter's career at each institution he was employed at and was apparently so severe at one of his jobs that he was terminated after two months. The verbal mistreatment, while unacceptable, was one issue; however, the physical contact with staff members was truly concerning and had been reported at each of his previous jobs. In retrospect, this situation became what I would come to understand as a truly defining moment for our new administrators. In my humble opinion, they chose to unilaterally hire a "top trained" and skilled surgeon, with an extensive history of toxic behavior, including several reported events involving physical contact with staff members ranging from pushing to grabbing ancillary staff and junior physicians. Not only did they disregard my opinion and that of others within the Heart Center regarding his hiring, but they chose to pay him handsomely and reward him with a long-term employment contract, and most importantly, they did so without establishing behavior guidelines in advance, thereby rendering the hospital defenseless should such behavior be displayed—meaning he could act as he pleased because his contract contained no clause stating that if he misbehaved then his contract could be terminated without the need to pay him. As a result, he could act as he pleased, as if telling the administration, "Go ahead, fire me; I will take my full ten million dollars and go elsewhere." A real rookie mistake made by desperate, first-time administrators.

Following Donald Henderson's email, Dr. Arnold, the chief surgical officer, was now experiencing a defining moment in his brief career at Children's Hospital of Biloxi as his response to Dr. Porter's behavior would elucidate the future direction of the program. Additionally, how he chose to respond to the situation would set the standard for the future, as there would almost certainly be behavior problems pertaining to Dr. Porter in the weeks and months to come. Days passed and it had been communicated to Ruth Hofstra, who had now been promoted to service line administrator for the Heart Center, that the situation had been "addressed," whatever that meant, although things continued as though nothing had happened, quite frankly because they hadn't! Following the root cause analysis, the ownership of ECMO repair and preventive maintenance was placed upon biomedical engineering and a protocol regarding the timing and frequency of maintenance was implemented. It felt reassuring that something positive resulted from this unfortunate event; however, I couldn't help but feel concerned about the secrecy regarding the administrative response to Dr. Porter's inappropriate behavior. Several staff members asked me what was being done to address such unacceptable behavior, to which I replied, "I am not sure," although I was certain the only action that had been performed was to sweep it under the rug. Nonetheless, we persevered.

Weeks passed, and as is natural when you spend a substantial amount of time with others personally or professionally, you tend to learn more about one another. You learn about their strengths and weaknesses, likes and dislikes, as well as their behaviors, including any odd or atypical ones. I began to identify factors that appeared to trigger anxiety or anger in Dr. Porter as well as telltale signs that such emotions were escalating. I found surgical rounds in the morning to be particularly agitating to Dr. Porter, and it was now clear how much he despised cardiac intensivists and in particular, inexperienced ones. If a cardiac intensivist had less than eight years experience, he would simply disregard and pick apart any input they had regarding the management of his surgical patients, or quite honestly, any input they had regarding anything. During surgical rounds he rudely interrupted the presentation of each patient by the intensivist who had been on call the evening before. The majority of the interruptions were to "correct" them or "educate" them for being stupid. The purpose of surgical rounds, which I had developed over the preceding years prior to his arrival, was to stimulate discussion and collaboration within the Heart Center while providing an opportunity to update the cardiologists and cardiac surgeons on the patient's clinical status, while also getting cardiology and surgical input on management. Instead, it transpired into a thirty-to-sixty-minute period of relentless criticism directed at CICU physicians and oftentimes the focus would shift to minutia such as whether or not we had corrected a low potassium, rather than discussing big picture problems that were occurring. As a result, my team began to complain, and rightfully so. I sat down on multiple occasions to discuss this matter with Dr. Porter; however, he was a master of mind manipulation, just as Dr. Rostri had been. He would often make me second-guess what I was saying and never admitted any fault, regardless of the situation. We used to carry out surgical rounds at the patient's bedside; however, families would often overhear our discussion and view our differences in opinion as arguments or lacking consensus rather than healthy collaboration, so once the new CICU opened with a brand-new conference room, I moved rounds into there. The downside was that being away from the families allowed a free-for-all in terms of malignant behavior by Dr. Porter. The ultimate result of this behavior became the development of unhappiness among the cardiac intensivists and advanced practice providers. He became downright nasty to some of my junior colleagues. He ignored their input during surgical rounds and at the bedside when caring for patients. He deliberately ignored them as if they ceased to exist, he told the nurses to ignore their orders, he changed medications and the plan at the bedside without their input, and to top it off he called them by the wrong name, which appeared to be deliberate. The nurturing environment we had worked so hard to create was actively being destroyed before my eyes, and it hurt, badly! He treated me differently, I actually worked well with him, and he respected my input for the most part, but how could I remain affable with the malignant treatment of my colleagues just because Dr. Porter and I worked well together? The answer is, I couldn't, that would go against everything I believed in. I also began to notice subtleties or patterns that preceded Dr. Porter's angry outbursts. They would appear as tics; however, I began to recognize a clear sequence that would develop and progress. The agitated sequence began with his face turning bright red, followed by the persistent rubbing of his head with his hand. This was subsequently followed by a second phase consisting of the sideward, rhythmic movement of his head as if he were the third Butabi brother from the movie *A Night at the Roxbury*. What happened next would depend on whether the inciting factor terminated or if it continued. If it was merely a grade 1 agitation sequence, it could simply terminate here and return to baseline without any major outburst. However, if not, the next phase was a grade 2 agitation sequence that consisted of Dr. Porter aggressively slapping his own leg underneath the conference room table one to three times in succession. However, if the inciting factor continued it would go on to initiate a grade 3 or greater agitation sequence. When this occurred, it triggered an entirely different algorithm. In this instance, the leg slapping would be replaced by a series of two to three rhythmic punches of the palm of his own hand. If it escalated beyond here, meaning a grade 4 agitation sequence, things got real because the hand punching would then escalate to an aggressive turn in his chair, followed by Dr. Porter screaming at the intensivist. I wish I was joking, but this was truly the "agitation sequence" that I decoded over about a six-month period of time, and it was reproducible. It became an inside joke among my CICU colleagues and me. The joking was clearly a coping mechanism for us, but it was truly awful to experience, and it saddened me because it represented that we had now regressed back to a toxic culture resembling the one I had worked so hard to eradicate.

CHAPTER 34

ADMINISTRATIVE CHANGES AND THE BEGINNING OF THE END

Several administrative staffing changes began to occur. It also became notable that the administrators began to show behavioral and philosophical changes or at least they became bolder in revealing their true intentions as time progressed. Following Michael Stringer's unfortunate departure, his replacement Joseph Bergeron was clearly inexperienced and tragically ignorant of the workings of a children's hospital and in particular the staffing needs and flow of a pediatric cardiac intensive care unit. John Wozniak, the chief nursing officer, who was instrumental in Ruth Hofstra and my success during our difficult times in the first two years at Children's Hospital of Biloxi, had left to take on the role as chief operating officer at another children's hospital. He was followed shortly after by the departure of Ben Washington, the chief development officer. Both were major losses to the hospital, and they had been huge supporters of the changes we were implementing in the CICU. While I was happy for their opportunities for career growth, I was admittedly sad as they left huge voids to fill. It was rumored that they started seeking other opportunities as time passed because they began to see the CEO, Antoine Boykins, for who he truly was, and they stopped believing in him as his true vision for the future of CHOB began to unfold. Two different administrative interns and the director of accounting, all of whom happened to be female, abruptly left due to sexual harassment allegations by men within Mr. Boykins administrative staff. The real scam here was that his right-hand man, Hector Ramirez, the chief financial officer, was married to the head of human resources. So strangely enough, the three women, who had all filed complaints to HR, ended up leaving "of their own free will," for lack of a better phrase, because they were threatened and verbally abused for reporting these individuals, who were married and had children. Ultimately there were no consequences for such egregious behavior and no trace documenting this sexual deviancy could be found. The true persona of Antoine Boykins and his shady thug, Hector Ramirez, began to reveal themselves. One day while I was on service in the CICU, the nurses shared an iPhone video captured during the most recent hurricane, which had been circulating, showing Antoine Boykins grinding on three of the environmental staff in the atrium of the hospital like a horny teenager on ecstasy at an electronic music festival. It was disgusting behavior for any rational adult, much less the married CEO of a children's hospital. Even more nauseating was that Hector began to ask through third parties for the contracts of all the physicians I had hired. My gut told me that administration was shifting toward cutting expenditures. Upon their arrival, the D.C. Children's administrators originally spoke of their dedication to investing in the Heart Center. However, I was concerned that I was beginning to see the early signs of a premature shift from a period of growth and development to one focusing on the return on investment. But how could this be? We were far from finished staffing several areas of the Heart Center, and I was just promised that we could recruit for eight cardiac intensivists. Were the comments regarding "investment in the Heart Center" merely a show? Antoine Boykins only two weeks prior shared with the Heart Center team that the hospital was $15 million in the black, yet we were putting the brakes on investment? I was confused and concerned.

I had obtained approval for eight pediatric cardiac intensivists and eight advanced practice providers. We were currently at six cardiac intensivists and six advanced practice providers. I had been waiting to recruit for the other two positions because I was trying to be financially responsible, and I felt that the workload was acceptable at the time. I was planning to delay the recruitment until I saw an increase in the cardiac surgical volume that was predicted following Dr. Porter's hiring. However, we began to be questioned regarding the extra night call per diem pay. Joseph Bergeron, the COO, also began questioning me regarding our work hours and asked "what we did with all of our spare time" and commented that when he would come by the CICU at nighttime, which was never by the way, he always found that the cardiac intensivist was sleeping so he asked why we need to be paid extra for working additional shifts? He also asked when I was going to start taking more night call and said that others were concerned that due to my health, I was incapable of doing my job. I explained to him that he had unreasonable expectations as it pertained to my staff and me. I reminded him that the CICU was the first unit in the history of CHOB to perform 24-7 in-house coverage and we did so with two cardiac intensivists. Following my success at improving outcomes, the pediatric intensive care unit and neonatal intensive care units were pressured to do the same; however, the PICU refused to do so until they had ten intensivists and the NICU refused to do so until they had twelve physicians. I explained that I did not have the luxury to do that; however, I felt that we were being taken advantage of because we had done it with fewer physicians and not once had we complained. I also explained that the staffing model needed to deliver 24-7 care was based on having a reasonable workload and not on patient volume. I stressed that it was shortsighted to look at hours per week and instead it was necessary to consider hours per month and that periods of rest were necessary to prevent physician burnout and other "free time" was actually dedicated to research, staff education, fellow and resident education as well as time needed for vacations, and so on. He was unimpressed by my explanation and said they would continue to monitor the situation. I also reiterated that my health situation was fragile and that while I may look well, following my last visit to Mayo Clinic, my cardiologist was concerned because my arrhythmia burden had significantly increased, and my PET scan showed progressively worsening inflammation. The reason I looked improved was because I was forced to increase my steroid dose despite being on three other immunosuppressants. The concern was that my side effects continued to increase and now I had officially become diabetic, my vision had deteriorated, and I now required glasses with an increasing prescription and had developed cataracts and severe insomnia and mood swings. As a result, my physician recommended that I stop doing night call. "Well, it sounds to me like you are unable to do your job," Joseph Bergeron said.

Meanwhile, there were whispers that Dr. Porter was the one suggesting that I was incapable of performing the job and he was secretly contacting a colleague of his from Children's Hospital of Pennsylvania who he wanted to replace me. When I directly asked Joseph Bergeron about this, he didn't deny it, but instead brushed it aside and said, "Well not necessarily to replace you, but perhaps to help you."

This is the type of leaders we were dealing with. At this point, my concerns were escalating by the minute. I saw what happened to Dr. Rostri and I felt as though it was a real possibility that I could be the next one escorted to my car by security. After everything I sacrificed for this institution, including my health, and my family, I couldn't believe that an institution would be so ungrateful and malignant. When Joseph sat down in my office to explain these concerns to me, I asked him bluntly, "Joseph, just so I understand your point of view, let me recap. There is concern among Heart Center and administrative leadership that I am 'unable to do my job anymore.' When I arrived, I did the job of six people and worked over one hundred hours a week for more than a year until I collapsed at my home and nearly died leaving me with an irreversible chronic medical condition that is likely to shorten my lifespan. Then, I recruited four other cardiac intensivists from 'top institutions' while this hospital had failed to recruit a single cardiac intensivist for many years. Then, I spent time developing each one of them after which I was able to reduce my workload to consist of doing the job of only four people. Now, after hiring an associate medical director, I am finally able to do the job of one to two people and I can actually try to focus on performing the job that I was hired to do, and that is to be the division chief of the cardiac intensive care unit. Yet you are questioning my ability to perform my job, you are asking me to work more hours, and you are questioning me as to when I can resume taking night call despite the recent deterioration in my health. Additionally, as a result of my hard work, you were finally able to recruit a new chief of cardiology from a 'top program,' which this hospital was unable to do for many years and subsequently, you were able to recruit a 'top trained' pediatric cardiac surgeon with a national reputation, which this hospital had failed to do for several years. Are you following me? Good, but please wait, I am not finished quite yet. Then, the 'top trained' cardiac surgeon who you hired without my input and without the input of any other member of the Heart Center outside that of Dr. Kowatch has decided that I am not capable of doing this job anymore and y'all have reached out to another cardiac intensivist whom you hope can replace me. Just so I can completely understand your perspective, you are supporting and taking the word of a man who has destroyed our culture in a brief period of time. Let me just compare what he has done since his arrival versus what we have achieved since my arrival. Has he improved our outcomes? No, he has not. We have experienced more patient mortalities this year than we have in the last two years combined. I reduced morbidity and took our hospital length of stay and other CICU metrics from the worst in the country to consistently performing among the top 25 percent when compared to other top programs. Has Dr. Porter improved our culture? No, he has not. In fact, he has destroyed it. My team worked exhaustively to eradicate the overwhelming toxicity that dominated the CICU for decades and now with his help, it has returned, and as a result job satisfaction has decreased, we have lost nurses and other staff are threatening to leave. In addition, we are struggling to recruit new staff because the only real 'national reputation' he has is as a world-class asshole." As I finished, I took a deep breath, perhaps the first breath I had taken in five minutes, I thought to myself, "Wow, that sure spiraled fast." Joseph sat silent, appearing pale and in a state of shock. "I am sorry for saying that so bluntly. However, I do not apologize for the content because that was all real. The long-term steroids have destroyed my filter and things just come out," I said after I had a moment to calm myself.

"It's OK. Let's see how things go," Joseph replied as he left my office.

As he left, I thought to myself, "I assume the odds of me getting escorted out by security just tripled."

Two other major challenges I was presented with were that Ruth Hofstra, the nurse manager who had moved to Biloxi with me from Fort Myers, had been promoted to service line administrator and Maddie Morgan, the nurse educator who also moved with me from Fort Myers, completed her Master of Healthcare Education and had moved to Tampa, Florida, to be closer to her family after a rough battle with breast cancer. Both were instrumental in the transformation of the CICU. They had not only improved the quality of nursing care being provided but they essentially closed the revolving door of nursing turnover that was rampant upon our arrival. Perhaps their greatest accomplishment, in my opinion, was their help in eradicating the toxicity that had infested the CICU upon our arrival, which they helped replace with a collegial and nurturing work environment. I was truly happy for them both and they deserved it; however, it left two huge voids in the CICU.

With the departure of John Wozniak, the administration quickly filled the chief nursing officer role with an internal candidate by the name of Laura Callahan. Laura was very nice and intelligent and had worked herself up through the organization, originally working as a bedside nurse and eventually being promoted, shortly after my arrival to CHOB, to director of critical care, which entailed her overseeing all three intensive care units. While I had a significant amount of respect for her, I realized that the true administrative talent that helped the institution thrive was now gone and we were left with Joseph Bergeron and Laura Callahan who were remnants of the old days. Here we were full circle back to being led by individuals whose experience was obtained during the "this is the way we have always done it," "we run thin" days. It was a cruel lesson, but I realized that when the true administrative leaders, Michael Stringer, John Wozniak, and Ben Washington departed, the invisible cloak was removed and the once prodigious CEO who was praised as the savior was exposed for who he truly was, which was nothing more than a shady, used car salesman. It was truly pathetic to see the illusive fallacies that had been used to fool a desperate organization into believing they had been blessed with an elite talent when in reality, they had been tricked by nothing more than an executive con man interested in running a not-for-profit organization as a business with the goal of making a profit at any cost, even if it meant compromising patient care.

With the promotion of Ruth Hofstra, the nursing manager position was vacant. Following the promotion of Laura Callahan, a nurse by the name of Andrea Colquit was hired as her replacement. Andrea was nice but emanated a vibe suggesting she had a tendency toward being a bit scatter-brained. Her experience and background were in the neonatal intensive care unit at a hospital within the same health-care system as Children's Hospital of Biloxi. To start with, I felt like she was a good addition to the team; however, as we began the process of searching for Ruth Hofstra's replacement, my opinion of her changed. When Ruth notified me of her promotion and eminent departure from the CICU, I immediately had two internal candidates in mind who I had heard may have mutual interest in the position. Ruth and I discussed these candidates at length and we both agreed that either one would be an excellent replacement. The first candidate's name was Mary Miller. Mary had been a CICU nurse at CHOB for the last eight years. She was loved and respected by her fellow nurses, and Ruth and I had a lot of respect for her knowledge, nursing skill, her calm demeanor, and the fact that she had significant experience functioning as the charge nurse in the CICU was invaluable. The second candidate's name was Cheryl Highborn. Cheryl was a veteran CICU nurse with more than fifteen years of bedside experience and was previously trained as a respiratory therapist. After working with Cheryl for the last few years, I could confidently say she was the strongest CICU nurse I had ever worked with, a title previously held by Ruth Hofstra. Cheryl had elite bedside skills combined with a natural instinct that allowed her to interpret data in real time and predict decompensation before it occurred thereby allowing us to intervene and prevent a cardiac arrest. Again, a gift and a skill that cannot be taught. In addition to her clinical acumen, she was among the most phenomenal human beings I had the pleasure of meeting in my life. She was beautiful inside and out. While I felt she would also be a great candidate for the position, I sensed she was uncertain about leaving the bedside as she was passionate about patient care.

Following Andrea Colquit's hiring, she asked to set up a meeting with me so that we may discuss the process of searching for candidates to replace Ruth as CICU nurse manager. As I entered her office, she greeted me. "Hi, Dr. Philson, thanks for agreeing to meet with me. I am impressed with all the work you have done to improve the care in the cardiac ICU over the last few years. You should be proud."

"Thank you, Andrea. It has been a lot of work, but I am proud of what we have accomplished so far," I replied.

"Have you had an opportunity to think about the qualifications you are looking for in a candidate, and do you have anyone in mind?"

"The answer is yes to both of your questions. There is one major qualification that is mandatory for this position and that is a minimum of five years of pediatric cardiac intensive care unit experience, preferably with experience as a charge nurse or a clinical lead. I have two internal candidates in mind, Mary Miller and Cheryl Highborn, both are solid candidates, both say they are potentially interested. Mary seems relatively certain she will apply while Cheryl is still contemplating whether she will apply or not. I also think we should post the position on the pediatric cardiac intensive care society website to see if there are any external candidates interested. Again, I want to stress that five years or more of CICU experience is mandatory. Leadership experience is wonderful, but our field is so specialized that even those with twenty years of PICU or NICU experience will struggle to understand the physiology, the staffing and the workflow of the CICU without experience. In fact, that is exactly what happened prior to Ruth and my arrival. The nurse manager who was hired had twenty years of NICU experience, but she struggled mightily in the role and eventually she resigned because it wasn't working," I said. "I felt so strongly about this requirement that when I was considering accepting the job, I negotiated a clause in my contract granting me a significant say in the final decision when determining who to hire for the position of CICU nurse manager. When I stressed that I wished to hire Ruth Hofstra for the position, I received a lot of pushback from the administration because she did not have previous leadership experience outside of being charge nurse. When I expressed that I would not accept the position without Ruth as nurse manager, they ultimately hired her. Ruth not only changed the quality of care and the culture, but she excelled to the point that they promoted her within the organization, which is why we are having this meeting today. I am only sharing this with you now to accentuate the importance of sticking to the criteria we have established, which is a minimum of five years of CICU experience," I stated passionately.

"I understand, Dr. Philson. I agree to follow your request," Andrea replied. Andrea followed up with me the following week to discuss an idea she had. She thought that since there was no "interim nurse manager" that it would be a good idea if Cheryl and Mary each spent a four-month "trial period" as the interim nurse manager, while being mentored by the current NICU nurse manager. I felt like this was a reasonable idea. Mary and Cheryl discussed their schedules, and it was determined that Mary would act as interim manager first. After Mary completed two months, Cheryl decided that she didn't want to leave the bedside and subsequently withdrew her application, which I supported, as I felt confident in Mary's ability to do the job. However, Andrea had other ideas. During Mary's interim trial period, the CICU had exploded in terms of patient volume and the staffing ratios were becoming unsafe; however, nurses were regularly being floated to the PICU as they were equally busy. Mary, being an experienced CICU nurse, understood that the number of patients was only a portion of the equation, the complexity in the CICU should warrant the cardiac unit keeping their own staff rather than having them pulled to the PICU. So, in my opinion, Mary did what a leader should do, she stood up for her staff and expressed her concerns to Andrea regarding the staffing situation in a professional yet assertive manner. Andrea did not like the fact that Mary challenged her decision-making. The next day, Andrea asked me to meet with her. "Dr. Philson, I don't think that Mary is mature enough for this role. We have another candidate. She doesn't have any CICU experience; however, she has been a house supervisor and has three years of experience as a NICU charge nurse. I would like to give her the same opportunity that we gave Mary as interim director. However, in order to give her some time to gain more CICU experience I would like to provide her six months in the interim role. What do you think?" Andrea asked.

I shook my head in utter disbelief. "Andrea, first of all, I am offended that you would even propose this to me after I stressed the importance of having at least five years of CICU experience. I am confused. Not only does this candidate have zero CICU experience but now you are asking me to allow her two months more in the interim role than Mary was given, simply because you don't like to be challenged about your decisions. Am I understanding this correctly?" I asked, clearly agitated.

"Dr. Philson, first of all, I don't need to ask your permission. I could just tell you that it is going to happen. I don't mind being challenged; Mary is just not ready for this position," she said.

"Based on what? And before you start making statements like 'I don't need to ask you permission,' I would ask you to go back four months and remember our discussion. The five years of experience is non-negotiable, and you agreed to it. In all honesty, if you are saying Mary is inexperienced and 'not ready' for this role, isn't that your job to mentor her and help her get ready to assume the position? You are giving me an applicant with no cardiac experience, and less overall experience, and asking me to provide her more time in the interim role so she may learn about cardiac physiology? Why not apply those extra two months toward 'mentoring Mary' to help her overcome whatever deficiency you are seeing in her leadership? What you are proposing is not what we agreed on, it is unfair to Mary, and beyond that it delays us filling this vacancy by six months. And, if you are going to threaten me by saying that you don't need to ask my permission, let me remind you that I have the authority, clearly outlined in my contract, allowing me the final say on the decision, which affects my unit. I don't want to have to utilize that authority; however, I will not be forced to hire an unqualified candidate to manage my unit just because you don't like Mary. I have known Mary for nearly four years now and I trust her and believe in her as a leader. The CICU is desperately missing a nursing leader and I don't want to prolong this process unnecessarily. If you want to give this candidate an opportunity as 'interim manager,' I will agree to four months, the same time as Mary, no more than that. I want to be clear that I will do my best to keep an open and unbiased frame of mind; however, it is extremely unlikely that I will deviate from my original belief that Mary is the right candidate for the job. So, this feels as though it is a waste of time and I want you to understand that you may experience a mutiny in the CICU, because they understand as well as I do, that the leader needs to have CICU experience because as I told you they have already seen a far more experienced NICU leader fail in the CICU," I replied.

"I understand and I agree to the four month trial," she replied. Over the next four months her candidate did a fantastic job and I really liked her but the lack of CICU experience was obvious and not something I was willing to forego, thereby placing the unit and patients at risk. She was a strong leader, but she even acknowledged herself that it would take a minimum of five years to obtain the necessary knowledge and understanding of the anatomy and physiology required to consider staffing and to assist at the bedside.

Ultimately, those involved in the interview process chose Mary and she was hired as the new nurse manager of the CICU. However, this pattern of behavior had clearly trickled down to the remaining administrators at Children's Hospital of Biloxi. Each of them became focused on trying to make decisions that they could say were their own, rather than making decisions that were best for the patients and the program. Yes, I was also a first-time leader, but I dedicated my life over the last four years at significant cost and I had developed a team that had a track record of outstanding results when it came to delivering quality CICU care. Why would they want to change that? Not only did they steal my nurse manager, of which I was supportive, but now they were trying to force me to hire unqualified people to manage the CICU nurses, and it appeared that they wanted to restrict the financial support necessary to continue recruiting staff. I did not feel good about the direction of the program or the hospital for that matter. The gifted leaders were gone, and the replacements were remnants of the past, and all had lost focus and become obsessed with making things about the individual rather than the collective and after all we had been through, here I was fighting again with the cardiac surgeon and the administration to keep things from completely regressing back to where I started. It was so upsetting, and it was wreaking havoc on my physical and mental health.

At this point of the story, we arrive back where we started. In case you don't recall, let me refresh your memory. "What is the fucking ACT?" Dr. Porter yelled at the top of his lungs as he stormed into room 3 of the pediatric cardiac intensive care unit.

"It is 140," said the ECMO technician.

"I told you I wanted it to be 160–180. Why isn't it 160–180?"

"Well, we are getting some conflicting orders regarding the goal ACT due to the massive amount of bleeding from the chest tubes," said the respiratory supervisor.

"What is your name? Who told you to think? I give the orders and you follow them, that's how this works," screamed Dr. Porter.

As I entered the room with Dr. Slovak, we looked at one another in utter disdain, we could see the pure rage on Dr. Porter's face, now cherry red, his surgical mask resting misplaced below his somewhat long, pointed nose, as sweat dripped from the tip as if falling from an aging, leaky farmhouse faucet. "Phil," I said quietly at first, followed by a louder "Phil," attempting to capture his attention. All five employees in the room, whose heads were directed downward toward the floor, offered a slight upward gaze of their eyes as they searched for the source of the voice. Their eyes resembled those of beaten dogs, once caring and innocent, now ambivalent and skeptical that I retained the influence I once had to protect them from the toxicity they once again found themselves exposed to, as a result of the lack of accountability displayed by our weak administrators. "Phil," I said, this time more sternly. "Let's go outside the room and discuss this." Phil finally made eye contact with me and stomped toward the door, exiting the room, all the while shaking his head and muttering to himself like a spoiled toddler who had just been told he cannot have ice cream before finishing his dinner.

I led Phil out of room 3 and around the corner of the cardiac intensive care unit, away from the patient rooms and the front desk, trying to minimize our exposure to the staff. "Eric, I told them I want the ACT 160–180, nobody is following my order!" Phil screamed.

I said, "Phil, the patient is hemorrhaging his entire blood volume every hour and has been doing so for the last five days."

"I want the fucking ACT 160–180," he stated. "Eric, when I say I want something done, I want it done, no questions asked. I said I want an ACT of 160–180, so God dammit, I want it 160–180," said Phil, now compulsively pulling his surgical mask up and down as he intermittently saturated it with the abundant sweat still prevalent on his nose.

Suddenly, I felt my steroid rage surging. I had just returned from Mayo Clinic the night before and had doubled my prednisone dose due to worsening of my autoimmune condition. I knew this feeling and it usually wasn't good. After three years of high-dose steroids, I still had not learned to control this feeling. "Phil, stop with the fucking ACT. The patient is hemorrhaging, we should be stopping the heparin infusion or at least be adjusting our anti-coagulation goals to be much lower and you should be performing a surgical exploration to look for the source of the bleeding. This patient is losing 500 milliliters out of the chest tubes every hour. That is equivalent to his entire blood volume every fucking hour. This is wrong and given the fact that we are in the middle of the COVID-19 pandemic and there is a nationwide blood shortage, this irresponsible use of blood is unethical! The other markers of anticoagulation show that our heparin dose is too much. We developed an anticoagulation protocol two years before your arrival because we had long-standing issues with bleeding due to the fact that people were following ACT alone and without oversight by a physician. Since we developed the proto-col, our bleeding complications have significantly reduced, our staff follow it very closely, and it keeps the anticoagulation standardized among all of the intensive care units. ACT is prehistoric so stop obsessing about it and quite frankly, in this particular scenario, forget about all of the anticoagulation markers, THE PATIENT IS EXSANGUINATING!" As I could feel my face now cherry red, I glimpsed over to see Tim Kowatch, the chief of cardiology peeking around the corner only to see him quickly recede behind the wall. Suddenly, I saw Ms. Lewis, the unit clerk, pushing Dr. Kowatch, against his will, toward Phil and me. Ms. Lewis was a sweet older woman but feisty. She had run to get Dr. Kowatch in an attempt to defuse the situation between Phil and me, but Dr. Kowatch attempted to flee the scene to avoid getting involved in the confrontation. Ms. Lewis had actually chased him down, and was now literally pushing Dr. Kowatch, against his will, forcing him to engage in the situation.

"Uh, guys, what's the problem?" Dr. Kowatch said nervously, his armpits stained with sweat the size of basketballs.

"Tim, I want the ACT 160–180 and they aren't listening," Phil obses-sively repeated.

"Tim, this is absurd, the patient is bleeding to death and he is obsessing about the ACT and insisting that we need more anticoagulation," I said.

"Guys let's take a deep breath; you both have valid points. Let's go to surgical rounds and discuss this later," Tim said as his voice cracked from extreme anxiety.

As we walked toward the conference room Phil looked back at me with pure rage, appearing to be in what I could only describe as a dissociative state, and said, "I want the ACT 160–180, I mean it, 160–180!" That was it, right there, I had seen that look before, three years earlier on the face of the previous cardiac surgeon, Dr. Rostri. That look of a sociopath. Yet Dr. Porter's look differed from that of Dr. Rostri. With Dr. Rostri, if you looked deeper, you could see that somewhere beyond the rage and obsession with control was a good man, an individual who had lost his way somewhere during their career. Being neglected the necessary resources to succeed had blinded him from seeing what was right for the patient, and instead he became capable of only focusing on "being right" and "remaining in control," but I knew the real Dr. Rostri was in there somewhere. Dr. Porter's rage, on the other hand, was different. I looked into his eyes and saw a rage so deep that it screamed pathology, perhaps a personality disorder. I was unsure of the etiology or the underlying diagnosis, but it was clearly not as simple as a man who had lost his way. Instead, his behavior screamed, give me "Haldol" or "lithium," or any other antipsychotic or mood stabilizing medication for that matter. He had been given every resource he needed to succeed so I refused to grant him any such excuse for his behavior. Strangely, while less obvious to others, I realized Mr. Boykins was actually displaying similar behaviors. He had become so focused on being the one responsible for making decisions, rather than making sure we were making the right decision as a team and as an institution. For Dr. Porter, it was more important to be right and to be in control than it was to have collaboration and intellectual discussion to determine the best possible avenue for a good patient outcome as a team. It was there in that moment after working together for only a period of months that I knew it was the beginning of the end for me and for the program. Does this ring a bell? Yeah, it's hard to forget, believe me. Well, unfortunately this poor baby did not survive. This unfortunate infant death set in motion the downward spiral and metaphoric death of the culture and cardiac program at Children's Hospital of Biloxi. During the tragic and traumatic two-week demise of this beautiful little baby, my colleagues and several of my fellow CICU staff members endured repeated verbal and emotional abuse at the hands of Dr. Porter. In the weeks that followed, two of my cardiac intensivists and four of my most experienced advanced practice providers resigned.

I stormed into Dr. Kowatch's office and unloaded on him. "Tim, this guy is a cancer, and he has metastasized and infiltrated the entire Heart Center. I am hemorrhaging staff members in the CICU as a result of his toxicity and atrocious decision-making. You need to fix this quickly, and you need to tell administration to get their heads out of their asses! I just returned from Mayo Clinic, and I had to go back up on my steroids again. This is not something I am going to tolerate for much longer. I told you when you hired him that I wouldn't be around for another Dr. Rostri, well I got news for you, he is far worse! I am very close to resigning, and I promise you that this is no joke."

Dr. Kowatch stuttered and nervously apologized. "Eric, I have been talking with Joseph Bergeron about possible interventions," Dr. Kowatch replied.

"Tim, I am leaving to San Diego Monday with my family, for vacation. I need to clear my mind and give careful consideration as to whether this program is right for me anymore. I am going to need to recruit new staff and retrain a whole new group of APPs that took me more than four years to do. As you have seen, it is already difficult enough to recruit to Biloxi but with Phil Porter's reputation of behavioral issues, it is going to be a real challenge to fill these positions. My team is going to be short-staffed, and I am dealing with a relapse of my cardiac sarcoidosis and am back on high doses of steroids. This cycle is not sustainable and at this pace may not be survivable for me. This job is going to kill me. You and administration need to get him under control and hold him accountable. When I return, I want to know what your plan is for holding him accountable and after some time to clear my head, I will let you know whether I am going to stick this out or not," I explained as I shook my head in disbelief. I couldn't fathom how we managed to find ourselves right back in the same environment as the one that was present when I arrived at Children's Hospital of Biloxi. I walked down to my office to finish out my last day before leaving on vacation. I didn't feel like being around anyone at the moment. My world and my hard work felt as though it was crumbling before my eyes. I had dedicated so much, and it cost me my health, possibly my marriage, and I lost precious years of my daughter's life and it hurt deeply to watch it be destroyed by others who were more interested in personal gain or recognition than building a team capable of delivering the highest level of care. As I contemplated my future, I heard a knock on the door. I turned around as my office door opened before I even said a word. It was Joseph Bergeron, the COO. I don't remember anything, it all happened so quickly as I turned and yelled, "No, uh uh. Get out! I don't want to talk to you or any other administrator right now. Get out!" I said loudly. The roid rage had kicked in and it all happened so fast. I immediately felt remorseful. I went to the hallway and said, "Joseph, I apologize. Please come back and have a seat." He sat in one of the chairs in my office. "Look, I am not in a good place mentally right now. I see my hard work and sacrifice crumbling before my eyes. I see a man who has destroyed our culture and I see no one holding him accountable," I explained as tears began to roll down my cheek.

"Eric, I can see you're bothered, but I honestly don't think Dr. Porter realizes that he is behaving like this. I have spoken with him, and he appears oblivious that others are viewing his behavior negatively," he said.

"Joseph, stop please. He is a grown man, and he is manipulating you, don't you see that? That is the problem, quit enabling him. What I saw during our disagreement was not a man who is passionate about his work, I saw a narcissistic sociopath that is interested in one thing and that is being right at all costs, and it has nothing to do with patient care. I am sorry for yelling at you, but I need to end this conversation now because I am mentally in a bad place, and I am afraid what I might say to you when I hear you say such things. I need to leave for vacation with my family and clear my mind. I will give you and Dr. Kowatch some time because I want to see if you can come up with a plan to control him and I need to decide if this program is still right for me. Let's talk when I get back in a week. Thanks for coming to talk with me and again, I am sorry I snapped at you," I said.

Ana, the kids and I landed in San Diego. We were all excited. I had been to San Diego many times before, but Ana and the kids had never been. It was my favorite city in the United States. My best friend and his family had lived there for twenty years before moving to Hawaii so I had visited him a number of times over the years, and I always promised them I would take them to visit. We rented a beautiful house in La Jolla, just two blocks from the Pacific Ocean. After a few days of touring downtown San Diego, the USS Midway Navy Museum, spending time at the zoo and the beach, I finally felt relaxed and as though I could think more clearly regarding the best option for me moving forward from both a career and a personal standpoint. "So, what do you think I should do?" I asked Ana as we strolled down the sidewalk along Windansea Beach in La Jolla.

"As I have always told you, I want you to do what is best for you personally and professionally. I do worry about the effect that this job has had on your mental and physical health. You know I love you no matter what, but this job has changed you, it has affected your health and I don't think that they have ever treated you kindly, even after everything you have done for them. You know I do not like Biloxi, but I will support your career and stick it out if you feel that it is right for you professionally," she replied with a sincere and loving look on her face.

"I need a little more time to think but I am beginning to consider that it may be best if I move on both professionally and for our family. I agree with you, it has taken a toll on all of us, and I am worried about the lasting effects it may have on me and us. It is clear that they don't respect or appreciate what I have done for this institution, and it has become obvious that they view me as expendable and replaceable," I replied. It felt good to have this conversation with Ana. It was the first time since we arrived in Biloxi that she had been that open with me regarding her thoughts. She was right, the administration at Children's Hospital of Biloxi did not respect me and it could be argued that they had taken advantage of my work ethic and ability to recruit for some time now. I felt it was best to keep an open mind and to continue to analyze the situation over the next few days. Since my arrival in Biloxi, I must have considered leaving at least a dozen times. Each time, my decision to stay was ultimately based on the effect it would have on the program and I felt guilty when I considered leaving others behind, particularly those who had moved to Biloxi for me and the experienced nurses and ancillary staff who not only decided to stick it out with me, but who also bought into the clinical changes, the nurturing environment and the programmatic philosophy that we had developed. Not once did I make a decision based on my family or me, yet here was an institution that couldn't care less about me, and other staff members for that matter, and who viewed us all as easily replaceable.

Prior to leaving for my vacation in San Diego, Joseph Bergeron, the COO, had questioned my ability to recruit physicians and advanced practice providers. "Eric, why are you having such difficulty recruiting cardiac intensivists? We administrators have been able to recruit more than eighty new providers over the last year," Joseph said boastingly.

"That is great, Joseph, congratulations! However, recruiting cardiac intensivists is an entirely different ballgame. This institution couldn't recruit anyone within the Heart Center for many years prior to my arrival. The previous administrations had zero success recruiting cardiac intensivists, a chief of pediatric cardiology, and pediatric cardiac surgeons. Now after the work we have done in the CICU, we have filled all of those positions, so we must be doing something right," I said, admittedly, with a slight undertone of passive-aggressiveness.

"Well, it appears that you are struggling to recruit at this time. Perhaps you need us to step in and take over," he replied arrogantly.

"Well, we had successfully filled all posted positions; however, since the recent events with Dr. Porter, and the departure of two cardiac intensivists and four APPs, we will now have to recruit for all of those openings. You suggested that you may need to step in and assist me in recruiting, do you know many cardiac intensivists around the country?" I asked.

"Not off the top of my head but we have our ways of recruiting," he replied.

"Oh, OK. Well, thanks for the offer but I think I am OK for now from a recruiting perspective. I am a firm believer that while 50 percent of finding the appropriate candidate is identifying an individual who is well trained, the other 50 percent involves finding someone with the right personality fit, who is collegial, who has a history of clinical competence, and a good work ethic. Just looking at someone's CV is not enough. That is why I am very particular about doing my own recruitment; however, if I am unsuccessful, I may take you up on your offer," I said.

By day five of vacation, I was feeling wonderful and fully relaxed. I was sleeping well for the first time in a while and was really enjoying spending time with my family. I had started to lean toward making the decision to leave Biloxi and move back to Fort Myers. I had been speaking with my colleagues from my previous job and they were elated with the prospect of my return. On the morning of my sixth day of vacation I made the mistake of opening my work email to find three messages that destroyed the tranquil peace of mind I had finally been able to establish while in San Diego. The first email I opened had been sent to the entire Heart Center staff, it contained a web link leading to a press release on behalf of Children's Hospital of Biloxi. The article detailed how CHOB was now on the cutting edge of technology by investing in a new type of risk analytic software that may help identify patients at risk of suffering a cardiac arrest in the CICU. The article went on to detail how CHOB was one of only a handful of programs around the country fortunate enough to have such breakthrough technology and how the administrative leaders had envisioned purchasing and utilizing this technology to ensure we were at the forefront in terms of innovation. The article went on to quote Dr. Kowatch who said, "I chose to pursue this technology with the goal of improving the quality of care that we provide to children undergoing cardiac surgery at Children's Hospital of Biloxi. I had performed exhaustive background research on this revolutionary software for some time now and felt that it was essential to implement this technology in our CICU."

"Wait, what?" I said to myself as I reflexively regurgitated my coffee and breakfast into the back of my mouth. Let me explain, for the last four years, I had campaigned and pushed for the hospital to purchase this software, spending countless hours researching, speaking with representatives from the company, obtaining quotes, taking with biomedical engineering and information technology, and more, desperately trying to convince hospital administration of its clinical value and that it was something that would set us apart from our local competitors. Yet, I was repeatedly turned down, until finally this year, it was grudgingly approved by the accounting department and administration. Interestingly, when Dr. Kowatch first started at CHOB, he spent a lot of time investigating the finances and the budget of the Heart Center, and one day he asked me what the purpose of this software was, because he had never heard of it and that he had been asked by administration if it was truly needed. I proceeded to explain the theory and evidence behind its growing use around the country and much to his surprise, I also detailed the fact that his previous organization, Mayo Children's, had been using this software for several years. He remained confused despite my simplistic explanation, and he ultimately questioned its utility and need. I again stressed its value and importance, particularly due to the fact that we had so many young staff members in the CICU, and I explained that it could help provide another layer of protection when it came to patient safety. So naturally, when I read the article, which had been emailed to the entire Heart Center team, you can understand why I was a bit annoyed. Truly, it was not in my character to concern myself with credit or attention, in fact I felt as though I lived my life quite the opposite, and wasn't all that comfortable with attention, tending to divert credit toward others. I had to admit though, having Dr. Kowatch provide a quote about technology that he had no clue about, followed by him and administration assuming credit for researching and implementing this software, really pissed me off. I became more enraged as I reviewed in my mind the persistent questioning I had endured regarding its clinical value and the resistance to purchasing such software by Dr. Kowatch and hospital administration, who now strangely enough appeared to be geniuses for their vision and expertise related to this revolutionary software. It was very irritating. This was the first of three emails that disrupted my mental peace on vacation. I read the email aloud to Ana as she shook her head in disbelief. "Am I overanalyzing this? Am I being petty that I am letting this bother me?" I asked her.

"Not at all, sweetie. It is absolutely insane that they would do such a thing. You have worked so hard to change that institution and have been pushing to purchase that software for four years. It is shameful that administration would ask Dr. Kowatch for a quote and even more insane that he wouldn't direct them back to you. It is even more distasteful that he would take credit, when he has no idea what it even is. This is what I have been trying to explain to you. This institution has used you to achieve things they have never been able to achieve. Not only have they taken advantage of you, but now they are trying to take credit for your work. Disgusting!" Ana replied, continuing to shake her head in disbelief. As I thought about her comments, I realized that she was right. Over the next few months, Ana's words would resonate with me as they proved to be premonitions as I witnessed Dr. Porter, Dr. Kowatch and Mr. Boykins continue to take credit for my hard work and that of Dr. Penton and so many others who had fought to make such substantial change, long before the three of them even worked at CHOB.

The second email that I subsequently read on that memorable morning in La Jolla, California, was a message forwarded to me individually from Joseph Bergeron, the COO, with the subject "New Recruit." His email read, "Hi Eric, I hope you are enjoying your vacation. Following our conversation, I asked Dr. Blount to use his recruiting tactics to find some new cardiac intensivists for you. He has had a lot of success recruiting physicians by performing google searches of the different medical specialties, so he performed a search for cardiac intensive care units at each of the 'top training' programs around the country and sent an email to each of the intensivists listed on their website to see if any of them would be interested in applying for one of our vacancies. Good news, we had one response. Please see below." The original email that he forwarded me was written by Gerry Blount, the CMO. It was a general email that he sent to countless cardiac intensivists he found on the Internet. The email read,

"Dear Dr. Shmo, my name is Dr. Gerry Blount. I am the chief medical officer of Children's Hospital of Biloxi. I am a nationally renowned pediatric radiologist and was the chief of radiology for more than twenty years at D.C. Children's Hospital. I am triple boarded in radiology, nephrology, and infectious disease. I have authored and published more than one hundred peer-reviewed articles over my illustrious career. Mr. Boykins, the CEO, and I came to Biloxi to transform the medical care here into that of a top children's hospital. Mr. Boykins was previously the COO at D.C. Children's and is nationally recognized. Since our arrival, Mr. Boykins and I have been able to recruit Dr. Tim Kowatch as the chief of cardiology. Dr. Kowatch was the medical director of cardiology at Mayo Children's for more than twenty years. Mr. Boykins and I were also able to recruit world-renowned pediatric cardiac surgeon Dr. Phil Porter as the new chief of pediatric cardiac surgery. The two of us have also recruited more than eighty new providers to join Children's Hospital of Biloxi over the last year. Our work has resulted in substantial improvement in the clinical care provided here at Children's Hospital of Biloxi. Mr. Boykins and I are now in the process of recruiting cardiac intensivists to staff our CICU. The current division chief and medical director of the CICU is Eric Philson. He is a nice guy. Should you decide that you are interested in this position, or if you have questions, please feel free to contact me. Sincerely, Gerald Blount, CMO, Children's Hospital of Biloxi."

OK. Please allow me a moment to take a few deep breaths so I don't LOSE MY FRICKIN' MIND! OK, I feel better, now please allow me to recap. So, before leaving for San Diego, Joseph Bergeron, the COO, asked me why I was unable to recruit cardiac intensivists, when in reality, not only was I able to recruit when the hospital had failed to do so for many years, I was able to do so in the middle of chaos and toxicity. He told me the administration could do better and that they would help me recruit. I thanked him for the offer but respectfully declined for the time being because my approach was different and involved finding clinically sound individuals who were also good people who had personalities that fit well with the team, rather than simply finding "top trained" individuals based on their CV. After I left for vacation, Joseph proceeded to ignore my request and then implored the assistance of the CMO who had been described as a "master recruiter." The CMO then proceeded to use his "master recruiting tactics," which now had been identified as google search engine, which he used to find the names of random cardiac intensivists around the country whom he then proceeded to spam with a generic email he had authored, highlighting his personal achievements and publications, Mr. Boykins's credentials and achievements, followed by the two of them taking credit for my hard work and for recruiting Dr. Kowatch and Dr. Porter. Oh, and how can I forget, the grand finale detailing the thoughtful and elaborate description of me as the CICU leader, consisting in its entirety of the five words "He is a nice guy." Is that really all they could come up with after four years of dedication, hard work, and clinical progress? I couldn't believe that the second email was even more disturbing than the first. Not only had they completely disregarded my request to handle the recruiting of my own staff, but they had also once again taken credit for my work, and now were randomly spam emailing colleagues of mine around the country—many of whom I knew and a few who actually reached out to me to ask me who the hell Gerald Blount was and why he was contacting them. It not only made me look bad as the division chief, but I also couldn't believe that the only positive thing he could muster on my behalf was that I was "a nice guy."

I shook my head as I read the email aloud to Ana. "What the hell is wrong with them? Again, taking credit for your work and how offensive that they are spamming your colleagues without your permission. And 'nice guy'? Who do they think they are?" Ana was upset, she never swore. I was annoyed but seeing her response made me realize once again that I should probably be more upset than I was. "Honestly, sweetie, you need to leave these fools. I want to see what they can truly do on their own, if you leave. Then they will actually have to perform and recruit rather than simply being able to take credit for all you have done. Honestly, the nerve of them," Ana said as she stood up from the table, too upset to sit. I was in agreement; it was going to be hard to continue on with leaders I didn't trust or believe in. To top it off, only one individual responded to their email. I spoke with this individual on the phone, and he seemed like a nice enough guy. My assistant spent days setting up his visit and then two days before his scheduled interview, he canceled via email and proceeded to ghost us by not responding to phone, text or email. Top trained yet validating my point that such behavior simply cannot be found on a CV or by using google search engine!

The third email while less offensive, was equally annoying and clueless. It was authored by Dr. Kowatch and addressed to the entire Heart Center staff. If you recall, I had challenged Dr. Kowatch and Joseph Bergeron prior to departing for vacation to find a way to get a handle on Dr. Porter's behavioral issues and find a way to restore the culture back to where it was prior to Dr. Porter and Dr. Kowatch's arrival. The third email outlined a "retreat" that Dr. Kowatch and Joseph Bergeron had arranged as a team-building exercise, and it included an "escape room." It was to be held on the Friday following my return, which happened to be the weekend of Father's Day. I was not asked if I was available and it was said to be an event for the entire team; however, I would come to find that only a select number of individuals would be invited, which obviously made no sense to me. The part of this email that annoyed me was that our attendance was implied, yet my family had already arranged special plans for that weekend and quite frankly I was disappointed that our planned resolution for dealing with Dr. Porter's inappropriate behavior was for the rest of the team to participate in "trust falls" and an "escape room." I was skeptical that this was nothing more than another smokescreen that would have little to no positive effect on the severe behavior issues displayed by Dr. Porter.

My peace of mind was lost for the remaining two days of my vacation. Yes, I enjoyed the time with my family, but I couldn't stop thinking about these emails and the lack of trust I had for the entire leadership team both within the Heart Center and at a hospital administrative level. I spent countless amounts of time thinking about the right move for me and my family. When I arrived back in Biloxi, I had convinced myself that it was time to move on. I called my old colleagues, and they were ecstatic that I wished to return. They quickly met my schedule and financial requests and had a contract emailed to me two days later. I spoke with Ana and told her that I was ready to move and that I had received an excellent offer to rejoin my old team in Fort Myers. She was elated. We shared the news with my daughters, Heather and Erica, who were so excited that they began to cry. Erica, my youngest daughter who was now eleven years of age, said to me with tears rolling down her face, "Thank you so much, Daddy. I never really liked it here in Biloxi. People in my class have been so mean to me since we arrived here, but I didn't want to tell you because I knew how important this job was to you."

I gave her a big hug as I began to cry, and said, "I am so sorry, Erica, I had no idea you didn't like it here. I am sorry I put you through that." As I cried, I couldn't help but think about all that had happened since we moved here. I had truly lost my way. How did I not know my own children were this unhappy here and how did I not realize that my baby girl was being bullied and that she was hurting in isolation, all because she didn't want to hurt my feelings? I was upset with myself for putting the institution ahead of my family and for allowing them to treat me in such a way.

The following day, I met with Lorraine McMaster, my friend whom I had hired as my associate director. I had been having ongoing discussions with her related to my feelings of uncertainty for more than a month and as a result, she had shared with me that she was starting to look around at other positions. Lorraine had been very honest with me from the very start, she came to Biloxi to help me, and we had always had an understanding that if one of us were to leave, then the other would be right behind. Lorraine told me she had interviewed for another position in Texas and that the job was hers if she wanted it, all I needed to do was say the word. On the eve before I was to meet with administration to notify them of my resignation, Lorraine called me. "Eric, let's talk this through. I know how much work you have put into this, and I want to be sure you have thought through all of your options," she said thoughtfully.

We talked for a while about all possibilities, even those that seemed ridiculous. The truth was, I was a bit concerned about the health insurance coverage I would receive if I were to accept my old position back in Fort Myers. I spent a lot of time researching whether or not I would be able to continue receiving medical care at Mayo Clinic, and eventually I determined that I would not, and the truth was that I was beginning to worry that my decision could have major repercussions on my health. I was yet to find an immunosuppressive regimen that kept me symptom-free with side effects that were tolerable. I did not have faith in the medical care in Fort Myers for something as rare as cardiac sarcoidosis and I worried that if I began to have issues, I would be stuck within the Fort Myers Hospital system and it would be very expensive for me to go back to Mayo Clinic, because it would be considered out of network by my health insurance. Equally, I couldn't retract my decision and destroy Ana and the girls' newfound happiness after just agreeing that we would move back to Florida. I was once again torn and spent the entire day obsessing about the decision at hand. Ultimately, I decided that I needed to be honest and transparent with my family. Ana and the girls had endured four-plus years of unhappiness that I had been ambivalent toward, just so I could complete the job I had undertaken. They had sacrificed so much and behaved in a selfless manner, all for my benefit, while I had told myself I was doing the same, yet my "sacrifice" was actually to their detriment. These complex thoughts were beginning to make me question the entire purpose I had used as fuel to persevere through the worst of times and push onward toward my goal. Had I lost my way just as Dr. Rostri had? I was confused. The truth was that I had completed the job, I had staffed and trained the CICU team and we were now providing care that was above the standard of care and I was proud of that. Additionally, the hospital was able to recruit a new chief of cardiology and new chief of pediatric cardiac surgery. It really didn't matter at this point whether I felt as though they were the appropriate leaders to take the program to the next level of pediatric cardiac care, I wanted to leave with my family and return to Fort Myers. While I still internalized concerns that the CICU could implode following my departure, my indecision this time had very little to do with the program at CHOB. Instead, I was concerned that accepting the job in Fort Myers would be the right professional fit for me and even more so, I was concerned about my ability to continue to receive the best medical care that I could, at least while I was trying to find a stable medical regimen to control my disease. I truly loved and respected the entire Heart Center team at Fort Myers Children's, yet I couldn't help but wonder if I would feel unchallenged professionally once again, or perhaps having less clinical responsibility would be good at this point. Since I had left the program more than four years ago, a lot had changed. Wesley Derosier, the chief of pediatric cardiac surgery who had built the program, had developed lung cancer, and though he was thankfully in remission, he now operated infrequently. The program had hired another cardiac surgeon two years prior, who was reportedly easy to work with; however, operating on newborns was not his expertise. Most recently they had hired a junior cardiac surgeon who had just completed training, and while he came with a good reputation, it would be years before he would be operating on complex newborns with regularity, which was a substantial portion of the program's surgical volume. Additionally, the chief of cardiology, Daniel Norton, who had also been instrumental in building the congenital heart program in Fort Myers, had been newly appointed chief medical officer for the entire Fort Myers health system and as a result, he announced his resignation as the chief of cardiology and had also notified the team that his clinical time would be reduced by 50 percent. As these changes were occurring, the CICU medical director, who had remained a good friend of mine, informed me that two of my previous colleagues were leaving and that the two remaining advanced practice providers had also submitted their resignation and the chief of cardiac anesthesia had announced his retirement, which would occur at the end of the year. Beyond my concerns regarding the health insurance that I would be provided, these staffing changes left me concerned. Lastly, I became concerned about the financial commitment to the cardiac program by the institution. During my contract negotiation with the COO of Fort Myers Children's, I sensed some hesitancy by the organization to invest in any of the pediatric programs while the COVID-19 pandemic was ongoing, and they were yet to approve refilling the vacancies that had been left by my two colleagues who had departed. This meant that I would be joining the program as the third cardiac intensivists and there was no plan to compensate for extra night shifts worked, nor was I certain that my body could tolerate working extra shifts. All of these factors weighed heavily on my mind, and seemed like a big risk to take, and had the potential to leave me in a tough situation that may be no better than the one I was in right now. I sat down with Ana and the girls. "Look, I just want to be open and honest with you, especially since you all had the courage to be honest with me regarding your unhappiness here. I have been struggling to make the right decision for us all. There have been substantial changes at my previous job in Fort Myers. While in theory the transition back to there would be simple, for several reasons, I feel my decision would be short-sighted, and it could put my health in jeopardy. However, I understand how much you have sacrificed for me, and I want you to be happy more than anything. Tomorrow Lorraine and I are scheduled to meet to discuss if there are any options for her and me to make it work here, at least in the short term," I explained.

"We don't want to leave without you," Ana replied with tears in her eyes.

"I know, and believe me, I don't want you to go either, but you have sacrificed enough for me, and this would be temporary until I sort out what my next step is," I said.

The following day, I met with Lorraine McMaster in my office. I explained my concerns to her regarding the personnel and insurance changes related to my previous program. "What if we call a meeting today and share all of our concerns with Dr. Porter, Dr. Kowatch, and the administration, and see what they propose as a solution? The way I see it is that there are two scenarios, the first is that they have no plan for controlling Dr. Porter's behavior and there is no financial support for the continued growth of the CICU, which will lead to our imminent departure and the likely exodus of many of the CICU staff, which will lead to the destruction of the CICU and all of the work we have done. The second scenario is that we both stay, the administration agrees to hold Dr. Porter accountable for his behavior and has some reasonable plan for doing so, and they agree to provide financing for the recruitment of our seventh and eighth cardiac intensivists, and two additional APPs. Also, I would like to assume the medical director position to help offload some of your work, while you remain division chief. Lastly, you and I will agree to provide senior backup, alternating every other week, allowing you to travel to Florida to see your family and we can split the administrative responsibilities and you can continue to join the surgical conference as well as any other required meeting via Zoom or Microsoft Teams," Lorraine suggested.

"Lorraine, that is a fantastic idea, and it just might work. Let's call a meeting for later today and if administration, Dr. Porter, and Dr. Kowatch are in agreement with your plan, I can share the news with Ana and the kids tonight. I don't know how long this option will be sustainable, but for now I think it's our best option," I replied excitedly.

Lorraine and I were able to arrange the meeting for later that afternoon, in the meantime, pressure was mounting for my colleagues and me to attend the "Heart Center retreat." I hadn't responded to the RSVP and neither had any of my colleagues. Dr. Kowatch called me prior to our meeting later that day, and said, "Hi, Eric, I really need your presence at the retreat. Your team has not RSVP'd and since the problems appear to be between Dr. Porter and the CICU physicians, the retreat won't have much meaning if your team doesn't attend."

"Tim, I appreciate what you're saying; however, if my presence and the presence of my team were truly that vital to the success of the retreat, perhaps you should have spoken with us to ensure our availability in advance. Not only did you choose to schedule it on Father's Day weekend without asking our availability, but you sent the email as though it was mandatory and would involve the whole team. Instead, you have selectively invited individuals who are unlikely to be vocal against Dr. Porter's behavior and it has been noticed by the entire staff, resulting in the appearance that the retreat is nothing more than a theatrical performance designed to make the staff believe that something is actually being done by hospital leaders to hold Dr. Porter accountable. I am sorry, but I have had plans for Father's Day for quite some time. Let's meet later today and if we can come to an agreement. I will send an email explaining that due to personal reasons, I cannot attend the retreat; however, I will offer my support as to its importance and state that I hope to participate in the next one," I explained.

"OK, Eric. But I really wish you would come," Dr. Kowatch replied nervously.

"Again, I understand but a little forethought and communication with those whose attendance you feel are vital could have avoided this problem. I will talk to you at the meeting later today at 4 p.m.," I said as I hung up the phone.

The day passed quickly and 4 p.m. arrived as we all entered the CICU conference room. Joseph Bergeron, the COO, had set up the meeting and I had suggested that we start the meeting by simply getting everything out on the table by sharing our concerns aloud, honestly, and without concerns for repercussion. I truly felt the only way this could succeed was if each of us were open, honest, and transparent regarding our concerns. Each person went around the room and shared something regarding the program that they felt needed to be changed or something that they felt was obstructive to progress within the Heart Center. Dr. Porter and Joseph Bergeron shared that they questioned my ability to do my job as a result of my unstable health. I responded by explaining that I had done the job of six staff members for years and now that I was working fewer clinical hours, I continued to work more hours than the typical division chief. I proceeded to share my concern that due to the excessive hours I worked in the past, without complaining, the institution now took my team and me for granted and expected us to do more with far less staff than the other intensive care units were being provided. I also spoke of my concern regarding the culture that had developed and that I was worried that the turnover in staff we were experiencing was just the beginning, and if we did not fix the culture, this would be a repeating cycle that would continue to occur every couple of years. I followed these words by explaining that I was very close to signing a contract to rejoin my old program in Fort Myers; however, Dr. McMaster had come up with a plan to try to make this work. Her plan included providing senior backup and would involve me traveling every other week to Fort Myers. The group agreed with our proposition. Joseph Bergeron and Dr. Kowatch assured us that the retreat was going to improve the culture as well as Dr. Porter's behavior. While Lorraine and I remained skeptical, we agreed to reevaluate progress in six months to determine if we would continue with the current plan, or if we would begin recruiting for my replacement. "Dr. Kowatch, I want to bring to your attention the perceived favoritism you display toward Tricia Cranton and Sherry Monroe. It is obvious among several of the cardiologists that they are treated differently than the others and that they feel untouchable, resulting in toxic behavior toward my staff, which has become problematic. I wish others would not come to me with their problems but for some reason they do, and more than a few have expressed their unhappiness with their behavior," I explained.

Dr. Kowatch's face turned beet red in anger as he spun his chair away from my direction and flipped his right leg over his left, crossing them with incredible flexibility, as if a circus contortionist. "Well, I don't know why they would come to you and not me, I am their boss. Let me explain a few things to everyone. Yes, I have favorites, it's true! Tricia, major fave! Kristin Tisloski (cardiac electrophysiology), totes fave! Sherry Monroe, not even close to being a fave! Ugh, as if!" Dr. Kowatch femininely explained while flapping his hands, resembling something between a high school girl and one of the Wayans Brothers from *In Living Color* performing the "Men on Films" skit where their characters routinely said, "Hated it!" as they reviewed movies they didn't like. The room was dead silent as everyone sat in awe at this eye-opening moment. Some of the administrators had heard of Dr. Kowatch's bizarre behavior but this was the first time they witnessed their "top trained" leader behave in such a manner. The meeting ended and I shared the news with Ana. So, I began to look for a furnished apartment to rent as we began to reach out to our realtor in preparation for listing our home for sale.

The first few weeks following our meeting and the Heart Center retreat gave the appearance that an effort was being made to strengthen the "culture" and to hold Dr. Porter and others accountable for their behavior. The term "culture" became used obsessively and often inappropriately, mostly by Dr. Kowatch and the hospital administration, eventually stripping the word of its meaning. We repeatedly heard how important "culture" was to our leaders; however, the take-home message from the retreat was that we were implementing something called an "above the line culture." This was essentially the idea that the staff needed to keep all comments positive and that it was our responsibility to remind anyone saying something negative that they were not conforming to the "above the line culture." Ultimately what this translated into was that it was now the staff's responsibility to hold Dr. Porter accountable by telling him that he was not acting in an "above the line" manner, essentially removing any such responsibility from Dr. Kowatch or hospital administration. This was absurd, reprimanding an individual with more than two decades of experience verbally, emotionally, and physically abusing staff, had now been placed on the bedside nurse, who may have a year or two of clinical experience, and the proposed plan for intervention was for them to say, "Excuse me, Dr. Porter, you're not practicing 'above the line' behavior." What a joke? It was a complete deflection of responsibility displayed by a bunch of cowards. One of the other staff cardiologists would later come to challenge the "above the line" culture philosophy, which as he masterfully explained, had been created by corporations in order to keep employees focused on speaking positive statements at all times, to maintain productivity and prevent disruption of revenue streams. He was right, this idea led to the perception that if you spoke of something negative, including reporting negative behaviors by others, then it was you who was the problem, and therefore you were behaving in a "below the line" manner. However, the reality is that if we never bring attention to negative events or people then it is impossible to change or improve upon them. Also, we are teaching the staff that they need to remain silent unless their comments are positive otherwise, they are the problem, a belief that is false. If you can't report a problem, there is zero chance of fixing it. It was a disgusting revelation, confirming my suspicions that the retreat and its after-effects were nothing more than a smokescreen, yet the malignancy and deception hidden within this "above the line" philosophy was at a level that was simply astonishing, yet it definitely fit the modus operandi of our shady leaders.

Following a brief honeymoon period without issue, Dr. Porter's behavioral issues reappeared with a vengeance. I began to identify some reproducible patterns of behavior exhibited by Dr. Porter. It became obvious that when his patients were doing well, he was easy to work with; however, conversely, if they were doing poorly, he displayed anger and would blame the CICU staff for the patient's worsening condition, a process that was mentally exhausting for all of us to endure. One such example involved an adolescent female who had been admitted with heart failure and endocarditis. She had previously undergone a valve replacement many years back and had been lost to follow up. She presented with fever as well as significant body and lung edema. She was placed on antibiotics and her blood cultures persistently grew Staphylococcus aureus, a common bacterial cause of endocarditis. Her echocardiogram showed a large vegetation on the mitral valve. She had renal insufficiency due to injury caused by small infectious clots that had dislodged from the vegetations on her heart valves and traveled to the kidneys. Fortunately, her brain MRI was normal and after a week we were able to clear the blood of bacteria as we had become concerned that we were going to be unable to do so. Her cardiac function, kidney function, and swelling all improved with medical therapy and she was subsequently taken to the operating room by Dr. Porter for a mitral valve replacement.

She returned to the CICU in critical condition and had persistent bleeding from her right chest tube that seemed out of proportion for the surgery she had just undergone; however, it was felt to be due to a coagulopathy resulting from liver dysfunction and the typical postsurgical bleeding seen with a complex surgery, which included a long cardiopulmonary bypass time. After thirty-six hours the bleeding slowed, and her hemodynamics improved. She tolerated extubation, her medication infusions were discontinued, and her chest tubes were scheduled to be removed the following day. That evening she was eating dinner and became nauseous as most patients do following cardiac surgery, and she began to retch. Suddenly her right chest tube began to fill with a large amount of blood. In a thirty-minute period her chest tube chamber had filled with 500 milliliters of blood, and it continued to do so at a rate of about 250 milliliters per hour, lasting for about three hours, during which time she was transfused blood. While the bleeding slowed, small amounts of fresh blood continued to drain at a rate of 10 milliliters per hour, lasting for approximately a week. Draining 10 milliliters per hour from a chest tube in a patient her size is not unusual; however, for the drainage to persist and to still consist of fresh blood more than a week after surgery was atypical. The patient was otherwise doing well and after much discussion among the team it was decided to take a conservative approach and continue to monitor the chest tube output. After ten days, the bloody output had ceased, and the patient was ambulating regularly and had just returned to her bed following a stroll around the CICU. Upon returning to bed, she coughed and suddenly the chest tube began draining large amounts of blood once again. This time the bleeding lasted for approximately twenty-four hours, and the entire team felt strongly that the patient needed to be surgically explored to search for the etiology of her persistent bleeding, that is except Dr. Porter, who insisted that this was nothing more than a tiny collateral vessel that would bleed each time the patient increased her intrathoracic pressure by coughing or vomiting. While we all acknowledged that this theory was plausible, it was still felt that the atypical presentation of three significant bleeding events, all of which were hemodynamically significant requiring transfusion of blood products, combined with the fact that the patient was far removed from surgery, warranted surgical exploration. However, Dr. Porter refused and the following day he left on a one-week vacation. Two days after Dr. Porter's departure, the patient bled once again following a coughing episode, so Dr. Penton scheduled to take the patient to the operating room the following day for surgical exploration. However, this time the bleeding consisted of a brief, one-time dump of 250 milliliters of blood, followed by its immediate cessation. Due to the brief nature of this event, it was felt that this could have been old blood that had accumulated in the chest that subsequently drained as the patient ambulated or changed position, therefore the scheduled surgical exploration was canceled. Over the next week, the patient did well without any recurrence of bleeding from the right chest tube, and it was finally removed. The patient progressed well and was nearing discharge when Dr. Porter returned from vacation. Three days following his return at 5:30 a.m., following her morning chest X-ray, which appeared pristine and without signs of pleural effusion, she developed a coughing episode and began complaining of chest pain. Seconds later she became acutely pale and hypotensive as she proceeded to lose consciousness. "Call Dr. Thorn," yelled the nurse.

Justin arrived almost immediately to the room as he was just outside reviewing the morning X-rays and found the patient unconscious with a weak pulse. "Call anesthesia and start CPR," Justin exclaimed. She was quickly intubated by anesthesia as Justin facilitated her resuscitation. Justin was able to stabilize her over a short period of time and immediately instructed the nurses to call for emergency blood. Dr. Porter was also called and arrived at the patient's bedside within ten minutes. They ordered a chest X-ray, which showed a large effusion surrounding the right lung that was not there thirty minutes prior on the morning X-ray. "This must be blood," Justin said.

"No, it's not blood. Get me the setup to place a chest tube," instructed Dr. Porter. The chest tube was quickly placed, and it resulted in the drainage of 500 milliliters of fresh blood. The patient was transfused and remained stable and sedated on the ventilator.

I was on service that week and as usual, I had reviewed all the patient's X-rays and labs at home prior to driving to the hospital. Therefore, the X-ray I reviewed that morning for this patient appeared normal. As I walked into the hospital and entered the elevator, I saw Donald Henderson, the ECMO director. "We almost had to put the patient in bed 25 on ECMO this morning. I think she bled into her chest," he said.

"What are you talking about, I just saw the chest X-ray it was completely normal?" I replied, confused.

"Yeah, she was fine then she coughed and dropped her blood pressure and became unconscious requiring CPR and intubation," he explained.

"What the hell? Alright. Thanks," I replied as I hurried to the CICU to see what was happening. When I arrived, Justin was at the bedside. The patient appeared stable and was starting to slowly awaken. Justin explained the preceding events and how Dr. Porter was in denial that the bleeding that had occurred was from the same source as the other events we had witnessed since undergoing surgery, despite the fact that it was in the same location and followed by the same coughing as the previous occurrences. "What are we doing about it? How does he explain the 500 milliliters of blood in the right pleural space that wasn't there on this morning's chest X-ray? We are lucky because we were going to send this patient home today and if this occurred at home, she would be dead. We need to explore this patient immediately before our luck runs out and we don't get another chance. Where is Dr. Porter, I want to talk with him?" I said, sensing a bit of developing "roid rage." I called Dr. Porter who came to the bedside to talk. "Phil, we need to surgically explore this patient, something is clearly not right here. This patient has bled in the same location at least four times since surgery. She is too far removed from her surgery for this to be still occurring. I can't feel comfortable sending her home in the near future knowing that this could happen," I exclaimed.

"Eric, you can't open a patient up this soon after a bleed, not to mention this blood resulted from the CPR performed by the CICU team," he replied in his typical accusatory fashion.

"Absolutely not, Phil. So, what is the reason explaining her cardiac arrest?" I asked rhetorically.

"I don't know, maybe infection. We are sending her for a STAT CT angiogram to look for any source of bleeding," he responded. I shook my head in disagreement.

"I don't think that is a good idea. She isn't actively bleeding so it is unlikely to reveal anything useful, not to mention the risk associated with the transport of a patient who just suffered a cardiac arrest. And I am sorry, but I disagree with your comment that you cannot open the chest of a patient who has just bled, I have seen it done on more than one occasion. In fact, Dr. Penton did it just two years ago in a patient who was actively hemorrhaging to death, and he saved her life. The patient was discharged home shortly after," I said angrily. The truth was that I had never seen such a skilled surgeon avoid and deny complications like I saw Phil Porter do. I had witnessed him fight and resist attempts by my CICU team to pursue postoperative complications in his patients such as diaphragm paralysis, vocal cord paralysis, and residual cardiac lesions. Even when we presented evidence of a problem we had identified, he would deny that it was having negative implications on the patient, even though every other member of the Heart Center knew such complications were a problem. It was so bizarre. It was as if he refused to admit that any of his patients could possibly have complications, narcissism at its finest. The reality is that congenital cardiac surgeons have one of the most difficult jobs in the world. They operate on the tiniest of hearts, the size of a walnut, with extreme precision, but the truth was, their job entailed so much more than just surgical precision, it required directing the entire OR team, as well as requiring the ability to render a 3D image in their mind of exactly how the repair should look upon completion, which was extremely difficult. In addition, the job required attention to the tiniest details ranging from addressing bleeding in the operating room to the type of stitch placed to secure a chest tube or intracardiac line. Every detail mattered and being a great technical surgeon while being sloppy in every other aspect doesn't make you an elite surgeon, it makes you a great technician. The combination just didn't add up for me, as I had seen average surgeons and I had seen great surgeons, and this combination was odd and didn't equate to the excellence that had been attached to his name. Beyond the clinical skill aspect, being a congenital cardiac surgeon requires critical thinking, being a leader, being a delegator, trusting in your teammates, and quite simply Phil Porter lacked all of these skills. Yes, they had an extremely hard job, but I am sorry, that's the job they chose. The truth was that performing a very complex surgery on the tiniest of newborns was tough and along with this difficult job comes complications. I viewed such complications over my career as expected, as did most others in the field. The literature was riddled with publications reporting the frequent occurrence of many of these complications. I had learned over the years the importance of rapidly identifying such complications and intervening when they impacted the patient's clinical progress. I had witnessed some average surgeons over the years deny complications, which resulted in patients lingering in the CICU for long periods of time as they accumulated morbidity, often eventually leading to mortality. As a cardiac intensivist, it was extremely frustrating to identify a complication that could be addressed and would likely make the patient better, yet we chose to deny or ignore it. I had to admit that I had never encountered a skilled surgeon who was so sloppy in every other aspect outside the cardiac surgery itself, and who denied and refused to acknowledge or address complications like Phil Porter. It didn't make sense to me.

"We are heading down to CT scan, Dr. Philson," the nurse reported.

"OK, the PA is going to go down with you to make sure everything is OK. Please make sure you take the unit of blood at the bedside down with you and take a couple doses of epinephrine with you just in case," I directed as I followed her into the room to peek at the patient one last time before they departed. Something just didn't feel right about this plan. The patient had awoken and was calmly sitting up in bed while still on the ventilator. She kept motioning for me to come closer to her, as she attempted say something to me but could not talk due to the fact that she had a breathing tube passing through her vocal cords. "Could you give her a pen and a piece of paper to write on? She is trying to ask me something," I said to the nurse.

The nurse handed her a pen and paper. She tried to write but it was barely legible because though she was awake, she was still sedated. The only part I thought I could decipher was, "Am I ..." The rest was illegible.

"You are fine, sweetie. We are just going to get some detailed pictures to see if we can find where this bleeding is coming from. The CT scan is very quick. The nurse and the PA will take care of you, then I will let you know what we find when you get back to the CICU," I explained. As I attempted to walk away the patient frantically grabbed at my scrubs and continued to mouth the same words over and over as she repeatedly pointed at the words she had attempted to write on the pad of paper. I thought I understood for a second but didn't want to say it aloud, so I did my best to reassure her that everything was going to be fine. I walked out of the room and joined the rest of the CICU team who had been waiting for me to resume medical rounds. Minutes later I heard the nurse yelling for help. I ran into the room and found the patient extremely agitated, pale and flailing around in the bed as she proceeded to stool and urinate on herself. Seconds later her arterial line went flat, and she became pulseless and unconscious. I immediately called for ECMO team activation and instructed the nurse to push the unit of blood as fast as possible as we began CPR. "Call for emergency blood and initiate the mass transfusion protocol," I instructed. Dr. Porter and the ECMO team arrived quickly, and we prepared for cannulation.

"What happened, Eric?" Dr. Porter asked.

"I am not sure, Phil, but I am suspicious that when she was disconnected from the ventilator to transport her to CT scan, the intrathoracic pressure must have dropped. I suspect the positive pressure provided by the ventilator must have been tamponading the source of bleeding and as soon as she was disconnected, the pressure decreased, leading to her exsanguination. We are giving blood and ordered the mass transfusion protocol but unfortunately, we haven't gotten a pulse back yet," I explained.

Dr. Porter proceeded to yell at everyone in the room for causing the patient to arrest as he struggled to cannulate the patient on ECMO. Dr. Porter placed the venous cannula followed by the arterial cannula as we continued to perform CPR and push blood as fast as we could. "Eric, I think the cannula is in the aorta, but I am not getting blood return," Dr. Porter said.

"Phil, we can't keep up with the bleeding so there is most likely no blood circulating in her body," I replied. The patient was ultimately placed on ECMO; however, unfortunately she expired. Death is always hard to take but this one hurt. The entire team witnessed her critical state upon admission and her significant improvement before the operation and then saw her literally on the cusp of going home with her family after spending more than one month in the hospital. Everyone was sad and angry. Most felt we should have intervened and that we missed more than one window of opportunity to help this patient, to whom we all inevitably became attached. She was a beautiful young woman, kind, intelligent and so genuine. She had decided during her hospitalization that she wanted to pursue a nursing degree because she was so impressed by the care she received from the nurses. It was tragic and many of the staff were angered by Dr. Porter's refusal to surgically explore for the source of repeated bleeding. Following the code, we performed our standard bedside review of the resuscitation where the team members involved detail the events and identify any areas where we thought we could have delivered better care or perhaps picked up on subtle cues that could have helped prevent the cardiac arrest from occurring. I brought up the idea of surgical exploration but was shot down immediately by Dr. Porter. I responded by saying that we would do a more detailed dive into the available data and review this case extensively next week at our monthly Morbidity and Mortality conference with the entire Heart Center team. Following that comment, I noted Dr. Kowatch and Dr. Porter make eye contact with one another. The entire event was disgusting and traumatic for the whole staff. I would later come to identify this patient's death as the defining moment where Dr. Porter officially lost the trust of the entire CICU staff and that of most of the other Heart Center team members, except Dr. Kowatch, who was too clueless to understand the significance of what had just happened. We subsequently lost two nurses who resigned that week due to the fact that they had become very close with this patient and as a result had arrived at the conclusion that they could not come to work each day and look Dr. Porter in the eyes without becoming infuriated. His refusal to address complications, or at least entertain the possibility of addressing them in this scenario, were unforgivable in my eyes and those of many others. It was indeed going to be a difficult situation for the team to recover from. The day following this patient's mortality, after the dust began to settle, I sought out Ariana Gore, one of our most experienced CICU nurses, who had been caring for the patient the day before, to ask her about one particular aspect of the preceding day's events that left me unsettled. When I arrived at the hospital, I immediately looked for her but didn't see her on the unit, so I decided to send her a text. "Good morning Ariana, are you at the hospital today? If so, could you please meet me in my office, I wanted to speak with you about something specific regarding yesterday's event. Thanks. Eric."

"Hey Dr. Philson. Yes, I am here. I will meet you in your office right now," she replied.

Within a matter of minutes, I heard a knock at my door. "Come in. Hi, Ariana, thanks for meeting me. Have a seat. First of all, I wanted to tell you what a phenomenal job you did caring for this patient yesterday. It was an awful experience for all of us and I know we are all still mentally digesting the events and the outcome, but you handled it like a seasoned professional and I am proud of you. I have been bothered by something specific about yesterday. Just before we disconnected the patient from the ventilator to transport her to CT scan, she was very agitated and was attempting to ask me something. I couldn't make out what she was mouthing, nor could I make out what she was writing because she was sedated. I barely slept at all last night because the image of her face mouthing those words haunted me. I wanted to see if you had any thoughts about what it was that she was trying so desperately to say? I have obsessively replayed that image in my mind, and I am convinced she was asking me, 'Am I going to die?' What do you think?" I asked.

"She was definitely saying that. She mouthed the same words to me before you arrived and after you left the room, just before we disconnected her from the ventilator. I am certain that is what she was asking, and it has haunted me as well," Ariana responded. She began to cry, and I struggled to hold back my tears but eventually I lost the battle. I stood up and gave her a big hug as we both cried.

"How terrified she must have been. I wonder how she knew?" I asked.

"I know, I am left wondering the same thing," Ariana replied as she wiped her tears away, attempting to regain her composure. It left an eerie feeling because during her entire hospitalization, even during her most critical hours pre- and post-surgery, not once had she voiced a concern about dying. How could she possibly have known? It was incredible to ponder that she seemed to somehow sense such an event moments before it occurred.

The following week came, and it was time for our scheduled Morbidity and Mortality conference. That morning, I heard a knock on my office door as I was reviewing the data for each of the CICU patients in preparation for medical rounds. Much to my surprise, it was Joseph Bergeron, the COO. "Good morning, Eric. I wanted to tell you that I have arranged a case review this morning at 11 a.m. in the conference room to involve you, me, Dr. Kowatch, Dr. Porter, and Dr. Penton to discuss the events of yesterday's code," he explained.

"Joseph today is Morbidity and Mortality conference; we will be discussing the events in detail from admission to decompensation and it should involve the entire Heart Center team not a select few. Why would we review it privately prior to M & M with only a select few? If you want to join, you are welcome to come," I said.

"I am concerned that you are going to blame Dr. Porter for this patient's demise in front of the Heart Center team and I am not going to allow that to happen," he explained as he pathetically attempted to appear authoritative.

"Joseph, that is false and an inappropriate comment. How many M & M conferences have you attended? Let me give you a little background. I started M & M conference three years ago and we were the first unit in the history of the organization to develop such a conference. The intention is to exhaustively review the data and present it to the group and identify potential areas where we may have been able to change the outcome and deliver better care. I have always started the meeting by stating that M & M conference is meant to be inclusive, and the discussion is intended to be open, nonjudgmental, and without concern for repercussion. We have discussed cases just as sensitive, if not more sensitive, than this one, and not once have I ever been accusatory in any manner whatsoever. Also, it is important that you understand that this process is necessary to provide closure for the staff and to allow them the opportunity to grieve. It is not appropriate to take that away from them. Instead, if we discuss the events in advance with only a select few, we are robbing the staff of these important opportunities," I replied, unable to hide my agitation.

"Nonetheless, I will see you in the conference room at 11 a.m.," he explained ignoring my request as he walked out of my office. I was infuriated and as I carried out medical rounds, I am certain my agitation was clear to the other team members who had joined me that morning. As I finished rounds, it was 11 a.m. so I headed to the conference room to join the other attendees already present and seated. "Eric, would you like to present the details of yesterday's events," Joseph asked.

"Sure. I guess I can present the details briefly since we will be discussing the case in more detail later today during M & M conference," I replied.

"Well, Eric, we are hoping we can come to more of a consensus regarding yesterday's events among this group this morning rather than during M & M," Dr. Kowatch said nervously, in a passive-aggressive manner, bearing a fake smile resembling someone suffering from severe constipation, wearing a polo shirt bearing armpit sweat resembling the People's Republic of China, both in shape and size.

I shook my head side to side in disgust and grudgingly gave a brief description of the events. As I finished, I focused on the obvious outliers, which were the multiple episodes of significant hemorrhage that occurred, far removed from surgery. I professionally raised the idea that I felt we had missed opportunities to surgically explore for the source of bleeding, despite the nearly unanimous belief by the team that we should do so. While several bleeding episodes had occurred, it was the final episode that resulted in a decompensation so profound that, in my opinion, it would be too unsafe to discharge the patient home due to the unpredictable and severe nature of this event. I explained that in my opinion, a patient who arrests due to bleeding, warrants surgical exploration. "That's absurd, Eric. As a surgeon, you cannot open the chest of a patient who has just hemorrhaged, it's far too risky," said Dr. Porter, clearly annoyed at the points for discussion that I had raised.

"Phil, I acknowledge the risk and I acknowledge that I am not a surgeon, but we need to be cautious when we make statements such as 'we cannot' or 'that's impossible.' We are in a very specialized and complex field of medicine, and we deal with risk and life-threatening events on a regular basis. Yes, to explore would be risky and difficult, but as I explained to you before, I have seen it, and in fact Dr. Penton has done so, and ultimately saved the patient's life. So, I acknowledge that it would be difficult, yes, but impossible, absolutely not," I replied passionately.

Dr. Penton being the professional he was tried to place the blame on himself by saying he should have explored the patient while Dr. Porter was away on vacation. Dr. Porter being the narcissist he was, quickly latched on to that and began to use it to control the narrative. He proceeded to direct the blame toward Dr. Penton for not surgically exploring the patient during the brief bleeding episode that occurred while he was away. He then proceeded to blame the CICU staff for being "careless" by detaching the patient from the ventilator, though it was necessary to do so in order to transport the patient to CT scan, which he had insisted on performing. I sat there angered by what was occurring before my eyes and felt as though I wanted to vomit. Dr. Kowatch then proceeded to incorrectly summarize the conclusion of the meeting aloud by saying, "Umm. OK, guys. So, the take-home point is that this was an unfortunate outcome, but clearly surgical intervention was not an option due to the risk and that is the message we should all relay to the team," he said, again with a fake grin as if still straining to evacuate a years' worth of impacted stool from his bowels.

"I disagree with all of these comments, and I will not be relaying a lie. I will not stir the pot by saying anything other than we cannot be certain if exploration was a viable option, but I refuse to lie," I said. The meeting ended and I stormed out of the room furious. M & M took place at the usual time that afternoon; however, I had been instructed by Joseph Bergeron that I could only mention that surgical exploration was deemed too risky to carry out. The true meaning of M & M had been stolen by Dr. Kowatch and Joseph Bergeron, so the conference finished much quicker than usual. I wasn't about to belabor a fictitious performance and felt like a phony with each word I spoke, as if an imposter who was nothing more than a puppet controlled by the administration, a feeling Dr. Kowatch must experience daily and had obviously come to terms with after selling his soul to Mr. Boykins. I vaguely concluded the meeting by saying what I was told to say, like an obedient puppet. This was the point where I began to see newfound immoralities displayed by our leaders, which no longer consisted only of toxicity and incompetence. I now feared I was witnessing the complete infiltration of our entire cardiac program by individuals who were more preoccupied with controlling the staff by spreading a false narrative and using illusory perception and theatrics to hide the reality, which was that they couldn't care less about "culture" and teamwork, nor did they care about delivering high-quality patient care. The administrators now openly displayed their unwavering support for Dr. Porter and Dr. Kowatch as the co-directors of the Heart Center, which signified that they would not be holding Dr. Porter accountable for any negative action, now, or in the future. I also began to become suspicious that the reason for their unrelenting support of Dr. Porter was the ridiculous contract they had desperately given him. I was certain that they had concluded that there was no chance they would ever terminate his employment as they would be required to pay him the entire $10 million. If they were to do so, they would be forced to explain to the hospital board members the idiotic contract they had given Dr. Porter, thereby exposing their incompetence by revealing that they had not only inappropriately convinced the board to terminate Dr. Rostri, but that they significantly over-paid a surgeon who was actually behaviorally far worse than Dr. Rostri. It was nonsensical and screamed of desperation and Antoine Boykins knew it! Additionally, the "return on investment" expectations that were being messaged by Mr. Boykins, to me meant that he understood Dr. Porter to be a major revenue stream for the hospital, at a level no other staff member could possibly match, thereby making him "irreplaceable" in his eyes, while render-ing the rest of the Heart Center staff as dispensable. Things had become so complicated and there always appeared to be unnecessary drama attached to everything. Instead of sharing the simple goal of working together to provide great care to the patients, everything appeared to have ulterior motives. From here onward, the hospital leaders hid behind the Heart Center leaders. It became clear that Dr. Porter was now the alpha male, directing the clueless administrators who subsequently manipulated Dr. Kowatch as their puppet to carry out the plan. I had never experienced such calculated deception, particularly at a hospital, and at such a skilled level. It seemed surreal, as if I was watching a live filming of the soap opera *Days of our Lives*. I had to give them credit, the great degree of skill required to design and implement such a calculated and immoral scheme was impressive, yet it left a foul taste in my mouth, and I began to question my ability to continue working in medicine for much longer.

Over the next several weeks the culture within the Heart Center rapidly deteriorated, as did my physical and mental health. I began experiencing shortness of breath once again and I began to feel palpitations, which were confirmed when my cardiologist from Mayo Clinic called to inform me that the loop recorder that they had implanted under the skin, above my heart to monitor for arrhythmias, was alerting them that I was having frequent peri-ods of tachycardia at a rate of two hundred beats per minute. Fortunately, it was supraventricular tachycardia I was experiencing, which is far better tolerated than ventricular tachycardia, the arrhythmia responsible for my previous collapse at home. Yes, the rapid heart rate felt uncomfortable and would worsen my shortness of breath if it persisted for more than a couple of hours, but it was unlikely to kill me in the short term. Foolishly, I tried to fight through the symptoms; however, I was subsequently taken off the night call schedule by my colleagues because I was told that I did not look well. So, the following day, I scheduled an urgent trip to Rochester, Minnesota, to see my cardiologist at Mayo Clinic.

35

CHARLATAN PLAGIARISM AND THE ILLUSION OF CULTURE

When I returned from Mayo Clinic, I was indecorously greeted by a text message from Justin and Lorraine that contained a link to a press release authored by the media relations department of Children's Hospital of Biloxi. As I read the article, I could feel the "roid rage" intensifying due to the increased prednisone dose prescribed by my physician. The article detailed the interviews of Dr. Porter, Dr. Kowatch, and Antoine Boykins. The three proceeded to elucidate how their work had evolved the care within the Heart Center far above the care that once existed. Antoine Boykins inaugurated the charlatan plagiarism by detailing how his leadership was the reason Dr. Kowatch and Dr. Porter decided to join CHOB. While it was true, his administrative team was partly responsible for initiating communication with Dr. Kowatch and Dr. Porter, both openly admitted on multiple occasions, that they joined CHOB due to the team we had assembled in the CICU and the

473

clinical results that subsequently followed. I had only read the first paragraph of the article and I already felt as though I was developing hypertensive encephalopathy and perhaps was on my way to a full-blown cerebral aneurysm as my head pulsated from the "roid rage." "The nerve of this guy," I thought to myself. I couldn't care less about personal credit, but at least give some credit to my team, who had busted their ass to move this program out of the dark ages. To defraud my team, in particular Justin, Dr. Penton, and Mark Borland, was infuriating and I stopped reading to take a few deep breaths, attempting to calm myself and lower my blood pressure before resuming. I reluctantly pressed on, reading the next paragraph of the article, which listed the multitude of "top trained" recruits that Dr. Kowatch had been responsible for adding to the Heart Center. The article read, "I have been able to successfully recruit a world-class fetal cardiologist and a nationally renowned pediatric heart failure/transplant specialist." Translation: "I have brought two young, inexperienced cardiologists who trained under me, who love to gossip like children, who have shown clinical weakness, a lack of work ethic, and who have displayed an absence of integrity, which has become destructive to the culture within the Heart Center." This is the chilling reality of medicine. The quality of care around the world is astonishingly variable and when incompetent leaders spit lies like venom and use subjectivity to describe care and base clinical ability on where individuals trained rather than on actual data, it leads to the dangerous concept of false advertising. In the article, Dr. Kowatch went on to spew additional lies, stating he was responsible for recruiting CICU staff, an adult congenital cardiologist, and a new interventional cardiologist, while also starting an adult congenital program that he had gotten certified. The truth was, I had recruited the CICU staff before Dr. Kowatch, Dr. Porter, and Mr. Boykins arrived. Mitch Borland who had worked at CHOB longer than me, had recently passed the Adult Congenital Board exam and had dedicated months of his time orchestrating and completing the painstaking requirements for the program to become "Adult Congenital Certified," which he successfully did, on his own! Not a single portion of this work was performed by Dr. Kowatch. I was nauseated and felt now that a cerebral aneurysm was imminent. The epitome of horrendous and disgusting leadership was on full display and sadly the entire Heart Center knew it; however, the poor families that may read this article had no idea that it was nothing more than bullshit propaganda. In my opinion, true leaders deflect credit and selflessly go above and beyond to recognize the work of their team and colleagues. The ineptitude of our leaders was flabbergasting. I forced myself to take three additional deep breaths prior to delving into the final paragraph of the article, which was now Dr. Porter's turn to display charlatan plagiarism. The article read, "Since my arrival to Children's Hospital of Biloxi, we have seen our cardiac surgical volume increase while our patient survival and clinical outcomes have also improved. Recently I had an extremely complex patient who I operated on and despite the fact that she required ECMO, we were able to successfully decannulate her and she is now home and doing well," Dr. Porter explained in words that could only be described as blatant lies.

First off, the year prior to his arrival, was the peak of the COVID-19 pandemic and for several months, all elective surgeries were canceled so we could focus our attention on caring for patients suffering from coronavirus. Dr. Porter's statement was in fact a shady misrepresentation of the real facts, which were that the previous year consisted of the fewest cardiac surgical cases in the more than twenty-year history of the cardiac surgery program at CHOB. So technically yes, the data the following year, which was void of COVID-19 surgical restrictions, showed that we had performed ten more cases than the previous year. However, if you removed the COVID-19 restricted year, then the volume during Dr. Porter's first year would have been the lowest surgical volume in the history of the program. A blatant misrepresentation of the truth, yet when you control the narrative, it is simple to spin it in any way you like. To suggest that his hiring had suddenly translated into more referrals and better outcomes was a lie and his words were repugnant and deceitful, just as Dr. Kowatch's and Mr. Boykins's were. The second portion of his interview displayed an equal, if not greater, degree of dishonesty. The complex patient Dr. Porter described in his quote was actually Dr.

Penton's patient and was operated on by Dr. Penton, not Dr. Porter. I was appalled and after gathering myself for a moment, I had to call Dr. Penton. "Hey, Terry, how are you? Yeah, I am good. Thanks for asking. Hey, I want to ask if you have seen the recent article released by CHOB's media department? No? OK, I will forward it to you. Please give me a call after you have had a chance to read it. I would highly recommend that you are seated while you read it and please remember to take some deep breaths," I said.

"Oh boy, I can hardly wait," Dr. Penton replied with blatant sarcasm. It couldn't have been more than five minutes before my phone rang. As I answered why phone, my ear became inundated by the angry voice of Dr. Penton, stating loudly, "The nerve of these people, after all of the hard work we put in to change things for the better, both clinically and culturally. I don't need credit, but the lies and the deception are despicable, and the sad part is that not only are they not responsible for any of these achievements, I think they truly believe that they are, while the real truth is that the only thing they are responsible for is destroying the same things they are assuming responsibility for. This is pathological lying and I don't know how much longer I can take this."

"I agree with you, Terry, these people are not only delusional, but the degree of narcissism they continue to display and the lies that they are spewing are astonishing and if I hear them use the words 'culture' or 'above the line' one more time, I will vomit. The word "culture" has become meaningless, yet Dr. Kowatch and Joseph Bergeron continue spreading their false narrative, claiming their tireless work at maintaining a healthy 'culture' within the Heart Center, yet Dr. Porter's behavior continues unabated. Each of his behavior issues, which are now several, has been reported to HR, yet miraculously, they have been swept under the carpet by administration. Now that Dr. Porter has discovered that his behavior carries no adverse consequence, and now that he understands that he has the unrelenting support of Mr. Boykins, the level of toxicity he displays is reaching all-time highs. He has continued to push his influence in the CICU despite the fact that he has no clue what he is doing, and this has quickly become evident by the steady deterioration of our

CICU data, over the last eight months. Terry, I agree with you. I don't think I can continue on like this. I have lost several of my staff and it has become increasingly difficult to recruit others to replace them because of Dr. Porter's national reputation for behavior problems, and quite frankly, I don't believe in the leadership within the Heart Center or at the hospital administrative level. The evolving deceit and continued need for their own self-recognition are not something I can be part of, and it is affecting patient care," I said as I shook my head in disbelief.

It was sad to watch our hard-earned CICU outcomes decline, and I felt defeated because my leadership position now lacked meaning due to Dr. Porter's empowerment by Mr. Boykins. I no longer had the influence I once had, which had previously allowed me to resist Dr. Porter's attempts at assuming primary control of patient care in the CICU. His CICU knowledge was limited, and he practiced in a very regimented manner, void of logic and made no attempt to think outside the box. I was now powerless and his infiltration of the CICU was inevitable. He regularly undermined my team and bullied them to the point where he now dictated the majority of clinical care, and I no longer had the authority or the will to resist. It crushed my soul as the staff repeatedly came to me with their concerns and complaints regarding Dr. Porter, and I had no choice but to be honest and look them in the eye as I said the words I had never spoken during my entire time at CHOB. "I am sorry, but there is nothing I can do. The administration has made it clear that they support Dr. Porter and whatever he chooses to do." The truth was, I knew what I needed to do as the leader of the CICU, I had done it for years when Dr. Rostri was here, but I no longer held the drive and intensity needed to do so, and even if I did, it would be unsustainable and now that I lacked influence, it would be a futile effort that could place my health at risk. In desperation, I shared my concerns with Dr. Potts and Luke Leblanc, showing them the dramatic decline in the quality of our CICU data since Dr. Porter's arrival. While they appeared supportive, by this point, with this new administration, it was clear that they too were powerless to help. I felt helpless as I could see what seemed to be the inevitable decline and destruction of everything we had worked so hard to achieve.

Dr. Marcus Blinder, the new CMO, who was recently hired by Antoine Boykins to replace the "world-renowned," triple-boarded, master of recruitment, google search engine expert, "chief medical officer," Gerry Blount. Dr. Blinder was indeed world-renowned. He was a pediatric pulmonologist in his sixties who was about six feet tall, slim in appearance with a full head of brown hair. He had developed a name for himself due to his extensive history of mission work in third world countries. He was the chief of pediatrics at D.C. Children's where the rest of the administrative posse had come from. While Dr. Blinder's name carried prestige, it also came accompanied by controversy, synonymous with each of Mr. Boykins's illustrious, "top trained" hires he so contemptuously patted himself on the back for. Dr. Blinder clearly deserved recognition for his many accomplishments, one of which included his prior nomination for a Nobel Peace Prize. However, prior to joining CHOB, he had been forced to resign from his position as the chief of pediatrics at D.C. Children's for unknown reasons. While I was skeptical that Dr. Blinder would be willing or able to help, I was desperate, so I scheduled a meeting with him to discuss my concerns regarding leadership, the trajectory of the program, and the toxic environment that was being allowed to flourish. When I arrived at Dr. Blinder's office I was greeted by handshakes and hugs from Luke Leblanc who had now assumed residency in the office across from Dr. Blinder. I was also graciously welcomed by Dr. Blinder's assistant who was previously Dr. Deeton's assistant. Dr. Blinder and I spoke for nearly an hour, introducing ourselves and giving one another a brief review of our respective backgrounds. I spent my time attempting to provide a detailed history of CHOB and the state of the institution when I arrived, including the dramatic evolution of the CICU that had occurred well before the D.C. administrators arrived. I stressed how important I felt it was for him to understand where we started clinically and culturally and how we had traversed the impossible to arrive at a point where we were finally able to compare the quality of our care to top institutions around the country, and the employees simultaneously thrived in the healthy new environment that we had constructed. I meticulously detailed the changes in culture that had transpired and how we had eradicated toxicity within the Heart Center and had finally established a culture of collaboration, respect and collegiality. I subtly suggested how things had drastically changed of late and how I was deeply concerned that the change in culture had rapidly metastasized and contaminated the entire institution. "Are you referring to the change in surgical leadership?" Dr. Blinder adeptly responded.

"Uh, yes that is definitely part of it, although in all honesty, Dr. Porter is behaving exactly how I envisioned he would, which is exactly the same as others around the country would have predicted he would behave, because it has been reproduced at every institution he has been employed at. I am far more disturbed by the inaction displayed by hospital leaders and their refusal to hold him accountable for his actions. I don't know how much more the staff can take. You have to understand that the toxicity of the past has resulted in significant PTSD for many of us and for the team to successfully emerge from this toxic environment and flourish in a newfound nurturing culture, only to be resubmerged in a toxic environment that is even worse than before, and appears immune of accountability, is too much for most of us to tolerate," I passionately explained.

"I understand. We went through a similar situation in D.C. I at least hope the surgical outcomes are exceptional. In D.C. we were able to harness this for a period of time; however, eventually vital staff members began to resign. You aren't planning on leaving are you?" he asked, appearing concerned.

"I have no intention of leaving; however, there is always a timeline of tolerance, which varies with each individual. That is why I am here, I am deeply concerned about my longevity and that of my team," I replied.

"Eric, I need to run to another meeting; however, I am grateful that you came to introduce yourself and to speak with me today," Dr. Blinder said as he stood to shake my hand.

"My pleasure," I said. As I left Dr. Blinder's office, I was definitely impressed by his intelligence and his ability to read people and situations. I truly wished he had started years ago when the rest of the D.C. posse arrived, as I felt his mentorship in the CMO role would have been invaluable. While I appreciated our time, I sensed his reluctance to offer solutions to the culture situation, and I assumed it was because he fully understood that Antoine Boykins held the ultimate authority and could veto any suggestion related to Dr. Porter, and wouldn't hesitate to do so, particularly when he had desperately overpaid him and enslaved the institution by delivering him a multi-year contract. I remained torn once again as to the best course of action as it pertained to my future, and while I was yet to conclude with certainty that I needed to leave CHOB, it became clear that at a minimum, I needed to consider developing an exit strategy, as everything around me appeared to be unraveling.

The word "culture" continued to be utilized exhaustively and inappropriately by Dr. Kowatch and hospital administrative leaders. And while the word had become meaningless, Mr. Boykins continued to spread his illusory message, which dramatized his tireless efforts to ensure a "healthy culture" for all employees. His latest attempt at sustaining this "culture illusion" involved the distribution of a miracle "snake oil" to the staff, in the form of Jerry Hyde, who as you may recall, had been hired by Mr. Boykins to implement "culture and values training," which was well underway. Mandatory training for all staff members had begun and consisted of small groups of employees who would spend three days in the conference room undergoing training on how to be a good teammate, how to be an optimistic and accountable employee, and how to prevent a toxic work environment. The hypocrisy was too much to bear, the institution was paying over a million dollars for Mr. Hyde to perform "values training" to "protect our culture," while they simultaneously paid $2 million a year for Dr. Porter to destroy it. It was a laughable facade, but instead I wanted to cry. Mr. Boykins's efforts to disguise the truth mirrored that of an amateur sideshow circus, where he had been performing the same disappearing act behind the same smokescreen for the last two years; each performance he attempted to distract his employees by diverting their gaze toward his theatrics and away from the truth, while Hector Ramirez scurried like a rat in the background, attempting to quietly cut financial support to the CICU and other areas throughout the hospital. However, the resilient employees who predated Mr. Boykins's arrival had learned from the tricks of the prior administration, refusing to be fooled by his low-budget performance, and rather than diverting their gaze, they instead intensified their focus, allowing them to see beyond the smoke, revealing Hector's pathetic attempts at hiding budget cuts, physician salary cuts, and his refusal to renew the contracts of valuable, well-paid physicians. More importantly, the veteran employees saw the most sensitive secret that he was attempting to hide, which was the fact that despite the hype, Mr. Boykins found himself surrounded by many of the same leaders who predated his arrival and that he had overpaid a surgeon nobody wanted, who in turn, nourished a toxic environment that now thrived and was far worse than the one that existed during the Rostri years. The truth was the circus had changed since Mr. Boykins arrived, but the performance remained dreadful. The circus tent was now a shiny new Children's Hospital, and the ringmaster was "top trained," while his supporting cast boasted elite skill, yet their performance remained amateur at best, despite the endless time and effort committed toward deceiving and convincing their patron employees otherwise. The employees merely wished to know the truth, and they fully understood it was being hidden from them, yet they sought transparency and honesty. The truth was that Mr. Boykins's arrogant and superficial plan had allowed the institution to regress to a state of toxicity exceeding that which had crippled the institution in the past. Their mistakes were so egregious that they had resulted in irreparable damage to the culture of the Heart Center and the hospital, and they now found themselves without a single viable option for resolution without exposing the blatant incompetence of Mr. Boykins and his staff. As a result, they clung desperately to their use of illusions and distractions to hide their failures from the staff and hospital board members. While the new hospital structure was indeed magnificent, sadly it housed nothing more than a weak group of administrators, some of whom were the same employees, now in more prominent roles, who restricted funding in the same manner as the old administration, which resulted in the same under-resourced and overworked staff, who were once again subject to the same toxic environment as the day I first arrived at CHOB. The irony was overwhelming, and this was the realization, after five long years, which finally led me to say the words, "Screw this place, screw this job, and quite possibly screw this career!" I was finally capable of metaphorically cleaning my glasses of the smoke and dust that had accumulated during my tenure in Biloxi, allowing me to become enlightened with lucid clarity, that the "savior" Antoine Boykins was nothing more than a phony. I refused to continue to work for such a soulless leader in an institution complicit with his lies and deception, which allows a culture that negatively impacts the mental health of its employees and affects the quality of clinical care provided to vulnerable children, all without displaying an ounce of remorse. I finally understood that it was all ... What's the word I am looking for? Oh yeah, now I remember, IT WAS ALL BULLSHIT! You cannot truly believe in "hospital culture" unless every single individual is held to the same expectation and each person is accountable for their actions. If a single employee is considered exempt, your words no longer contain meaning, and your actions will be viewed as nothing more than a theatrical performance, and if you add it all up, it will equate to a value that isn't worth the dog shit on the bottom of your shoe. It is an all or none, yes or no, strictly binary phenomenon, and the accountability that comes attached to the true meaning of the word "culture" is unbiased and blind to an individual's title, status, training, reputation, or salary. So, after five years, I was finally able to conclude with certainty, that Antoine Boykins was what we call in medicine FOS (full of shit), and when the CEO is full of shit, that shit drips down on all of us, and I wasn't going to stick around for the shit show! As I further dissected his elaborate scheme it all made sense. He hired Hector Ramirez as the CFO, empowering him to function without restriction, as he proceeded to cut resources to most specialties and salaries of higher-paid physicians, allowing Mr. Boykins to hide in the shadows, pretending to be unaware of Hector's actions, as the not-for-profit hospital made tens of millions of dollars annually. This financial performance in Mr. Boykins's eyes, allowed him to justify Dr. Porter's hefty salary, while providing the false perception to the hospital board that he had invested in the hospital and somehow was still magically making a lot of money for the institution, and if at any point his tactics were at risk of being exposed, he could deny knowledge of any wrongdoing, and proceed to throw Hector Ramirez under the bus. Hector being the greedy man he was, remained preoccupied with counting the bonuses he was being compensated for the money he continued to "save" the hospital, rendering him blind and unaware of the fact that he was the inevitable scapegoat. Even more disturbing was the hiring of Hector Ramirez's wife by Mr. Boykins, as the director of human resources, allowing him and those who benefited him in some way, such as Dr. Porter, to behave as they pleased without fear of repercussions, while also providing him complete control of the narrative at all times, when it came to reports of employee misconduct. This granted him full authority to destroy or prevent any trace or paper trail of evidence from ever forming, essentially ensuring he could never be incriminated. So, every one of the multiple staff complaints that were submitted to HR, each detailing repeated verbal, emotional and physical abuse by Dr. Porter, simply disappeared, swept under the rug, ceased to exist. So, if anyone demanded further action or sought legal action against the hospital, there was no evidence that such an event ever occurred. I felt as though I had just finished binge-watching five years of CSI Biloxi, and the series finale was now before me, and we had finally uncovered the shady scheme developed by an incompetent CEO of a children's hospital who had managed to scam the institution into believing he was the savior of the South as he and his hooligans completely destroyed the incredible work performed by an amazing group of individuals who simply wanted to improve the medical care for the children of Mississippi. Every single episode over the past five seasons will forever be remembered for the thought-provoking storylines, the new friendships developed, the monumental goals achieved, the horrendous failures, and the roller coaster of emotions, but the truth was that each episode, as painful as it may have been to watch, left me entertained and taught me a lot about life. It admittedly felt odd that the show had come to an end. And while the series finale provided me much-needed closure, I still wasn't sure that I liked the ending, but I certainly had no interest in rewatching it!

I spent the next week solidifying my return to Fort Myers, which included assurances regarding work schedule and health insurance. I informed Lorraine, my friend and medical director of the CICU, of my impending departure. She had rekindled the relationship with the institution she had considered joining previously. Once she had her contract in hand, I sent a text to Dr. Penton. "Hey Terry, can I stop by for a drink?"

"Sure. I am home all night," he replied.

Lorraine and I met at Dr. Penton's house to respectfully notify him of our decision to resign in person. As we entered his front gate, he met us outside and as he saw us both, he said, "Oh no. This can't be good."

We sat on the porch of his beautiful, old plantation-style home as he served us a Sazerac on the rocks. "Terry, I am really sad to say this, but tomorrow I am going to formally announce my resignation. It is time for me to move on for several reasons, which include my health, to be reunited with my family, and mostly because I no longer believe in the hospital and Heart Center leadership."

Dr. Penton shook his head in disbelief. "Honestly, I knew this was coming; however, it seems surreal that the day has finally arrived. Eric, what you have done for this program and for me individually and the friendship you have given me are irreplaceable. You have a gift. I have learned so much from you as a clinician and as a human being. My patients and the children of Mississippi have greatly benefited from your care and your vision. You are the only person who could have made this situation work. You blessed us with the perfect combination of patience, intelligence, integrity, compassion, clinical skill, and the leadership necessary to move this program forward.

Thank you for everything. I will miss you as a colleague and a friend," Dr. Penton said with tears running down his face.

At this point I had been in tears since his first word and replied, "Terry, thank you so much for those kind words. I equally want to thank you for believing in me. I have never met a congenital cardiac surgeon with your level of experience, capable of evolving his mindset and rapidly adapting to ongoing change. You gave me a chance, you learned to trust me, and you always believed in me to such an extent that you were willing to relinquish control of the CICU and allow me to run it in the way I saw fit. When I arrived, I was deeply concerned that you were going to be obstructive to my success; however, I came to understand how skilled you were as a clinician and a surgeon and you ended up becoming one of my best friends along the way."

What Dr. Penton said touched me deeply. It hurt that I was leaving the CICU and so many of my colleagues. I was deeply concerned about what would happen following my departure but right now I needed to be selfish with my decision and I needed to base it on what was best for me, my health and my family regardless of the impact it would have on the program. I had warned the administration for years of my concern for the repercussions of what could occur if I were to depart, but they ignored me. Now that I saw with great clarity the shortcomings of the leadership, I knew I was making the right decision, yet I couldn't help but feel sad.

The following day I met with Dr. Potts to respectfully tell him of my resignation before announcing it to the department. When I arrived back to my office, I constructed the email formally announcing my resignation, as did Lorraine. Our departures resonated throughout the Heart Center and the hospital. Dr. Kowatch and hospital administration desperately scrambled as they attempted to control the narrative. Dr. Kowatch followed our email with an email stating how he and Dr. Porter were "on it" and already had the names of potential candidates for the position of CICU medical director. He held an emergency meeting with the remaining cardiac intensivists where he essentially begged them to believe in him as their new leader and not to leave. He explained how he was going to now oversee the CICU and did not plan to recruit a new division chief and would instead only recruit for a new medical director whom he would be in charge of. "Guys, I want you to understand that Dr. Porter and I have this situation under control. Actually, this is probably a good thing because Eric really isolated you guys. I tried to help him, but he wouldn't let me. It's probably best for the program if Eric moves on anyway. I just don't want you to worry about our ability to recruit, because while I am a modest guy, I am VERY WELL-KNOWN and VERY WELL RESPECTED around the country, and I trained at one of the 'top training' programs, so believe me guys, we are good!" Dr. Kowatch said as he failed miserably at appearing confident. It was no more than two minutes following the conclusion of their meeting with Dr. Kowatch before Justin and Astrid were in my office. They were not surprised by my resignation and while they were sad, they congratulated Lorraine and me, and agreed that it was in our best interest. They then spent the next fifteen minutes sharing the ridiculous and insulting speech that Dr. Kowatch had just given them. The truth was that after twenty years at a prestigious institution, hardly anyone in the field knew of his existence and those who did, probably wished they didn't. The fact that Mayo Children's had passed on hiring him as their chief of cardiology as did other programs spoke volumes. Not all are born to lead and the behavior he had displayed suggested he was one who was not, and his response to my resignation further validated that. I was unaffected by the words he spoke about me, but I was astonished by his words to my team. Did he actually believe that they would ever see him as their leader, particularly in the cardiac intensive care unit? A man who could barely function as an outpatient cardiologist and whose clinical weakness was blatantly obvious to all when it came to inpatient medicine, much less as it pertained to the CICU. What a joke! It all could have been avoided but egos prevailed, and the resultant repercussions of my announcement were now solely on the shoulders of Dr. Kowatch, Dr. Porter, and Mr. Boykins.

Minutes after my email, Marcus Blinder, the CMO, called me on my cell phone. "Eric, I am shocked. I thought you were doing OK. What happened?"

"Marcus, I am sorry that you have to deal with this; however, it is time to take care of me. It is clear this institution views us all as replaceable. I can no longer continue to work in an environment that is not supportive financially and that allows a toxic environment to prevail. I need to take care of myself and begin placing my family and my health first," I replied.

"Eric, who is not being supportive? I need to know," he said desperately.

"I am not sure, I only know that I offered to help the hospital recruit for my replacement, which Hector Ramirez responded to by threatening me with a severance package if I did not agree to reduce my salary. Then Joseph Bergeron proceeded to insult my team's work ethic by saying we need to work more and that they will not support the use of locum tenens to help reduce the number of night calls that my understaffed team is providing. I can only guess that it is Joseph Bergeron or Hector Ramirez who are communicating the message, but I am pretty certain that Mr. Boykins is behind it all," I said.

"Eric, I am sorry to hear all of this. Please let me know if there is anything I can do," Dr. Blinder replied sincerely.

Dr. Kowatch spent the subsequent weeks humiliating himself by spam-calling random cardiac intensivists around the country. I became aware of his spam-calling tactic when I received a phone call from two colleagues of mine, at different institutions, asking me what was happening in Biloxi and why a pediatric cardiologist whom they knew nothing about was cold-calling them, to ask if they would be interested in the medical director position. His approach reeked of desperation and panic. It was a pathetic display but by this point it had become the expectation. Due to my concern for their future and for the well-being of my remaining CICU colleagues, I decided to share a list of potential candidates with Dr. Kowatch whom I felt could be a good fit as my replacement and who may be capable of surviving in the current environment.

The following day, Dr. Kowatch scurried tardily into the conference room to join the faculty meeting, which was already in progress. As he sat at the conference room table, the room was silent. "I want to thank Dr. Philson for his work over the last five years. The results he has produced have been crucial to the program and I personally wouldn't have taken this job were it not for his hard work and his presence. While I am saddened by his resignation, I respect the fact that he is leaving to be with his family. I also want to share some exciting news; Dr. Philson was kind enough to share some names with me as potential candidates for medical director of the CICU. I spent today calling each of them and there seems to be some interest from three of the candidates. So, stay tuned. I also want to share some other exciting news, Dr. Porter and I were able to secure approval to hire eight cardiac intensivists," Dr. Kowatch said anxiously as his voice cracked, wearing a yellow shirt, that looked as though it was once white and had changed color after accumulating a year's worth of armpit sweat. I was annoyed that he was again trying to control the narrative and I was especially bothered by the fact that he was doing so publicly. Yes, it was true, part of the reason I deiced to resign was related to my family, but the truth was that I was doing OK with the travel back and forth to Florida and quite honestly, I felt as though the time I was spending with them was higher quality and more substantive then when I was at home with them in Biloxi. For some reason I found I was able to detach from work much better when I was in Florida, which provided more balance between my work and home life. The truth was that the primary reason I was resigning was due to the fact that I no longer believed in the direction and support of the current leadership, and I refused to work in the toxic environment that had resurfaced and prevailed as a result of their inadequate leadership. When Dr. Kowatch finished speaking, he asked, "Eric, do you have anything you would like to share?" as he quickly tried to move on so that I would not respond to his comments.

"Uh, yes, actually I do. I want to thank everyone for the opportunity to work with you. While the workload was massive and it has had irreversible repercussions on my family and my health, I am proud of the care the CICU has provided and of the team we have built. I wouldn't change any of it. Accepting this job was what I have come to understand as 'the best and worst decision of my life.' I grew immeasurably as a human being during my tenure here and I was fortunate to meet many amazingly resilient people and I am grateful for the friendships that I have developed over the past five years. I just want to finish by saying two things. First, while it is true, part of the reason I am leaving is to be with my family, it is important for you all to understand that there are deficiencies within the Heart Center that need to be addressed and these factors have deteriorated to a point where I can no longer continue to tolerate them, and they are a substantial portion of the reason I have resigned; however, it is inappropriate for me to discuss specific details in a public forum such as this. Lastly, I want to clarify something. I have had approval for hiring eight cardiac intensivists for more than a year now, so the announcement of such information as if it were new and something we should celebrate is nothing more than an illusion. I wish to offer this piece of advice, the challenge is not in regurgitating the news related to the approval for hiring eight cardiac intensivists, instead the challenge lies in finding a way to successfully recruit the right intensivists to fill these vacancies, but even more importantly it lies in providing an environment where you can actually retain them! So, my advice is to save the celebration for when that occurs, otherwise it is simply more smoke and mirrors," I said initially agitated, but finishing in a mood I can only describe as relieved.

Dr. Penton could read my face like a book and could see I was annoyed. "I would like to say something. Eric, what you have done for this program and for me as a person and the friendship you have given me is irreplaceable. You have a gift. I have learned so much from you as a clinician and as a human being. My patients and the children of Mississippi have greatly benefited from your care and your vision. You are the only person who could have made this situation work. You blessed us with the perfect combination of patience, intelligence, integrity, compassion, clinical skill, and the leadership necessary to move this program forward, and you are irreplaceable. Thank you for everything. I will miss you as a colleague and a friend." Dr. Penton graciously repeated the words aloud that he spoke to me individually on his porch and they resonated with me even more the second time I heard them.

"Here, here! Totally agree! Thanks, Eric. We love you! We will miss you!" were the words spoken aloud by several of my Heart Center colleagues who had been with me from the start, who were present during the faculty meeting. Dr. Porter and Joseph Bergeron said nothing. As the meeting ended, I rushed out of the room and headed to my vehicle, trying my hardest to hold back the tears.

In total, four cardiac intensivists, five advanced practice providers, and three of our most experienced cardiac nurses resigned. Six months later Mitch Borland resigned and joined me in Fort Myers and others were strongly considering leaving, as the hospital continued to struggle to find a new leader for the CICU. It was sad to see; however, I no longer recognized the CICU I had once built and outside of Justin, Astrid, the pharmacist, and the remaining nurses, I no longer felt responsible for the future of the program. Ruth Hofstra continued on as service line director and I understood her need to persevere for her son who was finishing high school and for her career; however, I suspected that she would leave shortly after her son graduated. It was a harsh reality, but I finally understood that the only person truly looking out for you in life is YOU and equally, the only person who you are responsible for is YOU!

36

VALIDATION OF MY DECISION

University policy stated that it was mandatory to give ninety days notice prior to your last date of employment. I had previously had several discussions with Dr. Potts who was formally considered my boss. He had reiterated his gratitude for the work I had performed and the adversity I had overcome to successfully build the CICU. "You completed the job you were hired to do and so much more! You have nothing left to prove, Eric! You can leave at any point with your head held high. Those of us who were present from the beginning know what you did for this institution. Regardless of what happens from here onward, it is no longer your concern or responsibility. From my standpoint, you don't need to complete your ninety days, you can leave now if you would like," Dr. Potts explained.

"I truly appreciate that, and I am grateful for your unwavering support over the last five years; however, I know my colleagues who will remain after my departure have a rough road ahead of them, so I will complete my ninety days and help them fill the schedule as much as my mind and body will allow," I replied.

Over the next ninety days I observed and participated in events that mentally helped me validate that indeed I was making the right decision to resign from Children's Hospital of Biloxi. The first such event occurred during my second-to-last service week. The CICU was busy, the patient acuity was high, and we were struggling to staff the unit, as a few of our experienced CICU nurses had resigned and as a result, the majority of the nurses staffing the unit were inexperienced or were float nurses from other units within the hospital, and therefore had no cardiac intensive care experience. We were also struggling to cover the nights from a physician standpoint because we had already lost two intensivists and I was still advised by my physician not to work nights, so I was only covering day shifts. The unit was full of critical patients but in particular we had three neonates with single ventricle physiology who had recently undergone stage one surgical palliation. Each of these fragile newborns underwent placement of a small shunt from the systemic circulation to the pulmonary circulation. This shunt is typically between three and four millimeters in size, and this small Gore-Tex tube is responsible for carrying all blood flow directed to the lungs, which means the baby is constantly at risk of thrombosis, which can be fatal. One of these fragile babies was born with a chromosomal anomaly of uncertain clinical significance and after much discussion, the baby underwent placement of a systemic to pulmonary shunt and was in critical condition following cardiac surgery. After three days the patient improved and underwent attempted chest closure. During the procedure, she acutely decompensated and required reopening of her sternum and twenty minutes of CPR, including several defibrillations and administration of antiarrhythmic medications. When I took over the daytime service that week, there was a lengthy discussion by the team regarding potential cardiac catheterization due to the fact that there was no clear etiology for the cardiac arrest, although it was proposed that there was an ischemic episode (decreased blood flow to the coronary arteries) leading to ventricular tachycardia and fibrillation. Since the baby appeared to be recovering, the plan was to allow a period of time for the kidneys, liver, and cardiac function to recover, followed by a cardiac catheterization later in the week or first thing the following week. The baby struggled to make progress during the week; in fact, the amount of support required to maintain stability increased each day. He had two episodes of profound hypoxia during the week that raised suspicion of a problem with pulmonary blood flow, suggesting either a narrowing of the shunt or significant reactivity of the pulmonary vasculature due to a restrictive atrial septum present at birth. Daily discussions occurred regarding timing of the catheterization; however, the kidneys were slow to recover and there remained concerns that the contrast required for the procedure could push the baby into renal failure. The catheterization was finally set for Monday. By Sunday we had reached a period of quasi-stability, which meant that there were no episodes of profound hypoxia that day; however, the patient was on high mechanical ventilator settings, requiring 90 percent oxygen just to maintain his oxygen saturations at 75 percent (goal saturations 75–85%). He was on a therapeutic heparin infusion to help prevent shunt thrombosis and was requiring heavy sedation and medical paralysis to keep him motionless, in order to prevent hypoxia. As the day ended, I gave a detailed hand off of all the patients to Astrid who was covering the night shift. "Any questions about the patients?" I asked as I completed hand off.

"No, I am good. If I think of something, I will call you," she replied and waved goodnight as I walked with my backpack down the hallway toward the exit. Suddenly, the door leading from the CICU to the wing of offices was opened with urgency.

"Astrid, they need you in bed 14, STAT!" said the charge nurse with a tone of panic.

I turned around, dropped my bag in my office and followed Astrid back into the patient's room. We both arrived to room 14 of the CICU to find three nurses and a respiratory therapist at the bedside and the patient with an oxygen saturation of 40 percent. "Were there any precipitating factors leading up to this?" I asked the nurses.

"No, nothing! We were standing here as the oxygen saturations acutely dropped. We bagged and suctioned the patient, gave sedation and another dose of paralytic but nothing has helped," the nurse explained.

"Astrid, why don't you grab the echo machine and try to take a look at the shunt," I said.

We proceeded to try the usual algorithm for management of hypoxia in a shunted patient including fluid boluses, additional doses of sedation/ paralysis, ordering a chest X-ray, as well as small doses of vasoconstrictor medications, which can help force blood into the shunt; however, the CXR looked normal although the lungs did appear somewhat oligemic (dark appearing lungs) suggesting there may be decreased pulmonary blood flow. "I don't see any flow reversal in the descending aorta," Astrid exclaimed as she performed a bedside echocardiogram.

"It's likely a compromised shunt. Let's bolus 75 units per kilogram of heparin. I realize he is already on a therapeutic heparin infusion; however, if the shunt is compromised, it's clearly not enough," I said aloud. The heparin had no effect on the oxygen saturations; in fact, the hypoxia worsened, and we were now seeing saturations of 20–30 percent. I grabbed my phone from my pocket and called Dr. Porter, as I said aloud, "Activate the ECMO team and draw me up two doses of tissue plasminogen activator (tPA = clot buster)." The first dose of tPA had no effect. "Hey, Phil, it's Eric. I need you here. Bed 14, the Norwood/BT shunt patient became acutely hypoxic with oxygen saturations now around 20–30 percent, which has been unresponsive to our resuscitation. The echo shows absence of flow reversal and there was no response to nitric oxide, an additional heparin bolus, or tPA."

"Eric, I am driving, and I am about thirty minutes from the hospital. Did you call the ECMO team?" Dr. Porter asked.

"Yes, the team is on the way and so is interventional cardiology. I am going to give another dose of tPA and I will call you back with an update in a bit," I replied.

"OK, Eric. Sounds good," Dr. Porter replied.

As I asked the nurse to draw up another dose of tPA I thought to myself, "Phil sounded different. He appeared to be slurring his speech. No, you are imagining things. It is a stressful situation, and he was on speakerphone, so it was probably just the connection." I shook off the thought and chalked it up to a stressful situation at hand and a bad phone connection. "I would like you to also draw up a dose of phenylephrine (a vasoconstrictor) in addition to the tPA. I will follow the dose of tPA with a dose of phenylephrine to see if a higher blood pressure will push the clot buster with force toward any potential clot within the shunt," I explained. The staff was ready to initiate CPR if needed as the patient's saturations were now 20 percent at best. As I pushed the two medications back-to-back the oxygen saturations acutely rose to 75 percent, which clinically suggested there was at least a partial thrombosis of the shunt. I picked up my phone to update Dr. Porter on the clinical change of the patient. "Phil, so with the second dose of tPA we had an acute improvement in the baby's oxygen saturations to the low seventies. He is requiring a higher than typical blood pressure to maintain those saturations, so I believe there is a narrowing of the shunt as we are now seeing flow reversal on echocardiogram and there is a 70 mm Hg gradient across the shunt. The catheterization and ECMO teams are both here at bedside," I explained.

"Eric, I am twenty minutes away. Have the OR team ready to cannulate the baby to ECMO," Dr. Porter said.

"Sure, see you shortly," I replied.

"Wow, Phil sure seems calm," I thought to myself. It was during periods of stress and patient decompensation such as this where Dr. Porter would notoriously lose his composure and begin to yell and blame the CICU for the patient's deterioration, although admittedly, he tended to behave this way toward my junior colleagues and had not treated me in such a manner in the past. I had to admit, he appeared calmer than typical nonetheless, and I became more convinced that his speech was indeed slurred. Again, I shook off the possibility that he could be under the influence and focused on keeping the patient in stable condition until he arrived.

Over the next twenty minutes the baby continued to require intermittent boluses of vasoconstrictors to maintain a higher than typical blood pressure so that we could maintain oxygen saturations in the low seventies. By this time, it was 7 p.m. which meant it was change of shift for the nursing staff, so they so were attempting to give hand-off report as the OR team prepared the patient for ECMO cannulation and Astrid and I remained at the patient's bedside. "Here comes Jimmy Buffet!" I heard the incoming bedside nurse say aloud.

"What the hell is she talking about?" I thought to myself, unable to divert my gaze from the patient to investigate the reason for such a comment.

Seconds later, Dr. Porter entered the patient room wearing flip-flops, swim trunks, a backward ball cap, and oddly he was wearing sunglasses inside the CICU. I summarized the sequence of events that had occurred as well as what the current clinical status of the patient was. I can only assume that my expression appeared baffled as I explained the details and stared at Dr. Porter wearing his sunglasses and looking like the classic suburban dad who had been hanging by the pool all day. "We are going to milk the shunt. That's what we are going to do. OR team, let's get set up and if there is no clear improvement after I milk any clot out of the shunt, then we will cannulate the baby directly to ECMO."

It was now obvious that Dr. Porter was slurring his words. I made eye contact with Astrid and we both exchanged confused and concerned looks as the OR team continued to set up. I didn't know what to do. There was no conclusive way for me to confirm that he was indeed under the influence; however, I had worked with him daily, so I knew this behavior was atypical. I thought about possible solutions. Dr. Penton was out of town so I could not call him. I considered pushing for the patient to go to the catheterization lab; however, by this point the risk of cardiac arrest during the procedure was high, so ECMO cannulation appeared to be the best course of action. It all progressed quickly, and the OR team was ready. Dr. Porter scrubbed his hands and once he was dressed in sterile surgical attire, he asked the nurse to remove his sunglasses and replace them with his surgical loops. During the exchange, it was blatantly obvious that his eyes were bloodshot. "Phil, you feeling OK? I just want to make sure you are OK to do this," I asked.

"What do you mean? Of course I am OK. Why wouldn't I be?" he asked in an agitated voice.

"Just making sure," I replied. Dr. Porter proceeded to milk the shunt without any clinical improvement, so he began cannulating the baby to ECMO. Dr. Porter's coordination appeared normal during the procedure and the first cannula was placed without complication. As he began to place the other cannula, he appeared unaware that his elbow was putting pressure on the endotracheal tube, which was covered by the sterile drape. "Phil, watch your elbow!" I said. Suddenly, the ventilator began to alarm that there was no tidal volume returning from the patient and we lost end-tidal CO2 monitoring. "Phil, I think you dislodged the endotracheal tube with your elbow. The baby has become desaturated and is starting to brady (bradycardia=slow heart rate)," I said with urgency.

"Don't worry, I almost have the cannula in place," he said, as the heart rate and blood pressure progressively dropped. We prepared to begin chest compressions, just as the cannula was placed. "Start ECMO flow," he said urgently. The ECMO pump began to flow, and the vital signs stabilized as we narrowly escaped the need for CPR.

Dr. Porter removed his sterile gown and his loops, replacing them immediately with his sunglasses once again. "So, what do you think? Should we take the patient to the catheterization lab now or tomorrow?" I asked Dr. Porter, Astrid and the interventional catheterization team. As I thought about the situation a bit more, I decided to follow my questions up with the statement, "I think since he is stable on ECMO, we should do the procedure tomorrow," after coming to the realization that if we identified a problem in the cath lab that required surgery, I was concerned about Dr. Porter's current ability to perform a complex surgery while clearly under the influence of something. Dr. Porter was quickly in agreement that tomorrow would be better for the catheterization to take place. Dr. Porter hung around the CICU for the next thirty minutes to ensure the patient was stable prior to leaving for home, during which he continued wearing his sunglasses, indoors. I couldn't believe the events that had just transpired. I could hear the nurses whispering about the odd behavior displayed by our chief of pediatric cardiac surgery. "Astrid, can we go into my office for a second? I want to ask you something," I said shaking my head in disbelief. We walked to my office and shut the door. "What the hell was that? He is under the influence of something," I exclaimed.

"Yes, I agree his behavior was odd. Are you sure he was under the influence?" she asked.

"I was suspicious at first; however, after the ECMO cannulation, while standing next to him, I clearly heard slurred speech and saw bloodshot eyes. So yes, I am pretty certain," I replied.

"What are you going to do?" she asked.

"I don't know, it all seems so surreal right now, I am still in shock, and have never been in such an uncomfortable situation before. I need to go home and think about this," I replied. I knew the right thing to do, which was to report the incident; however, I had lost all faith that Dr. Kowatch and Mr. Boykins would do anything to hold him accountable, as all previous complaints regarding his behavior were quietly swept under the rug without any consequence. I had also recently resigned, and the administration was well aware of my disdain for them, so I fully expected that any complaint originating from me would likely be met with skepticism and the narrative would be spun to label me as the jaded cardiac intensivist that was "out to get" Dr. Porter. I knew morally what I needed to do; however, I decided to sleep on it. Part of me thought, "This leadership team has consistently disregarded all previous complaints, they created this environment and have failed to hold

BURNED OUT

this man accountable from the beginning, this is their problem, I should just forget about this event and move on with my life." That night, I couldn't sleep. My conscience clearly disagreed with my initial plan, which was being based solely on my angry reaction to the repeated unethical behavior displayed by Mr. Boykins over the last few years, rather than being based on the philosophy I had always tried to follow, and that was "do the right thing." When morning came, I knew I needed to report the event, despite the fact that I had little faith any punitive actions would result. By this point, Dr. Potts and Luke Leblanc were the only members of leadership that I trusted. I wanted to trust Dr. Blinder, the new CMO; however, I hadn't known him long enough to establish such a relationship, so I decided to start by calling Dr. Potts. "Hi, Richard, it's Eric Philson. Listen, I have been struggling with this for the last twenty-four hours and I need to get it off my chest. I entertained the idea of saying nothing due to the lack of faith I have in hospital administration, but I can no longer concern myself as it relates to their reaction, I need to do what's right and I need to get this off my chest," I explained in a clearly distressed tone of voice. I proceeded to detail the precise sequence of events that had occurred with Dr. Porter during the patient's decompensation.

"Eric, you could have easily and justifiably said nothing, but as you have done during your entire time here, you did the right thing, even when the right thing is the most difficult path to take. I will relay this information to Luke Leblanc who may give you a call to ascertain more detail. Following that conversation, you need to report this to the CMO, Marcus Blinder. Are you OK with that?" he asked.

"Yes, I am fine with that plan, I simply need to get this off my chest. Then it becomes the hospital's problem and I have no control over their response; however, at least I will have carried out my moral obligation as a physician and hopefully that will be sufficient to appease my conscience." I spent the next hour reproducing the exact sequence of events to Luke Leblanc and Dr. Blinder. They both thanked me for doing the right thing. Dr. Blinder said he would be escalating this offense directly to the top, meaning Antoine Boykins would be made aware, which was the right thing for Dr. Blinder to do, but I also knew what that meant when it came to punitive measures, and that was that nothing would be done to Dr. Porter, but at least I did my part and as I had learned at CHOB, that is all I can be responsible for! The following morning, I received a call from the chief surgical officer, Dr. Eddie Arnold. I once again reproduced the exact same story detailing the events that occurred. "Yes, Eddie, I am certain. I tried to convince myself otherwise but once I heard the slurred speech and saw the bloodshot eyes, I am certain that Dr. Porter was under the influence," I explained confidently.

"Have you ever noticed, or have you had concerns about this type of behavior by Dr. Porter in the past?" Eddie asked.

"No, never," I replied.

"Thank you, Eric. We will take it from here," he answered. Those words validated my concerns and, in my mind, assured that no disciplinary action would occur. I sensed that Eddie's focus was on the idea that this was a one-time mistake, and it wasn't going to happen again, which sounded very familiar, as those same words had been spoken following his first display of abusive behavior toward the staff. The truth was, I had never seen Dr. Porter behave like this. I tried to justify in my mind that he was forced to cover several days consecutively on call while Dr. Penton was out of town, and perhaps he was simply having a couple of drinks to relax on the weekend. Maybe that was true; however, regardless of the reason, I couldn't arrive at any meaningful justification for what had just occurred. The fact that he was under the influence, likely led to the endotracheal tube becoming dislodged, which resulted in unnecessary morbidity to the patient, and could quite possibly have led to patient mortality. I truly didn't want anything to happen to Dr. Porter; however, this needed to be reported and I felt relieved to get it off my chest. During my remaining days at Children's Hospital of Biloxi, sadly, no disciplinary action occurred and once again, Dr. Porter continued operating without recourse. It was truly disappointing on an entirely different level. I now knew that Antoine Boykins was the roadblock responsible for obstructing any attempts at disciplinary action when it came to Dr. Porter, and I am certain there was no evidence to incriminate him and even if there was, Hector's wife had clearly taken care of that. Sad but expected, and the inaction displayed only validated that my resignation was the right move for me. The immoral behavior displayed by the CEO in this instance took on a whole new level, as a patient had suffered morbidity at the hands of Dr. Porter, and while there was no immediate adverse outcome, that is not the point; he had operated under the influence, and that was unacceptable, yet Mr. Boykins did nothing, validating my other concern, which was that he functioned without regard to the effects his inaction had on patient care and on staff well-being, and I couldn't possibly work for such an individual while continuing to look myself in the mirror every day. My newfound comprehension that such behavior could exist at the highest level within a children's hospital had left me pondering how long I could mentally and physically endure working in such a career. Is this what medicine and hospital politics have evolved to become? Had our obsession with the hospital and specialty rankings published annually by the U.S. News & World report become a popularity contest that nonmedical administrators view as a true measure of success when it comes to patient care? My observations over the past few years would suggest that they did not understand what it was that defined true patient care, nor did they wish to understand it; instead, their focus was on their own individual success, defined by simplistic measures such as this annual popularity contest by U.S. News, which required investing money into many unnecessary resources for a program of this size, just so they could simply check the box off and add another point to the algorithm used to determine the ranking. The other measure of individual success for them was obviously money! I believe just as Dr. Rostri, the CEO of the hospital and the leaders of the Heart Center had lost their way. They had become more focused on control and achieving their own measures of success and had completely forgotten the core reason we pursued this career, and that was to help children.

The next behavior exhibited by hospital leadership validating my decision to resign was the suppression of negative feedback from their employees. The "above the line" bullshit that was regurgitated following the "Heart Center retreat" had been grasped on to tightly by the administration and it had been contorted to match their goals, which consisted of spreading the words of "culture and support," again providing the smokescreen meant to distract us all from the truth, which was that unabated toxicity and negativity were rampant within the Heart Center, and their obvious focus was on financial gain, irrespective of its effects on patient care. Employees were now being told that they were "below the line" or excessively negative if they brought a concern or complaint to their director's attention. The COO and CFO began to monitor social media postings where they would befriend employees and quietly observe their postings, watching for any postings that could be perceived as negative or inflammatory toward CHOB. One of the perfusionists commented on a post on LinkedIn that had been shared by the perfusionist at another institution, who was congratulating the staff on their teamwork. The perfusionist at CHOB posted a congratulatory comment regarding the poster's success and wrote, "I hope that our program can get there as a team someday." He was terminated the next day. At least five other employees were warned about comments that could be construed as inflammatory and one other staff member was terminated, despite the fact that their posting did nothing to expose patient information, nor did it detail any individual as the problem, they were merely general philosophical comments regarding toxicity.

Meanwhile, the administration created a public post stating, "Congratulations to Hector Ramirez for being nominated as one of Biloxi's biggest moneymakers!" More than five hundred individuals throughout the health system and across the country, mostly administrators, liked and reposted his nomination.

I was appalled and proceeded to send a screenshot and text to Dr. Penton asking, "Am I missing something here? We work for a nonprofit organization with the goal of providing a high level of care to every child in the state of Mississippi, irrespective of whether or not they have health insurance, not to make money. I understand that being frugal financially is vital to long-term success but quite frankly, I find it inappropriate for our administration to publicly congratulate our CFO for 'making money' while he is actively restricting resources, cutting salaries, and refusing to renew contracts of vital employees. If they want to high-five one another behind closed doors, by all means enjoy yourselves, hell while you're at it why don't you slap each other on the ass as well, as a sign of good measure. But in my opinion, to publicly congratulate the CFO of a nonprofit organization on social media for 'making a lot of money' appears tone deaf to me, and quite frankly, it highlights the disconnect between physicians and hospital administrators."

"No, you are not missing anything. It is pathetic and embarrassing that they would post such a thing on social media," Dr. Penton responded.

"Is the message we are sending to people, 'We are making shitloads of money on your sick children, but please don't forget to donate generously to us!' Absolutely disgusting!" I responded.

The third event during my final days at Children's Hospital of Biloxi that validated my decision to resign came as a result of my own bitterness and anger, which led to a poor decision on my behalf. While I have been open and honest about my disdain for the actions of our leaders it is only fair to reflect on my own poor decision. Back when I had offered to help the institution recruit for my replacement and to help mentor this person and support them while they learned to navigate the complexities of dealing with Dr. Porter, I had been informed by Hector Ramirez and Dr. Kowatch that I would need to accept a pay cut. I had previously informed the two of them that in exchange for helping them recruit my replacement and subsequently mentor this individual, I would ask for a three-year commitment from the hospital to maintain my current salary, while I continued to mentor the candidate, after which time I would be willing to renegotiate my contact. Hector Ramirez responding in a threatening manner by saying, "Dr. Philson, if you are not amenable to a salary reduction, we will have no choice but to create a package for you."

"Can you please elaborate as to what you mean by the term 'package'? Because I view that as a threat and I interpret it to mean 'severance package,'" I replied angrily, to which Hector did not respond. I was bewildered by the obvious threat, as I quickly recalled the memory of watching Dr. Rostri being escorted from the premises by security. If he could be terminated, there was no doubt in my mind that I could be handled in the same manner.

I decided to proactively seek the advice of a labor and contract attorney to help me understand my options in case they intended to terminate my employment. During my meeting with the attorney, he outlined my options as they related to severance and also volunteered his legal opinion pertaining to a clear path for legal action based on the health issues I had suffered as a result of the unacceptable work hours I was forced to endure. It was already unlikely that I would be terminated because I had officially resigned and quite frankly, they needed my help to cover the unit. However, I was upset regarding the continued lack of accountability displayed by the hospital leaders, but in particular, the lack of response related to the most recent event consisting of Dr. Porter's operating under the influence, which had left me in a dark and angry place psychologically. I saw my hard work crumbling before my eyes, the team I had built was also being destroyed as more and more staff continued to resign. The culture was at an all-time low and when combined with the complete lack of leadership, it was resulting in deteriorating care that was being provided to the patients. After all I had done for this institution, this is how they treated me; it was likely they no longer saw any remaining value that they could suck from my damaged body and no more of my results that they could take credit for, which rendered me useless in their eyes. They had aligned with Dr. Porter, and Dr. Kowatch was incapable of confronting and controlling Dr. Porter. How did I end up back in a situation that was actually worse than the one present upon my arrival to Biloxi? The factors responsible for provoking my agitation were numerous and cumulative. In retrospect, I let this flurry of emotions lead me to a decision I am not proud of and I ultimately regret, yet it would reveal surprising information further validating my resignation. I won't blame the steroids because as I said earlier, I am responsible for me; however, they amplified true emotions and dealing with complex emotions was something I already struggled with. As I attempted to understand and dissect these feelings, my anger repeatedly invoked memories of my attorney saying, "You definitely have a case when it comes to damages related to your health." Quite honestly, I couldn't care less about any financial compensation, I wanted to expose Antoine Boykins for the phony he was, and I wanted to expose Dr. Deeton for his lies and deceit during my recruitment and during the early days of my employment, and I was angry about the irreversible effects it all had on my health and my family.

I called the attorney to discuss the possibility of legal action against Children's Hospital of Biloxi. "Look, Vincent, I would like to pursue legal action against Antoine Boykins, James Deeton, and Children's Hospital of Biloxi," I said.

"Eric, your contract says your employer is Dr. Potts and the University of Southeastern Mississippi, not CHOB," said Vincent Polanzo, my attorney.

"I understand, Vincent; however, the relationship between CHOB and the university is complex. I am employed by the university; however, 80 percent of my salary is paid by the children's hospital. The way the decision-making process works is that I answer directly to Dr. Potts. If he approves something such as a new hire, it subsequently needs final approval by the administration of CHOB. So yes, the university writes my check; however, they are subsequently reimbursed by CHOB. I know, it is confusing. Additionally, Dr. Potts has been the only leader that has offered his unwavering support for me over the last five years, and I really do not wish to involve him in any legal action," I explained.

"OK, Dr. Philson, we can give it a shot; however, I am skeptical that we will be able to proceed with anything meaningful without including Dr. Potts and the university in any legal proceedings," Vincent explained.

"I understand," I replied. Vincent spent the next weeks gathering all pertinent information related to my case, including my health records from Mayo Clinic, email correspondence with Hector, Dr. Kowatch, Joseph

Bergeron, and other administrators. He also reviewed my contract in detail as well as documentation I was able to dig up detailing each of the previous complaints that had been submitted regarding Dr. Porter's verbal, emotional, and physical abuse. He also included my statement outlining the event where Dr. Porter had operated on a patient under the influence. Vincent suggested that we send a settlement letter that he constructed, stating that if CHOB did not respond to our demands of $1 million, or offer a negotiated settlement, we would report these infractions to the state board of labor relations. He outlined the one hundred hours a week I worked for over a year, which was documented on university timesheets, leading up to my collapse at home, and ultimately leading to my diagnosis of cardiac sarcoidosis. He also detailed the toxic environment that had been allowed to thrive as a result of inadequate leadership and a refusal to hold Dr. Porter accountable. Again, I honestly couldn't have cared less about any financial reward, I wanted to expose Antoine Boykins and Dr. Deeton in a court of law and share the unethical behavior they displayed with the public. I wanted to testify under oath and hear them defend their immoral actions. Two days prior to the deadline we had placed, we received a response from the attorney representing Children's Hospital of Biloxi. The letter outlined what I would classify as disturbing details that I appropriately termed the "Southern Conspiracy," as it detailed a system that holds university employees captive, leaving them defenseless and exposed to abuse at the hands of Children's Hospital leaders, without fear of recourse, the same system Mr. Boykins had set up for himself with his HR scheme, but on a much grander scale. In a sense, when an employee signs a contract with the University of Southeastern Mississippi, they are hired as a "third-party" contractor, and therefore any dispute related to Children's Hospital was essentially "not their problem" and inferred it was the university's problem, yet the university would argue that they were not the one responsible for final decisions or causing said problems, they were merely paying the salary, and therefore were not responsible. It created a legal loophole that allowed one party to play good cop, while the other played bad cop, while both could claim they were not responsible. It was mind-blowing to reveal that such deep and ingrained deception could exist simultaneously within a children's hospital and medical university and for decades.

The letter from the hospital attorney read as follows: "*Please be advised that Dr. Philson was not an employee of Children's Hospital of Biloxi. At all times, he was an employee solely of CHOB's Contractor, the University of Southeastern Mississippi pursuant to a Professional Services Agreement, the terms of which expressly provide that: Each Contracted Physician (Dr. Philson) and employee assigned in any capacity to CHOB shall be an employee solely of the Contractor and shall not, for any purpose whatsoever, be or be considered an employee, representative, or agent of the Hospital …*" I was in awe. This was the ultimate scam that had secretly occurred unchallenged for decades. The truth of this situation was that while the university logo appeared on my paycheck, their contribution toward my salary was minuscule, yet they paid the entire amount of my salary, and were subsequently reimbursed by CHOB for the entire amount of the paycheck, a confusing process indeed, which now appeared to be intentional as to maintain this "contracted employee" concept that was void of any responsibility for their actions, while simultaneously granting them universal authority and veto power over ALL decisions related to my employment, which was nonsensical and deceptive. So let me summarize to be sure you understand the "Southern Conspiracy" and the depth of its intentional deception. Children's Hospital administration is responsible for making all the staffing and financial decisions and they also reimburse the university for the entirety of my salary, yet they are void of any legal or financial responsibility because my contract is issued by the university, so in essence, they are allowed to treat employees however they please, and therefore can function as the bad cop, freely abusing the staff as they wish, without concern for repercussion because we are all considered third-party, contracted employees. Equally concerning is that the university can play the good cop, and say look, we are paying your salary, we tried to approve and address your concerns but ultimately the problem is coming from Children's Hospital administration, not us, sorry. This lack of accountability on behalf of both parties renders any disgruntled employee virtually helpless. This was the ultimate scam, highlighting the shady underworking in the Deep South, without employee knowledge of their vulnerability to mistreatment.

The second paragraph of the letter was equally, if not more, disturbing than the first and lacked even the faintest hint of empathy, despite all I had sacrificed for the hospital. The second paragraph read as follows: "*Notwithstanding the lack of employment relationship with my client, your client's allegations lack even a modicum of discrimination. His contention that he was "forced" to work long hours is false. Dr. Philson was a highly compensated physician whose terms and conditions of employment are governed by his contract with a third party. Dr. Philson voluntarily and unilaterally placed himself on the night call schedule and was compensated for his work. There is simply no evidence of any adverse action or discrimination, therefore your financial demands are rejected…*"

The icing on the cake was when I noticed that the email message from the hospital attorney had copied none other than Hector Ramirez's wife, the head of human resources, whose responsibility it was to make Mr. Boykins's paper trails, which could tie him to any wrongdoing, disappear into thin air! There it was, a harsh lesson as it relates to the real world, including such cutthroat behavior in the world of health care. We are nothing more than a contracted employee to this institution, there is no loyalty or concern for your mental or physical well-being, you are hired with the sole purpose of working for the benefit of the hospital until you no longer are able to serve the needs of the administration, or until you attempt to expose the scam. In either scenario, you will be subsequently chewed up and spat out by the CHOB administration and if you are lucky, you will still have your health and your family intact; unfortunately for me, that was not the case. There was a total lack of concern for my well-being, after sacrificing my health and my family, from an institution that without my hard work during the early years following my hiring was without doubt at risk of having their congenital cardiac program shut down. Not only had I suffered irreversible damage to my health, I lost invaluable years of my children's lives, which are forever gone, and my marriage was unlikely to survive. I had been scammed into believing I was working for actual human beings with a conscience, but I was foolishly wrong! I spoke with Vincent that evening. The reality was that beyond the contractual scam that rendered my suit against CHOB hopeless, the hospital administration couldn't care less about my health, and they were doubling down on my weakness, which was my love and respect for Dr. Potts. They were essentially saying, "We aren't responsible, and we dare you to sue your mentor and the university." They had used me to evolve the clinical care in the CICU, which was necessary for the hospital to emerge from the dark ages and to avoid being shut down, and then they used the exceptional care that my team provided and the impeccable outcomes they produced as well as my ability to recruit quality staff, all to benefit the hospital, that had failed miserably to recruit anyone for many years. It was now clear that once they had finished using me for their benefit and once I began questioning hospital leadership, I became an annoyance and dispensable. I felt dirty, used and defeated. While I regretted initiating the lawsuit, I was grateful that I was able to reveal and enlighten myself regarding the "Southern Conspiracy." Discovering this scam provided further validation that indeed, resigning was the correct decision for me, as I had no desire to work for such a corrupt institution. Vincent urged me to pursue legal action against the university and believed in the strength of my case as it related to the irreversible damages suffered to my health. He also cited the fact that the dean of the medical school had recently been thrust into the national spotlight, leading to his forced resignation and was currently under investigation for allegedly spending millions of university dollars on lavish vacations and first-class airfare. Vincent explained that the university was going to do whatever it could to keep controversy out of the media. However, I refused to pursue further legal action as my love and respect for Dr. Potts would not allow me to put him in that position. So, at least for the time being, I decided to drop the case and move on with my life.

These were the events that occurred during my final ninety days of employment at Children's Hospital of Biloxi, painfully validating my decision to resign. The institution had chewed me up, spat me out, and left me with a broken family and a health condition that would likely alter my ability to practice cardiac intensive care in the future. My career would definitely be shortened as excessive night call had wreaked havoc on my immune system. This would have massive financial implications on my ability to retire and I was left wondering if I could continue to perform this career for the next couple of years, and how I would be able to maintain the necessary health insurance that I will require for life. The only gift I received from Children's Hospital of Biloxi administration was that I finally understood what it meant to feel "burned out." For my entire career, professionals in my field have discussed the importance of establishing a healthy work-life balance, otherwise we place ourselves at risk for "burnout." Over my career I had heard these words with increasing frequency, particularly in the field of critical care medicine, which consistently had physicians who reported the highest rates of burnout among all specialties. Some individuals in the field dedicated time and research to understand the root cause of burnout. Some have suggested working excessive hours with an unhealthy work-life balance is the primary cause. Other potential contributing risk factors that have been suggested include a lack of ancillary support, stress, lack of sleep, and incompetent bosses who do not value their employees' well-being. After hearing several colleagues casually throw around the term "burnout," I always felt the term was overused and wondered, how do you know if you're "burned out"? I can tell you this with certainty, I don't know how to describe the feeling, but I promise, you will know what it feels like when it hits you, because it is not subtle. You are left feeling helpless and miserable, you no longer wake up excited to go to work, you understand that you are being manipulated by others and you become overwhelmed by hospital bureaucracy. It feels as though you have been violated by administrators who have robbed you of your passion for helping children. The same passion that drove you to become a physician or health-care provider is replaced with mistrust, negativity and hopeless skepticism. What I am still figuring out is whether becoming "burned out" is a reversible or irreversible phenomenon. Perhaps once it occurs, it is too late and the progression becomes inevitable and irreversible, like a disease process that once diagnosed, imminently details the timeline of your demise, without hope for a cure. Or perhaps by undergoing lifestyle changes such as adjusting your priorities, obtaining a work-life balance, and finding a job that provides a collegial and nurturing environment while valuing you as an employee, can arrest the progression toward an irreversible stage of burnout, and even better, perhaps with time it can be fully reversed, reinvigorating the happiness and passion you once felt. Maybe it's not too late. I guess only time and, in this instance, finding a job with a healthy environment, strong leadership, and work-life balance can answer these questions for me.

As for my opinion pertaining to the etiology of physician burnout, I would say it's multifactorial. I now believe that monitoring your work hours is essential. The body and eventually the mind can only take so much, take it from me. Equally, most families can only endure the repercussions of your persistent absence for a finite period of time, which I can only assume is variable with each family but underlines the importance of the work-life balance concept. My advice is that a young physician should focus on understanding and achieving such a balance early in their career, as it only becomes more complicated to do so as time goes on. Based on my experience at CHOB, I would like to suggest another type of imbalance that most individuals are unaware of, yet I now believe to be a tremendously important cause of physician burnout. That consists of a balance between your commitment toward an institution and the expectations placed upon you by the institution. Meaning if you naturally give everything to the institution because of your dedication to patient care, while admirable, be wary, because the institution will take advantage of such dedication and ultimately take advantage of you as well, without any concern for your well-being. Before you know it, your dedication has turned into an everyday expectation that becomes impossible to escape, skewing the balance heavily in favor of the institution, at your own expense, for free, without reward, and to your own detriment, until it is too late, and you are left with nothing. For example, there was a clear imbalance between what I provided to CHOB when compared to what they provided me. They benefited immensely from my work; however, my selfless and quiet dedication became the expectation and suddenly the administration felt entitled to not only use the fruits of my labor to their advantage, but to pass them off as their own. I believe that working in a toxic environment combined with an imbalance between the service I provided to the institution and the demands placed upon me by the institution were the ultimate cause of my burnout. This imbalance ultimately spirals and leads to all the other factors that contribute to burnout, including feeling helpless, disrupting work-life balance, losing passion for your job, and mistrusting others. The future remains uncertain for me, and I needed some time off before starting my new job, so I could hit the reset button and clear my mind. I hoped some time off would provide a fresh perspective, allowing me to recapture my passion for medicine; however, I couldn't help but feel uncertain as to whether my physical or mental health was amenable to a long-term future in medicine.

As I prepared to leave Biloxi, consumed by a mixture of emotions, there was one last event that occurred that I couldn't help but feel was the universe sending me a message, one that would provide me closure as well as some new hope that the path before me could still end in lifelong happiness. I had never been a believer in social media, as I was barely social in real life, much less via the Internet; however, the one website I was part of was the professional platform "LinkedIn." As I was packing to leave Biloxi, my phone suddenly vibrated, notifying me that I had received a new professional colleague request on LinkedIn and as I opened my phone to investigate further, I was surprised to reveal that the request was from none other than Dr. Rostri himself. I was shocked but also excited, because I had always assumed he despised my existence, and somehow felt as though I was responsible for the despicable manner in which his illustrious career had come to an end at CHOB. I immediately accepted his request and over the next couple of days, as I continued to pack my bags, I felt the overwhelming desire to reach out to him and ask if he would be willing to meet me in person for a cup of coffee, in the exact same manner we had both marked the beginning of my five-plus-year adventure at CHOB. He graciously accepted my invitation and we planned to meet at the exact same coffee shop we had met years before. When I arrived, Dr. Rostri was already seated, at the exact same table we sat more than five years ago, and he appeared physically identical to the man I remembered. I grabbed an espresso and sat directly across from him as we shook hands. "Dr. Rostri, it is wonderful to see you. Thank you so much for meeting me, you have no idea how much this means to me. I am leaving CHOB, and I not only wanted to see you before I head to Florida, but I had also been thinking for some time now, how much I could really use your advice," I explained.

"Eric, great to see you too. I was pleased that you accepted my colleague request," he replied.

"Dr. Rostri, so much has changed since you left, and I wish I could tell you that it was all for the better; however, that would be nothing more than a lie. I was devastated by your departure and even more so, the manner in which it happened. I don't know if you are aware, but I actually witnessed security escorting you to your car as I was returning to the hospital after meeting with Dr. Potts across the street that fateful morning. It was traumatic to watch you be treated in that way, after everything you had done for the city and the hospital. I remember telling Justin what I had just witnessed, and I remember vividly the words I spoke to him that morning, which were, 'One day you are king of your domain, the next you are being escorted from the premises by security.' Those words have resonated with me, and I have wondered each day, if I will be the next one escorted off the premises. The three years since you left have been rough. Once we overcame the shock of your departure, we found a comfortable period of time where the team was functioning well together; however, the new CEO showed his true colors, which has led the program into a downward spiral. There are two main reasons I really wanted to speak with you. The first is that I wanted to tell you that I am sorry for the way you were treated. I had no part in that. You and I may not have always seen eye to eye in terms of our vision for patient care in the CICU, but I always harnessed an immense amount of respect for you, for all you had built, and for the incredible passion and dedication you displayed toward the patients over a very long period of time, despite the many obstacles that were placed in your path by a clueless administration. You deserved to be treated with respect and honor. The second thing I wanted to discuss with you was your opinion regarding my departure from CHOB."

I went on to detail all of the problems I had encountered since he left, including the superficial attempts by administration to cover the same lack of support that he had experienced, as I watched them initially provide resources that were prematurely retracted before delivering on what they had promised. I also shared the details of the lopsided contract they had offered Dr. Porter and as a result, we were now held hostage as we suffered the consequences of his toxic behavior while the CEO did nothing to hold him accountable. I went on to share my eventual discovery of the layer upon layer of deception displayed by Mr. Boykins and his administration as they attempted to hide the truth from the staff, as well as the deeper deception on the part of the hospital and university as I uncovered the "Southern Conspiracy." As I finished summarizing three years of drama, he looked at me with a very peaceful and supportive smile. "Eric, I am sorry you had to deal with all of that. It sounds as though things are not much different from when I was there. The most important thing is that you are leaving, and you are doing so on your own terms, even if it may not feel that way at this moment. You figured out the source of all of the problems you just explained to me, entirely on your own, though I know it must have been a painful process. I failed to recognize the hopeless situation I was trapped in for more than twenty years. I was blessed the day they walked me off the premises; however, it took me nearly two years to realize that, following my termination. When you are in the middle of it all, and you are fighting hard for the patients, it is impossible to recognize futility, even when it is staring you right in the face. I initially felt angry that Dr. Penton, you, and Dr. Saltiel didn't immediately resign in protest of my termination. However, I now understand that this was not a feasible expectation. Everyone has mouths to feed and careers to consider, so I now understand that making emotional decisions in the moment is not a good approach, and I recognize that my anger was misdirected. When I finally had time to spend with my family, which was rarely possible over my twenty-plus years at CHOB, I began to understand the importance of establishing a work-life balance. It provided me clarity, allowing me the opportunity to process my termination and eventually I realized the same important lesson that you just shared with me, which was that I had been used by the institution, because they needed me, yet they made me survive on scraps, and before I knew it, my excessive hours and dedication had become the expectation, and carrying on such an unhealthy and unsustainable lifestyle had major repercussions on every aspect of my life, which I had somehow found a way to deal with by telling myself it was for the betterment of the patients. So, if you are asking me, did you make the right decision to leave? I think you already discovered the answer, but my response is an overwhelming yes!" said Dr. Rostri in such a peaceful and self-actualized manner. His words made me feel so much better about the possibility for the future. I had always sensed the presence of a kind and genuine man, buried deep beneath the hardened, war-torn exterior I observed the first time we had met in this very coffee shop at this very table. He seemed so different, though his body appeared identical. He had taken the awful circumstances he was forced to endure and had used it to undergo a spiritual awakening and rebirth, allowing him to discover a new life purpose, one focusing on his own happiness, which was now defined by the time he spent with his family—an enlightening realization that could only be discovered by cutting the umbilical cord directly connecting us to the source of manipulation that had led to our misery and unhappiness. He helped me realize how fortunate I was to discover the source of such negativity that had left me feeling "burned out" after only five years. Discovering the source allowed me to cut the umbilical cord, releasing me from the toxicity which had resulted from an incompetent administration. Dr. Rostri's umbilical cord, connecting him to his source of misery and unhappiness, was involuntarily severed, without warning. Two years later, he was able to recognize that his source of unhappiness and mistreatment was actually the same as mine. The clarity, happiness and peace he subsequently found and now displayed before my eyes, reborn as the person he had been many years ago, was precisely what I needed to witness at that exact moment in my life. It provided me hope for the future, as I now understood that I simply needed to allow time for the trauma that my body and soul had endured over the last five years to heal and doing so in the warming presence of my beautiful family, which I had carelessly neglected, was the recipe for success that he had so kindly laid out before me. We finished our coffee and went our separate ways. I was grateful that the universe had brought us back together, one last time, providing me closure and a chance to tell him how much I respected and admired him, while he passed on this important message of hope for a future filled with happiness, which would surely be reborn when in the healing confines and presence of my family.

37

FINAL WORDS

There are numerous types of leadership styles, and the truth of the matter is, that regardless of how many courses you take, or how many leadership positions you have held, no one can prepare you to lead at an institution that is still recovering from a natural disaster that occurred nearly two decades ago. I was certainly unprepared, and if I had attempted to prepare in advance, I would have aborted that plan on day one or two of employment after it most certainly would have failed. I discovered that the only way I could possibly reach a group of people who had endured immense loss and suffering at a level incomprehensible by most people in this country was to put my head down, keep my mouth shut, keep my mind open, and lead by example. When enough time had passed, permitting others to conclude that my sacrifice and commitment were indeed sincere, and that I would not abandon them, as so many others had done following Hurricane Kelly's destruction, the staff began to buy into the concept of a team. The no-nonsense, blue-collar approach translated into trust and teamwork, which resulted in objective data, validating the clinical results we saw at the bedside. It wasn't what I envisioned when I accepted the job, or even one year into the job, but I did my best to adjust based on each success and failure. I realized early on that forcing my beliefs on a resilient group of people who had seen atrocities most of us will never see in our lives, would fail. Not to mention, the authoritative approach was simply not who I am! However, over time I came to the conclusion that our success likely had little to do with the leadership style I adopted, instead, it had more to do with me finally understanding the importance of taking the time to get to know the staff by hearing their stories and their experiences, both during the hurricane and at the bedside. Once I was capable of understanding and grasping what it was that they had endured, it led to the realization that the one who needed to embrace change first was, in fact, me. I needed to change my perspective and prove that I was committed, that I was not going to leave or abandon them, and I was not going to criticize or blame them for any perceived inadequacies, because they were not stupid, in fact they were far wiser than I could ever be. They didn't need me to tell them that the care that was being provided needed to evolve, and that they desperately needed more resources, they were all more aware of that than I was. One of the greatest realizations that I clumsily stumbled upon during this process, was that these people didn't need someone like me to tell them what to do; they needed someone like me to show them what can be done, together. The pieces were there; they just needed a fresh set of eyes to help them assemble the puzzle. It took me at least one to two years to fully grasp this complex concept. I stand wholeheartedly by the statement that during my five and a half years in Biloxi, I was responsible for nothing, other than building a team and providing a spark, which lit a fire that empowered a team, who were responsible for everything. The experience was awful, it was magical, it was horrifying, and it was magnificent. I lived the dream while I lived the nightmare, simultaneously! As I type these final words, tears roll down my cheek, but much to my surprise, and delight, they are tears of joy, not sadness. I will miss Biloxi and its incredible people, for they have forever changed me as an individual and how I perceive the world, and I am overwhelmingly grateful for that. Even as the rampant toxicity rabidly feasts on the endless incompetence of the hospital leaders, thriving unopposed as it finalizes the destruction of the team we once built, I walk out the doors of Children's Hospital of Biloxi for the last time, knowing that they can never destroy the love and admiration I feel toward my friends and colleagues whose acquaintance I was fortunate enough to make and learn from over the last five years.

The next morning as I drove beyond the Biloxi City limits toward Fort Myers, I reflected on another achievement I attained during my time at CHOB, one that I had no idea I was pursuing, and that was learning the important life lessons that were revealed to me over the last five and a half years. First, nothing is impossible. As cliché as this statement may be, it is true. The reality that I learned is that the only obstacle to success is the false perception created by your mind that an obstacle actually exists. However, I must warn you that pursuing the "impossible" at all costs can have significant and irreversible repercussions on your own well-being, so be sure to set boundaries in advance, to protect yourself and your loved ones.

Secondly, we all deserve to be happy. If you are fortunate enough to find a job you are passionate about, don't let others be the reason you lose that passion. Leadership is everything. If you find yourself at a job with incompetent leaders or find yourself in a toxic environment, FIND A NEW JOB! There is no amount of money or personal achievement that can overcome these factors and if you wait too long, you risk becoming burned out!

Lastly, as the city of Biloxi disappeared into the distance, no longer visible in my rearview mirror, I found myself pondering one final question, one which each individual needs to answer for themself. What is sacrifice? It can be defined as "surrendering or giving up for the sake of something else." My five and a half years in Biloxi were the epitome of human sacrifice. I sacrificed my time, my health, and my family for the well-being and success of the program. I was fueled by my desire to build the CICU, increase the resources available to the staff and patients, leading to the selfless goal of evolving the clinical care we provided to the children of the state to a level that they deserved. I explained to my kids as I missed birthdays, holidays, vacations, school events, etc. that I thought of each of the children I cared for as if they were my own. As a result, I explained to them that I imagined that if they were unfortunate enough to have a cardiac condition, that I would want their doctor to be dedicated and be willing to sacrifice for the benefit of their well-being. This belief provided me peace of mind and gave me purpose as I missed years of my children's life and progressively damaged by marriage. However, when sacrifice for others results in damage to your health, family, or results in other problems pertaining to your personal well-being, it crosses a line, and as I came to understand, it may actually signify an addiction. Can you be addicted to sacrifice? I don't know the answer, but the obsessive pursuit of obtaining a selfless goal that results in destruction of your personal life, health, and family, sure sounds like an addiction to me. I lost years of my daughter's lives which I can never recapture, and I am skeptical that my marriage is salvageable, and I acquired an irreversible chronic medical condition that will likely shorten my life span and require lifelong immuno-suppression, all in order to evolve the cardiac care for the children of Missis-sippi, which was ultimately destroyed in a matter of months by the failures of others. So, was it all worth it? I am still unsure of that answer. I struggle to this day, even as I ponder these thoughts on my drive to Fort Myers to be reunited with my family, with the most elementary quandary related to the concept of sacrificing time. Is sacrificing time away from my own children in order to help other parents' children survive, worth it? To further complicate this internal struggle, I repeatedly ask myself, was the time I sacrificed ever truly mine to sacrifice, or did I steal it from my family? I suspect I will only truly obtain these answers by dedicating every minute I can to being pres-ent in their lives right now, in this moment, and hoping that they will grow to become strong selfless women, who, as a result of my own shortcomings, understand the importance of balancing selfless goals at home with selfless goals in whatever profession they choose to pursue.

Lastly, family is everything! There is nothing more important. It is essential to develop a work-life balance NOW, or if there is an imbalance, skew it towards your family. Please don't wait!